Love is in the Air

Joanna Knowles –

Author, Writer, Prolific Reader, Lover of Cake.

Joanna lives in the south of England with her family, in a house with far too many books, and a cat who often ignores her. She hates to fly but loves to travel; she prefers paperbacks to eBooks, and she adores American sitcoms.

Alongside her writing, she has a love of movies, eating out, and socialising with her friends. Her family are her world and her husband is the love of her life (that is, until Dwayne Johnson comes along…) Her love of literature comes from a young age, when seated cross-legged on the classroom floor, reading book after book in the book corner. It was then that she realised the power of words, visualised imagined worlds captured on paper, and made friends with the fictional characters who became real in her mind.

These days, she can often be found sitting at her desk, with copious amounts of tea and a stack of beautiful, but unused notepads.

Love is in the Air

Joanna Knowles

ORION

First published in Great Britain in 2023 by Orion Fiction,
an imprint of The Orion Publishing Group Ltd.
Carmelite House, 50 Victoria Embankment
London EC4Y ODZ

An Hachette UK Company

1 3 5 7 9 10 8 6 4 2

A CIP catalogue record for this book is
available from the British Library.

ISBN (Mass Market Paperback) 978 1 3987 1764 0
ISBN (eBook) 978 1 3987 1763 3

Typeset by Born Group

To my darling three that make me, me.

I love you more than cups of tea.

Chapter One

'Sir? I won't ask again. If you could please take your seat with immediate effect.'

Cabin crew, please take your seats for take-off . . .

Maya's smile was so frozen in place that it felt like tiny shards of ice were splintering inside her cheeks. She slammed the overhead compartment slightly harder than she'd meant to and the child in 27C jumped in his seat, his bottom lip wobbling precariously. That was all she needed. Her left shoe was already rubbing on the back of her heel and the collar of her blouse felt tighter than usual. Looking down the aisle, she watched as Chloe replaced the plane phone into its cradle, straightened her skirt and took her seat. Maya closed her eyes for a second and took a deep breath, hoping to calm her already frayed emotions.

'Sir?' Maya was starting to lose her cool. This passenger had had the audacity to arrive late onto the plane, sauntering on with the speed of a sloth and an attitude that, quite frankly, stank. He hadn't removed his ridiculously large coat, or his black baseball cap and she knew that she had about ninety seconds before they became airborne. He was faffing around with his backpack that was sitting in the plane seat instead of being pushed under it and he had his back to her. She leant forward to take hold of one of the straps of his bag in assistance.

'Let me help you.'

'Please don't touch my bag,' he hissed, his voice deep. His fists tightened on the bag, his knuckles whitening. She moved her hand away and resisted the urge to throw the damn bag off the plane.

I

'Then please could you place the bag under your seat and sit down with immediate effect. The plane is now taxiing,' she responded tersely. Still facing away from her, he threw the bag unceremoniously under his seat and slumped down, pushing his bulky frame into the narrow plane seat, and fumbled with his seat belt. He was muttering under his breath, and she swore she could hear the words, 'bloody woman'. His head was facing downwards, but she noted week-old, dark stubble and thick-rimmed, black glasses.

Good morning, ladies and gentlemen and welcome on board Oasis Airlines, Flight 340, direct from London, Heathrow to JFK International, New York. The flight time today will be seven hours, forty-five minutes and the weather in New York is currently a festive minus seven. This is Captain Anderson speaking, and on behalf of the Oasis crew, may we take this opportunity to wish you all a very happy Christmas and thank you for choosing Oasis Airlines as your travel choice for today, the 25th of December! With clear skies ahead of us, our arrival time in New York should be one fifteen in the afternoon – just in time for a traditional Christmas lunch! Please take a moment to read the safety leaflet in the front pocket of the seat . . .

With a quick, frustrated glance at bulky coat man, she made her way back to the front of the plane and pushed down her folding seat next to Chloe as the pilot completed his spiel.

'What an arsehole,' she muttered as she pulled her seat belt across her chest, careful not to relax her fixed smile. She tugged down her dark green pencil skirt so that it was within protocol, its hem sitting just on the knee. One hundred and eighty-seven beady eyes were watching them both intently. She felt the familiar judder of the plane being pushed back from the gate.

'Who?' Chloe said, giving a reassuring thumbs up to a clearly anxious passenger in the second row.

'28C. Strolls in late, ignores me completely. I hate men like him. All arrogance and misogyny dressed in an oversized coat.'

'Ah babe. Want to swap sections then? I know this is a difficult day for you.' She moved her hand across and closed it over Maya's, giving it a squeeze. Maya noticed the anxious woman's eyes in the second row widen at the mistaken gesture of concern. She mirrored Chloe's thumbs up with her free hand to show her all was well.

'No, I'll be fine. I just want this shift to pass quickly and for me to pass out drunkenly in my hotel room later.' She tried to make light of the situation, but the annoying lump in her throat was back with a vengeance. She pulled at the collar of her blouse again and gave Chloe a reassuring wink. There was a young boy in the first row who was wearing a bright red reindeer jumper and had a green paper hat sitting at an angle on his head that looked like it was straight out of a cracker. He was staring out of the window at the slowly moving tarmac and singing gently to himself. The sweet lyrics of 'Jingle Bells' drifted towards her, and she felt her eyes glisten. Keep it together, she chided herself.

For the first time since her shift started, Maya allowed her eyes to glance over at seat 1E. It stared vacantly back, its unoccupied seat taunting her. He should have been sitting there. He should be smiling at her, lovingly. She would have slipped him free champagne throughout the flight, and they would have shared excited whispers and eager glances.

'Some Christmas this is turning out to be,' she muttered as the engines roared into life and the plane began to accelerate. She leant her head back onto the wall behind her and tried to leave all the thoughts of what this day should have been on the retreating damp, grey tarmac. Christmas Day three thousand miles away from home, working and alone. As the plane rose into the air, she wondered if this day could get any worse. It turns out it could.

Chapter Two

Within moments, the plane was airborne, and the familiar 'ding' brought Maya back into the moment. Chloe had already unclipped her seat belt and was on the phone to their colleagues at the back of the plane. It was business as usual. The next few hours crawled by as they served the passengers a lukewarm, mediocre plastic excuse of a Christmas dinner and smiled through every concerned question, demand, and crisis. Even before she'd had a chance for her break, Maya had already dealt with two sick bags, one hypochondriac with an aversion to air conditioning, one marriage breakdown and two inebriated grannies who'd spent the best part of their airport hours clearly propping up the bar. She'd stealthily transformed into nurse, psychiatrist, serving officer and guidance counsellor faster than an unblinking chameleon, and they weren't even halfway.

She had just disposed of the second sick bag and grabbed her bag from the locker to take her cherished break when the call-bell rang. She ignored it, unzipping her bag to check for her phone. It rang again. Repeatedly. She peeped through the curtain from the galley, careful not to make eye contact with any of the passengers for fear of getting beckoned. She could see Chloe was busy setting up a cot for a frazzled mother and crying baby. She looked at the other cabin crew, but they were all either busy with passengers or hiding behind their curtain, like actors unwilling to perform for their audience. Sighing, she popped her bag back into the locker, pulled at her seemingly ever-tightening collar and answered the call.

It was 28C.

'Yes, sir?' Maya leant over the seat to press the button and cancel the call. She inhaled a strong waft of sandalwood. The familiar scent reminded her so strongly of Michael that her legs almost buckled with grief. She closed her eyes for a moment, but her smile never faltered. The man adjusted his baseball cap and she could finally see his face clearly.

'I need to move seats,' he demanded rudely. 'I have zero leg room here and my legs are cramping up.' He had a cool, husky voice that dripped with irritation. When he looked up at her, she noticed a strong chin, chiselled cheekbones and, behind his glasses, dark eyes that were unfairly swimming in long, dark lashes. Annoyingly he was actually very handsome, in a rough-cut way, possibly mid-thirties. He gestured to his legs which, Maya noted, were long, muscular, and hidden in dark denim. In between those legs was his backpack.

'I'm afraid that is not an option. You see, the flight today is full.' Maya motioned to the rest of the plane, unwilling to mention one particular seat that remained empty at the front of the aircraft. It was too painful.

'What about in first class?'

'You purchased a ticket for our standard economy class, sir, and this seat has been allocated for you—'

'This is total elitist nonsense,' he said, interrupting her. 'I am uncomfortable and cramped and demand that you move me.' He jostled the bag between his legs to prove his point.

'Sir, it is just not possible to move you right now, we are at capacity on this flight, with no available seats for you to move to. However, your bag can be placed in the overhead compartment which will free up some room for you.' She pointed at the offending bag and opened the overhead compartment to check for available space. There was lots.

'My bag stays with me,' he said abruptly, his legs clamping shut.

'Your belongings will be perfectly safe in here and right above your seat, sir. I am happy to place it in there for you.' Maya pointed to the bag, but he took hold of one strap in his hand as if to stop her grabbing it. She felt accused, as if he thought her a thief.

'My bag stays with me,' he repeated, and he adjusted his cap again, this time pushing it lower onto his head.

Maya sighed. What an infuriating man. She found that her smile was beginning to straighten into more of a grimace.

'Then may I suggest that you stretch your legs by taking a walk to the bathroom? At this point in time, there is nothing more we can do to help you. We are airborne, if it hadn't escaped your notice.' As she spoke, she knew those last words were just past the line of being professional, and bordering on sarcasm, but she really didn't care. She wanted to lie down in the dark on one of the bunks in the rest area, switch off from everything for a blissful hour, and he was delaying it. He'd noticed the sarcasm though, she could tell. She gave him one last overly positive smile and walked away.

'Sod him,' she muttered to herself, before whipping aside the curtain to the galley with a little more force than she intended.

An hour in the darkness of the rest area had done little to improve her mood. If anything, it had lowered it faster than the cabin pressure on fast descent.

Maya blinked as she entered the brightness of the galley and smiled weakly at Chloe, who gave her arm a quick, sympathetic squeeze before continuing to load the trolley. Maya shoved her bag back into the overhead locker and placed a hand onto the trolley.

'You go. I'll take it from here.'

Chloe looked up. 'Are you sure? Take a few more minutes if you need it . . .' the kindness almost started Maya off again, but she smiled resolutely before shaking her head, her tightly bound curls desperate to escape the achingly tight bun required by the airline.

'I'm sure. Go.'

Chloe didn't need telling twice. She disappeared into the rest area, leaving Maya to check the trolley was fully stocked before stepping out through the curtain and into the sea of festive, but weary passengers.

'Anything from the trolley?' she repeated methodically to each row, walking slowly along the aisle. The winter sun was bright in the sky now, streaming through the left side of the plane and causing her to squint. Three-quarters of the way there, she told herself. Not long now.

She reached row twenty-eight.

'Can I get you anything from the drinks trolley?' She deliberately addressed the window seat, a lady who looked to be in her eighties, dressed fabulously in a shocking red kaftan and with white hair fashioned in an updo that rivalled Joan Collins. She had the biggest sunglasses on her face and pillar-box-red lipstick. Her style screamed 'fabulous'. The lady shook her head, lifting a nearly full glass of champagne in Maya's direction. The seat next to her was occupied by a thin man with a receding hairline and three-piece suit, who was quietly snoring. There was a trail of dribble hanging precariously close to his left shoulder as his head stooped sideways. Maya's gaze moved across to seat 28C.

'Anything to drink, sir?' She noted the three empty miniature bottles of whiskey already on his folded-down tray and that his plastic tumbler was also empty, bar a couple of ice cubes sitting dejectedly at the base. One look at his unfocused eyes as they narrowed in on her confirmed her silent deduction – he was drunk.

'Double whiskey with Coke. Thanks.' He raised his empty glass at her, shaking it in her direction, the ice cubes clashing together. Maya sighed. She could see he had reached his limit. Damage limitation was key and remaining diplomatic was what she had been trained to do.

'How about a hot coffee first? Or a cup of tea? We have a range of milks available.'

Silence hovered in the air between them as her words took a moment to register.

'No thanks. I asked for a whiskey. I would like a double whiskey. With Coke.' Slurring, she noted.

7

'How about a complimentary bottle of water, sir. Flying can cause dehydration, especially for long durations, such as today.' Maya pulled out a bottle of still water and placed it onto his tray. He looked at it.

'I don't want a water. I would like a double whiskey, with Coke.' He raised his voice. 'Can you not hear me?'

The lady in the red kaftan rose a perfectly manicured eyebrow in his direction, tutting quietly.

'I can hear you perfectly well, sir. Let me check the trolley for you.' Maya pretended to check the trolley by bending down and rummaging her hand through the neatly stacked miniature bottles, ensuring their clinking together was sufficient to convince him.

'I'm afraid we are all out of whiskey on this trolley. Perhaps my other colleagues have some on theirs. Bear with me.' She walked down the aisle towards Andreas who was bent over his trolley.

'Shake your head and mouth *No*, please. Drunk man in row twenty-eight,' she whispered into Andreas's ear and, ever the professional, he did exactly as asked. With flair. Maya loved Andreas, aspiring actor, and all-round eccentric. Arm gestures and apologetic facial expressions were directed towards row twenty-eight, and she squeezed Andreas's hand in thanks. She walked back to her trolley.

'I'm afraid we are all out of whiskey on this flight, sir. But please accept this complimentary coffee as an apology.' She poured him a coffee and placed it onto his tray, along with some milk and sugar. He looked at the beverage as if it was heated sewer water.

'This is quite frankly appalling service. What is your name?'

Maya pointed at her pin; the name clear to see. 'It's Maya, sir.'

'Well, Maya. Look forward to my complaint.' He picked up the coffee and handed it back to her, before reclining his seat with some force. A yelp from behind him alerted Maya to the fact that seat 29C had had his book flung into his face.

'Sir . . .' she began, but he pulled his cap far down over his face, crossed his arms over his chest and feigned sleep. With every inch of her body wanting to cry, she took a deep breath and moved onto the row behind.

The plane touched down at JFK airport.

Ladies and gentlemen, we have landed safely at JFK airport ahead of schedule and the local time is midday. May I take this opportunity to thank you for travelling with Oasis Airlines and, on behalf of all the staff travelling with you today, may I wish you all a very happy Christmas . . .

Maya had never been more delighted that a shift had ended, and she quickly fulfilled her ground duties, emptying the plane of its passengers as quickly as possible. She spoke on autopilot, wishing each passenger a monochrome *Happy Christmas, enjoy your stay.*

She noticed that seat 28C had exited the plane through the doors at the back and she felt ridiculously relieved. Her throat ached, her head was throbbing, and she just wanted to collapse into her hotel bed and order room service, while binge watching Hallmark Christmas movies. Chloe and the other cabin crew had different plans entirely.

'You're not going to sit in your room all day like some jilted bride on her wedding day.'

'Chloe, I am a jilted bride, that's exactly what I am!' Maya exclaimed.

Chloe's eyes widened at her mistake but brushed off her error.

'But it's not your wedding day, though. It's Christmas! It's against the law to not celebrate Christmas!'

'That is in no way correct or factual—'

'Shhhh!' Chloe said, raising a finger and pursing her lips. 'I said it is, so there you go. And anyway, who wouldn't want to spend Christmas in New York?'

★

Me.

That's who, Maya thought. She didn't want to spend Christmas in New York, or Barcelona, or Antarctica . . . anywhere, quite frankly. Not without Michael.

Maya was crammed onto the shuttle bus that was headed into New York City at an alarming speed, with splodges of dirty slush splashing up against the side of the window. It was early afternoon, yet the sky was a dark hue of orangish grey with huge flurries of snow whizzing past her steamy window as she stared at the familiar sight of the New York skyline as it loomed ever nearer. The highway was covered in grimy, grey slush; with dirty snow piled up at the sides.

Thankfully, the traffic was light, and the driver seemed completely unperturbed by the weather. She tried to relax, subconsciously rubbing her ring finger as she always did to calm herself and remembered with a lurch of her stomach that she no longer had a ring on that finger. That beautiful, princess cut diamond ring, surrounded on either side by emeralds, was now back in Michael's possession. She swallowed down a sob and rummaged in her bag until she found her sunglasses. Despite the wintery weather and darkening skies, she put them on. Chloe was sitting next to her but was chattering away with the other cabin crew who were all squeezed onto the shuttle bus, her long legs stretched out into the aisle and her gaze fully focused on the pilot sitting across from her. Chloe laughed at something he said, throwing her head back and puffing out her chest like a peacock, her mountain of blonde curls whipping Maya in the face. Maya rolled her eyes from behind the glasses. She had been friends with Chloe for over a decade now, having first met on their second training day when teamed up together to complete a safety challenge. One shared innuendo about a failed inflatable life jacket and they were in fits of giggles. A drink later that evening in the hotel lobby bar had seen them cement their friendship over a shared love of 1980s classic films and an obsession with shoes. They had been firm friends ever since. Chloe was even meant to be a bridesmaid at Maya's wedding and she knew how important this flight had been to Maya.

Another stray tear escaped her lid and slipped silently down her cheek. As they crossed the Queensboro Bridge, Maya took in the lights of the city, the twinkling blurring from her tears. No matter how many times she visited this city, it always took her breath away. Once in the Upper East Side, it was hard to ignore that it was Christmas. All the shops, restaurants, and cafés were ablaze with Christmas tinsel, lights, and plastic Santas. There were Christmas trees in most windows they passed, with families huddled together in the warmth, enjoying the festive magic that the world had been building up to for the last five weeks since Thanksgiving. Americans sure did love Christmas.

As did Michael. He was crazy about Christmas. The minute Halloween was done with, and the last plastic skeleton was packed away back in the loft, Michael was there, up his rickety old ladder, installing Christmas lights to the roof of their terraced, three-bedroom, red-brick house. *Correction*, Maya thought, *his house*. It was never 'their' house, she realised. Despite paying half the mortgage and bills for the last three years, Michael had bought the house before he had met Maya, with an inheritance left by an uncle and she'd never thought to query it. She'd just felt so lucky to have met someone with a ready-made family home, all equipped with a box room which was primed, in her mind, to be kitted out as a nursery. It was his idea to get married in New York. In Belvedere Castle, Central Park, to be precise. Not for the beauty of the castle or for the stunning location, but for the fact it was once a renowned weather station and Michael was absolutely crazy about weather. Obsessive even. It came with the day job.

Michael worked in television. He was the local weatherman for one of the most prestigious regional news stations in the country. He had started off with just a two-minute slot at the end of the main news bulletin on weeknights, but his on-screen chemistry with the rest of the team meant the ratings had soared and he was soon more than just the weatherman, sometimes standing in for the other presenters when they were away, or poorly. It helped that he was stupidly chiselled, with a sharp jawline and skin that constantly glowed. Maya used to joke that he looked like he was standing under a giant buttercup all day long as he exuded this golden hue, but he never found it funny; especially as he was lactose intolerant.

He was almost thirty, but his body didn't show it. He went to the gym five times a week and only ate carbs on a weekend, resulting in a toned upper torso with biceps that nicely stretched the cotton of his shirt. His legs were also toned, but looked good in skinny jeans, almost feminine, not bulky.

Not like the guy from seat 28C, his legs were huge, Maya thought.

Wait, what? Where did that come from? Why did he pop into my head? An image of those denim jeans stretched over those long legs appeared suddenly, unwanted, and Maya shook her head forcefully. Chloe glanced over at her, concerned. But before she had a chance to comment, the bus made a sudden stop, the brakes squealing under the effort, and they both fell forward, knocking Maya's sunglasses off her head.

'What the . . .' Maya complained.

'Shit driver,' Chloe called out, far louder than Maya would have liked, and Maya looked outside to see that they had reached their destination, home for the next three nights. They had stopped directly outside a tower block of a building, all glass and stone, with an elegant neon sign, lit up in a brilliant white hue with the name scrawled in italics – The Lexington Lodge.

Chapter Three

Once unpacked, Maya sat on the edge of the white linen bed and stared out of the floor-to-ceiling window at the ever-darkening skies. Towering buildings blocked the horizon, but in between the skyscrapers, she could just see Central Park in the distance. She checked her watch, noting she hadn't changed it from London time yet. It was just after 8pm in the UK. She should call her father and wish him a Merry Christmas before he got too drunk on the whiskey she had given him yesterday. But she just couldn't. She felt too deflated to speak to anyone.

I'll email him, she thought. *Let him know I'm OK.*

She unzipped the inside compartment of her pull-along and pulled out her iPad, which was encased in a lovely, new marble-effect jacket that had been a reciprocal present from her dad yesterday. She ran her fingers gently over the engraved, gold initials, M.M. He might be a single father, with no common sense or awareness into the inner workings of a daughter, but he did have a mighty fine assistant, Gayle, who was epic at gift-giving. Gayle was ten years his junior, but equal to him in every other sense, including her knowledge and affection towards Maya – she had actually cried when Maya had told her the wedding was off. Lovely Gayle. With her affection for fashion magazines and flair for hunting down vintage classics, she was a total legend. She was loyal, attentive to Maya's father and had worked with him for almost a decade now, coming on board a few years after Maya's mum died. She had been divorced twice and now lived in an apartment in the centre of town, spending her days working and her evenings socialising, but Maya suspected that there was more to their relationship than just a working one.

Once the tablet had booted up, Maya quickly fired off an email to Gayle thanking her for the lovely present and wishing her season's greetings. She realised that she hadn't even asked Gayle what her plans were this year, she'd been so engulfed in her grief. But secretly she hoped Gayle was spending it with her dad. She then emailed her dad with a reassuring, upbeat and clearly phoney message, telling him she had arrived safely and that she:

i)   Had had an enjoyable shift with an easy flight (total lie),
ii)   Was feeling much more positive now she was in New York (blatantly untrue), and finally,
iii)   Hoped that Michael was having a good Christmas, them being so amicable and all (totally untrue, she hoped he got food poisoning from a mouldy turkey)

She pressed send and slumped back onto the bed, feeling exhausted. Noting the remote on the bedside table, she switched on the TV and an old black-and-white movie flashed up, *It's a Wonderful Life*. George Bailey was trying not to flip out completely in the bank, despite having lost huge sums of money. His eyes were frantic, desperate to keep it together. To not fall apart. Much like her, ever since that awful day.

Three weeks earlier . . .

'And now over to Michael for this weekend's weather forecast. So, Michael, are we in for any snow this weekend? Does Father Christmas need to start de-icing his sledge in time for Christmas?'

Amanda Avary turned slightly in her presenting chair, her toned arms resting on her desk and her mega-watt smile glinting in the studio lights. Her blonde hair was coiffed into a pristine side bun and her professional make-up highlighted her sharp cheekbones and large, blue eyes. Her slender body was squeezed into a powder-blue bodycon dress. Her colleague, Samuel Stinson, was looking equally pristine, in his dark suit and matching powder-blue tie. Both in their thirties, they made a striking couple and were the main reason the ratings were so high.

'Thank you, Amanda. Unfortunately, there is no snow on the horizon for this weekend, just sporadic, heavy rain showers for most of the country, with higher-than-average temperatures.' Michael gestured to the green screen behind him with ease, before turning to the camera. 'However, we are going to see a surprise phenomenon tonight.'

Michael was wearing dark trousers and a navy shirt that Maya had picked out and ironed for him only that morning. His face was lit up with excitement, a flush spreading up from his neck, visible even through his made-up face. The make-up artist currently watching off screen had her make-up bag ready to try and correct this before the next weather section.

'We are?' Amanda looked confused, but her smile never faltered. She looked over at Samuel, who just shrugged in confusion.

'Shooting stars?' he asked, theatrically raising his hands towards the camera, ever the professional.

'A lightning storm?' she questioned.

Michael shook his head. 'Something much more local.'

He took a step forward from his small podium, causing the crew to panic and mouth frantic words to one another. Cameraman Two followed him as he made his way across the studio floor towards Amanda. She let out a nervous giggle, all high pitched and feminine, her hand raised to her earpiece, hoping for some guidance. Michael stopped beside her desk, before turning to the cameraman that had followed him. There was an awkward atmosphere in the air, with the teleprompter being pushed forward in the vain hope that Michael would revert to the script. He ignored it completely and looked directly into the camera before speaking, his voice breaking slightly.

'No, Amanda, tonight I am going to tell the world how my life has been changed dramatically by the phenomenon that is Amanda Avary.' He gestured to her with a flourish.

'This amazing woman, this beautiful, gifted, talented woman who lights up the lives of millions of people watching her each and every day . . .' he paused for dramatic effect and Amanda was starting to match him on the blushing front, while Samuel looked on gormlessly '. . . is the same woman that I have fallen hopelessly in love with.'

A gasp went up around the studio, with Samuel's gasp being the most dramatic. Michael continued, his gaze solely on Amanda and his voice rising.

'This woman is someone I want to spend the rest of my life with, and I can no longer keep it a secret from our friends, our families . . . indeed, the world!' At this, he made a grand, circular motion with his hands, before lowering himself down onto one knee. He pulled a small, square box from his trouser pocket and slid it onto the desk, making sure the diamond was clearly in shot. The single solitaire glinted in the bright studio lights.

'Amanda Avary. Will you do me the greatest honour of becoming my wife?'

The studio went totally silent, with an assistant floor manager standing there with a sign saying, '*cut to break*'. Amanda just looked completely shocked, her eyes wide and unblinking, her mouth open as if catching flies. Seconds passed, which, in television time, was dead air.

'Amanda?' Michael looked less confident now, his shoulders slumping slightly.

Samuel, kicked back into action by the screaming in his earpiece, turned to his camera and said quietly, 'We'll be right back after this quick break.'

In their shared house ten miles away, Maya was sitting on the sofa in the lounge, a large glass of wine remaining untouched on the coffee table in front of her and a sizeable artificial tree twinkling merrily in the bay window. She had been wrapping Michael's Christmas presents in bright green wrapping paper and was surrounded by gold ribbon and bows. Now her shiny, unblinking eyes were filling fast with tears and her gaze was focused on their flat-screen television; the adverts barely penetrating her shock. Her hand was frozen mid-cut, the scissors still in her left hand, and her own diamond engagement ring looked dull as it caught the light from the extinguishing embers from the fire in the hearth.

The phone rang, causing her to jump, tears now flowing silently down her face. She went to stand, her present to Michael sliding off her lap and landing with a thud on the wooden floor. The large box opened as it hit the ground, revealing a vintage weathervane that she had bid for on eBay and travelled over fifty miles to collect. A Christmas present for a fiancé that had just proposed to someone else. Live on air. Broadcasting to potentially millions of viewers.

She looked down at the partially wrapped present, the metal of the weathervane reflecting the shimmering Christmas tree lights. She leant down and picked up her wine glass before glugging the contents in one go, her eyes fixed to the television. The adverts had finished, and an image of Michael flashed up large on the screen. Maya could no longer hear any voices nor the constant ringing of the telephone, only the pounding of her own heart as her world began to swim in front of her.

The last thing she remembered was Michael's face gleefully placing the (much larger) engagement ring onto Amanda's finger and them embracing. Then Maya's world went completely dark.

Chapter Four

Maya was finding George Bailey's frantic soul-searching too much to cope with and she switched channels before heading over to the hotel minibar and pulling out a mini bottle of vodka. She opened it and downed the bottle in three gulps. Without pausing, she pulled another from the fridge and drank that too. Closing her eyes, she leant back onto the bed, hitting her head on her tablet. She pulled it from beneath her hair and noticed the screen was still lit with an unread email from her line manager. She read it.

From: NigelJEdwards@oasisairlines.com
Sent: Tuesday, December 25th 2018 20:31:23
Subject: Complaint
Dear Maya,
I didn't feel it fair to raise it at the debrief earlier in front of the entire crew, especially due to the personal circumstances you have recently had to endure, but I am obligated to inform you that a formal complaint has been made against you from a passenger travelling today on flight HK490 from London to New York. He was seated in Seat 28C.

He states that you were, and I quote, 'rude, sarcastic, and unwilling to oblige with his requests' and that he 'did not receive the level of service that one would expect from Oasis Airlines'.

I know you have experienced a traumatic relationship breakdown recently, which is why I don't want to take this any further. Your record with Oasis Airlines is superb and your level of professionalism has, to date, been exemplary.

*However, I do have to adhere to our complaints procedure
and therefore please can you acknowledge, by return email, that
you have received this and will endeavour to improve, going
forward.*

*Sorry, Maya. I know this is the last thing you want to read
at Christmas. Let's speak properly on your return from your
current trip.*

Regards,
Nigel Edwards
Line Manager – Oasis Airlines

Maya read the email twice. Then she grabbed a third mini
bottle from the fridge, no longer caring what it was as long as
there was a high alcohol content. She drank the bottle, feeling
the comforting burn at the back of her throat.

Seat 28C. That total arsehole had the audacity to complain
about her when his attitude had been so dreadful. She felt tears
sting the backs of her eyes and she pressed her palms into her
eyes, pushing hard. How dare he? How dare Michael? She
didn't deserve this.

The anger from the last few weeks rose internally; frustration, humiliation, shock – all bubbling away in her stomach
like searing bile. She had such anger, yet it didn't seem to want
to come out as tears or screams. She thought about ringing
her dad, but she didn't want to voice the words out loud.
Staring at the television screen, she noticed she'd inadvertently
switched onto an old black-and-white American movie, and
the main character was sitting at a desk, writing a letter, the
tears flowing onto the parchment and blotting the ink.

Then Maya had an idea.

She sat upright and pulled the tablet onto her lap. The
three bottles of alcohol had simultaneously relaxed her body
but heightened her senses.

She started to type, then deleted it, pressing the delete
button repeatedly. She rubbed her fingers over the slim dent
on her ring finger, where her engagement ring had sat until

only recently, thinking. She then began to type again. This time, just two words into the heading. She then underlined it, before crossing her arms across her chest and staring at the screen. She felt defiant. She smiled. The two words read,

<u>Flying Solo</u>

Chapter Five

Over an hour later and Maya was interrupted from her typing by a knock at her hotel room door. Four taps: one quiet, two loud and fast, and the final tap quiet again; a greeting synonymous with Chloe. They had decided on this coded knock early on in their careers together. It felt safer to them both when answering their respective hotel doors, especially when travelling globally and having to sleep alone. However, as time went on, it became clear that Chloe was more often not alone in her hotel room, through choice, and Maya's polite knocking was more of a chance for Chloe to hide/show off her most recent conquest and get dressed. She still hadn't managed to get the image of Chloe from last summer out of her mind, answering the door in nothing but a tiny hand towel covering her nether regions and a smear of black eyeliner across her cheek.

Maya rolled off the bed and slumped onto the floor. The alcohol and lack of sleep were beginning to kick in and she heard her stomach growl irately at her. Chloe knocked again.

'I'm coming,' she yelled, standing up, wincing at the head-ache that was forming at her temples already. She unlocked the door. Chloe was standing there looking fresh-faced, wearing a little black dress that emphasised her slim figure, and heels that instantly made her tower over Maya's short frame. She would have looked graceful if it wasn't for the tacky, plastic Christmas hairband that sat in her golden, wavy hair. The headband declared '*It's Christmas!*' in gold glitter and there were three Christmas trees adorning the wording, wrapped in tinsel.

'Ta dah!' Chloe exclaimed, pressing some hidden button behind her ear. The headband began to flash manically, while blaring out the sounds of 'We Wish You a Merry Christmas'. It was both tacky and brilliant. Maya burst into laughter, her headache retreating just for a second. But Chloe's delighted face soon straightened out when she took in Maya's appearance.

'Why aren't you dressed? Everyone is already in the lobby.' She crossed her bare arms across her chest, her pretty face furrowed in annoyance. Maya looked down at her creased uniform; her crumpled skirt and her white blouse had whiskey stains dried onto it. She had completely lost track of the time.

'Sorry, sorry, I got distracted. I received an email from Nigel Edwards.'

'Why? After our debrief, didn't he head straight off to spend Christmas with his American in-laws over in New Jersey?' Chloe asked, walking into the room and taking a seat on the bed, her headband still flashing. Maya nodded, closing the door.

'Apparently a complaint was made against me today on the flight, and he didn't want to mention it in front of the crew.'

'Are you kidding me?' Chloe said, her face filled with annoyance. She gripped her hairband and swiftly turned it off, the sound of Christmas cutting out. There was a knock on the door again, and Maya answered it to find Andreas standing in the corridor, his own pillar-box-red Christmas jumper flashing with lights that put Times Square in the dark. Maya had to squint as he passed by and joined Chloe on the bed. She barely acknowledged Andreas, still angry, and yelled, 'How dare he?!'

Andreas turned his eyes towards Maya. 'Do I detect a little drama here?' he said, crossing one leg over the other on the bed and resting his chin in the palm of his hand with his elbow balanced on his knee. Maya rolled her eyes, closed the door to her hotel room, and turned her attention to Chloe.

'Chloe, please keep it down. I don't want everyone knowing about this,' she said quietly. At times like this, she wished Chloe had a 'discreet' button she could activate.

'Who made the complaint? And what for?' Chloe asked, this time more quietly.

'A complaint? Against whom?' Andreas looked at Chloe and she pointed at Maya directly.

'28C,' Maya said, an instant image of that guy with his sexy stubble and ridiculously long eyelashes popping into her head uninvited.

'The drunk guy with the attitude problem?' Chloe asked. Maya nodded. 'Well, we'll back you up, I saw how drunk he was, as did Andreas. The airline won't take this any further.' She shook her head convincingly.

'I know, but it still doesn't help me feeling like shit. He acted like the total moron and yet I'm the one that gets punished.' She sighed. 'That seems fair,' she said, sarcastically. 'Why is it all men seem destined to be total arseholes in my company at the moment? Do I have this effect on men?' Now it was her turn for her voice to rise and Andreas suddenly held out his palm, encouraging her to stop.

'Honey. You need to listen to yourself!' He threw his hands up in theatrical grandeur. 'You're amazing! A beauty, inside and out. These men are horrid creatures, with bad taste and awful dress sense. I'm sorry, but you can do so much better. Trust me, I'm a man—'

'A gay one,' Chloe interrupted.

Andreas shot her a warning look. 'A gay one, yes. But I can still appreciate the beauty of a woman, even if I don't want to date her. And this dear girl here' – he pointed at Maya – 'is a true gem.' Maya felt her cheeks grow hot and felt a rush of affection for the two people sitting in front of her. She may not have a man, but she had two pretty awesome friends.

'Thank you, Andreas. I appreciate your support.'

He blew her a kiss and turned back to Chloe. 'Give me ten minutes and I'll be ready. Sod them,' she said resolutely, heading straight into the bathroom.

'Sod them!' she heard Chloe and Andreas shout back in unison and couldn't help but laugh as she hopped into the shower, suddenly feeling a lot lighter.

Fifteen minutes later, scrubbed clean and with a rush-job of make-up applied to her pretty face, she emerged from the bathroom in a haze of steam, her natural curls scrunch-dried with a towel, and headed over towards the wardrobe. Chloe was arched over the tablet that Maya had left on the bed, her body spread out on the satin bedspread.

'Where's Andreas gone?' Maya asked.

'To hunt down a taxi. Did you write this?' she asked, not taking her eyes from the screen. Maya felt a rush of heat flush her cheeks as she realised that Chloe was reading her words from earlier. She pulled a blue dress from its hanger with a little more force than she intended.

'Oi. That's private. Stop reading my stuff,' she said, stepping into her blue bodycon dress, her curves filling it out. She was glad she hadn't eaten the microwaveable turkey on the flight earlier – this dress barely allowed room for breathing, let alone eating. She pushed her arms through the straps and tried to zip the dress up from behind. Her ribs felt like they were in a vice. The last few weeks of elasticated waistbands and repeated calls to her local takeaway were clearly taking their toll. Maya had always been curvy. Puberty arrived at the age of twelve, and with it came the embarrassing gift of a 34C bra size almost overnight and hips that she inherited from her mother. She had spent most of her teenage years envying her friends with their flat stomachs and narrow hips, while she always seemed to have a soft roundness to her stomach that defied the many diets she attempted. While everyone around her opted for crop tops and skinny jeans, Maya was always in baggy T-shirts and floaty skirts. It wasn't until her late teens and the loss of her lovely mum that she finally accepted her curves and embraced her body for what it was – healthy. But even she had to admit that since Michael's shock departure from her life last month, she had veered off the healthy track and fallen deep into the 'chocolate and wine' pit of despair. She sucked in her gut, looking into the hotel's full-length mirror, held it for a second, before blowing out loudly and letting her stomach expand. Its response was to grumble angrily. She realised it had been hours since she last ate anything substantial, not even a purple Quality Street, her favourite.

'It's really good though,' Chloe said, tapping a perfectly manicured nail onto the screen. 'This diary entry. Sad and desperate, obviously, but not badly written at all.'

Maya rolled her eyes into the mirror, 'Gee, thanks, honey. A real compliment.'

'Flying Solo – I like it. Are you thinking of writing a blog?' Chloe looked up at Maya.

'Nope. I just needed to vent,' Maya replied, shrugging her shoulders. She lifted her arms and made air-quotes in front of her face and spoke in a fake, monochrome voice. 'Inspired by heartache, fuelled by alcohol. Neither recommended".'

Chloe looked over sympathetically from the bed, pushing out her bottom lip before turning back to the lit screen, her attention diverted.

'Did you mean it when you said, and I quote, "I'm going to begin a twelve-month rule of singledom, starting December 26th. No dates, no relationships, no romance. One year of finding time for myself, learning new skills, and avoiding men at all costs." Is this what you really want?'

'Yep,' Maya said defiantly.

'But what will you do for a whole year? Who will I double date with?'

'You don't need my help, missy. You're quite capable on your own. I'll still be your wing girl.'

'I bet you won't stick to it.'

'I bet I will,' Maya replied.

'You'll need support,' Chloe answered, tapping her mani-cured index finger on the glass screen.

'I have you for that.' Maya smiled briefly as she bent down to pull some silver strappy sandals from her luggage.

'We could make this big,' Chloe murmured. 'This could catch on.'

'What did you say?' Maya's hair was dangling around her face, her wet curls still dripping onto the hotel carpet. She was slightly flushed, the tightness of her dress restricted her breathing as she was bent double.

'Nothing!' Chloe trilled. 'Mind if I just check my emails on your tablet?'

'No!' Maya exclaimed, holding up her left sandal in her hand. 'Look at the heel. Look at it! I can't wear these now.'

Chloe looked up to see the offending shoe had a silver heel that was hanging awkwardly to one side, like a broken tooth. She winced but then shrugged her shoulders.

'Don't panic. I brought three pairs, and one will match your outfit perfectly.' She pulled her room key from her tiny purse and threw it towards Maya. 'Go and help yourself to mine.'

Maya sighed. 'But these were my favourites. I have worn them for years.'

'The answer to why they are broken becomes clear . . .' She rolled her eyes. 'Maya, I love you dearly, but you have some awful affliction that hinders you from buying shoes. I just do not understand you sometimes. Go. Take my shoes. But promise me that on Monday, we go shoe shopping.'

Maya placed the offending shoe back into her suitcase and sighed. 'Sure.' She stood up and hobbled, one foot encased in the sandal and the other on tiptoe, inelegantly out of the room. Once the door had closed behind her, Chloe turned back to the screen and began typing away, the only sound in the room being the tap-tapping of her nails on the keyboard. A good ten minutes later, she tapped the space bar with a flourish and leant back, a pleased smile stretching across her face. Maya walked back in, this time more elegantly in two matching shoes and no limp and threw the lonesome, unbroken shoe into her suitcase to join its mate.

'You could have warned me about the state of your room. It took me ages to find this pair. One shoe was in the bathtub and the other one was under the bed! How can any singular person make such a mess in such a short space of time?'

'It's a talent, I know.' Chloe ignored the insult. 'Good choice, too. They're relatively new.'

Maya walked to the full-length mirror and pointed her toe. 'Seriously though, thanks. These are actually gorgeous.'

'Well, they should be, they cost £385,' Chloe said, hopping up from the bed and straightening her dress. 'Shall we go?'

'Sure. Let me just turn off my tablet.' Maya made a move towards the bed, but Chloe quickly grabbed the tablet and pressed the off button.

'All done. Let's go!' She grabbed Maya's elbow and marched them both towards the door, while surreptitiously popping the tablet into Maya's holdall as she passed it. Maya allowed herself to be led out of the room, but Chloe stopped suddenly at the threshold.

'Wait!' she exclaimed, causing Maya to stumble slightly on her newly acquired heels.

'What's wrong?' Maya said.

Chloe reached up and switched on her headband. It began flashing excitedly again and she said, 'Now I'm ready.'

The two women giggled as they made their way down the corridor and into one of the hotel lifts, with Maya pressing for the ground floor. As they whizzed down nineteen flights at an alarming speed, Maya was completely unaware that her blog post was also whizzing at an alarming speed via the wonder that is social media. Little did she know that in the ten minutes she had been absent from her room, Chloe had set up a new blog page and uploaded the blog post, under the heading, *A Single Girl's Guide to Flying Solo* and it was now visible for all the world to see.

Chapter Six

They reached the restaurant ten minutes later, after a very festive cab journey downtown. Their cab driver had adorned the interior of the taxi in twinkling lights, with Christmas tunes blaring out of the speaker and a nodding Santa situated on the dashboard, its white beard almost shimmering under the glare of New York as it whizzed by their window. Maya almost forgot her heartache under the beauty of the city. Almost. She loved this place. No matter how many times she visited, there was always a new restaurant, a new skyscraper, and a new experience for her to be astonished by. But knowing she should be seeing this with Michael still smarted. Images of him cuddling up to Amanda Avary, after a perfect Christmas together, still made her chest ache and her throat tighten.

'We're here!'

Chloe's shout brought her back into the present and she looked out of the cab window to see a sleek new conservatory, jutting out from a typical New York brownstone building. It was all glass and metal, with a neon blue sign resting on the roof, highlighting the four letters, *NYFB*. There was a large queue lining the sidewalk with a white rope blocking the entrance, and two men in grey suits checking off names. She spotted the other cabin crew already in the line.

'Chloe, this doesn't look much like a relaxed, casual restaurant to me,' Maya said, but Chloe had already thrown some notes at the taxi driver and exited the car with a squeal. A cheer went up as she tottered over to join the rest of the crew. Maya leant back into her seat and exhaled. She was tired, hungover, and really hungry. She did not fancy a hoity-toity dinner.

'You goin' in?' The cab driver turned in his seat, and for the first time Maya noticed his red, reindeer jumper protruding over his large stomach. He had a kind face though, with a nice smile that emphasised his two missing front teeth.

'I don't know,' Maya muttered. Half of her was debating whether to get him to take her back to the hotel and lock herself away in her room until their return flight. She suddenly felt exhausted. Her hand rose and touched her throat, finding the tightness in it incessant. She swallowed, but it was more of a gulp. *Don't cry*, she thought, *don't cry*, but she could feel her face growing hot.

The cab driver was watching her, and without speaking, he switched off the meter and turned the ignition key. The car fell silent.

'Take as long as you need, doll. I ain't going anywhere.' He smiled again. 'I ain't just a driver, you know. I'm a glorified therapist, counsellor, lost luggage locater, translator . . . heck, I've even helped deliver a baby in this cab. I've seen it all right here and nothing can shock me. Wanna talk about it?'

Maya felt touched by this American stranger but didn't trust herself to speak. She just shook her head side to side, her curls bouncing as she did so. She fiddled with the strap of her bag on her lap, looking down.

'Heartache? I can tell.' He went on, 'Guy or girl?'

'Guy,' she said, her voice coming out as a croak. A tear fell onto her left hand, now devoid of any ring. There was still a slight indent where it had once proudly sat.

'Was it recent?' he asked, his tone softer now.

She nodded, taking a deep breath to steady herself.

'We were meant to be getting married the day after tomorrow, at Belvedere Castle, Central Park, at sunset. But instead, he proposed to someone else three weeks ago, live on air.'

As she spoke the words aloud, it just sounded so surreal. Was she sure she wasn't stuck in some nightmare, and she would wake up with Michael still loving her, still planning to marry her? She pinched the flesh on the back of her hand to test herself. It hurt. The nightmare was real, then. Another tear fell.

The cab driver leant back in his seat and whistled to himself in disgust before muttering, 'What a total asshole.' Maya nodded silently in agreement.

'Problem is, I still love him,' she said. She bolstered the courage to look up at him and could see the sympathy in his eyes, his big, bushy eyebrows creased in concern.

'Course you do. Love ain't something you can wash away, like a stain on the paintwork of a car,' he said, 'it's ingrained in your heart. You gotta wait until it fades away. And, doll? It will fade away. It just takes time.'

'What if it never goes away?' she asked him. He paused for a moment.

'Ah, you see, the thing is, love requires momentum. It's a partnership. You need to work at love and if one side isn't willing to, then it loses its spark and begins to fade.'

She listened to him, the noise outside the cab seeming to disappear. She hadn't spoken to anyone properly since Michael dumped her, not even Chloe. She couldn't, she was utterly humiliated. She just spewed out the same old line, *I'm OK, honestly. At least he did this before the wedding. I'm lucky really.* Except she didn't mean a word of it, she just couldn't face the sympathetic glances and the consoling words. Yet, talking to this complete stranger felt comforting and the tightness in her throat relaxed just a notch and she took a deep breath.

'Look,' he continued, 'it's Christmas, and as far as I can see, you have three choices. I can take you back to your hotel alone, we can sit in this cab all night while my wife's brisket gets tough, or you can wipe away those tears, exit this smelly, old cab and have a great time with your buddies out there.' He pointed in their direction and Maya noticed they were almost at the front of the queue now. 'I know which one I would rather do.' He leant over and grabbed some tissues from the glove compartment and handed them through the little gap in the partition. She took them and wiped underneath her eyes, careful not to smudge her make-up.

'I got two gals, just around your age. I spend my life carrying tissues and chocolate. If they want one, they sure as heck want the other.' He guffawed, pulling down his sun visor above his head and pointing at a Polaroid image of three woman, two young brunettes with long, wavy hair past their shoulders. They were standing arm in arm with an older woman, late fifties, with the same long hair, but with streaks of silver sliced through. She had even darker skin and her eyes were the deepest amber, like liquid gold. They made a beautiful image. The cab driver's face lit up with pride, his own light blue eyes full of life.

'Men are a dime a dozen,' he said, turning back to her. 'Surely you can find another that ain't gonna dump you like some cheap ass whiskey into the trash.' He shook his head, muttering to himself. 'And live on air too . . . what a loser.'

Maya jumped as there was a loud knocking on her window. She looked out into the dark to see Chloe gesturing at her, her face quizzical and her arms thrown up in confusion.

'Are you coming?' she shouted, she turned to indicate that they were at the front of the queue.

Maya looked to Chloe, then to the cab driver, who shrugged his shoulders and smiled. 'It's your call, lady. What do you want to do?'

'I want to eat.' She sighed, her tummy grumbling again.

'Then, go! Remember, no man has a right to ruin your Christmas.' He ushered her to get out of the cab, which she did, exiting the car and turning back to him as he wound down his window.

'Merry Christmas, British girl,' he said, his breath hitting the cold air like steam from a kettle.

'Merry Christmas to you too,' Maya answered, smiling her first genuine smile in what seemed like forever.

Chapter Seven

Maya opened one eye tentatively and took a moment to navigate where she was. Then she remembered. New York. Hotel room. Alone. She lifted her head slightly, ignoring her brain screaming at her to lie back and fall into a comatose state until she had to fly home again. Her vision widened as she took in the room. She was lying on top of the white, cotton sheets of the hotel bed, side on, as if she had just fallen from a standing position, which she probably had. And as her body sensations appeared to return, she realised she was still wearing her dress from last night, along with just one sandal. She sat up painfully and looked around her for her phone, noting with a wince that her pillow was covered with smudges of black mascara and red lipstick. She attempted to rake a hand through her curls, but they were knotted and frizzy. She winced again. She was still none the wiser for where her phone was. A groan arose next to her, under the covers and she yelped, jumping out of bed, a wave of panic rising through her dehydrated body. As she did so, she tripped on her one shoed foot and fell flat onto her face.

'Ow,' she groaned, clutching at her nose.

'Ow,' came a muffled moan from under the covers. 'Someone get me a strong coffee. Black. Now.'

With the sound of Chloe's pained voice, memories of last night flooded Maya's mind, and she felt nauseated. The two of them in a hip restaurant with the rest of the crew, nibbling on trendy sushi and mochi, then stumbling into a dimly lit bar, then a taxi ride with neon, flashing fairy lights and finally, an image of her and Chloe drinking the remnants of her room's minibar. She groaned again. From her current position on the

32

floor, she spotted the empty bottles scattered around her. She crawled over to the desk and poured two glasses of water from the decanter in the room and tried standing. It wasn't hugely terrible, and she didn't vomit, so she attempted walking to the bed, her head pounding with each step.

'Here, drink. It's not coffee, but it'll help.' She nudged the glass onto the mound, and it moved, the covers flipping back and Chloe revealing herself in all her hungover glory. Her make-up matched Maya's in that it was streaked across her cheeks, and she also had a sheen of glitter across her face, no doubt remnants of her festive hairband. She took the glass and gulped it down eagerly.

'Some night, eh?' she said, her voice croaky.

'It was great, actually,' Maya said. 'From what I can actually remember.' They both laughed, then winced.

'You ready for food, yet?' Maya asked.

'I'm always ready for food,' Chloe said, pulling aside the covers and climbing out. 'Just give me two minutes to change.'

Maya pulled open the hotel room door to the corridor and yelped in surprise. Standing in front of her was Nigel Edwards, wearing a beige woollen vest, with brown lines criss-crossing over it, over an even more beige shirt. He was wearing straight-cut jeans, with loafers, and Maya's first thought was that she had never thought a pair of jeans could look wrong on a man, until now. He was carrying a satchel over his shoulder, and she spotted the familiar Oasis Airlines logo on the bag.

'Nigel!' she exclaimed, causing her head to pound even louder. 'What are you doing here? Outside my room? In New York?' Her mind went immediately to his complaint email yesterday. 'Look, if it's about that complaint made, I promise you that I didn't mean to cause any upset—' She stopped mid-sentence as Nigel held up a hand indicating for her to stop talking.

'May I come in?' he said, looking past her into her room, his eyebrows rising as he clocked the mess on the floor and the state of the room in general.

'Um, I was actually just going down for breakfast,' she said, hoping that would get rid of him for a few minutes, so she could compose herself and not throw up all down that horrid vest of his. All that cross-hatching, and it appeared to be swaying. Or maybe that was just her.

'That's OK, this won't take more than a few minutes of your time,' he said, walking past her and into the room, uninvited. At that moment, Chloe released herself from the bathroom and almost collided with Nigel. Surprisingly, Maya noticed, neither seemed shocked to see the other one there. 'Good morning, Chloe,' he said, walking forward and taking a seat at the hotel desk chair that was in Maya's room, clearing some space by sweeping his arm sideways, her cosmetics and toiletries making a clatter as they were all shoved to the side. He lifted his satchel onto the desk and began extracting items from inside.

'If you could close the door, Maya, and come in?' It was a question that sounded like a demand, and Maya dutifully did as she was told, her mind appearing to have emptied of all its thoughts. She sat down on the edge of the bed, and Chloe sat beside her. There was silence for a moment as Nigel pulled out some paperwork and his glasses case from inside the satchel and arranged the glasses on the end of his pointy nose.

'By the look on your face, I assume that Chloe has not informed you of why I am here this morning,' he said, looking across at Chloe, who shook her head in unison with Maya. Nigel rolled his eyes, and then continued. 'Maya, last night Chloe forwarded me a blog post, written by yourself, see here.' He picked up a piece of paper and showed her a printout of her own words from last night, her own thoughts, and she blushed at the idea that Nigel might have read them. 'Can you confirm that this is writing that you yourself have produced?' Maya nodded mutely. He seemed satisfied and smiled. Maya was not used to seeing him smile. It was not a comfortable sight. 'Well then, I have to say, Maya, that I am very impressed. And with Chloe's help, we think your blog could have huge benefits, both for yourself and Oasis Airlines.'

Nigel looked from her to Chloe, waiting for some kind of response. When he didn't get any, he continued.

'Chloe has come up with an idea and the PR team have agreed that it is a good one,' he said, leaning in towards them both, his elbows on his knees. 'Her idea is to use this blog post, and any further posts written by yourself to boost the airline's social media profile—'

'And get you out of any potential trouble with your complaint,' Chloe butted in.

'Yes, and that. She came up with the idea of letting the airline run with it.' He waved the printout in the air in front of him. 'The anonymous cabin crew pitch. "Follow soaring highs and turbulent lows of one female crew member who is 'Flying Solo'".' With those last two words, he raised his voice to add gravitas. Chloe nodded enthusiastically and he continued, 'I forwarded it to Helen in PR last night, and, despite it being Christmas, she thought it was a brilliant idea and drew up a press release off the back of the post within the hour. Before we could say "Happy Holidays", it was emailed to me, along with the Executive Director's agreement for immediate publication.' He looked triumphant; his veiny cheeks flushed with excitement. 'It really is very good, Maya. You definitely have a way with words.'

Maya didn't know what to say. The thoughts in her head were whizzing around faster than a Boeing 777. Her words, on the company website? Her words being promoted worldwide? She didn't know what to think.

'So, I'm here this morning just to get you to sign a little bit of paperwork,' Nigel said, whipping out some folded papers from his satchel beside his chair. 'It's just some legal jargon to say that you give Oasis Airlines permission to use your posts as part of their marketing, that we will keep you anonymous as per your request, and that social media sites can run with it with immediate effect, blah, blah, blah . . .' he said, tailing off and leaning down into his satchel for a pen.

'Of course she agrees!' Chloe said, leaning forward to yank the pen out of Nigel's hand and holding it out for Maya. 'On the proviso that the complaint is wiped off her record and she is duly compensated for any additional traffic that the airline receives because of her blog.'

'Of course, of course . . .' Nigel said, rifling through the pages to find the right section, finding it and then reading it aloud, '"Clause 1.2 – with your agreement as the content creator, Oasis Airlines Limited request that you continue writing blog posts no less than one a month, but not exceeding more than one a week, over the subsequent twelve months, and that the company is given full permission to post any writings on their platform first, and then any social media accounts related to Oasis Airlines Ltd thereafter. Any copyright will remain with the content creator, being Maya Madeski. On agreement, the company are delighted to clear any complaints currently against you, and in addition, offer you four complimentary flights, anywhere in the world, at economy level or equivalent for yourself and your spouse—" oh, um.' He looked flustered at his error, looked up at Maya, blushed a deep crimson red, and then looked back down to the paperwork on his lap. He cleared his throat and continued, 'Um, "your spouse, or, in the case of there being no spouse, one member of your immediate family".' He removed a handkerchief from his shirt pocket and wiped his balding hairline. 'There's more, but that's the general gist of it. How does that sound?'

How does it sound? It sounds unbelievable, Maya thought. Incredible. Maya Madeski, an Oasis Airlines blogger? She just stared at the paperwork in his hands, her own hands limp by her sides.

Chloe took the paperwork from him and began reading through it, her manicured fingernail combing each line with precision. 'And she remains anonymous throughout?' she asked Nigel and he nodded.

'As part of the agreement, only Maya can reveal herself, as and when she wants to. The company agree that they will not disclose her identity at any point. And she is under no obligation to ever do so, though. That's part of the campaign, the anonymity of it all, it keeps the reader wanting more. Keeps them guessing.' He spoke directly to Chloe, but kept glancing at Maya, hoping for some sort of sign from her that she was onboard. The room was silent for a few minutes while Chloe finished reading.

'I can't see anything wrong with this,' she said, turning to Maya. 'You get to write, which you love, your complaint is resolved, and you hold both the copyright and the control of what, when, and how you write. And four free flights! One of which I will obviously steal from you! It's a no-brainer in my eyes.' Maya turned to look at her, willing her to make the decision for her. She hated making decisions.

Chloe could see her struggling. She spoke more softly. 'What would your mum say?' she asked.

At the mention of her mother, Maya instantly recalled the moments of spontaneity with her mum; the last-minute trips chosen by the pick of a letter, them catching a train to London to see a show with Maya missing a whole day of school, the random pets brought home, the experiments with hair dye, the jokes, the fun — she could hear her mum's voice now, urging her on, telling her to be courageous.

'She'd say go for it,' she said, looking at Chloe, before turning to Nigel and signing the first dotted line. 'What have I got to lose?'

Chapter Eight

After breakfast, the whole team decided to wrap up warm and take a walk around Manhattan. With it being Boxing Day, they knew that the streets would be quiet. Ten minutes later, after collecting as many layers as they could wrap themselves into, they stepped outside of the hotel en masse. Maya was immediately hit by the cold, the freezing air smarting her cheeks and nose. She wrapped her scarf even tighter around her face and dug her gloved hands deeper into her coat pockets. The snow had finally stopped, but it lay thick and grey across the streets, like a dog-eared, once-loved white blanket, and each step Maya took was like stepping into a shallow ice bucket that had been sat out for a while. Thank goodness for her trusty walking boots, she thought as she glanced over towards Chloe who was attempting not to slide around in her three-inch, knee-high boots. Maya rolled her eyes.

They walked towards Saks on Fifth Avenue, which would normally only be around a fifteen-minute walk, but with the sidewalks like ice-rinks, it took double the time and included two slippage incidents involving Andreas and the co-pilot, Graham, who were both now sporting wet bottoms and rosy cheeks.

The roads were quiet and there was an eerie calm over Manhattan, the streets almost deserted. Maya never tired of looking skywards at the huge buildings that towered over them and it made her feel so tiny, like a grain of sand surrounded by huge sandcastles. She was looking up when she felt an arm slip through hers.

'Hey you,' Chloe whispered, her nose bright red and her glossy lips pale under the grey skies. 'How are you really doing? Are you OK?'

Maya looked over at her, noting the concern in her eyes and the hint of worry lines across what forehead she could see under Chloe's woollen hat. She squeezed her arm.

'Honestly? I don't know. It feels surreal, you know? Being here, without him.'

'Of course it does,' Chloe said. 'But I'm here and I'll always be here for you. I love you, darling girl.'

'I know,' Maya replied, quietly. 'So much has happened in such a short space of time and my emotions are all over the place. And then this morning just, well, that all came as a bit of a shock.'

'You mean seeing Nigel in jeans?!' Chloe joked, and they both laughed, with Chloe tightening her hold on Maya's arm. They walked in companionable silence before Chloe asked,

'Are you going to tell the others about your blog?'

Maya had been thinking about that since breakfast. 'Not yet. I need some time. My whole world has been turned on its head and I feel like I need a moment to process it all.'

Chloe didn't answer, she just leant over (rather dangerously in her heels) and kissed Maya on the cheek. Andreas was walking slightly ahead of them both, turning periodically to check on them. They all trudged on through the slush for another few minutes, the noise of the traffic occupying their thoughts, and then turned a corner. They gasped at the sight before them.

Saks Fifth Avenue stood proud in all its festive glory, each window lit up in an array of beautiful colours, fabrics, and styles. One window was full to the brim, right to the ceiling, with gold boxes. Each box had a tiny window cut into it along the side that faced the world and was lit from the inside, so that passers-by could glimpse their hidden contents. Another window was set with a giant Christmas tree, adorned with flags that looked like every country of the world was represented from its branches. Behind it was a giant world map on the wall, with twinkling lights on nearly every continent and a metal Father Christmas hanging from the ceiling over Europe, as if he was in flight. Maya noted a further window that made her mouth water; it was a huge dining table adorned with every tasty Christmas treat imaginable, a giant Christmas turkey with all the trimmings, a large trifle, a Christmas pudding, with crackers of every colour, and plastic candles that flickered and made the room glow. There were two small mannequin children, positioned at each end of the table, reaching up to the tall table in an effort to touch the food. It looked like a vintage Polaroid image capturing a moment in time.

The building itself was adorned in beautiful twinkling, white lights. There was a huge, flashing *Happy Holidays* sign hanging from the roof and a giant red and gold sash hanging both across and down the building, with a gargantuan bow in the centre; the shop itself was a huge Christmas gift. It was like a Hallmark Christmas movie, but with real snow and actual, real-life people. Chloe and Andreas squealed. Maya just gawped at it, noting the beauty, but also the gaping lack of festive spirit in her soul. Her heart ached for what could have been. Michael had not only broken her heart that day, he'd also stamped out Christmas for her, too. She wondered if Christmas would ever hold the same magic it once had . . . or if it was lost to her forever.

Chapter Nine

The next morning, both Maya and Chloe entered the hotel restaurant to find the rest of the crew already seated, with coffee and waffles piled up on the large table. Chloe went to sit with the co-pilot and Maya headed towards Andreas. He was seated between Sarah and Gabrielle, and they were all huddled together, staring at his phone. Maya took a seat opposite as a waiter magically appeared.

'Can I take your order?' he asked in a strong southern accent. Maya looked up at him, noting his good looks and nice smile.

'Yes please. An espresso, with scrambled eggs, spinach and gluten-free toast. Toast cooked on a grill please. Thanks.'

'Coeliac?' he asked. Maya nodded. 'Sure thing.' And he moved on to Chloe, who was seated at the other end of the table whispering with the pilot and co-pilot. They appeared deep in discussion. She looked over at Andreas to find they were all staring at her, eyebrows raised and silent.

'Are you OK?' she asked them.

'Are you?' Gabrielle asked. 'When were you going to tell us?' she exclaimed, thrusting her phone screen towards her. Maya could see what appeared to be the airline's social media page, with small text indecipherable from across the table.

'Oh, that,' she said, realising her anonymity was no longer a thing among the crew sitting all gawking at her. She looked over at Andreas and he had the decency to blush.

'That?! That?! You mean the blog post written by one of our crew, that is now on the front page of its website, trending on social media, and appears to be the biggest trending blog post this side of Christmas!' she exclaimed.

'Why didn't you mention it?' Sarah said.

Maya shrugged as the waiter appeared with her coffee, and she could have kissed him. She took a sip. 'It's no big deal.'

'Maya Madeski, will you stop being so coy? Not once at dinner last night did you mention that you were about to become the next big internet sensation. And the company's cover girl! So bold! You're a genius. Letting Oasis Airlines run your story as part of their latest campaign, just brilliant. Incredibly sad, but brilliant!'

'Eleven thousand shares already—' Andreas said, his eyes on his phone.

'Picked up and shared by *Blogging Weekly*, this morning,' Gabrielle interrupted.

'On *Best Blogs*, too!'

'Darling, you're famous!' Andreas exclaimed. 'Your blog post has gone viral. VI-RAL.' He emphasised that last word, stretching it out. He handed her his phone and she could see on the screen that her post had been pinned to the top of the airline's social media pages, with a link taking her directly to their website. She scrolled down and noticed the 'share' option statistics at the bottom. It had been shared 11,071 times since the post went live over twelve hours ago. She could feel panic in the pit of her stomach, and her hand rose to her throat, willing herself to take a deeper breath. The waiter appeared with her eggs, but she pushed back her chair, almost knocking him to the floor, and walked over to Chloe.

Kneeling down beside her chair, she whispered, 'I think I've made a mistake.'

'Well, I didn't want to say anything, but that top really doesn't go with those trousers,' Chloe said, taking a bite of her bagel. Maya looked down at her top and shook her head.

'No, with the blog post. It's all a bit much. I'm not ready for this.' She could feel beads of sweat forming under her arms, so she grabbed the menu off the table and began fanning herself. 'Shall I see if Nigel will get them to take it all down?'

Chloe lowered her bagel slowly back onto her plate, licked her lips, and sighed. She turned to face Maya directly, placing both hands on Maya's shoulders.

'Maya, I love you dearly, you're my best friend, but I think it's time for a few home truths. I get that it's been shit with all the Michael stuff, and cancelling the wedding, and losing your home and so on, but even before this, you'd become . . . dare I say it, he sucked all the confidence from you. You never went out, never partied, never smiled. In the last few months, you've been as much fun as a parking inspector in a sandstorm.' She paused, searching Maya's face for a reaction. 'This is your moment to shine. Your reward. You have so much talent and you just need to believe in yourself. You need a boost and now you've got it — in the hundreds. Look at the comments at the bottom of the post!' She grabbed her phone and scrolled down to the bottom of the airline page where Maya could see row upon row of comments. She didn't know what to say, she felt so befuddled.

'There are so many comments,' she whispered.

'I know! You're a hit, baby. The internet loves you. As do I.' Chloe kissed the top of Maya's head and let go. 'Now, go and eat your breakfast, it's going cold. I don't want to hear another word about cancelling or removing anything.' She grabbed her bagel and took a huge bite, with cream cheese coating her lips. She licked it off with her tongue, completely aware that the co-pilot was staring at her lustfully. Maya rolled her eyes; Chloe really did have no shame.

She returned to her seat, opposite Andreas.

'She's right, you know,' he said. 'Annoying, yes; but right. You are extremely talented, darling girl. This blog has potential.' He took a big gulp of his orange juice. 'But I still think you're crazy to swear off men for a whole year. I couldn't do it.'

'You couldn't last a week!' Sarah joked, elbowing him in the ribs. She turned her attention back to Maya. 'But do you really think you can do it, Maya? A whole year.'

Maya looked at her, noticing the flash of the two rings on her wedding finger. Sarah had been happily married to a great guy called Stanford for over five years and being single was a distant memory to her, Maya imagined.

'I do. I've had enough heartache to last me a lifetime, let alone a year. It'll be easy.'

After breakfast, Maya retreated to her room and spent the next hour reading through the numerous comments. She was shocked at how many people could relate to this single post. Comments like,

> Twelve months – try four years and counting! Who needs men when we can buy shoes?!

> Dumped and divorced here. A year of singledom sounds great! Can I join the club?!

> Multiple dater here and tired of always dating Mr Wrong, hoping for Mr Right. Your idea sounds brilliant. Please keep writing. I need ideas!

Maya began to realise that there was a whole world of women (and men) out there who were tired of searching for their soulmate and getting let down. The comments made it clear that people wanted to feel they weren't alone, that there was a solidarity that came with being single. An oxymoron at best, a seemingly lonely prospect at worst. Perhaps she could help fill the void that existed for those lonely like-minded people out there. Perhaps she should keep writing.

Maya looked at her watch and realised that in a parallel universe, where Michael wasn't a total cheating cad, she would have been slipping into her wedding dress about now. Instead, she had an empty day ahead of her as Chloe had a hair appointment booked and Maya didn't fancy joining the rest of the crew to watch a hit new Broadway show – that's even if she could have got hold of a ticket, which was unlikely.

44

Her fingers hovered over the keyboard, itching to move. It's not like she had anything else to occupy her mind. She began to type.

Day One.
Dear Diary,
Today should have been my wedding day. The eve of a new chapter of my life. Today should have been full of excitement, drama, and pampering. Instead, I am sat here eating chocolate, with unwashed hair and chipped nails. There will be no ceremony, no grand celebrations or sweet-smelling flowers, or creamy vanilla frosting on a three-tiered cake. No white, fairy tale dress hugging my curves and sparkling in the light. No tiara atop my curls, no fancy footwear or three-course dinners. Instead, I'm about to embark on an eight-hour flight, with greasy hair and under-eye bags so big that I feel I should check them into the hold.

I need a plan, a focus. A reason to pull myself up and remove my elasticated trousers. So what if I'm single? And now technically homeless. With joint ownership of a turtle called Tennyson. At twenty-eight. That's still young, right? Mum always used to say, 'Life is like a Victoria sponge. Often sweet but sometimes disappointing.' Ironic really, with me being strictly gluten-free.

So, looking at the positives . . . I love my job. Adore it. How many people can say that? And I love to write. One diary entry a day keeps the insomnia at bay. Agreed? This is the first time I've ever written in anything other than my trusty grey diaries. I'm going to document my thoughts here and with every passing day, I hope to climb out of the fug that is my life. The ups, the downs, the joy, the tears. Searching for the positives of each day, without having to think about anyone else. The bed is all mine, and so is my life.

My first job? To get a manicure. The ring may be gone, but the nails can still look fabulous, right?

Maya emailed the blog post to the PR team at Oasis Airlines and sat back. Did she mean everything she said? Or was she hoping that by saying it, she would start believing it?

'That is the million-dollar question,' she said aloud to the empty room.

The silence was disturbed by Chloe's trademark knock at the door, with Chloe bellowing at her to open it. Maya did and was greeted by Chloe leaning on the doorframe tapping her foot on the floor.

'You have ten minutes to improve the shit-show I see before me,' she declared, pointing a finger at Maya and waving it from head to foot.

'Until what?' Maya questioned.

'Until you take my hair appointment.'

Maya shook her head in confusion. 'Why would I take your hair appointment?'

'Because your hair is a disaster, your roots are horrid, and I'm the best friend in the whole world,' Chloe said, walking into the room and picking up a towel from the floor, her nose screwed up in disgust.

'I couldn't, it's your appointment!' Maya protested.

'Listen, today was meant to be your wedding day! To arse-hole Michael, which is now not happening due to said arse-hole. Darling, I love my hair, but I love you more and right now, you need to be pampered more than I do.' She threw the damp towel onto the bed and looked straight at Maya; her expression more serious. 'Please take it. You deserve it. I want you to have it.'

Maya was speechless. She lifted a hand to her hair. Her natural curls felt dry and frizzy, and her added highlights had now grown out at least three inches. She hadn't felt the need to maintain them when she had a man who loved her uncon-ditionally. How ironic.

'Are you sure?'

'I am,' Chloe said. 'But only for another ten minutes and then I might completely reverse my offer and leave you and your roots high and dry.' She smiled and winked. 'C'mon, throw some clothes on and meet me downstairs, I'll hail a taxi.'

46

Chapter Ten

An hour later and Maya was sat under the hairdryer hood, her head covered in tinfoil and colour, and a glass of champagne in her hand. This was some stylish hairdresser, she thought, as she took another cool sip in an effort to counteract the heat around her head, the bubbles hitting the top of her mouth satisfyingly.

Chloe had agreed to meet her at the Rockefeller Christmas tree in an hour. Maya knew she was making a concerted effort to cheer her up by keeping her busy and she really appreciated it. Her phone beeped and she lifted her black gown to retrieve it from her jeans pocket. It was a voicemail from her dad. She lifted it to her ear, hovering it there gently so as not to touch her wet hair, and listened to the message. It wasn't the best connection, and she could hear someone in the background clattering around.

'Hello, poppet, Dad here. How are you? I miss you. Christmas just wasn't the same without you and we both said we wish you'd changed your mind. I hope you're enjoying New York, and the snow, I saw it on the news! It's a frosty two degrees here in Bridport, but grey skies, no hint of snow as yet—'

'Levi! Don't mention the weather!'

'Eh?'

'Don't mention the weather, you old fool! She'll think of Michael!'

'What? Oh . . . sorry, poppet. Anyway, ring me tomorrow, hey? I'd like to hear your voice. Remember, I'll be at the airport to collect you on Friday, as planned. Better go now. Love you.'

Maya couldn't help but smile. She recognised Gayle's voice in the background, berating him for mentioning any tenuous link that might make her think of Michael, as if she wasn't thinking about him all the time as it was. Despite them hiding it disastrously, she knew they were in a relationship, and she was so pleased for her dad. He'd been devastated when her mum died seventeen years ago and had bravely stepped into the role of full-time parent and carer for Maya, yet she knew he had been lonely. Gayle was a good match for him. She went to call back, but her hairdresser appeared next to her and whipped her over to the washbasins and all thoughts of her father disappeared from her mind.

Ninety minutes later, Maya was walking towards Rockefeller Center, a lightness to her step as her freshly coiffed curls bounced around her face. Despite it being absolutely freezing, she couldn't bear the idea of flattening her hair with her woollen hat and so she walked quickly, looking out for Chloe as she did so. It was busy, as expected, and she really had to meander her way through the crowds towards the huge tree that was like a lit beacon to them all. She spotted Chloe standing alone, wrapped in a hot-pink duffel coat and bright blue mittens, trying to hold what looked like a steaming hot chocolate between her hands. A silk gold and purple scarf was wrapped around her head, and she was wearing large sunglasses, blocking out the wintery sunshine. She looked like a movie star. On Maya it would look ridiculous, but on Chloe, it just screamed fabulous, and Maya felt instantly plain, dressed in her ripped jeans, old boots, and grey duffel coat.

'Chloe, over here.'

Chloe turned in her direction, her eyes passing over Maya completely, and then doubling back, widening in surprise.

'Maya, you look fan-bloody-tastic! Wow, the colour! The cut! You look amazing.' She walked over and touched Maya's hair, feeling the curls, and getting her to turn full circle so she could have a look.

'All thanks to you!' Maya said, blushing. 'It does look good, doesn't it?' A man walked past her and winked. She looked at her boots, feeling flushed. She couldn't remember the last time she had felt attractive. Gone was her dark brown, dull, dry frizz and in its place were golden-streaked, well-defined curls that now sat at least three inches shorter on her shoulders.

'It looks great. You look great. A total knockout.' Chloe put her arm around her and gave her a squeeze. 'Now let's go and get a festive cocktail.'

Chapter Eleven

Two rounds of mulled wine later, and Maya was feeling a little more cheerful. Chloe had an infectious spirit, and it was hard not to get caught up in her enthusiasm, and she'd also managed to find them a table at an outdoor café right beside the Rockefeller Tree itself. They'd been playing a game where they had to guess the contents of people's shopping bags, and their answers were becoming more outrageous the more they drank. A handsome man approached and started talking to Chloe, her attention diverted by his sexy eyes, leaving Maya to take in the festive atmosphere around her.

Her phone rang. It was barely audible above the hubbub and excitement of the city around her, but she pulled it out of her pocket and froze. A name was flashing brightly in the shadows of the sparkling Christmas tree lights above them. A name that she hadn't seen in almost a month.

Michael.

Her heart went from beating regularly to suddenly pounding and her vision began to spin. She sat upright and stared at the phone as if it was a piece of burning lava, holding it in her flattened palm. Michael's face stared back at her, his profile photo taken on their holiday to Crete last year, with him standing on the beach with a surfboard and a baseball cap saying, *I love Crete*. He looked annoyingly geeky and gorgeous.

She stared at the screen while the phone continued humming in her hand. Should she answer? Why was he calling? She hastily worked out the time difference and noted that he was calling on what would still have been their scheduled wedding day in the UK. Did he regret what he had done? On the seventh ring, the phone fell silent, and his image disappeared. The screen turned black. Maya continued staring at her phone for a good few moments after the call, but it didn't ring again. And there was no new voicemail message. Whatever Michael had wanted, he didn't anymore.

Maya felt bruised, exhausted, numb. She gazed over at Chloe who had been too distracted to even notice, and she let herself flop back into her chair. Her limbs felt heavy, the phone still grasped in her shaky fingers. Images of her wedding dress, still hanging in their spare room wardrobe, appeared unwanted in her mind. The intricate lace trim that enveloped the soft satin skirt and had been made from her mother's own veil. The fitted, off-white bodice with the sweetheart neckline and detailed pearl finish. It had actually shimmered as she moved for each of her fittings. She had felt beautiful wearing it, even in the shop with her make-up free face and frizzy hair. It was a dress that accentuated her curves, rather than hid them. And she would have felt beautiful today if she had been getting married as planned.

Should she ring him back? She knew what Chloe's response would be. And what her mum would say too. No. Move on. He's not worth it. He hurt you. She sighed, her breath visible in the cold air, rising towards the giant tree above them.

Instinctively, she stood up, needing to escape her thoughts. Her left knee hit the sharp edge of the café table in doing so, and Chloe glanced over at her in shock. Slamming both hands onto the table in her effort to not scream out in pain, her knee throbbing, she muttered a hasty 'I need the loo,' and hobbled away, through the crowds, away from the festivities, and towards the welcome darkness of a quiet side street. However, with her mind elsewhere, she didn't spot the brightly decorated Manhattan rickshaw coming towards her at speed, didn't hear his horn or his yells.

There was no time for him to stop and nowhere for him to swerve, and with a sharp, stabbing pain, her elbow made contact with the wing mirror, and her phone flew out of her hand and towards the ground. The driver yelled angrily back at her as he drove unsteadily on, but she neither heard nor replied. Instead, she stared at the phone, now submersed in a dirty puddle, its screen shattered and blank. Picking it up, she tried restarting it, but nothing, it was dead. Now the decision to find out why Michael was calling was out of her hands. Even if she had wanted to call him back, she couldn't. She felt broken. And Michael felt lost to her forever.

'I think this is a bad idea,' Chloe said for the umpteenth time since leaving the electrical store where Maya had reluctantly purchased a new phone, under Chloe's insistence. Her face was screwed up in concern.

'I need to do it,' Maya replied, her eyes straight ahead on her target. She walked, with Chloe struggling to keep up with her in her ridiculous high heels. A strong wind whipped around them, the snow flurries beginning again, and the park was glistening under a snowy white blanket, the evening sun dropping lower in the peach-stained sky.

'How about we go and get a drink instead, hey?' Chloe puffed, turning to look behind her and pointing. 'I spotted a nice-looking bar just before we entered the . . . argh!' Chloe yelled as she slipped on an icy patch of gravel and almost fell. Maya made a grab for her, guiding Chloe to a park bench only a few feet away.

'Why don't you take a seat here and I'll go on alone. I won't be long.'

Chloe refused, shaking her head sideways vehemently. 'No, no. If you are going, I am going. You chose me as your maid of honour, and the maid of honour's pact is to never leave a bride alone, especially if they have been jilted, dumped, cheated on or humiliated . . .'

'Three out of four ain't bad,' Maya muttered sarcastically.

Chloe continued. '. . . and therefore, it is my duty to stay by your side.' She went to stand again, resolute in her duty, but slipped again and fell back onto the bench with a slam.

'Ow!'

'Seriously, you're no good to me with a broken leg, duty or no duty. Stay here, I'll be back before you know it. And I have my new phone to keep me safe,' she said, wagging the newly purchased phone in Chloe's face.

Before Chloe had a chance to argue her case, Maya turned and strode off as quickly as she could on the slippery path. She didn't need Chloe for this. It was something she had to do for herself.

Ten precarious, icy minutes later and Maya arrived at her destination. It was blissfully quiet in the park, the weather keeping people away, although there were a few hardy visitors standing on the terraces, looking out. Despite being in the centre of the city, there was a stillness that hung in the air like magic, as if time had slowed. All the city noise was muted by a thick blanket of pure, white snow, and with every step, Maya could feel the soft crunch beneath her feet. There was a comfort in the stillness. She inhaled deeply, her lungs filling with icy, crisp air. She was standing in front of Turtle Pond, the water completely frozen over, towards the Vista Rock, on which Belvedere Castle stood proud. Its corner tower had a coat of snow, but its American flag was flapping gently in the winter breeze, its colours contrasting against the stone building and white snow. A couple of resilient ducks waddled past her legs and jumped onto the pond, their flat feet skidding on the frozen ice and they quacked at each other in consternation.

She walked around the pond slowly, her eyes staring up at the huge rock and impressive castle, the mock-medieval structure looking like something straight from a film set. Not that Michael had chosen it for its architectural design or dreamy connotations. At first, when he had suggested getting married here, she was bowled over by his romantic gesture, until he calmly informed her that Belvedere Castle had always been on his radar since he'd visited as an eight-year-old boy and he'd learnt of its scientific and meteorological significance.

'What better place to marry than where some of the most extreme weather phenomena have been recorded in the last one hundred years!' he'd said, over a year ago when they first started planning their wedding. 'Imagine saying your vows next to a century-old anemometer or walking the same steps that some of the best climatologists might have themselves walked. Wow.'

'And the fact that it is extremely romantic, getting married in Central Park in the winter,' Maya interjected.

'Well, yeah, that too. But we could coincide it with a tour of the Rockefeller Center and its Meteorological Observatory. We could even try and secure a meeting with a climatologist to gauge their opinions on the predictions of the next El Nino phenomenon . . .' he had continued excitedly, but Maya had zoned out, just pleased that at least he had agreed a Christmas wedding in Central Park. Their separate reasons why, at that point, seemed irrelevant.

This memory stayed with her as she approached the entrance to the castle, and she looked up at the thick, grey clouds above her. Michael would have loved this weather; snow was his favourite. She joined a short queue of people waiting to gain access. A couple in front of her were holding hands, and she spotted a huge diamond on the woman's ring finger.

'Just imagine getting married here!' the woman exclaimed with a little squeal. 'What a magical place.' Her fiancé nodded in agreement, and they hurried on inside, leaving Maya to follow behind into the darkness of the castle. She followed the signs and made her way up towards the terrace, climbing the shallow stone steps, imagining herself climbing them holding onto her dad's arm, her dress trailing behind her, a faux fur bolero to keep her warm and Michael waiting nervously at the top. But as she reached the top step, she saw only strangers taking selfies and staring at the panoramic view of the park as the sunset lit everything up with an amber hue. She stood under one of the beautifully designed archways of the roof structure and looked out towards the Great Lawn. It really was exquisite, Maya thought. There was a woman sitting on a gold chair, playing a large cello, its deep sound reverberating around the terrace. The cellist was playing 'Silent Night' and Maya could imagine how beautiful this spot would be for a wedding. A couple next to her began to kiss.

'OK, I think I'm done,' she said, turning on her heel and making her way back down the stairs. She'd hoped visiting today would have given her some sort of closure, but it actually just made her feel sad for what could have been. In a parallel universe, she would now be a married twenty-eight-year-old, with a stable job and a comfortable life. Instead, she was a single woman, in her late twenties, wearing a T-shirt stained with this morning's latte and who'd just made some crazy-arsed pact to not date another guy for a whole year. What was she thinking? She sped up, now wanting to leave the place as quickly as possible, find Chloe and get a drink. Preferably alcoholic, preferably large.

She was reaching into her pocket for her phone to call Chloe, when she stepped off the last step and bumped straight into a huge chest and protruding stomach, which knocked her backwards and onto the wet steps behind her. Her phone went flying out of her hand for the second time that day.

'Ow!' she exclaimed, the horrid sensation of damp ice seeping into her jeans. She looked up to see who the human bollard was, ready to voice her frustration, when she jolted in surprise.

'Hello, British Girl, I thought I might find you here. It might do you good to watch where you're going though.' His body blocked out the late afternoon light, but as she looked up, she found herself looking straight into the warm eyes of the cab driver from two nights ago. He picked up her phone first, then held out a huge, gloved hand and she took it gratefully, pulling herself to standing, groaning at the large damp patch on her bottom. But as she turned back, she noticed he was holding a small, rectangular box in his other hand, and he pushed it towards her.

'You mentioned in the cab the other night that you were due to get married at sunset at Belvedere Castle and I just had a hunch you would be here. When I finished my shift, I mentioned it to the wife and we both agreed that no bride should be without their flowers, whether the groom turns up or not. So, on the off chance that you might turn up, we wanted to be here to hand you this.'

Maya looked down at the brown paper box and took it from him carefully. She opened the lid and gasped. Inside was the most beautiful corsage comprised of winter honeysuckle, ivy, holly and mistletoe, all encasing the most delicate of white snowdrops. It was so beautiful; the freshness of the green leaves and the vividness of the red berries a contrast to the delicate, snow-white petals of the snowdrops. Maya felt tears prickle the backs of her eyes.

'You, you did this for . . . me?' she stumbled, her voice a whisper. He nodded, looking over to the left of him.

'Well, it was mostly the missus,' he said, pointing at an attractive lady in her late fifties, wrapped in a beautiful, cream coat. She had long, salt and pepper hair that blew softly in the wind and a warm smile. She waved towards them.

'She's gotta heart of gold, that one.'

Maya felt that familiar lump appear in her throat and she didn't trust herself to speak. Instead, she lifted the box up to her face and took a deep breath in. It smelt like Christmas, sweet and woody and she was instantly transported back to her childhood, decorating their freshly cut Christmas tree with her dad.

'It's beautiful,' she managed, a tear rolling down her cheek. 'Thank you.'

He noted her tears and shifted his feet, clearly feeling uncomfortable. 'We didn't mean to make you cry. We just couldn't bear the idea of a girl our daughters' age being all alone in New York City at Christmastime. We only live twenty minutes' walk from here, and often take our walks through the park, so it really was no effort. And the flowers were nothing really,

56

my wife's a florist, you see, so she put it together,' he rambled, trying to make light of his gesture. 'I just had a hunch you'd be here.'

Maya nodded, smiling. She looked at his face, blotchy skin patchworked with spots, and a chin that almost disappeared into his neck. He had bushy eyebrows and dark stubble shadowing his cheeks, but his eyes radiated kindness. He was wearing a huge, brown button-up coat that reminded her of a big brown bear. Instinctively, she walked forward and kissed him gently on his cold cheek.

'I love it, thank you,' she said, smelling strong cologne and honey roasted nuts. 'Would you help me put it on?'

His smile showed relief and he nodded. 'Sure can, British Girl, but not with these clumsy hands. I've got just the person.' He gestured to his wife, who appeared to have been waiting in the wings for his call. She walked over and took the box from Maya.

'Hello, doll. My name's Dorothea and you are just the sweetest thing since candied apples. Will you take a look at that face?' She looked from Maya to her husband, and he nodded. 'What man would be fool enough to say no to you?' She made a disapproving, clicking noise with her tongue and shook her head from side to side.

Maya noted the southern accent. 'My name's Maya and can I just say thank you for making such a beautiful gift? You are truly talented.' She allowed Dorothea to take the corsage from the box and, with slim, perfectly manicured fingers, she watched as she deftly threaded it through Maya's buttonhole.

'Ah, my pleasure, sweetie. Ain't nothing more soothing for the mind as putting together some of God's greatest creations. Flowers are gifts from heaven for the eyes, senses, and soul.' She finished adjusting it and took a step back to admire her handiwork. 'Just perfect.'

She looked up at Maya, her face softening. 'He ain't worth it, darlin'. Clearly has the mind of a gnat if he let you go. There'll be another one waiting just around the corner, you mark my words.' They moved aside from the steps to let a large party walk past and Maya noticed that dusk was falling.

'Look at me and my Ron here. I was dating this quarter-back in college, thought himself the big man on campus, but he treated me like the dried-on dirt on the bottom of his boot. This charmer here' – she nudged him with her delicate shoulder, and he put a huge arm around her narrow waist – 'he noticed me crying in the garden of some frat party in our third year and offered me a hanky from his blazer pocket. What kid carries around hankies at college?' She threw both arms up questioningly and they chuckled at the memory. 'But this kid here comes up to me and tells me that I'm too good for quarterbacks and jockeys and men who couldn't see me for who I was – the most beautiful girl in the room. *And would I honour him with a date?* On our first date, he turned up at my dorm room with a big pot holding these purple flowers; *Dorothea flowers*, he tells me, I tell ya, darlin', I was hooked from that point onwards.' She knotted her arm through his, giving him a squeeze.

'You've gotta find a man who'll love you the way my Ron loves me. Who looks at you as though he can't believe his luck. Who makes you feel like every day is your wedding day. Sure, you'll have your bad times, your rough patches, but you need a man who is the only person you want to dine with, lie with, argue with and laugh with. If you can find a man like that, stick to him like mustard on a hot dog. You got that?'

Maya loved her instantly. What an amazing woman. They seemed like an unlikely couple, her striking beauty and lean body against his blotchy face and doughy body. But she noticed their body language, the way she leant into him comfortably and the adoration on his face as he looked at her.

'I've got it,' Maya said, smiling. 'Thank you.' She leant forward and kissed her on the cheek, careful not to knock her corsage. Her phone rang suddenly, Chloe's face lighting up the new screen. Maya mouthed a silent apology to the couple and answered it.

'Where are you, chick? I couldn't bear the idea of you walking to that castle, so I managed to get a ride on a horse-drawn carriage. Are you there?' Maya could hear the neigh of a horse in the background and chuckled. Only Chloe would flag down a horse-drawn carriage like she was catching a bus.

'Yes, I'm still here. Actually, I'm just leaving. I'll come out.'

'I'm to the left of Turtle Pond,' Chloe said, and Maya hung up before turning back to Ron and Dorothea.

'That was my friend. She's outside. Turns out I'm not totally alone in New York.'

'Well, ain't that just great,' said Dorothea. 'Boys come and go, but your girlfriends, well, they're there for life.' Dorothea gave her a quick kiss and gently nudged her to leave them. Ron gently patted her on the shoulder and indicated for her to leave.

'Goodbye, British Girl.'

Maya smiled at them both, feeling like this was the first time she had really, genuinely felt her shoulders relax in weeks.

'Bye. And thank you.'

Chapter Twelve

'Oh, don't be so ridiculous,' Chloe exclaimed as she pulled the rug a little higher around her torso.

'I'm just saying . . .'

'You're just saying that you want to head back to the hotel and sulk in your room, watching old movies and despairing about the state of your life.'

Maya said nothing, blushing, despite the arctic temperatures and the fact that the snow was now whipping around them as they trotted through Central Park in their carriage. Chloe had totally hit the nail on the head there. She did want to go back to the hotel and climb into bed. She felt exhausted. She looked ahead at the looming Manhattan skyline, the city lights so artificially bright compared to the quietness and serenity of Central Park. The festive atmosphere surrounded them but she just felt immune to it all. She desperately wanted to leave, so she tried a different tack.

'But we fly home tomorrow, we need to be at our briefing at 11am. Bright-eyed and bushy-tailed, not red-eyed and scruffy-tailed. I've already been given a written warning,' she reminded Chloe but could see it was making not one iota of difference. Chloe simply rolled her eyes.

'Nigel Edwards has already written off that complaint. And he knows you're the most dedicated crew member we have on our team. He's more likely to fire the pilot mid-flight, during a snowstorm, and with two engines down, than he is to get rid of you. Now stop acting like an old-lady spinster, show off that fabulous hair and let's go to that art gallery tonight. Who wouldn't want to see some dull art and try and wrangle as many free cocktails as we can? Not us!'

Maya sighed. 'What is this art exhibition even about?'

Chloe shrugged. 'How should I know? All I know is, Graham will be there and invited us to come along, so we have to go.' She gave Maya the look that meant she wouldn't take no for an answer and Maya could begin to see her resolve crumble. Once Chloe had a plan, there was no deviating, no diverging. Just like their recent flight to Vancouver that was re-routed to Edmonton because of bad weather, she knew she could do nothing to change Chloe's flight path once she'd set her mind to it.

One very hot bath to warm her extremities, two hot chocolates in her room and three hours later, Maya and Chloe walked from the cold night air into the warmth of Alto Art, supposedly Manhattan's swankiest new art gallery. Tonight was opening night. There was a cellist playing to the left of them, dressed totally in pale green, including the cello, and there were waiting staff milling around them, also dressed in green, this time in an emerald shade. One waitress appeared in front of them like a magician's assistant, with a sea-green tray filled with bright green cocktails, with sprigs of mint garnishing each glass.

'Chloe,' Maya whispered, 'why is everything green?' Chloe didn't speak, but simply pointed at the printed poster on the pillar beside her that had the title, *Establishing a Green Environment, An Art Movement* by M. M. Milner.

'Crazy,' she said, taking a sip from the glass in her hand. It was surprisingly good. She tasted apple juice and vodka.

'Shall we peruse the room?' Chloe said in a fake-American drawl and Maya nodded, taking a step forward to the closest canvas on their left. It was a white canvas with a large, single brushstroke of vivid green across it and specs of brown paint splashed over the top. In the top right corner were some actual real leaves glued onto the canvas, strategically aligned so they looked like they had been caught in motion as they fell but were frozen in time. In the bottom left corner was a painted clock face, in what looked like fountain pen, its lines deliberately smudged downwards. It looked to Maya like it had been completed by a bunch of pre-schoolers, and in a matter of minutes at that. She looked across at Chloe, whose eyebrows were knitted together in mock concentration. They moved onto the next canvas silently, which involved a large, brown splodge in the centre, with five thin, wavy, emerald-green lines passing horizontally through it.

'Is this for real? Are we meant to take this seriously?' Maya whispered to Chloe.

'As seriously as climate change, supposedly,' a voice answered from behind, his British accent standing out against the low hum of American chatter.

Both Maya and Chloe turned to see a man standing there, his red T-shirt contrasting against the green room like a beacon, his face serious but the lines around his eyes creasing as if he were trying not to laugh. Maya noted his eyes were a deep brown, almost as dark as his pupils and he had thick, wavy hair that flopped over his forehead and around his ears. It looked unkempt and unbrushed, yet sexy. He took a sip from his matching green glass, and Maya couldn't help noting his soft lips. It was ridiculously sensual, yet he seemed completely unaware. Maya could feel her cheeks heat slightly under the harsh gallery lights. With his left hand, he popped some thick-rimmed, black glasses back onto his face to scrutinise the canvas behind her and it was then that something mentally 'dinged' inside her head. Those glasses, that face. Yes, the thick stubble had gone, as had the stupid faded black baseball cap from his head, but it was definitely him. He turned slightly, revealing the peak of his baseball cap tucked into the back pocket of his jeans. 28C.

She gasped and took a step back. Chloe stared at her in confusion, looking from Maya to the man. Seeing how attractive he was, she giggled at his joke coquettishly.

'Oh, my friend was kidding. I can totally see how the artist was articulating the haunting decline of nature versus urban city life. The clever use of tones and shapes highlight how the landscape of our natural world is being dragged down by human selfishness. It really is enlightening.' She held out a hand towards him, her gold bracelets jangling as she did so. 'Hi, I'm Chloe. And this . . .' she nodded her head in Maya's direction '. . . is Maya. Isn't this exhibition just wonderful?' Her smile was switched on to full beam, matching the strip lights above them. He shook her hand briefly before letting go.

'Theo. Nice to meet you both. And in answer to your question, no, it's crap. All of it. Pretentious drivel, created by a privileged millennial who has no desire to work or indeed campaign against environmental change.' He smiled at her, to show he was speaking in jest. 'Kidding. The artist is actually great. A true gem. I'm only here for the free drinks and because I promised my cousin I would come.' He turned and gestured to an equally attractive man who was grabbing a couple more glasses from a passing waiter. He walked over to them and handed one to Theo.

'Hey, here you go, bud.'

'Thanks, Dave.' He turned and pointed to the girls. 'I'd like to introduce you to Chloe and Maya. Chloe loves the art here, she's a huge fan.'

Dave looked surprised, but politely shook their hands. 'Really?' He looked a little bemused and Chloe blushed.

'Well, not a *huge* fan . . .' she began, taking a long gulp of her drink, emphasis on the huge.

'Because I personally know the artist, so if you like, I could make an introduction?' Dave indicated towards the back of the gallery, a mock-serious expression on his face.

Chloe looked panicked. 'Oh, who am I kidding, this art is crap! If I wanted to see muddy marks on a piece of paper, I could just head to Central Park and look for a soggy newspaper on a park bench!' She leant in closer to both men, surreptitiously making sure her low-cut dress showed off her assets to full advantage. 'Does anyone actually buy this stuff?'

'Well, judging by the price tag, I should think perhaps they do.' Theo moved past Chloe and stood shoulder to shoulder with Maya. She could smell his aftershave again, sandalwood and a hint of mint. He smelt clean and appealing. Up close, she noticed his broad shoulders and the three tiny moles on his neck positioned like a triangle. He needed a haircut and he looked tired, the bags under his eyes slightly purplish and deep, yet he was still annoyingly sexy. She followed his gaze to the tiny little white strip underneath the canvas that bore the title, 'The Haunting Heath'. Written in even smaller print was the price: $34,750.

'Are you kidding me?' she exclaimed.

'That's more than I earn in a year,' Chloe said.

'Yep. Madness,' Dave said. 'Fancy another and we can all play a game of guess the most pretentious price?'

Chloe laughed, 'I'm in.'

'Sure,' said Theo.

'Um . . .' began Maya but no one seemed to be listening. Dave had already disappeared off to find a tray and Chloe was fluffing up her already fluffed-up hair.

'Chloe, can I have a word?' Maya said, trying to surreptitiously indicate to her that she meant in private.

'Hmm?' Chloe answered, moving closer, leaving Theo stuck between them.

'Let me go and see if Dave needs a hand,' he said, sensing the atmosphere and disappearing into the throng of people.

'What's up, buttercup? How cute are these guys?' Chloe said. 'I like the American one, you can have the British boy.'

Maya rolled her eyes. 'Chloe, do you know who he is?' she said, pointing at Theo's perfectly formed, retreating bottom.

'Ooh, someone famous? A celebrity? Although with that accent— Ooh, a duke?' she squealed in excitement. Maya grabbed both her wrists to calm her and to potentially stop her from bouncing on the spot.

'No, Chloe. That man is 28C.'

'Who?' Chloe said, confused.

'That arse from the flight that made a complaint about me! The reason I had the email from Nigel Edwards. The reason my Christmas was hideous!'

Maya watched as realisation dawned on her face.

'*That* guy? No! He seems so nice!'

'Because he doesn't recognise or remember me. And because he's probably hot on you, like most men.'

Chloe shrugged. They both knew that she picked up more men than a London Uber driver.

'Are you going to say anything?' This time it was Maya's time to shrug.

'I don't know. Shall we just leave before they get back?'

'But his cousin is so hot!' Chloe's bottom lip plunged out. 'Do we have to? Couldn't we just have one more drink and then move on?' she pleaded with Maya; her eyes bright. Maya went to respond with a no, but the two men appeared at their sides with fresh glasses in each hand.

'Two ultra-bright cocktails for two ultra-gorgeous girls,' said Dave, handing his over to Chloe, his eyes focused on her. Theo handed one to Maya and she took it with a sigh. Chloe was silently pleading with her and Maya conceded. One drink, that was all.

'Let's move around the room, and every time we hear or see the word *tone*, we must take a sip of our drinks. Got it?' Dave nodded excitedly and Chloe giggled, and they moved collectively onto the next painting. This one looked like a cat had vomited onto a blank canvas and then rolled in it; a yellowy-green splodge that had been splattered onto the canvas with bits of grass and moss stuck on. The price was $28,950. The four of them stood side by side, staring at it. A couple approached from behind and talked loud enough for them all to hear.

'Now take this one, for example. The artist has captured the tone perfectly, each brush stroke mimicking the decline of the rainforests . . .' They all took a sip, eyes facing forward. '. . . and I heard Milner speak of how she spent two weeks in a rainforest, with nothing but his survival backpack, a paintbrush and notepad and the clothes on her back. All for the sake of his art . . .' They moved on, the balding man still blathering on. The four stood there as another couple came close.

'. . . you see, for me the artist has a wonderful eye for detail. See how the tone of his work is reminiscent of Picasso in its melancholy portrayal of the power of mankind . . .' They all took another sip.

'This is fun!' Chloe said. 'But, Dave? We're going to need bigger glasses.'

Chapter Thirteen

An hour later and Maya was feeling decidedly tipsy. They had carried on with their game through two more glasses of green liquid and Maya was starting to worry that her pee would literally glow in the dark. One more drink had turned into two and Chloe was currently arm in arm with Dave, laughing coquettishly at something he said. Maya noticed that Theo was definitely the quieter of the two, although that might also be because she had barely said two words to him.

'Would you like another?' he asked, waving his empty glass from side to side like a pendulum.

'No thanks,' Maya answered curtly, 'I have an early start tomorrow for work.'

'Oh, yes? What is it you do?'

He really didn't recognise her, she realised. It made her feel ridiculously tiny and insignificant. And cross.

'I'm a flight attendant. For Oasis Airlines. We are returning home tomorrow on the midday flight.' She gestured to Chloe.

'Oh wow. That must be such a cool job, meeting famous people, jet-setting all over the world . . .' He tailed off animatedly.

'Not all of it is glamorous, I assure you,' she said wryly, but he didn't seem to be listening, his brow creasing in thought.

'I flew over with Oasis Airlines, actually. A few days ago. I don't suppose . . .' This time he tailed off quietly, looking disconcerted.

'Christmas Day flight, by any chance? Seat 28C?' Maya looked him straight on, one eyebrow raised suggestively.

'Um, perhaps? Wait . . .'

'No, you wait,' Maya spat, her anger from the last few weeks spilling over. 'How could you make a complaint about me, when all I was trying to do was my job? You were rude, arrogant, ridiculously drunk and could have cost me my job.' Her voice shook at the last words, her resolve wanting to crumble. But she wouldn't let him see her cry. 'Chloe? Can we leave, please? I have a terrible headache.' She leant around him to speak directly to Chloe, who had her head resting on Dave's shoulder. She looked shocked.

'Now?' Her eyes darted from Theo to Maya, and she clocked the atmosphere. She sighed. 'Sure, babe. Let's go.' Maya felt ridiculously relieved. However much of a flirt Chloe was, she was as loyal as they come when it came to friendship. 'I'll call you next time I'm in town, yeah?' She turned to Dave, and he nodded, completely taken aback by the sudden change of events, but too drunk to keep up.

'Sure, darlin'. Here, take my card.' He fumbled drunkenly in his wallet and pulled out a card for her. He gave Theo a glare of disapproval. Maya couldn't look at either of them, she just began walking towards the exit, desperate to feel the icy, cool air on her face and to get some distance between her and Theo. She felt Chloe's hand take hers from behind in sisterly support but didn't look back. They left the gallery and stepped onto the busy street. There was now a queue forming to get into the gallery and two more girls their age, wearing skimpy dresses, were allowed in by the bouncer.

'You OK, Maya?' Chloe asked.

'I'm fine,' Maya responded. 'Let's just get a cab and go back to the hotel.' She began to shiver. Her cotton playsuit was no match for the below-freezing temperatures and she could hear Chloe's teeth chattering beside her. She felt a huge surge of anger. It was men. Always men. They treated her like dirt, like she was some sort of disposable object. She could feel the frustration and anger from the last few weeks building, ready to burst out of her.

'Sure thing, sweetie,' Chloe said, looking concerned. She stepped onto the edge of the kerb to hail a passing cab.

'Maya!' a voice called from behind her and she turned to see Theo bursting out of the gallery, his face screwed up in guilt and concern. 'Please, let me apologise.'

She shook her head, her curls bouncing side to side. 'Just leave us alone.' She couldn't deal with any drama at this point. She needed to calm down, before she said something she'd regret. He had now reached her side and touched her hand gently. She recoiled. 'Don't touch me.' He let go instantly.

'Please. At least let me explain why I behaved the way I did. I promise I'm not normally like that. It was just a really bad time. I am a nice guy normally, really.'

'Do nice guys normally insult women? Do nice guys get drunk and make a formal complaint about someone, despite them being in the wrong?' Maya was aware that she was almost shouting now, and the people in the queue were beginning to stare. She barely noticed Dave had come to stand next to Chloe, his jacket now wrapped around her shoulders protectively. She just felt furious. At Theo, at Michael, at the unfairness of it all.

'No, they don't. But then nice guys don't always have to carry the ashes of their beloved grandmother on a long-haul flight,' he said, causing her to stop short, her mouth open to retort but no words forthcoming. He took the silence as a chance to continue. 'I'm in no way excusing the way I behaved. I was a total arsehole, I know. And I will retract that complaint first thing tomorrow, I promise. But I was scared, lonely, and if I'm honest, heartbroken. My grandmother was like my mother. She is' – he paused to correct himself – 'was, the only close family I had left in the UK. I'd already been in an argument at check-in as they wanted me to put her in the hold with my main luggage, but I had a permission slip to carry her with me in hand luggage, so when you started yelling at me—'

'I wasn't yelling,' Maya interrupted.

'Right, sorry. When you tried to take my bag from me to pop it in the overhead lockers, something just snapped. I couldn't let her go. I was scared the airline would lose her.'

His voice cracked a little and Dave came over to him and put a consoling arm around his shoulders. He smiled appreciatively at him. 'It's OK.' He turned back to Maya.

'Look, I'm not trying to give you a sob story or make you feel guilty, but I couldn't let you go without at least explaining to you why I acted like I did. I am not a bad guy, I promise. But I am sorry.' He stopped and took a deep breath, his shoulders seeming to droop a little, like the air had escaped his body and he was deflating slowly. He was clearly in pain. Maya immediately felt the anger melt away. It wasn't his fault.

'Wow,' she said quietly, her rage leaving her body like a deflated balloon. 'I'm so sorry for your loss.' She reached out and squeezed his cold hand. His face lit up with relief and he held her hand for a moment longer. 'And yes, I accept your apology.' She continued, watching him as a smile stretched across his face. 'But I do have one caveat,' she said, looking serious again, and he nodded, the smile vanishing in an instant.

'Sure, of course. What is it?' he asked.

'If you ever decide to fly Oasis Airlines again, can you ditch that baseball cap?' She pointed at his head. 'Or better, burn it?!'

There was a nanosecond of silence before they all burst into laughter and the tension was broken.

'What's wrong with my baseball cap? I've had it since my university days,' he protested, touching it fondly, its frayed edges and threadbare cotton visible, even in the darkness.

'Clearly!' Maya replied, causing him to laugh again.

'Fine. I promise I won't wear my baseball cap again,' he said, in mock salute, 'providing you agree to come for one more drink with me now.' He indicated to Dave and Chloe. 'All of us.'

Chloe looked delighted and ran over to Dave, nodding ferociously at her. Maya thought of her pact, but then he wasn't suggesting anything more than an apology drink and he had invited Chloe and Dave too, so it was clear there was no romantic intention in sight. Just how she wanted it.

'Sure,' she said. 'But we'd better stop somewhere along the way for a pizza slice, I'm starving.'

If she wasn't on a date, she didn't need to worry about how she looked, or what she ate. And this girl sure was hungry.

Chapter Fourteen

Maya walked through the safety talk while the plane taxied on the runway with renewed vigour. She was so grateful to be going home and last night had actually turned out to be surprisingly great. The four of them had headed to this tiny deli about four blocks from the gallery, as recommended by Dave, and she had had two slices of the best pizza she had ever tasted. With full tummies, they'd then abandoned any thought of cocktails and found a cute little ice cream parlour where they sat until closing time, sharing ice cream sundaes and comparing notes on UK living versus New York living. It turned out that Dave and Theo were cousins, but had lost contact with each other when they were both very young, and had only recently had the opportunity to reconnect via some family incident. Since then, they had become almost long-distance brothers. Dave would either fly over to the UK, or Theo over to New York, whenever they had the chance. Theo was staying with Dave while he sorted out various things. Maya noticed that he didn't elaborate on what 'things' or what 'incident' had occurred, though.

At the end of the night, they'd been perfect gentlemen and walked both the girls back to the hotel before saying goodbye. Maya had never enjoyed a double non-date more.

Cabin crew, please take your seats for take-off.

She sat down beside Chloe and buckled her seat belt, smiling at the nervous teenage boy in the fourth row who was looking decidedly green around the gills. She gave him a thumbs up and turned to Andreas who was buckled in beside her.

'Glad to be going home, honey?' he asked over the roar of the engines and the raucous rattling of the air larders in the galley.

'Actually, I really am,' she said. 'It's time to start a new chapter.' She looked at him and he placed a big, soft hand over hers and squeezed it sympathetically. His face was pure compassion, and she could see his worry for her etched across his forehead. 'I'm fine.' But he didn't move his hand, just rubbed his thumb gently across the back of her hand, his mouth turned down in a frown.

'Honestly, I am,' she said, patting his hand, looking over at the fourth row again, 'but I won't be in a minute when that teenager in the fourth row throws up. I bet you he hurls before we've even made it to thirty-five thousand feet.' At which point the plane's nose pulled off the ground and they began their ascent into the air to the sounds of engines roaring and, as if on cue, the sound of a teenage boy vomiting.

Ten hours later, Maya pulled up in front of her shared home with Michael and noticed the familiar ache in the back of her throat had reappeared. She hoped her time away would have alleviated it somewhat, but it turned out her stupid heart had a great internal GPS system and had tracked that she was back at the scene of the crime.

'Want me to come in, Maya Moo?' her dad asked, switching off the engine of his Volvo and unclipping his seat belt. Maya hesitated. Did she? Or should she face Michael alone? She hadn't heard anything from him since that missed call on their supposed wedding day.

'No, I'll be alright, Dad. But thanks.' She smiled at him and got out of the car, the frosty air hitting her skin, causing goosebumps to spring up on her bare wrists and the back of her neck. She was still wearing her uniform from the flight and her hair was shoved up in a messy bun. Her winter coat and gloves were still zipped inside her holdall in the boot of the car. She hadn't expected to return to the UK to snow. They hadn't had snow in over five years and even then, it was some disappointing flutter that barely settled or turned instantly to slush. Michael must be having a field day, she thought wryly.

Then, like an ironic lightning bolt, she realised that if she was still with him, she would have known about the snow in advance, she would have been prepared. The irritating lump in her throat grew a little larger, her airway felt a little tighter. She closed her eyes for a second and focused on the sensation of snowflakes landing on her face. All around her was quiet and still, the weather having brought the country to a standstill.

'Just get this over with and you'll be back at Dad's eating cake' she muttered, visualising her dad's iconic Christmas cake which he absurdly made in September, but was actually phenomenal. Instead of brandy, he infused it with his own homemade mulled wine and his icing was rolled with candied clementine peel. Maya had been known to eat a whole one by herself, and so it was a running joke that he now made one whole cake especially for her. She turned to give him a reassuring thumbs up, and he returned the gesture before pulling out a folded newspaper from the side door pocket. She knew he was trying to remain nonchalant, and she appreciated it. If he weakened, she knew she would.

She made her way forward and opened the wooden gate that led the way up their tiny front path to their shared green front door. She loved their front door, its deep, rich colour offset by the stained-glass frosted window that depicted a beautiful sunrise. It contrasted beautifully against the red brick, and she tutted when she saw that her two small pots that stood either side of the door and were thriving with cyclamen when she was last here over a month ago, had long since withered away and died. Much like their relationship, she thought wryly.

She pulled out her key from her bag and was surprised to see a real Christmas wreath hanging from a red ribbon across the stained glass. It was lush and full, its red berries vibrant against the ivy and gold bows that looked a little ostentatious. It was definitely not their usual, garden centre artificial wreath that they had bought together three years back and stored in the loft from January until November. She pushed it aside in an effort to slide her key into the lock but found that the key wouldn't fit. Probably the frost, she thought, perhaps it had frozen the lock. Michael knew she was coming though, so she rang the doorbell, hearing the familiar chime and hating the fact that she had to ring the bell rather than walk right in, like a common house guest.

The door swung open, and a series of events hit her senses like a slap in the face. First, the overly sweet, pungent aroma of orange and spices, as if someone was boiling up a huge vat of marmalade. Second was the low hum of dance music emanating from the lounge, its thudding matching the quickening of Maya's heart rate. Last was Amanda Avary standing in her doorway, holding a cocktail glass of clear liquid, and wearing nothing but a sheer satin and lace, cream, thigh-length dressing gown.

'Maya?' Amanda said, a practised smile plastered on her face, a smile that didn't quite reach her eyes. 'Great, you're here. Come in, come in.' She ushered Maya inside what had been her home for so long. Shocked, Maya did as she was told.

'Where's Michael?' she said, her voice a little croaky and weak. She tried to clear it with a cough. 'He said he would be here. We arranged a time.' She looked away from Amanda and into the living room to the left. It was set up ready for what looked to be a party. The large dining table was full of empty platters and glasses, and a huge silver champagne bucket stood proud in the centre with a magnum of champagne plonked inside.

'He just popped out for some ice,' Amanda trilled, as she walked away and opened the door to the cupboard under the stairs. 'But don't worry, here are your things.'

She dragged out four large cardboard boxes from the cupboard and placed them at Maya's feet, careful not to damage her long, painted nails. A flash of sparkle caught Maya's eye and she noted the huge engagement ring on her hand.

'I packed them up for you. Sometimes it's better if a girl does it, you know? Michael would have just thrown *everything* in there, whereas I was a bit more considerate.'

Maya had no idea what she was talking about, but just shook her head in confusion, bending down and opening each box in turn. One was full of books, photo frames and a couple of ornaments, while the other three were a mix of make-up, clothes, and shoes.

'Where are the rest of my belongings? All my clothes? My handbags?'

Amanda wafted a hand in the air as if she was swatting away a fly.

'Well. Obviously, I only packed the current clothes. The rest were all either too old, too dowdy, or . . .' She paused, passing her eye fully over Maya, from her shoes to her face. 'Just unsuitable.' She pointed at the boxes. 'The rest I donated to the charity chain associated with the news channel. We must think of others, mustn't we?' she said, checking her nails.

A phone pinged and she pulled it from her dressing-gown pocket and checked the message. She squealed and typed a return message, the tapping of her nails on the glass and the sheer ignorance of her words hitting Maya like machine-gun fire.

'Too unsuitable?' Maya said, quietly, her cold fingers balling up into the palms of her hands, her nails digging into her skin painfully.

'That's right. You're lucky, really. I used to be a personal stylist before I got my big break, and people paid a fortune for my services. I did you for free.' She smiled again proudly, as if Maya should be grateful. Maya was at a total loss for words and her mouth gaped open as Amanda continued, 'You need to accentuate those curves of yours by wearing items that draw the eye towards them, and cover up those areas that don't work, such as your thighs and the tops of your arms. The clothes in these boxes will do just that.' Her phone pinged again, and she rushed to check it.

'Look, I don't mean to be rude, but between the removal men arriving tomorrow, and the party here tonight, I really don't have the time for chit-chat. I need to focus on my own outfit, not give out free advice on yours.' She chuckled, before picking up one of the boxes and heading towards the front door.

'You're having a party?' Maya said, her voice tight as she fought the urge to pick up a box and smash it into Amanda's pretty little face. Amanda looked surprised, her botoxed forehead almost showing the hint of a crease.

'Michael didn't call you?'

Maya shook her head, thinking back to the missed call a few days ago and how he didn't leave any message or try again. Amanda's expression changed; her face now full of pity.

'Oh, well – we're having a little soiree tonight for family and friends. A celebration. You see, we're selling the house! Moving on to bigger and better things.' The inference was clear, Amanda was the better thing all round.

'You're selling my house?' Maya whispered, her voice gruff.

'Well, it's never actually, legally, been your house now, has it?'

'Well, I contributed to the mortgage and bills for years . . .'

'Yes, you did. Effectively making you a live-in tenant,' Amanda said, her smile never slipping. 'Now, I don't mean to rush you, but I need to crack on. If you could just pick up your stuff and I'll see you out.' She pointed at the boxes and Maya's eyes were drawn towards her engagement ring. She blinked slowly, the diamond seemingly growing larger and larger as the room started to spin. Amanda was still talking, but her voice faded away into the background to be replaced by a roaring sound, as if she was holding a seashell up to her ear. She tried to focus on the four boxes, but noticed they were now swimming in and out of focus. Her skin prickled and burned, and a rush of heat was spreading slowly up her spine towards her head, feeling like a firework ready to explode. She had to get out of there.

Using all her strength, she picked up one of the boxes and blindly made her way to the open front door, focusing all her efforts on not letting her knees buckle. Her dad was leaning on the passenger door, clearly having abandoned his façade of reading his paper as soon as she vanished into the house and came immediately forward when he saw her leave. Maya said nothing, simply handed him the first box and turned for the others. The uncomplicated act of this repeated task gave her a focus and she handed all four boxes over to him, cradling each box like a newborn child. When the last box had been handed over to him, she turned back for one last look at the house that she had shared with Michael. Amanda was standing in the doorway, her slim silhouette like a blot on her many memories within those walls. Her eyes finally rested on Amanda's face. There was so much she wanted to say, but the words seemed to be jammed. She turned away for the final time and made her way down the front path. When she reached the gate, she heard Amanda call out,

'Maya? Can I just say one thing before you leave?'

Maya let her head drop down and sighed, her hand still on the latch of the gate. Taking a breath, she turned to look at Amanda, noticing the concern etched on her face.

'What?' she said, gruffly, knowing deep down that no apology would suffice for the pain Amanda was causing her. Amanda took a deep breath in, her satin dressing gown loosening slightly, and spoke.

'I just want to say . . .' Amanda paused as her phone pinged, but this time she ignored it '. . . that going forward, I really recommend that you avoid the colour yellow. With your skin tone and hair colour, it simply washes you out. Stick to duller tones and you'll be just fine.' And with her pearls of wisdom bestowed, she smiled and waved, before closing the door with one final thud, leaving Maya standing in the dark, cold night.

Chapter Fifteen

The journey home was silent, bar her dad occasionally clearing his throat. Maya couldn't bring herself to say anything. They'd piled her boxes into the back seat of his car and set off towards his house, with Amanda's voice still trilling in her ear. *Selling. Moving.* The week of Maya's cancelled wedding. She absent-mindedly rubbed her bare ring finger, while her eyes stared emptily forward.

'Things will be better when we get home,' he said. 'We'll sit down and make a plan of action.' Maya didn't respond, she just nodded mutely. 'You'll always have a place to stay with us,' he continued as he turned left into his tree-lined street and headed for his house. The snow was falling heavily now, with his windscreen wipers on full.

'What the . . .' he began, pulling up outside his house, forgetting to indicate, which was unheard of for him. Maya snapped out of her stupor at his tone and looked up. Her eyes sprang open in surprise. Gayle was standing outside the house in a baby-pink towelling dressing gown and fluffy slippers, her hair wrapped in a towel and her hands firmly planted on her hips as she shouted silently at a flustered-looking middle-aged bald man. Maya lowered her window a smidge, a flurry of snow coming into the car, and in flew Gayle's angry voice.

'I simply will not vacate until I find Smithy. First you get me out of the bath, then you tell me I need to leave my home, and now you want me to leave my beloved cat behind! All for the sake of some supposed gas leak . . .'

'Madam, it simply isn't safe . . .' the gas man tried to reason.

'Safe? Sod the gas leak, I'll freeze to death from hypothermia in a bit and it'll all be your fault.'

'I'm just doing my job. Until we have eliminated all risk at your property and next door, we have a responsibility to remove all persons to a place of safety.'

Maya's dad got out and joined them both on the pavement. He removed his coat and wrapped it around Gayle's shoulders and turned to negotiate with the gas man. Maya stayed in the car, listening to the man reveal the news that their next-door neighbours had smelt gas while preparing for a post-Christmas party and called out the gas board. On further inspection, they had detected a faulty boiler, and ordered everyone to evacuate until further notice. Because the two houses were semi-detached, they were forced to advise both properties be vacated. Maya's dad was taking the news more calmly than Gayle, whose colourful choice of language was heating up the air by a fair few degrees.

Maya shivered and looked over at number seventy-nine, the offending house with the supposed gas leak. Its façade matched next door almost identically, except it was decorated with enough gaudy festive lights to deplete the national grid. She noticed the Ashers had already left, their car no longer in the driveway. In its place sat Smithy, his white paws neatly facing forward, his ears turned backwards as he listened in to the scene unfolding next door. Maya quietly climbed out of the car and walked over to him. He meowed in greeting and allowed her to scoop him up in her arms. She walked towards Gayle, before holding him up like a trophy.

'Found him,' she said. Gayle's face changed from anger to delight.

'Oh, Smithy! My darling boy, you're safe.' The gas man visibly relaxed and checked his watch.

'We'll call you as soon as it is safe to return to the property,' he said, eager to get on with his job, and with a quick nod, he was gone.

★

An hour later and they pulled up outside a dilapidated but picturesque cottage on the outskirts of the city. Maya's heart sunk a little lower, which was no mean feat as she already thought she had hit rock bottom.

'I really am so sorry about this, darling girl,' Maya's dad said for the umpteenth time, his face creased in concern, his white beard matching the pale landscape outside.

'It's fine, Dad. Honestly.'

'It'll just be for one night,' he continued, trying to alleviate his guilt.

'I know.'

'If we could have squeezed you in, we would have done,' Gayle said, turning in her seat, her makeshift towelling head-dress leaning to one side, Smithy curled up on her lap. 'It's just my brother already has family staying for Christmas, and with it being almost New Year, I'm surprised he could even fit us two in last minute . . .'

'Really, it's fine. I'll be fine.'

'As it is, we're sleeping on the sofa bed,' he continued, trying to make her feel better. It didn't.

'I'll ring you both tomorrow. It's only one night, like you said.'

But she didn't make a move to get out. She felt nervous. She hadn't seen her Aunt Sophia. Aunt Sophia was her mother's sister and was just as beautiful, but also completely bonkers. She was an unmarried artist who lived on an old farm and was a sight to behold. She made all her own clothes from material she salvaged from charity shops or spare bits of material found around the home. She had a penchant for making wide-legged trousers and matching waistcoats, with multiple pockets that were always brimming with odd items. Maya could remember falling over when she was little, and Aunt Sophia pulled a small jar of honey from her trouser pocket and rubbed some of it over the graze. Her pockets were like treasure troves, filled with coins, buttons, paintbrushes and packets of seeds. She had lived on this farm since she was a baby, having been adopted along with Maya's mum when they were both small children by a wonderful couple called the Montgomeries.

Maya's mother, Tess, and Aunt Sophia had always been really close, with the same thick, curly hair and beautiful smiles. Neither sister knew of their heritage, having been abandoned at a police station soon after birth. They were dark-haired unknowns with large brown eyes and rosebud lips who grew into beautiful girls. Maya's mum was quiet and sensible whereas Sophia was wild and unpredictable and while Maya's mum had settled down into marriage, Sophia had remained as she was, single and eccentric. But she was fiercely loyal and a dedicated aunt to Maya, with people often mistaking them for mother and daughter. However, Aunt Sophia had never really taken to Michael and because of this, they'd lost touch. Before she knew it, three years had gone by. But when she'd called, only an hour ago, to ask if she could stay, Aunt Sophia appeared delighted and told her to come straight over.

A light came on in the hallway of the cottage, causing Maya's dad to shift nervously. He and Aunt Sophia didn't see eye to eye, but Maya had never been able to understand why. Whenever she tried to ask, they both brushed her off with some weak response, revealing nothing.

'We'd better get on then. The clock is ticking, and the weather is getting worse.' He climbed out of the car and swiftly emptied the boxes onto the kerb. Maya clambered out and stood facing him. She gulped so as not to cry.

'Thanks, Dad.'

He shuffled his feet, kicking the tyre of his car with his left toe. 'Love you, Maya Moo. We'll see you tomorrow, OK?' He engulfed her in a huge bear hug, and she could feel her resolve crumble; she wanted him to hold her forever. But in a few seconds, he let go.

'Love you, Dad,' she whispered, wondering what tonight had in store for her. One thing was for sure, it couldn't get any worse.

82

Chapter Sixteen

The next morning, Maya was up with the lark. Quite literally. And the cockerel. And the chickens. Their crowing, clucking, and singing was like an animal opera outside her window. In her early grogginess, she'd forgotten she was essentially staying on a working farm. She gingerly lifted her head off the pillow and noticed she was in Aunt Sophia's spare room and was covered in a colourful patchwork quilt that resembled the trousers Aunt Sophia had been wearing last night. Despite the beginnings of a hangover scratching at her temples, she smiled. It had been a great evening in the end.

She'd been ushered into the cottage by a welcoming Aunt Sophia late last night and they'd shared the evening with a bottle of fifty-year-old Scotch and a gluten-free spaghetti dish that was actually rather wonderful. Maya had divulged all her woes to Aunt Sophia over dinner and Aunt Sophia had answered in her usual tact-free manner.

'You're better off without that imbecilic fool. I always knew he was no good, I could tell by his weak shoulders and lack of discernible chin,' she said, raising her glass and swinging it around so that the Scotch sloshed all over the kitchen table. 'Plus, he always talked down to you, like you were his inferior.'

'Did he?' Maya asked, shocked. Aunt Sophia nodded.

'He certainly did.' She put on an accent, '"*Maya, I don't think you're quite ready. Maya, don't stretch yourself, Maya you're not quite suitable . . .*" He played on your insecurities. I couldn't stand him for that.' She looked Maya straight in the eye. 'You're worth so much more than what he saw you as. What I see you capable of achieving.'

Maya had been ridiculously flattered. Her dad always complimented her, but he was her dad, whereas Aunt Sophia was not known for her praise. She was straight-talking, argumentative, and brash, so any words of encouragement could be taken with the sincerity they were said. On the back of this, Maya told her all about her blog, *Flying Solo*, which Aunt Sophia found hysterical.

'Bloody marvellous, girl!' she said, throwing her head back, her salt and pepper curls reaching almost down to her lower back, and laughing raucously. 'I love it! Who needs men, anyway? I bet you'll find this will be the best year of your life!'

Buoyed by her infectious excitement, Maya found herself pulling out her laptop, newly rescued from Michael's house, and began writing another blog post. It read:

Day Four

I'm getting in early before the chaos of New Year's Eve and writing to you all now. I know I'm only meant to write one post a week, but hey, here's an extra one. Call it a belated Christmas present. In the voice of the awesomely talented Brian Blessed, 'Happy New Year to one and all!' Or, in the voice of the recently dumped, sayonara to the crappiest year to date. New beginnings, new resolutions . . . all that bollocks that the media spins to get people to feel it necessary to re-evaluate their lives. All I know is that yesterday I was single, and the same applies tomorrow. And the next day. Nothing has changed, and nothing is going to. The same clock will strike midnight on New Year's Eve, like it does every single day.

I will still be single, still be angry.

I found out today that my ex is selling the house we shared and moving on. With the woman he left me for. He didn't even have the courage to tell me himself, I had to hear it from her. Yep, directly from her, face to face, in MY house. I'd like to say I was dignified, calm, and eloquent in our conversation, but alas, any witty retorts or snappy replies disappeared from my lips quicker than a leaf in a hurricane.

84

I get it though. People can fall in and out of love, like the seasons; people change, adapt, evolve and love might not always bend with those variations. It's how you handle the change that matters. And my ex handled it catastrophically. Could he have handled it better? Oh, yes. Could he have treated me with a little more respect and compassion? Also, yes. The last few weeks have resembled a rager of a storm, but I see a new season evolving. My hopeful prediction is that the forecast for the next twelve months will be warm, sunny, and bright.

So, happy new year, all. However you spend your NYE this year, just remember you'll still be the same person as you are today. Just one day older and most probably hungover.

Aunt Sophie had cackled at the last few lines, and drunkenly, they both pressed the key to upload the post, and both toasted the new post with an old dusty champagne bottle Aunt Sophia had found in the back of her larder. Being with Aunt Sophia made her feel closer to her mum again and Maya found herself happy, in spite of the fact that she was about to embark on a new year recently dumped, single, and homeless.

Chapter Seventeen

'Maya! Breakfast is ready,' Aunt Sophia yelled from the kitchen, interrupting Maya from her thoughts. 'C'mon down, it's going cold.'

Maya rolled out of bed, her feet wincing at the cold, wooden floor and she realised she only had her cabin crew uniform available. Everything else was still packed in boxes or in her holdall. She walked over to the wooden wardrobe standing next to the washbasin and opened it. It was packed tight with clothes and an instant waft of mustiness hit her square in the face. She rifled through the hangers and found a cute tea dress with puff sleeves, a pulled-in waist and a flattering knee-length skirt. She pulled it over her underwear and was relieved to see it fit her well, her curves filling out the dress. She did a little twirl in it and giggled. It was perfect. Even more so for the fact it was the colour of canary yellow.

'Up yours, Amanda,' she said to the empty room and headed downstairs.

'Ta dah,' Aunt Sophia said, placing a huge plate of pancakes in front of Maya. They were dripping in maple syrup and piled high with fresh strawberries and blueberries. 'This is for the stomach.' Aunt Sophia then handed her a huge, chipped mug of black coffee. 'And this is for the sore head.' Maya's hungover, parched mouth watered at the sight. 'Don't worry, it's gluten-free. I never make anything else.'

Maya looked at her with gratitude. 'Thank you.' Maya had been diagnosed with coeliac disease as a small child, which was no surprise as she had inherited the condition from her mother,

86

who had also been diagnosed in her teens. Aunt Sophia had grown up making sure that her sister remained healthy and was vigilant when it came to watching her diet, so cooking and baking gluten-free came easily to her. Maya took a big bite and groaned appreciatively.

'These are phenomenal, thank you.' Her stomach seemed to wake up on first bite and she dug in ravenously. She was down to the last pancake when she got up to pour herself another coffee from the pot. When she turned, her plate was empty.

'What the . . .?'

'Matilda, NO!' Aunt Sophia yelled, and attempted to shoo a brown, scraggly goat away out of the kitchen. It bleated at her, not moving. Instead, it threw its neck back and finished off Maya's pancake in a few gulps. 'Naughty goat!' Aunt Sophia scolded, rolling her eyes. The goat stuck out its purple tongue in response.

'Matilda?'

'Her full name is Lady Matilda, Countess of Home Farm. She rules the roost on the farm. I adore her. But she's a nightmare when it comes to my underwear; she's forever stealing it, along with my cookies.' Maya laughed.

'And does she live outside?'

'Oh no,' Aunt Sophia said seriously, 'Lady Matilda is too good for the outside. She lives with me and sleeps in the office. She's a great natural paper shredder for my accounts.' Her voice was serious, but her eyes twinkled, and they both erupted into laughter.

'So, what's your plan for today?' she asked Maya, wrapping a purple and gold scarf around her head to contain her flowing curls. She was dressed in oversized, wide-leg denim trousers and a blue and white striped shirt that she tucked into the trousers. Over the top she wore a bright purple, knit jumper that reached almost to the floor and dirty, mud-stained boots with yellow laces. Her face was free of make-up, yet she looked far younger than her age, her face almost entirely free of wrinkles, apart from around her eyes. She plonked herself down at the large kitchen table opposite Maya and took a big gulp of coffee, the steam rising as she did so. 'I take it you haven't heard from your father yet.'

Maya shook her head, realising she hadn't even checked her phone this morning. She couldn't decide if that was a good or a bad thing.

'I have absolutely no plans. Not one. I should be on my honeymoon, so to speak, so I have no flights scheduled either.'

'Ah, shit, of course, sorry,' Aunt Sophia said, her mouth wincing at the faux pas. 'Well, what shall we do instead, then? My father always said that *freedom is a gift and free time is a delight*. We must make the most of it. Fancy a drive to the lakes today?'

'The lakes? Have you seen outside?' Maya gestured to the window, where the fields were covered in a layer of snow and the farmyard was empty of animals.

'And?' Aunt Sophia said, shrugging her shoulders.

'And driving is an impossibility in this weather,' Maya said, draining the last dregs of her coffee, her headache receding slightly. Aunt Sophia smiled, and a familiar twinkle returned to her face.

'Nothing is an impossibility, babe. Not with me around. Meet me outside the front door in five minutes. Dress warm.' She pushed back her chair and got up, grabbing some keys from a bowl on a sideboard, and made for the back door. She paused, turning back to Maya. 'Great choice of dress, by the way, I remember her wearing it.'

'Who wearing it?' Maya said, running her hand along the frilly lace collar.

'Your mother. She loved that dress. I think she wore it the first time she met your father.'

And with that she left the house and disappeared into the courtyard, leaving Maya staring after her, her mouth agape and her hand frozen on the frill of the pretty yellow dress.

★

'You have got to be kidding me!' Maya yelled over the din of the engine as it approached her along the road.

'Climb aboard!' Aunt Sophia yelled back, her head hanging out of the open left window, her hands wrapped in huge, yellow workman's gloves. Maya burst into laughter at the sight. Coming towards her was a huge, red tractor, with giant black tyres that were slushing through the snow and leaving black tyre marks in its path. Aunt Sophia was bouncing around in the cab positioned high up; her face lit up in delight. She had wrapped fairy lights around the huge steering wheel and controls, and they were flashing merrily as she chugged closer towards Maya. It was such a sight to see, and Maya felt her belly aching, an unfamiliar feeling of late. It felt good. The tractor stopped a few feet away from her, the engine rattling to a halt.

'Are you getting in, or what?' Aunt Sophia said.

'You know how to drive this thing?' Maya asked, her body staying firmly put, flakes of snow drifting around her. Aunt Sophia looked affronted.

'Darling girl, I have lived on this farm since I was a baby, and ten years of it alone. If I don't drive this thing, I go hungry. Of course I can drive it! Now get in before I drive off and you can walk to the lakes.'

Maya didn't need to be told twice, her feet were already beginning to freeze in Aunt Sophia's spare wellington boots, and she climbed up the three huge steps and sat beside her. She slammed the door closed and with a jolt and a rumble of the engine, they were off down the country track, the tractor the only red dot in a sea of white snow.

Twenty minutes later and with a sore bum from all the bouncing, they pulled into a layby alongside a car park and stepped out of the tractor. Maya looked out in awe towards the beauty that stood beneath them in the valley; a frozen lake that sparkled in the bright winter sunlight. The lake was huge but from their elevated height, they could just about see all around it and there was a small island in the centre that was occupied by oak trees and bushes. The hazy midday sun glistened off the water like tiny touches of shimmering gold and the frozen water reflected the clear blue sky above. There was a sense of calm that emanated from the lake, a peaceful silence. Aunt Sophia came beside her and linked her arm through Maya's.

'It's beautiful, isn't it?'

Maya nodded, staring far out into the distance. A far cry from the sandy beaches of the Greek island where she should have been standing.

'I often come here, to think, to draw.' Maya looked at her questioningly. 'It has healing powers, nature. When my shoulders get a little heavy and my mind gets a little full, I come here. It's like therapy, only free and self-administered. I recommend it to everyone. Nature has a damn fine way of healing all stresses and worries.' She looked at Maya. 'You're welcome here whenever you want, you know. To stay with me, for however long you need to.' Her eyes met Maya's. 'I miss you, Maya.'

Maya leant her head on Aunt Sophia's shoulder. 'I miss you too.'

They stood that way for a few minutes in companionable silence before Maya turned to her.

'Can I ask you a question?'

'Sure, go ahead.'

'Can I stay with you a little longer?'

Aunt Sophia's face broke into a wide smile, 'Honey, you can stay as long as you like.'

Chapter Eighteen

Cabin crew, please take your seats for take-off.
'And then what happened?'
'And then I left. What else could I do?'
'You didn't react? Swear? Scream? Pull out her tacky hair extensions?'
'Nope.'
'You just got in your car and left?'
'Well, technically it was my dad's car, but yep. In a nutshell.'
'And now you're homeless and living with your crazy aunt.'
'Again, yes.'
'Wow.'

Chloe stared straight ahead as the plane's nose tipped upwards and left the runway, ascending towards the clouds. As Maya felt the full force of the engines pull her back into her seat, she found herself being pulled back into the memory of last week.

After the lake trip with Aunt Sophia, she'd headed back to the cottage and found herself being drawn to her laptop. In her sad state, she had searched the internet for Michael and Amanda. And just as she expected, the news channel had repeatedly run coverage on the whole elaborate proposal with gusto. There had even been a full ten-minute segment on their supposed love affair, which Maya noted with irony did not include the third wheel in their relationship – her. An elaborate engagement party had taken place in central London, in some garish bar just after Christmas. The bastard even had the audacity to wear the suit he was going to wear to their wedding. What a cheapskate, low-life scumbag. Her anger over the next few weeks had made her fingers itch again, resulting in her next blog post This one she titled *Surprise!*

Day Eighteen
Surprise!
Who doesn't love a surprise? 'Surprise — you're going to be an auntie!', 'Surprise — we're off to Paris for the weekend!', 'Surprise — you got that job promotion!' But what if the surprise is slightly less positive, such as 'Surprise — I'm marrying someone else!'

Who doesn't love a surprise? Me, that's who.

My surprise last month was less of a Kodak moment and more of a scratch-this-surprise-from-my-memory-forever-more moment. Not so good. The only positive to come out of this was that I spilt my huge glass of Merlot all over his creamy white carpet on finding out, and I know it'll never come out. How do I know? Because I was the one who stupidly chose white carpet and it meant we only ever ate beige food downstairs. Plus, I managed to sell the stupid, but oh-so thoughtful Christmas present I bought him online for double the price I paid for it. So, who's the loser now?

Based on recent events, I have decided to take control of my surprises from now on.

So, for the next twelve months of singledom, along with my ban on dating, I realise I am going to have a LOT of free time! How will I fill it? I hear you ask. My plan is to finish this year having learnt twelve new things. It could be an activity, a skill, anything really — providing it doesn't involve dating, men, or matters of the heart. I want to feel proud of myself.

So, throw me some ideas as to what I could learn! Cooking? Art lessons? Scuba diving? The crazier the better. For one thing recent events have taught me is that who knows what is around the corner? No point waiting for others to steer your boat for you, you need to become the captain of your own boat.

NB: Despite the boating analogy, please don't recommend boating/sailing lessons — I get seasick just having a bath. No joke.

★

Maya had emailed the blog post to the airline and then had a little look at the airline's social media page, to see what traffic it had received since her blog began. She was amazed to see she now had over fifteen thousand followers. The comments alone on her previous blog posts were over two pages. There had been something strangely comforting about knowing her words were connecting with so many people.

In addition, Oasis Airlines were seeing a huge surge in online traffic due to her blog posts and they had decided to incorporate her into their brand awareness scheme. She was now the faceless figure on the front of their inflight magazines, and only yesterday she had heard her blog being mentioned when working onboard. The idea of an anonymous Oasis employee baring their soul for all the world to read meant that their flights were filled with inquisitive eyes, and the airline had already begun to see a rise in their ticket sales. Passengers were keen to catch the eye of the secret blogger or guess their identity.

Andreas was in his element. He'd been mistaken for the secret blogger numerous times, and he revelled in the attention, often adding little hints and shooting rhetorical questions back at the passengers, making the whole thing into a game. And Nigel Edwards was delighted too. He had latched onto Maya's coat-tails and used her blog as a springboard for a potential promotion. Which meant he was now pleasant to Maya and often gave her upper class to work or turned a blind eye to any minor errors. Work had never been so enjoyable, and she felt grateful to be back in her favourite place – the skies.

'So, your New Year must have been pretty shit, then?' Chloe's question over the roar of the engines brought her back into the present. 'Sorry I couldn't be with you.'

Chloe's face filled with guilt at the fact she hadn't been around for Maya after they landed from New York. But when Maya had originally booked her honeymoon all those months ago, Chloe had decided to book a two-week retreat in Switzerland with her mother to celebrate the New Year and had only flown back a week ago.

'Don't be silly. I don't expect you to cancel all of your plans, just because mine were.' She patted Chloe's hand. 'And actually, it was a pretty hilarious New Year, all things said.'

And as the plane accelerated up to thirty-five thousand feet, she told Chloe all about the evening with Aunt Sophia; how they'd cooked a delicious steak dinner together and shared a brilliant bottle of red, before moving back into her mother's old bedroom and going through her clothes, with Maya trying on outfits that were so old-fashioned, they'd now come back in style. They'd turned on the radio and taken it in turns to catwalk down the hallway, tottering in vintage heels. Aunt Sophia had told her to keep anything she loved, so she felt like she now had a brand-new wardrobe. Maybe Amanda had done her a favour by throwing away all her old dowdy, comfortable clothing.

Then Aunt Sophia had shown her photo albums of them as children together, and they'd found an old chest of her mother's that was like opening a treasure trove into her mother's soul – costume jewellery, poetry she'd written as a teenager, pencil drawings, trinkets – Maya had loved it. They'd opened another bottle by this point and moved downstairs. Aunt Sophia had plonked herself down at the grand piano in the living room and they'd had a good old-fashioned, drunken singalong, with even Matilda the goat joining in, her bleating almost an improvement on Maya's tone-deaf singing. It had been both hilarious and uplifting, and Maya found that she barely even thought about Michael the whole evening.

'Sounds better than my New Year,' said Chloe, as the call bell rang to alert them that they were safe to begin duties. She unclipped her seat belt and stood up, straightening her skirt, catching herself deftly as a violent bump of turbulence caught her off guard. 'Mum met some Austrian douchebag in a bar on our first night there and I didn't see her again until New Year's Day. I ended up seeing in the new year with room service and watching a fireworks display from my hotel bedroom window. Totally rubbish. Mother never fails to disappoint.'

She shrugged and moved into the galley, the trolleys knocking together as the plane navigated sharp bumps of continued turbulence. Maya went to respond, but the call bell rang again, and she turned to see a green-faced teenager in the seventh row vomit into the sick bag provided and she had to leave Chloe to deal with that.

'Nothing like handling a bag of warm vomit at 6am to make you feel alive,' she muttered under her breath as she switched on her most sympathetic smile and went to assist.

Chapter Nineteen

'Should I text him?'

'Totally up to you. Did you like him enough to want to see him again?'

Chloe shrugged. 'Maybe? But what else is there to do? I'm bored, it's freezing, and we have no other plans, as you are on this stupid no-dating ban.'

'Wow, you're all romance,' Maya quipped, nudging her in the ribs as they unloaded their luggage from the coach outside the Lexington Lodge. Chloe shrugged.

'We're here for three days. There's no time for romance.'

'Now you're beginning to sound like me. Hey! Why don't you join my rule of singledom? We could do it together!' Maya exclaimed, looking at Chloe with excitement, eyes wide. She returned the look, minus the excitement and pulled out her phone from her coat pocket without responding, dumping her luggage onto the slush-covered sidewalk. She dialled a number and held it up to her ear, with Maya looking at her questioningly. After a few seconds, her face lit up and she spoke.

'Dave? Hi, it's me, Chloe. From the UK. I don't suppose you're free tonight, are you?' A pause. 'That's great!' Another pause, and she winked at Maya. 'Sure, sounds good, meet you there. Bye!' She popped the phone back into her pocket and picked up her luggage again as the coach drove away from them.

'Thanks for the offer, Maya, but I'd rather pluck out my eyelashes one by one than join you on your twelve-month ban.' With that, she walked into the hotel, Maya chuckling and following behind her.

'Fine by me. I am busy anyway.' Chloe stopped in her tracks. 'Why? What are you doing?'

'It's a surprise,' Maya said, walking straight past her towards the lift, leaving Chloe staring after her.

'Maybe this wasn't such a great idea,' Maya muttered quietly to no one in particular.

'If you can just step forward a notch, and we'll clip you on.' A boy with a southern American drawl said, pulling her harness forward. Maya did as she was told and looked up for what seemed like the thousandth time. The climbing wall looked much higher than it did online, and no one was smiling like they were in the brochure. In fact, the man next to her was sweating profusely through his T-shirt, despite the minus temperatures outside.

'Now, as we've already briefed you, take it slow and steady; find your footing securely before you inch any higher, and if you get stuck or panicked, just holler. We are fully trained here and will assist you where necessary.'

The only thing they are all trained in is being recently potty trained, Maya thought to herself, looking around the building, her heart pounding in her chest. The staff of Stepping Stones looked like they had been plucked straight out of high school, with their matching acne and hungover eyes. Being a legally registered adult was clearly not a prerequisite to working there. She did not feel at all safe as her trainer, Chad, gently pushed her forward to the wall.

'Just find your first footing, and the rest will follow naturally,' he said, grinning at her with pearly white teeth. Maya gulped, feeling ridiculously nervous. She looked at the wall, chose a bright blue stepping stone and placed her left foot onto it.

'You chose to do this. You chose to do this,' she muttered to herself, closing her eyes just for a second to gather herself. Then, with one seemingly momentous effort, she lifted herself off the ground and placed her right foot onto an orange stone. She was off.

'Hey, way to go, Maya! Now just keep on climbing!' Chad hollered at her, holding tightly onto the safety line. She didn't look back at him, she just looked for the next step and kept on going. She could hear the other man huffing and puffing below her as she continued to climb, but she didn't look down. Or up. She just focused all her efforts on finding the next step. Her arms began to ache first, the muscles tense from holding her weight, and then her legs. Soon enough her whole body was beginning to shake with the exertion, and she had sweat dripping down her back and face, causing her wet hair to stick to her head under the safety helmet. The harness was rubbing her in all the wrong places and her body felt so heavy, it was taking all her concentration to not let go. Blue step, orange rock, green step . . . her whole body was screaming at her. Yellow rock. Sweat was dripping into her eyes now, she felt exhausted. Green rock . . .

'One more, and you've done it!' called a voice from above. She looked up to see the heavy boot of one of the instructors in her eyeline, a boy who was smiling down at her and offering his hand. She couldn't believe it; she had reached the top! With one final step that had her muscles screaming at her in protest, she moved up and he grabbed her harness, pulling her to safety on the butte of the man-made rock. She flopped ungracefully onto her back, staring up at the ceiling. The instructor bent down and patted her on the shoulder.

'Well done! Not many reach the top on their first ascent! Rock climbing clearly comes naturally to you.' If she could have actually made any sound at all, she would have laughed. Instead, she just made some sort of snorting noise and shook her head. He continued, oblivious to her apparent total body shutdown. 'Whenever you're ready, just let me know and we'll show you how to descend safely.'

The instructor moved aside to concentrate his efforts on shouting encouraging words at others trying to reach the summit. Still panting, Maya found the energy to raise herself up so she was seated, and looked out at the building around her. She could almost touch the ceiling of what appeared to be an aircraft hangar and when she leant slightly over the edge, her stomach flipped nauseously. But there was something else coursing through her veins too – adrenaline. She had done it! She had learnt a new skill and, not only that, she had also succeeded in climbing the highest artificial rock-climbing wall in Manhattan. She felt elated. Mentally ticking off her first challenge in her head, she said aloud: *New Skill – Rock climbing – COMPLETED.*

Chapter Twenty

Maya was still buzzing when she entered the hotel lobby and headed for the lift. But as she looked left towards the hotel bar area, she noticed Chloe and Dave seated at the bar, their barstools close together, their shoulders touching. Maya thought it best to leave them to it, but Chloe turned around, as if sensing her there, and called out excitedly, waving both hands to gesture her towards them. Maya did so reluctantly, realising that her gym outfit, consisting of threadbare leggings that had a hole in one knee, her oversized Garfield T-shirt, and a purple fleece wrapped around her waist, was probably not in line with the dress code required for entry. She noticed, with no surprise, that Chloe looked stunning in a pencil skirt and oversized shirt. She smiled at Dave, who, as always, seemed just content being anywhere near Chloe.

'Maya!' Chloe exclaimed, not caring that her volume was enough for the residents on the first floor to hear. 'You are not going to believe this! Sit!' she demanded, patting the stool next to her, throwing her poor, neglected Gucci bag onto the floor with abandon. Maya looked down at her own bag; an actual bumbag from the 1980s, in neon purple, yellow, and green, that she hoped came across as vintage and ironic. She slid onto the stool carefully, nodding her greeting to Dave, and he waved back. Neither could get a word in over Chloe, who had barely stopped to breathe, her eyes sparkling as she spoke.

'. . . and then after the bottle was empty, we decided to walk to this new hot spot but ended up passing by the art gallery from last week. Remember? Alto Art? Pre-school artwork at Manhattan apartment-style prices? A focus on green . . .?' She kept looking at Maya, her eyebrows raised questioningly, but not waiting for a response, 'Anyway, the artist was inside the gallery, and saw us passing, so we popped in to say hello. We got to chatting and it turns out that this most recent exhibition of hers is not actually her usual style. She was trying something new.' She leant forward theatrically, her voice dropping a few decibels. 'Clearly she should stick to what she knows . . .'

Her voice rose again, 'Anyway, it turns out she is a portrait artist. A very talented and fantastic portrait artist. Of the naked variety. Showing life form in all its natural glory, in nature. All very tasteful, blah, blah, blah . . .' She tailed off to take a huge gulp from her glass. 'Anyways, it turns out that Theo knew the artist on a more personal note,' Maya's face looked troubled, and Chloe shook her head, 'no, no, not like that! Ew! No, she has a base in London as well as New York, and a few years back she put out a call for models in most university sites surrounding London. She needed models who were the average, everyday man. And guess who saw the advertisement pinned on the university board and decided to go for it?!' Maya shook her head, not understanding where this was going, Chloe rolled her eyes, 'guess who was in his final year and was totally skint, and needed funds?'

Chloe was looking at Maya, waiting for her to catch on. Maya was lost, and just shook her head. Chloe threw up her hands in frustration, 'Theo! Your Theo! 28C! Boy with the baseball cap and a vase full of ashes!' she exclaimed and then slumped back into her stool, clearly triumphant. It took Maya a moment.

'Wait, Theo posed as a model for Alto Art? A naked model?' She looked at Dave for confirmation, and he nodded.

'It was all very tasteful though,' he said, in mock-serious tones. 'No private parts were exposed in the making of the exhibition.' He laughed, and Chloe joined him. 'M. M. Milner did some wonderful work with Theo. It made him quite the star for a while too. And it certainly financed him when he started his own business.'

Maya listened in shock. Theo, the annoying, untidy, baseball cap-wearing man had posed as a model? She instantly felt the need to know more.

'Show me,' she said, waiting for either of them to whip out their phones and show her some images.

'Oh, we intend to,' Chloe said, sliding down off her chair and picking up her scuffed bag from the floor. 'Follow us.'

Twenty minutes later, the three of them climbed out of a taxi and walked towards the entrance of the art gallery. Maya thought how different it looked in the daylight. Dave walked inside first, holding the door for both Maya and Chloe, and before Maya had even had a chance to take in the cavernous room, there was a large shout of joy,

'Dave, my darling boy. You're back!' There was a rustling sound from behind one of the many large, exposed brick columns in the gallery, and suddenly a woman appeared. Maya instantly liked her. She was much older, Maya guessed late sixties, and was heading towards them wearing a pale yellow linen suit over a blue bow shirt that enveloped her entire chest. The swishing noise came from her large canary-yellow cape that swept the floor behind her and appeared to be made of some sort of crinkle fabric. Around the collar of the cape was a white ruffle that stretched up towards her chin. She was tall and lithe, like a yellow daffodil. Her hair was white, with what looked like paint splatters in her fringe, and was tied back untidily with a paintbrush. She was holding a bright blue cane in her left hand but held out her right to shake theirs. Maya shook it and was surprised at her strength.

'Welcome, welcome.' Her face was warm and inviting, the lines on her face so delicate, they looked like they had been painted on with a fine-tipped paintbrush. She had the most unusual eyes, a sort of cloudy grey, and she smelt of acrylic paint and roses.

'Thank you,' Maya said, watching as she kissed Dave on both cheeks.

'My darlings, twice in one day! And with another beautiful face too. Dave, you really are a magnet for the ladies.' She chortled at her own joke and gestured for them to follow, which they did. She didn't seem like someone you disobeyed. 'Now, what is it you want to see?'

'We're interested in some of your older work actually,' Dave began. 'Work with Theo in.'

At the mention of his name, she turned around, her face full of wonder. 'Oh, darling Theo. My muse, my finest model, oh, how I wish he'd return just the once for one more show . . .' She tailed off, still walking forward, but now gesturing for them to follow her out to the back, where Maya assumed the workshop was. She tried hard not to step on the artist's cape as it trailed behind. They meandered around a long, white counter in the gallery and towards a hidden door that Maya never would have noticed if it wasn't for the fact the artist was walking through. The room they entered was in darkness, and Maya found her eyes trying hard to adjust.

'Ready, my honeysuckles?' the artist said from the shadows, and Maya heard the flick of a light switch, and the room was suddenly flooded with light. Looking around, Maya was stunned at how large the workshop was, with lines of canvases all covered with dust sheets on the floors around them. In the centre of the workshop were long trestle tables, full of paints, pots, spray cans, and multiple paintbrushes and sponges. There were also easels scattered around with half-finished paintings. Maya watched as the artist waltzed over to one of the tables and threw back a dust sheet revealing a pile of canvases. 'Here they are. Some are originals, some are prints. And some are mine.'

They weren't paintings, they were photographs, but with ink pen images drawn over the top. Maya gasped and moved forward to the table. The canvases were all of Theo, in various poses, and in both black and white and sepia. Minus any visible clothing. The images were startling, and stunning. Maya couldn't take her eyes off them. The artist began shifting the canvases so that each one was visible and the table was totally covered.

'Told you,' Chloe whispered, knocking shoulders with Maya, and winking. 'How hot is he?'

Maya didn't respond. She couldn't. She was staring down at Theo and feeling conflicted. The images were beautiful, but his vulnerability shone through each one. His body was strong, with muscular thighs and taut skin that stretched over his stomach, back, and biceps, depending on the various positions being held. His chest had a smattering of hair, as did his lower stomach, and the artist had drawn over the top of his image, adding age-lines, wrinkles, and age spots, to give the appearance of time passing.

'I call it, the *Haunting Juxtaposition of Time*. It really was one of my best exhibitions,' the artist said, staring at a particular canvas, which was solely of Theo's torso and arms. Maya took her time filing through canvas after canvas. While he held each pose, she could see the tenseness in his shoulders, and the tautness of his jawbone. He was clearly uncomfortable, definitely not a natural, but this only added a vulnerability to the image. There was a depth to him there that seemed to hold an entire unspoken story. The addition of the ink pen lines and shading offered the viewer a chance to visualise two timelines in one place; one at his age now, and one where one could envisage him decades older, but still handsome. The duality of time overlapping intentionally was haunting, emotive, but beautiful, and Maya was speechless.

'He was a total nightmare to work with, but boy, just look at what we achieved. His susceptibility was eventually his strength, and I think we can all agree that he ended up being the perfect model.' She was staring wistfully at a canvas in her hands, sighed, and then passed it along to Maya. 'This one will never be sold.'

Maya took it and stared. It was Theo, but not any Theo that she had encountered before. In the image, he was sitting on a bare, wooden stool, his elbows resting on his knees, his body facing forward. His head had dropped down, as if in defeat, but his eyes were looking upwards, directly into the lens of the camera, and his gaze was strong, confident, defiant. One eyebrow was raised, questioning the camera. It was sexy, she realised. The image was in black and white, with dimmed lighting, so that only his upper torso and legs were visible, but Maya could still make out the toned chest and the rippling stomach. How had she not noticed this before? The artist had barely touched this canvas, other than a tattoo drawn onto his left biceps, an image of an eagle. She looked deep into his eyes, his gaze honest and open. Chloe handed her another one.

'Check out this one!' The artist placed a second canvas into Maya's hands, overlapping the one she was already holding. Maya stared at it, taking in the curves and ripples of his torso, this time from behind. Again, the lighting was cleverly angled, so that his backside was shadowed, and his most exposed part was his upper back and shoulders. His face was turned sideways, looking off-camera, his cheekbone and outline accentuated. This image had been vividly sketched over by the artist, with excess shadowing and contours. She had painted on the torso an outline of Theo's supposed skeletal spine visible through the skin and white ink flecks added into his hair, indicating grey hairs. It was both an image of strength and fragility. Of youth contrasted with inevitable age. It was stunning. She felt something stir in her, and she found it difficult to draw her eyes away from his image. She wanted to stroke his skin, feel his strength. The images were sensual, and she found herself reacting to them.

A jolt brought her back into the present, and Maya looked over to see the artist watching her, her own expression gleeful and silent. She could see that it had awoken a stirring in Maya that wasn't there before. She winked and walked over to talk to both Dave and Chloe, leaving Maya alone with the canvas. As Maya continued staring, her eyes tracing his body, she could feel a blush rising from the pit of her stomach, upwards towards her cheeks. She was attracted to him. Theo was sexy. Very sexy. And not just because of his firefighter-style body, but because she knew he was both vulnerable and attractive. She could feel her cheeks flushing and suddenly she was acutely aware that there were others around her, and she wanted to be alone. She lowered the canvas and excused herself, under the pretence that she needed the loo. Once alone, she splashed some cold water onto her wrists and behind her ears, hoping to cool down and slow her racing heart. Her flushed reflection in the bathroom mirror told her everything she needed to know. She knew this feeling, she remembered it. She was falling head first down a rabbit hole of a high-school crush.

'C'mon, Maya,' she said aloud, into the mirror. 'Stay strong.' But as she left the bathroom, she realised two things. One, that she hadn't thought about Michael now for hours, maybe even since that morning; two, she really, really wanted to see all the canvases again.

Chapter Twenty-One

The flight home so far had been uneventful. Most of the passengers had either dosed off or were happily watching the in-flight movie, with their headphones in and their eyes forward. Maya loved the evening flights, despite the jet lag, as it meant an easy shift. She was busy in the galley, getting ready to serve the dinner trays, when Chloe burst through the curtain.

'Will you watch my section for me for two minutes? I'm desperate for a wee!' she said, bouncing up and down on her toes.

'Where's Simon? Why can't he watch it for you?'

'He's dealing with some arse in first class, leaving me on my own. Go on, please? I'll be two seconds. Everyone is mostly asleep anyway,' she pleaded, her jiggling intensifying. Maya sighed.

'Go on, then.'

Chloe kissed her on the cheek and ran off into the break area. Maya left the galley and wandered towards the back of the plane to Chloe's section, walking the aisle slowly, checking each row as she did so. The call bell rang, and she noticed it was for a window seat towards the back of the plane. The person was staring downwards, wearing a tired, black baseball cap. She walked towards them, glancing out of the passing windows at the clear night sky, and when she reached the row, she leant over to switch off the bell. It was seat 28C. As she did so, she asked politely,

'How can I help?'

The eyes under the baseball cap lifted to look at her, and a deep voice asked,

'Any chance of a double whiskey and Coke?'

The voice was Theo's. And he was smiling.

Chapter Twenty-Two

'What are you doing here?' Maya whispered, her eyes wide in shock.

'I have a rare, but tragic sleepwalking condition,' he said, mock serious. 'It seems I sleepwalked into the airport, bought a ticket, somehow made my way onto the aeroplane, and now I find myself halfway to London.'

Maya laughed loudly, and the old man in the middle seat next to Theo jolted awake from his dozing. He mumbled incoherently about turbulence and closed his eyes, before nodding off again, with Theo placing a finger over his lips to shush her. She wasn't sure why, but this made her instantly blush. She'd never noticed how sexy his lips were, and as if on cue, he unknowingly licked his upper lip, and she had to turn away to stop herself from leaning in. He took that as his cue to follow her, and before she had time to protest, he had unclipped his seat belt and stood up, joining her in the aisle. Maya cleared her throat, aware that she needed to remain professional.

'But seriously, how come you're on this particular flight?' Maya said.

'Just by chance,' he said, but his eyes darted away from hers towards the aisle behind her. Instinctively, she turned around to see Chloe walking towards them. She was smiling.

'Will you look at that! What are the chances,' she said, all faux innocence.

'Chloe, did you know that Theo was going to be on this flight?'

'I might have done.'

'And is that why you asked me to cover your section?'

'I have no idea what you're talking about.'

'Chloe . . .' Maya warned.

'I won't answer any further questions without my lawyer present,' Chloe said straight-faced, and Maya could hear Theo laughing behind her. She shot Chloe a warning look.

'OK, OK, I *may* have seen Theo the other night back at Dave's apartment and he *may* have said he was flying home on the same flight. So, I thought it would be a nice surprise for you! It is, right?'

'Well, it is a nice surprise, obviously . . .' Maya began, shooting awkward glances towards Theo. 'Are you heading back home?'

He nodded. 'Just for a few weeks, then I'm back over again. Lots to sort out.' His face looked pained, and he looked to speak again, but then closed his mouth. Maya felt a pang of sympathy for him.

'I bet you do. How are you?'

'I'm OK, thanks. Just finding it all slightly overwhelming. I seem to have inherited a business, along with a huge amount of legal stuff that needs sorting. Along with trying to juggle my day job, too. Oh, the fun,' he said sarcastically, sighing.

'What do you do?' Maya asked, leaning into him as a passenger tried to squeeze past her on their way to the toilet. As she did so, her legs pressed against his, and she could feel his heat radiating through her skirt. So she pulled back quickly and straightened down her hem.

'I'm a self-employed cartographer,' he said, seemingly a little flushed himself.

'A what?' she asked, ignoring the call of a bell further down the aisle.

'A cartographer. I design and draw maps,' he said, pulling the sleeve of his jumper up slightly, revealing the inside of his wrist, where Maya spotted an elaborately inked tattoo of a compass. At the sight of his muscular forearm, she blushed, with images of the artist's portraits appearing into her mind. She had to hold her hands behind her back in an effort to stop herself stroking his skin.

'That's a step above a weatherman,' Chloe said, winking at Maya openly. Maya gave her a look, but thankfully Chloe was called away to answer the call from a passenger. But as she moved away, the air between Maya and Theo changed, and not just due to a slight drop in cabin pressure. The hairs on her neck felt charged as she turned to look at him and noticed he was staring intently at her.

'I'd best get back to my section,' she said, 'but it was so good to see you again.'

He nodded, his eyes warm and inviting. 'It really was.' She turned away from him, but he called out to her, 'Do you fancy grabbing a coffee sometime?'

Instinctively she went to nod an excitable yes, but then remembered her twelve-month rule of singledom. Could she just pause it for one, tiny little insignificant date? Would anyone even know? And it wasn't like she was interested in him like that at all. Was she? She thought of her last post and how many likes it had got, how many comments of support and gratitude that someone was brave enough to post about heartache. People were relating to her words, her thoughts. She couldn't drop everything at the first sign of a hot guy or a potential for romance. No, she couldn't give in, even if those lips were causing her a serious case of the trembles.

'Thanks, Theo. But now is just not the right time for me. I'm still recovering from a recent break-up—'

'Say no more,' he said, interrupting her. 'Let's just leave it at that.' He smiled sweetly and pulled out the in-flight magazine from the seat pocket in front of him and began rifling through the pages. Maya went to say something else, but found herself at a loss, so paused, before saying,

'Well, I'd better get back.'

'Sure,' he said, not looking up from the magazine, his concentrated gaze supposedly on an article on the effects of flying when struggling with haemorrhoids. Maya walked away, feeling decidedly sadder than half an hour ago.

Chapter Twenty-Three

Day Thirty-One
One month down already. Time flies when you spend most of it knee-deep in a vat of your own tears, while trying to simultaneously work and function like a normal human. Thank goodness for concealer and dry shampoo. The last month has been tough, I won't lie. I've cried enough tears that I've given myself conjunctivitis twice and found that my entire life fits into seven regular-sized boxes. I've moved house (not by choice), ridden a tractor, climbed a precipice, and drunk more wine than my liver can proactively process. I've laughed unexpectedly, found kindness in the unlikeliest of places and experienced loyalty that makes me eternally grateful. To put it lightly, it's been a roller-coaster of a month!

Am I still a dumped, twenty-something, single girl addicted to chocolate? Yes.

Am I still fighting the urge to ring my ex every day and beg him to take me back? Also, yes.

But am I determined to complete this year of singledom with positive thoughts? Heck, yes!

So, moving on from that point – this month's new challenge. I have decided to attend a . . . (drum roll, please) . . .
Glass Blowing Lesson!
Yep, you heard that right, I'm off to learn how to blow glass. My gorgeous aunt is joining me on this adventure. She organised it all. Apparently, it all takes place in a cave cut into the cliffs somewhere along the coast and the requirements are no skirts or long sleeves, and flat shoes. We are specialising in lampworking (nope, I'd never heard of it either and yes, I can

hear you all furiously tapping away to look it up). It's the process of making glass beads which can then be fashioned into a bracelet or some ornate jewellery. It's all sounding very medieval and dauting and just a tiny bit fabulous! I will either make some enchanting bracelet that will forever be the topic of conversation whenever I wear it, or I'll end up scorching my hair and walking away smelling like a toasted marshmallow. Time will tell . . .

'Maya, put that thing away and listen, will you?'

'In a second,' Maya whispered back, typing quickly before slipping her phone back into her pocket and smiling at Aunt Sophia. To be honest, this class wasn't as fun as she thought it was going to be. The teacher, a middle-aged, slightly paunchy man called Henry, had a voice as monotonous as the speaking clock, and she couldn't help but feel herself drifting off when he was giving them their introductory talk. But he'd spent twenty minutes already discussing the optimum temperature of the kilns and the names of each instrument that they would use today, and Maya was bored. She just wanted to make pretty things.

She looked around the cave, which was actually pretty amazing. And huge. She'd imagined a small, confined place carved into the rockface, but this was a vast open space, accessible through an enormous, seven-foot-tall wooden door that shut out the coastline beyond it. The cave itself was at least a hundred feet in diameter and was lit by large candles positioned in the walls around them. Six long tables sat around the periphery of the cave, with a ginormous opening lit by an actual, real fire. Next to that sat a giant, grey kiln. The heat didn't quite reach her table though, and she shivered a little. The cave was cool, quite literally. She looked up and could see condensation running down the walls.

'So, as I said, if you all grab your torch and your chosen instrument, you can begin.' Henry's voice suddenly shot back into earshot, and she looked around to spot the other ten participants all nodding and springing into action. Maya looked across at Aunt Sophia, who had already popped on her goggles and slipped on her gloves. She then switched on her glass-blowing torch as if she was a seasoned pro, the bluey flame bursting from its point like a jet engine. Maya noted she was actually humming. She copied her by sliding on her own goggles and gloves, a feeling of anxiety twisting in her stomach.

'I'm not sure I heard everything he said,' she whispered to Aunt Sophia.

'That's because you were too busy on your phone,' Aunt Sophia chided, picking up a red and a gold glass rod from the table in front of her and placing an end of each rod into the flame. Her greying hair was held back in a tight bun, the curls so like Maya's, desperate to escape the multitude of clips that were holding them back. Maya chose a green and blue rod and placed them into her own, now burning, flame in front of her.

'Make sure the rods are properly heated before you try to merge the colours together,' Henry called out to the class as he slowly walked around the cave, stopping to inspect and help each table in turn. Aunt Sophia nodded and slowly turned each rod in the flame. Maya followed suit. After a few moments, Aunt Sophia began to fuse the ends of the two rods together, their colours almost black in the flame and Maya shamelessly copied.

'Keep an eye on your own flame here, Miss Madeski. Please do not get complacent, your torch here can heat up to temperatures exceeding 900 degrees.' Maya jumped in her chair to find Henry standing directly in front of her table, his chiding, halitosis-fuelled breath causing her to hold her own.

'Sorry, sorry,' she said, focusing her eyes on her own work. The cave fell silent as every participant concentrated on their glass work, bar the odd comment from Henry advising them of the next steps. Before she knew what was happening, she had one perfectly cyclical bead sitting on the stone plate beside her. She felt ridiculously proud. It was stunning, a tiny glass bead of green and blue infused together, that reminded her of the sea. She looked across at Aunt Sophia's desk (surreptitiously making sure that Henry was nowhere within eyeshot) to see that she had already completed two beads and was choosing her coloured rods for her third. She was humming quietly, her eyes focused downwards on her task. Maya moved onto the second bead and found that this time she was a little quicker, and by her third bead, she had found her groove. It was such a relaxing, but focused task. It required high levels of concentration and Maya noticed that her mind didn't have time to roam off with worries or concerns, she simply completed each bead with a clear head and a calm mind.

An hour later, the whole class had completed twelve beads, each unique to them. Not all of Maya's were perfectly round or smooth, but they were beautiful to look at, the glass catching in the candlelight.

'You have all done extremely well,' said Henry, standing in front of the large kiln. 'Your beads will now need to be annealed within the kiln which we will do after the class has ended. Your beads, once cooled correctly, will be boxed, and sent out to you at the addresses provided. I hope you have all had an enjoyable class and thank you all for attending.'

Both Maya and Aunt Sophia stood up to leave, each looking at the creations of others as they headed towards the exit. Maya's eyes were drawn to a man seated behind a bench by the door. She hadn't noticed him before, but then they had been late and had scooted in, all apologies and embarrassment straight to their table. But now she couldn't take her eyes off him. He was gorgeous. All naturally bronzed and sandy haired, like he'd stepped straight off a California beach and his eyes were warm and inviting. He was laughing politely with the elderly lady he'd been partnered with, and Maya spotted a deep dimple in his right cheek that she just wanted to reach up and press. He reminded her of Michael with his tanned skin and tight shirt, however this man's tan looked natural while Michael required a spray tan every fortnight in an effort to stop his make-up artist having to pile on the foundation with a cement trowel every night. This man was dressed in a crisp, white shirt and jeans, yet they looked expensive, and she could easily spot the athletic physique through the shirt. As she walked past his table, he looked up at her and winked. She looked away, embarrassed that he had caught her staring, but laughed. She went to grab her coat from the rack by the front door and looked back at him. Aunt Sophia nudged her in the ribs as she slipped on her coat.

'That dish is eyeing you up over there,' she said, nodding in cute guy's direction. 'Ooh, he's lovely,' she said, making no effort to be discreet and bending right round Maya's shoulder.

'Aunt Sophia,' she said, a warning tone to her voice, 'stop it. I am not engaging with men at the moment. Remember my twelve-month rule.'

'Oh, come on. You can still look,' Aunt Sophia answered, her bottom lip sticking out childishly.

'Looking leads to talking, which inevitably leads to dating, which undoubtedly leads to romance,' Maya said, tying the belt around her waist. Someone had opened the huge wooden door and an icy sea breeze was blasting in. 'C'mon.'

'Hi.' A deep, male voice caused Maya to jump. She looked behind her to see the man had left his bench and was now standing close to her. He smelt amazing, she noted, and she had to tell herself not to reach up to touch that endearing dimple again. It was impossibly cute.

'Hi,' she stammered, smiling. She felt Aunt Sophia pull at her hand, but she stood firm.

'I didn't want you to leave . . .' he began but was interrupted by the arrival of Henry who came and stood next to him.

'Well done, you two. A very successful class tonight,' he exclaimed, bits of spittle flying from his lips and landing on cute guy's white shirt. He didn't seem to notice.

'Yes, thank you so much,' Maya said. 'But we had better get going before it's too late.' She emphasised the words *too late* for Aunt Sophia's ears.

'But it's only 9pm,' Aunt Sophia argued, turning back to Maya and giving her a glare.

'Yes, but you need to get home to Matilda. She does worry if you're not there for her bedtime milk.'

Both the guy and Henry looked a little shocked at this, especially as Aunt Sophia was nearing sixty.

'Matilda is her goat,' Maya explained, which didn't seem to help.

'Yes, well, I'd best get back on with popping the beads in the kiln before they cool down too quickly,' Henry said, clearing his throat. He then reached out and touched the man's shoulder affectionately, 'Will you help me?'

'Of course,' the cute guy answered, turning to Henry, and kissing him on the cheek. 'I'll be right with you.' Henry walked off, leaving Maya staring at his retreating back in shock.

'As I was saying,' the cute guy began, holding out Maya's blue gloves in his hand, 'you dropped these when you rushed in earlier and threw your coat onto the coat rack. I picked them up for you and didn't want you to leave without them.'

His smile was sweet, and Maya's stomach took a plunge.

'Thank you. That's so kind.'

'My pleasure,' he said. 'They are gorgeous and go wonderfully with your coat. Bye then.' And with that, he turned to walk towards Henry, placing one of his strong arms around Henry's waist and pulling him in for a hug. Maya looked at Aunt Sophia who proceeded to burst into raucous laughter as she walked out of the cave.

'Turns out he's definitely not your type anyway, honey,' she said, walking into the darkness of the night, still laughing, leaving Maya trailing grumpily behind.

Chapter Twenty-Four

'Remind me why you are watching this, again?'

'Shhh . . . just listen to them both. It's sickening.'

Maya's eyes didn't leave the TV screen and she felt compelled to watch, even though it was as painful as having her teeth pulled out by a blunt pair of scissors. Amanda Avary was smiling directly into the camera.

'Michael, tell us what we have in store for this weekend. Are we finally going to see the signs of spring in the air?'

'Thanks, Amanda.' Maya noted a cheeky wink in Amanda's direction. 'This weekend is finally showing promise, with a large warm front moving in from the west which should bring with it elevated temperatures and blue skies. Don those lighter jackets folks, as this weekend will potentially see highs of 15 degrees centigrade and sunny skies.' Maya watched as he moved his hands across the green screen, gesticulating over particular areas of the UK. She noticed the small scar on his wrist that he'd obtained from a skiing accident on holiday with her a few years back. She remembered nursing it affectionately. Amanda's voice brought her back into the present.

'And what about next week, Michael? Will this sunny spell stick around?' Amanda was keeping it professional, but Maya was watching her suggestive smile and flick of the over-styled, bouffant hair.

'Good news, Amanda. This weather looks set to stick for a good ten days, with this high pressure, slow-moving front remaining with us. The temperatures might even climb above higher than average in some southern areas. My advice would be to dig out your gardening gloves this weekend and start searching for your daffodils, it looks like the worst of winter is now behind us.'

His smile was infectious and the air between them was charged, Maya couldn't help but notice.

'Thank you, Michael. Now back to Samuel for a sports update.' Amanda turned her head towards her left and Maya froze the screen with the remote control. She moved off the sofa and walked up close to the screen, scanning Amanda's left hand at the huge ring that was sitting proud: the diamond catching the lights of the studio.

'Maya, stop this.' Aunt Sophia came forward from the doorway of the lounge and switched off the TV completely. 'This is so unhealthy.'

'I don't do it every day,' Maya tried to argue.

'That's because you physically can't when you're not in the country. You do watch it when you're here. It's not healthy.'

'I'm just interested in the weather, that's all.'

'Then get yourself the weather app installed on your phone. Enough is enough. I do read your blog posts, you know, I know you're spying on them both.' Maya looked down at the floor in shame, Aunt Sophia's face softened a little. 'From now on, I ban the news channel from my house.'

'You ban the news?'

'Not *all* news, just the news channel. *That* channel,' she said, pointing at the dark TV screen. 'Now go and finish packing, we leave in five minutes.' Aunt Sophia walked out, leaving Maya standing there.

Maya did as she was told and made her way back upstairs to pack for her next work trip. She made sure she packed a few swimming costumes and summer dresses. She gulped at the thought of what she had signed up to do. Would she really be brave enough? Was she insane? She hadn't told anyone about her next challenge, not even Chloe. Aunt Sophia might have been supportive, but at the end of the day, she was the closest thing she had to a mother right now, and her instinct told her that Aunt Sophia would try to dissuade her from doing it.

No, she'd be best off getting through the challenge and telling everyone afterwards. That is, if she didn't get killed or become fish food first.

Day Sixty-One

As I embark on the third month of my twelve-month ban of dating, I can't help but sometimes think about my ex. What is he up to? Is he happy? Has he gained weight? Has his annoying nose hair grown into a handlebar moustache? Does he still think about me at all? Questions that spin around my mind like a taunting merry-go-round of 'what ifs'.

Sadly, or luckily, (depending on how I feel that day), I actually have a way of finding out. Which I do. Every day. And his new fiancée too. I can study them from afar; her in her tight, little dresses, fake nails and equally fake laugh and him, with his newly sculpted eyebrows and spray-on trousers all from the [dis]comfort of my own home . . .

But I think this needs to stop. It doesn't feel healthy and with each viewing of their sickly sweet smiles and his sub-par presenting I feel my positive energy fading quicker than his phoney fake tan. It brings me pain and, as my Aunt Sophia says, 'Pain is optional, pleasure is essential. It's all about choices.'

Therefore, I choose to go pain-free from now on . . . Wish me luck (and please someone hide the remote control).

Chapter Twenty-Five

They'd landed in Los Angeles to brilliant blue skies and a heat that hit Maya in the face when she stepped off the plane. Despite having flown out to California too many times to count, the heat and scent always surprised her when coming from cold England. She lifted her face towards the skies and enjoyed the feeling of dry warmth bathing her skin. She took a deep breath. Instantly, her shoulders relaxed.

The flight had been uneventful, but she felt tired. The night flights were always great to work on, but hard to recover from afterwards. She could already feel her eyelids growing heavy behind her dark sunglasses. She wasn't working with any of her regulars, no Chloe, Andreas, or Graham this time, instead she was working with some new members of staff that were just exhausting with their high energy levels and positivity. But it did mean that today was free for her to do as she pleased. No one need know. She gulped at this realisation. No one would know. Not until afterwards.

She arrived at the hotel and checked in robotically. The plan was to sleep for four hours before the pre-arranged taxi picked her up to take her the two hours out of Los Angeles towards La Jolla, but she couldn't sleep a wink. She lay on the comfy bed, the air conditioning causing the hairs on her arms to stand on end, while her stiff body lay frozen in trepidation. She ended up scrolling through social media and checking the clock umpteen times before finally giving up and getting dressed. The preparatory email had been very clear in its instructions: bikini or one piece, water shoes if available, and everything else would be provided on arrival. She lathered on the sunscreen and made sure she had her sunglasses packed in her little bag and checked the time again, still thirty minutes to go. Her fingers tapping on the bed in angst, she decided to do what had become so natural to her recently, she pulled out her phone and began to write.

Day Sixty-Two

My hands are actually trembling as I write this, but today I am taking part in my third challenge. Now this one I am doing on my own. Mainly because,

- *No one else I know would willingly participate.*
- *My insurance won't cover this activity.*
- *If my family found out, they'd try to stop me.*
- *If I do happen to lose a limb, pushing the airline service trolley might prove difficult on the journey home.*

For today, believe it or not, today I am going swimming with sharks! What was I thinking? It all seemed like such a good idea a week ago, when I was buoyed by a great bottle of chardonnay and a particular desire to 'do something spontaneous'.

Note to self — never book anything involving deep water, heights, or the need to fill out a next of kin form without adult supervision again.

I thought about cancelling (or should that be counselling?!), I really did, but something inside told me not to — a death wish perhaps? And now it's too late. The bus to collect me will be here in less than half an hour and I haven't even had time to paint my nails. At least if I'm going to lose a limb then it may as well have beautiful, manicured nails at the end of it.

So, if I do get eaten by a great white shark today, please can someone ensure that my dad receives a message of how much I adore him, that my vintage collection of My Little Ponies are gifted to a worthy recipient, and that my friends throw me a gloriously exuberant wake, in which my ex is forced to sit in the front row with a flashing, neon sign over his head, stating 'Cheater'.

Wish me luck . . .

Maya uploaded it and read through the comments from her blog posted yesterday. It still amazed her that so many people had taken a liking to her silly old blog. But the numbers didn't lie – 18,564 views and 154 comments already. But she didn't have time to read them now, she had to get downstairs to meet her pick-up.

As she made her way out of the hotel lobby and into the beautiful American sunshine, she felt her phone ping in the pocket of her shorts. More to distract herself than anything, she pulled it out and read the notification. It was from an unrecognised number. She opened the message to read it.

Hi Maya, I hope you don't mind me messaging you, Chloe gave me your number. If you happen to be on the OAS37 flight this coming Friday to NY, I just wanted to let you know that I will be on it too. I hope that's OK. Take care, Theo.

As she read the message, the minibus pulled up outside her hotel, and she climbed in almost without thought, taking a seat thankfully alone on a row of two. She barely noticed that the minibus was almost full. Theo was messaging her, reaching out. They hadn't spoken since that awkward encounter on the flight home from New York over six weeks ago, where she had turned him down flat. She'd felt so guilty afterwards but knew that it was the right thing to do at that time. She had felt too fragile. She still did, she reminded herself as the minibus shot through the stunning American countryside of lush green fields that led towards the steep inclines of the hills in the distance. They whizzed past vineyards and orange groves, with the sweet, citrusy smells wafting through the open windows of the minibus as the countryside blurred past. But Maya didn't seem to notice, she was too busy thinking of Theo, with his sandalwood smell and silly baseball cap. And the way his eyes looked only at her when he was talking to her, as if the rest of the world had faded away.

She sent a quick message to Chloe.

You gave Theo my number?

She waited only a minute before a message trilled back.

I did. Are you mad? Dave asked for it when we last spoke. Apparently, Theo had made plans to fly back to New York, but was worried about surprising you on the flight. You're flying Friday, right?

Maya hesitated before responding. Was she mad? Or was she secretly excited about seeing his face again?

No, not mad. It'll be nice to see him again. This time, hopefully without a complaint being made against me.

She joked, but her heart did a little leap as she thought about him. Or it could have just been the fact that she had spotted the ocean, with the boats and the harbour and, she gulped, big waves with the multitude of white tips that made it hard to distinguish between wave and shark.

'So, just stay calm in the water, do not panic or flail about. While the sharks are totally harmless, we have a duty to protect them, and if you begin to panic, it might cause them to become stressed and they will disappear quickly. We are in their territory, so respect that. And above all, enjoy yourself!'

The team leader, Scarlett, was smiling broadly, her face relaxed and bronzed, her freckles spreading wide across her make-up-free face. She was dressed in a bright blue and purple wetsuit that did the unthinkable and emphasised her athletic figure, while Maya was acutely aware of her multitude of curves stretching her own plain black wetsuit to its limits. She kept pulling at the rubber collar but could feel the skin around her neck becoming irritated and sore.

Scarlett waded out into the water, with Maya's group following behind. There were twelve of them in total, of varying ages and varying excitability levels. Maya realised she was the last to enter the water.

'Stick close to the shore until you feel comfortable with the sea,' Scarlett called back, as she pulled down her scuba mask over her face and, with one graceful dive, went under the water. The rest followed suit, albeit slightly less gracefully. Maya gulped, taking tentative steps forward, her toes sinking into the soft sand on the seabed. The water was warm, and the waves weren't too terrifying, and Maya found herself both wanting to retreat onto the warm sand but also stay with the others in her group.

'Safety in numbers,' she kept whispering to herself as she waded out further, the water reaching waist level. She pulled down her scuba mask – more so that she had a reason to keep her hands out of the water than anything else – and began to look around her. Through the foggy haze of her mask, she turned to see a terrifying sight: two small, dark fins heading straight towards her. She screamed into her mask, her vision fogging up even more. She felt frozen in place, her skin tingling beneath the water, her heart racing.

'Maya, just stay as you are, you'll be fine.' A calming voice appeared at her side, and she whipped her head around to find Scarlett next to her. Scarlett pulled her mask up onto her head and reached out to grab Maya's shaking hand, squeezing it tight. 'They are harmless. And beautiful,' she said, looking Maya right in the eyes. 'Just look.'

Maya looked down to find two leopard sharks swimming silently around them both, their snouts pressed low onto the seabed, in hunt of their lunch. They weren't bothered at all by Maya's presence. In fact, as they navigated around her legs to continue their hunt, it was clear that she was of no interest to them. She let herself exhale, realising she'd been holding her breath for far too long.

'Look at how gracefully they move, Maya,' Scarlett said, her soothing voice and presence bringing down Maya's heart rate to a more acceptable level. Maya did, following the two sharks in the crystal-clear waters. 'Do you want to try placing your head under yet?'

Maya, still following the sharks' movements, nodded silently and Scarlett let go of her hand, so that she could pop her mask back down over her mouth and nose, and lowered herself down into a seated position, the top of her head now bobbing on the surface, the breathing tube pointing upwards. Maya slowly copied her, lowering herself down into the cooling water, so that she was sitting cross-legged on the sea floor. The panic was still raging through her veins, but Scarlett was right, there was something so immensely calming about the sharks' slow, measured actions and the dull quietness surrounding her underwater. Scarlett made a hand signal towards Maya, checking she was OK, and Maya returned it. She was. She could see at least a dozen sharks now, all gliding around the group's bodies as they swam or hovered in the water. Maya gently allowed herself to reach out and her hand softly brushed past one of the sharks. It felt cold and smooth. It reacted by shifting sharply away from her, more frightened of her than she was of it. Scarlett was right, Maya realised. She didn't lower her hand, but let it float in the water, the sun streaming through the water, glistening and sparkling off her hand. Just as she was admiring the beauty of the water, a lone leopard shark appeared from nowhere and hovered by her fingers; its body sideways, but its eye focused solely on her. It was huge, at least double the size of the other sharks nearby, and its movements seemed measured and slow. Maya didn't flinch or move, just stared back; their eyes searched each other, communicating, learning. Its eyes were black, yet there seemed an intensity to them, a wisdom that came from years of observing things. They floated in unison and something deep inside Maya's gut felt soothed, like a hairline crack that was fusing back together.

Suddenly, the shark's eye darted away from her to a shadow to the left and in a moment, it was gone, swimming away from her into the darkness of the deeper ocean. Maya turned to see the cause of the shadow and found herself staring at the hairy, muscular legs of one of the team. A Brad, or Chad, or something Maya couldn't remember. She stood up, her body rising from the water, and she pulled off her mask.

'That dude was a whopper!' Brad/Chad said, his mask on his head and an underwater camera in his hand, his face wide with astonishment. She smiled back, realising her own smile was as wide as his. Her body was still tingling, but this time with exhilaration.

'Wasn't he? Or she, I think it was a female.'

'How'd you know?' he said, fiddling with the lens of his camera, ready to duck down again into the water. She shrugged.

'I could just sense it.'

He looked at her a little disdainfully but was distracted by a call from someone in the other group. They had spotted what looked like a whale far out in the waters and everyone was standing together, looking out into the vastness of the sea. But Maya turned and headed back to shore, feeling strangely content. Today had been a good day.

Chapter Twenty-Six

Day Sixty-Five
Buoyed by the fact I am clearly the world's next shark-whisperer,
I am on the hunt (pun intended) for my next challenge. What
do you lovely people of the internet think I should attempt next?
And while I thank you for some recent suggestions, may I
remind you all that while I am lucky enough to travel the world,
I am limited by my lowly cabin crew salary of what to do when
I'm there and a lack of desire to break the law, which means
I am unable to complete any of the following,

- *Dinner at a Michelin star restaurant, pretending to be a food critic.*
- *Run the red carpet and give Tom Cruise a big, fat kiss.*
- *Parkour through supermarket aisles. I'm not safe to be left unattended in supermarkets. I'd end up in the chocolate aisle, and never leave.*
- *Go for an extreme makeover/haircut. Those that have seen my hair, will understand. My tangled web of curls are reminiscent of Medusa on a damp day in November. They are a force to be reckoned with. And a makeover? – not my style. I'm more of a stick-to-what-you-know girl. I've been wearing the same mascara now for over two decades, and no one, and I mean no one, can convince me that I could pull off an eyeliner flick.*
- *Speed-dating – er, hello! Twelve-month rule of singledom ring a bell?!*
- *Jump out of a plane – I may work in planes for a living, but I prefer to remain inside them, with correct cabin pressure*

and with full control of my limbs please. Jumping out of them is reserved for emergencies only.

- *Graffiti the ex's car – not only did I fail GCSE Art, I also have terrible aim. I'd end up graffitiing everything but the car, me included. It would not be pretty. And yeah, also illegal.*

Let's keep it cheap, above board and legal, shall we?

I have two New York flights coming up, each with a one-night stopover, so any suggestions of something easy, fun and bookable, please let me know in the comments below.

Maya uploaded the post and pushed her phone back into her holdall, before slamming shut the overhead compartment. Passengers were due to board any minute and she felt immensely nervous, and not because of the huge storm currently over their flight path in the Atlantic.

'Maya? Are you ready? They're about to come on board.'

'Sure am.' Maya smiled at Andreas and headed towards the back of the plane where the plane door was being opened. Andreas headed towards the front for his greeting of the passengers. She straightened her pencil skirt and adjusted her collar before turning towards the stairs that had been attached to the plane. The first passengers began to board, and she switched on her professional smile. One by one, they passed her by, and she waited, searching for the one face in the crowd. Finally, she spotted him. Theo.

'Hi, Maya,' he said, stepping into the plane, his holdall thrown over his shoulder. She noted he was wearing a gorgeous bright blue jumper and fitted denim jeans. 'How are you?'

'Good, thanks,' she said, her smile turning genuine. 'And you?'

'Yep, much better than last time I stepped on a flight to New York,' he quipped but was jostled forward by a tired and angsty businessman behind him. He moved forward, away from her. 'Hopefully speak later.' She nodded at his retreating back.

The next twenty minutes or so were the usual chaotic mess of seat confusion, lack of storage solutions, crying children and the all-important safety talk. She was walking her section, the final check before take-off when she felt a tap on her shoulder. It was Andreas. He looked worried.

'Everything OK?' she asked him quietly, so as not to draw the passengers' attention to a potential problem. He was smiling, but she could see it was strained.

'After take-off, come and find me in the galley,' he whispered, before turning and heading back to his own seat. It was a smooth take-off, and once they had reached cruising altitude, she unclipped her belt and headed straight for the galley at the front of the economy part of the plane.

'What's going on, then? Why the sombre face?' she asked him, and he looked at her before rolling his eyes theatrically.

'Oh, darling girl. Emma wasn't sure whether to tell you or not, but I thought it only fair, just in case you're called up front . . .' he paused, placing his hand over his lips as if still debating whether to speak on.

She shook her head, '. . . and?"

'And it looks like we have a passenger flying with us today who you have met before.'

'OK. Who is it?' Maya asked, beginning to lose patience. She had a whole section to start on and this gossiping was not professional. Andreas touched her arm gently.

'It's Amanda Avary. Emma has her in seat 1A.'

Maya suddenly felt nauseous, which had nothing to do with any air turbulence, and placed a steadying hand against an air larder. Her throat felt tight again. She tried to speak.

'Are you sure it's her?'

Andreas nodded. 'She's bleating on and on with her foghorn voice all about her recent promotion and how the TV station were flying her out to New York for some special news report that is all hush-hush, yet she won't shut up about it . . .'

She nodded but wasn't really listening anymore. Amanda Avary was actually on this flight. And she was stuck with her for the next eight hours.

'Was I wrong to tell you?' he asked her, concern etched onto his handsome face.

Maya thought about her answer. The woman who effectively destroyed her life and ended her chance of happiness was sitting only inches away from her, no doubt sipping champagne. The woman was a reminder of everything that Maya had lost. Her stomach ached and she felt suddenly exhausted. But, despite this, she would rather know than be kept in the dark.

'No,' Maya answered quietly. 'I'm glad I know.'

She left the galley at this point and made her way back to her section, routinely beginning her shift without thought and, much like the cockpit of the plane, on autopilot.

'Maya? Do you have a minute?'

A voice spoke softly to her from behind, and she turned to see Theo standing beside the galley and adjacent to the airplane toilet, his hand leaning on the wall for support. They had hit the Atlantic, and, as expected, hit some quite serious turbulence. Since Andreas's shock announcement about Amanda, Maya hadn't given Theo a second thought, which made her feel slightly bad.

'Sure,' she said, emptying out the coffee remnants of the jug she was holding into a bin and continuing with her task. She gave him an encouraging smile though which seemed to reassure him.

'I just wanted to check we're OK, after last time, you know, when I asked you out.' He looked sheepish and uncomfortable. And extremely adorable, she found herself noting. They both wobbled as a large bump of turbulence hit the plane and Maya leant on the sink next to her, propping her elbow into a gap between the cupboard and sink to steady herself while she poured boiling water back into the jug.

'We are,' she said, stopping her task and looking at him. 'Sorry if I came across a bit of a bitch last time' – he shook his head to disagree, but she continued – 'it's just that I'd been recently dumped and was feeling so vulnerable.'

'Well, that's understandable,' he said. The plane hit another air pocket and Maya held herself firm, but Theo stumbled forward, banging his head on one of the galley cupboards, its metal door letting off a loud clang as his forehead made contact with it forcibly.

'Fuck!' he hissed, holding a hand over his forehead as he struggled to get his footing, Maya quickly sprang into action, placing the hot jug into the sink, ensuring its contents were draining away, and turned to help him.

'Are you OK?' she helped prise his hand away from his forehead and as she did so, she could see a trickle of blood on his skin, coming from a cut that lay just under his hairline. There were also the beginnings of a big, angry bump forming under the gash. 'Stand still, you're bleeding,' she ordered, grabbing some tissues, and handing them to him. 'Hold that firm on your head and wait there.'

He did as he was told silently, the tissues already turning red, and she stepped out of the galley towards the phone and placed a call to the back of the aircraft, requesting assistance. A male voice answered.

'Andreas? We have an injured passenger in the galley. Head wound due to turbulence. Can you assist?' She placed the phone back into the receiver and walked back to Theo, placing a gentle arm onto his back. 'Now this is why we have a very clear seat belt sign!' she berated him. 'Why is it, whenever you're on one of my flights, you end up being a big pain in my ass?' she joked, as Andreas stepped into the galley and pulled the blue curtain across to give them privacy and not cause alarm.

'What do we have here, then?' he asked, eyeing up Theo in a less than professional manner. Maya couldn't help but roll her eyes.

'He bashed his head into one of the cupboard doors,' she said, unlocking a nearby cabinet and pulling out a bright red first aid box. 'It looks like the metal handle caught him on the hairline.' She indicated to the tissue-covered area and began pulling on some latex gloves. Andreas nodded and walked past her to where there was a pull-down seat.

'Here, sit down.' He gestured to the seat and pulled on his own pair of medical gloves. Theo gladly accepted, his face a little ashen now. The plane was still jolting around. Maya gently pulled away the tissues and examined the cut. It seemed mostly superficial, more of a graze than a deep cut, so she began cleaning the wound with some antiseptic. Theo winced.

'Ow, that really bloody hurts,' he said, his body tensing as she dabbed the wound.

'Ah, you big baby, you're fine,' Maya answered. Andreas looked at her in shock, before speaking.

'What she means, sir, is that the cut doesn't look too major. You'll be just fine.' He shot Maya a warning look.

'It's his own fault for not staying seated,' she continued, but Andreas interrupted her.

'Maya. Perhaps our passenger needed to use the bathroom—'

'Or perhaps he just a big idiot with a flair for causing trouble,' she interjected, smiling back. Poor Andreas looked positively flummoxed when Maya continued. 'It's OK, Andreas. I know him. This is Theo. Theo meet Andreas.'

'Nice to meet you, Andreas,' Theo said, wincing again as Maya placed a plaster across the cut, and held out a hand. Andreas took it.

'Well, thank goodness for that. I thought Maya must have bumped her own head in the process,' he said, shaking it gratefully. 'How do you two know each other?' he asked, looking from one to the other.

'Theo here was the guy that made the formal complaint about me at Christmas,' Maya said, having fun now. Theo groaned and put his now-bandaged head into his hand.

'You're *that* guy?' Andreas said. 'Now I'm really confused.' Maya couldn't help but laugh.

'Don't worry, it was all a misunderstanding. The complaint was withdrawn, and Theo has since made it up to me,' she explained.

'Yes, and I was just in the process of asking her out for a drink tomorrow when I decided to smash my own head in—'

'And I was going to decline politely before you did that,' Maya said, ripping off her gloves and reaching for the accident book.

'You'd decline a wounded man a small token of one simple coffee?' Theo asked, looking to Andreas for support.

'I'll have coffee with you,' Andreas replied helpfully, and a tad too eagerly, Maya noted.

'Sure, the more the merrier,' Theo said, shrugging, with Andreas looking very pleased. 'One coffee, Maya. Come on, I hardly know anyone in New York, and it'll be all business otherwise.' He was pleading with her. Maya could feel her resolve melting. Surely one drink wouldn't hurt. Especially if Andreas came along too.

'Fine. But we fly home again in the evening, so it'll have to be in the morning,' she said, throwing her arms up into the air. 'One coffee, that's it.' Theo looked victorious.

'Fantastic. I know just the place. I'll message you the details.' He stood up gingerly, testing his balance, and smiled. 'Andreas, I look forward to seeing you tomorrow.' Andreas looked positively delighted and pulled back the curtain with flair to allow Theo to walk back down the aisle towards his seat.

'Honey, you have some explaining to do,' he said, before whipping the curtain shut again and sidling towards her. Maya returned the first aid box to its locker, ensuring it was locked, and turned to him.

'Later. We have a shift to finish first.'

Chapter Twenty-Seven

On the bus ride across town to their hotel, Maya got the low-down from Emma about Amanda. She wasn't sure if she wanted to know, yet her maudlin curiosity got the better of her and she had asked Emma outright.

'Turns out she is guest reporting on some American Television Awards taking place in the city this weekend. She wouldn't shut up about her dress, and her hair and her make-up . . . blah, blah, blah. She refused all meals on the plane, saying she' – Emma stuck up her hands to air-quote – '"*couldn't possibly eat anything that wasn't organic*".' Emma rolled her eyes. 'And she was really rude to Chanelle when it was suggested she take a nap along with the other passengers who were trying to sleep. Talk about high maintenance, good luck to whoever gets her on the return flight home.'

Emma didn't know about Michael or the history behind Amanda's connection to Maya, and Maya really didn't want to have to explain it, so she just stayed quiet. But knowing that Amanda was in New York felt oddly unsettling. She liked flying because it gave her a short period away from all the problems at home, if only temporarily, but now it felt like Amanda's shadow was following her.

Once settled at the Lexington Lodge, she couldn't help but type Amanda's name into her phone and press search. Up popped details of her previous boyfriends, her engagement to Michael, sugar-coating it with some fairy tale make-believe romance, where she studied, what her first television job opportunity was, who her favourite designer was – Maya found herself falling down the rabbit hole of gossip websites and entertainment pages. She couldn't find anything on why Amanda was flying to America though and that frustrated her. She wanted to know where she was, and make sure there was no opportunity to accidentally bump into her.

Her phone beeped at her, and a message popped up, it was from Theo.

Hi Maya, are you and Andreas still free tomorrow morning for a coffee? I have just the place in mind, if so. It's called Clementine's Bakery, at the corner of West 59th Street and Amsterdam Avenue at 10am. Hopefully see you there! Theo

Maya smiled before shooting back a quick response.

Sounds great! See you tomorrow. X

She pressed send, before realising that she had added a kiss at the end of the message; her default response to almost everyone. But what if he misconstrued her kiss as something other than friendly? She really hoped not. She went to bed worried, and, after a restless night's sleep, she found herself dressed and ready to leave in the morning, sat waiting for Andreas. Her fingers itching, she decided to console herself with writing another blog post. She was beginning to find great comfort in writing these days.

Day Sixty-Six
Sealed with a kiss . . . or not?
Can a man and a woman ever just be friends?

The age-old dilemma. Is it OK to send any type of message and sign off with a simple kiss or does that imply that something more might come of it? Where does the line lie between just being friendly or hinting at something more? I've already made it quite clear that I am not looking for a relationship, but have I just confused things? I want to stay in the friend-zone. Don't I?

I am now into my third month of my twelve-month rule of singledom, and I must admit that I am not missing being in a relationship at all. Is it because I am still hurting? Probably.

Or because I am finding the freedom and independence refreshing? I hadn't been properly single for years and realise now that I also hadn't been myself for years either. Much like a chameleon, I adapted myself to suit my environment and areas of my character that I didn't feel suited the relationship I hid deep down inside, to keep the relationship going. But what did my ex do? Did he worry constantly about adapting himself to suit me? No. Did he feel he had to hide his areas of improvement so as not to put me off? No. And nor should he. And nor should have I. We are who we are, and no relationship should ever make you feel you have to change yourself to fit. Don't you agree?

There was a knock at the door, so she quickly uploaded the post and closed her tablet and answered the hotel room door. There was Andreas, standing in smart, freshly ironed jeans and a tight white T-shirt under an equally freshly ironed pale orange shirt, the colour of the spring sky outside her window. His hair was styled with enough gel that even a hurricane couldn't shift a hair out of place. His handsome face was freshly shaved, and she could just see the hint of a double chin, which just made him more adorable.

'Well, don't you look handsome,' she said, giving him a kiss on the cheek and pulling the door behind her as they headed towards the hotel lift.

'One must always make an effort, darling,' he said, checking his reflection in the mirror as they both entered the lift, 'I like to match my outfit to my destination. Clementine shirt for our Clementine Bakery.'

Maya suddenly felt very aware of her outfit – creased jeans that had been shoved into her holdall and a 1970s vintage pale blue knit jumper that had been her mother's, along with her trusted, comfy white trainers that were brilliant for traipsing around the never-ending long streets of New York. Not exactly filling the brief on 'making an effort' as Andreas said. Just as the doors were closing to, she jumped out and shouted back,

'I'll meet you in the lobby.' And before he had a chance to respond, she had run back to her room and let herself in. Ten minutes later, she appeared in the lobby, to a low whistle from Andreas.

'Wow, you look amazing,' he said, taking in the halter-neck yellow-and-blue tea dress that accentuated her curves beautifully. It had a flattering V-neck that showed off her large chest and she had decided on a simple gold chain with a locket that sat comfortably at her collarbone. She'd let her hair down from its messy ponytail and quickly spritzed her curls into some shape in the bathroom, so that they now sat framing her face. She had also sharpened the eyeliner around her eyes, added some blusher and applied some nude lipstick with gloss to her plump lips. A collection of gold bangles jingled on her arm, along with a folded denim jacket that could be thrown on if she wanted to. But her trusty trainers remained stubbornly on her feet – she didn't want to overdo it and Maya was never one for style over comfort. She looked pretty, but not over the top.

'Thank you,' she said, blushing. 'It's your fault. I couldn't possibly step out with you looking like that, and me looking like a frumpy old maid.'

'Maya,' Andreas said, stepping forward and taking her hand, affection in his eyes, 'you could never be frumpy. You are gorgeous.'

'I don't know about that,' she began, but he squeezed her hand tight, interrupting her.

'You are. You just don't realise it.' His gaze was serious, and she didn't know what to say, so she just stayed quiet. He snapped out of his serious expression quickly though, as his eyes came alive, and he declared, 'Now, let's go on the hunt for some cake.' He yanked her into the cold New York street and scanned around in an effort to hail a taxi. 'This boy needs to eat!'

Chapter Twenty-Eight

They could have walked the few blocks to the bakery, but Maya was glad they hadn't. The spring weather had turned wet, and the heavy rain pummelled the roof of the taxi as they made their slow way towards West 59th Street. She slipped on her jacket and shivered a little. As they approached the corner of Amsterdam Avenue, Maya noticed a queue of people standing in the rain, huddled under umbrellas, bags, or newspapers in an effort to stay dry. The queue must have stretched at least fifty people long.

'What are they all queuing for?' she said to Andreas, as the taxi began to slow at their destination. He shrugged as the taxi came to a stop at what appeared to be the front of the queue. Amazed, Maya looked out of her window to see a very pretty, pale orange sign, lit-up with white wording and surrounded by beautiful artificial flowers of spring colours, spelling out the name *Clementine*. The shop itself appeared quite large, with two huge glass windows lighting up the inside of the bakery and a massive artificial flower arch of matching spring flowers over the front door. As they exited the car, the sweet smell of baked goods reached their senses and Maya's stomach rumbled in hopeful anticipation.

'This place looks amazing,' she said, paying the taxi driver.

'It really does,' Andreas said, immediately turning and taking a selfie with the bakery in the background. They turned to begin the long walk to the back of the queue when Maya heard her name being called out by a familiar British voice.

'Maya! Over here.'

She turned to see Theo standing at the entrance and was beckoning them inside. He still had a plaster on his forehead where he'd banged it yesterday and the memory of her touching him gave her a feeling she tried to ignore.

'I have a table already. Come on in.' He was smiling excitedly and seemed completely oblivious to the huge queue that were glaring at him as he blocked the entrance. Maya felt a bit sheepish avoiding the queue altogether, but Andreas didn't give it a second thought and walked under the flowered arch and into the darkness of the bakery, so she followed behind.

As she stepped into the bakery, she found herself pressed against a crowd three deep at the counter, and she could see why. The counter closest to her was full of the most delicious bakes of every type imaginable; cupcakes with multi-coloured icing and sprinkles, lines of iced doughnuts, cookies so large they looked to Maya like she'd need two hands to hold one, various muffins that looked like blueberry, chocolate, and banana; baked cheesecake slices topped with vibrant berries or just plain lime slices. Maya could feel her mouth watering at the sight. The second counter was brimming with stuffed bagels of every type imaginable; American hams and sliced salami, chicken and avocado, delicious thin slices of smoked salmon and thick cream cheese, the typical lettuce, bacon, and tomato; Maya could see why this bakery was so popular. But what really excited her was the third counter, which stood separate to the other counters with a plastic screen that stood almost floor to ceiling between them. Behind the third counter was a large sign, written in the same font as the shop name that stated, 'All gluten-free.' At this counter were the same delicious-looking cakes and bagels, that Maya couldn't quite believe the variety.

Theo led them to the back of the bakery where there were booths that lined the back wall and she slid herself onto the soft, plush orange seat next to Andreas, and Theo slid in opposite.

'This place looks amazing,' Maya repeated, realising that the high back of the booth seats meant that the noise and hubbub of the bakery actually felt a little muted. It felt intimate and like they could chat in peace.

'It is quite special, isn't it?' Theo said, blushing a little.

'How's the head?' she asked, looking at his slightly tired-looking plaster.

'Oh, much better thanks. Barely hurts at all now unless I touch it,' he said, pulling his floppy fringe down to try and hide the plaster.

'Glad to hear it,' she said, realising she really was glad he was OK.

'How early did you have to get here to grab this booth?' Andreas asked, leaning forward to take the menu from the table. Theo seemed to blush a little more.

'I have been here a little while,' he said, before tapping the menu with his finger. 'Decide what you want, and we'll get the order put in. I'm starving.'

Maya didn't need telling twice. She had already spotted a delicious-looking cheesecake slice, topped with fresh strawberries and white chocolate shavings inside the gluten-free counter.

'I know what I want,' she said.

'Great,' Theo said, and he caught the eye of a waitress who wandered over, pulling her pad and pencil from her apron pocket.

'Hi guys, what can I get you?' she said, giving them a megawatt smile and, Maya noted, Theo a cheeky wink, which, for some reason, really irritated her. She spoke first to get the waitress's attention.

'I'll have the gluten-free strawberry cheesecake with a black coffee, please,' she said, turning to Andreas.

'BLT sesame seed bagel please, followed by a cranberry and oat muffin. White coffee. Thank you,' he said, licking his lips in anticipation. The waitress nodded, writing it down and turned to Theo.

'And what can I get you?' she said, her smile overly familiar, but Theo seemed oblivious.

'The double chocolate chip cookie please, with a hot chocolate and white chocolate sprinkles.'

She wrote it down. 'Sure thing, guys. Be back shortly.' She disappeared and Maya had to ask,

'You like chocolate then?'

'I sure do,' he said. 'Unapologetically. Chocolate is my happy place.'

'I have to say, this is a really great place,' Andreas said, 'and I can't believe I hadn't heard of it before. How did you hear about it?' he asked Theo.

'Oh, I've known about this place for years. They make the best chocolate cheesecake this side of Manhattan. An age-old family recipe. This place feels like home to me.'

The waitress reappeared with a big plate of drinks and plates and set them down in front of them. With each plate was a tiny fork with a clementine engraved into the metal, Maya noted. She didn't hesitate, she dug the fork into the cheesecake and took a huge bite. The softness of the cream cheese melted on her tongue and complimented the sharpness of the strawberries perfectly. The base was a combination of buttery crunch and saltiness that set her taste buds alight. It was simply phenomenal, and she couldn't help but let out a groan.

'This is just fantastic,' she said, as she shoved in a second large mouthful of cheesecake.

'It really is!' Andreas exclaimed as he squirted more mustard onto his bagel, having already taken a large bite. Theo's smile grew larger.

'I thought you'd like it here,' he said, tearing off a chunk of cookie and dipping it into the whipped cream of his hot chocolate. He popped it into his mouth in one go. Maya took a sip of her coffee, and it was delicious.

'OK, I'll admit it, this was a good call. I'm glad I agreed to come,' Maya said, looking between them both with Andreas nodding vehemently.

'Absolutely.'

'So how long are you in New York for?'

'Just a week, I'm flying back on Sunday as I have a deadline on Monday.'

'Are you here to sort out things from your grandmother?' Maya asked. She regretted it instantly though when she saw his face crumble quicker than the cookie on his plate. 'Sorry, you don't need to say,' she added quickly.

'It's OK,' he said. 'Yeah, I am. I have some big decisions to make and some legal stuff to sort out, which needs to happen this week, ideally.' He took another huge bite of his cookie. 'But I'm not going to worry about that today. Today is for chocolate. Now, Andreas, tell me all about you. How long have you been flying?'

The next two hours flew by as they fell into comfortable conversation with each other and drank second rounds of coffee and hot chocolate. They barely noticed the hordes of people swarming in and out of the bakery and before they even noticed the time, Maya's phone pinged with a message. She read it and turned to Andreas.

'That was Michelle. The airport coach is going to be at the hotel in an hour.' She felt genuinely disappointed. 'We'd better get going.' Both Theo and Andreas looked saddened, but they began to gather their things. 'Shall we get the bill?'

'No need,' Theo said. 'I've got this.'

'Oh no, let us pay our share.' They both tried to argue, but he simply shook his head.

'Seriously, it's on me. It's the least I can do for having to bandage up my knucklehead of a forehead,' he joked, touching his forehead gingerly.

'That's very kind, thank you,' she said, looking at him and not quite knowing what to do next to say goodbye. Should she hug him? Pop a kiss on his cheek? She could see that he was shifting awkwardly from foot to foot, so she wondered if he felt as unsure as she did. Andreas helped the situation by stepping forward and enveloping Theo in a big hug.

'Thanks for a fabulous morning, I love this place!' he said. When he pulled away, he looked at her questioningly and nodded in Theo's direction as if to say, what are you waiting for? She stepped forward and gave Theo a quick hug, her skin barely touching his, yet she felt charged. At his touch, she closed her eyes, and her body pulsed with a wave of heat that stretched from her head to her toes. Inhaling his scent, the combination of sandalwood and sugary sweetness almost made her legs buckle. She wanted him. The realisation hit hard, and she pulled away with a little too much force, causing him to stare at her, confused. She cleared her throat and said, 'Yes, thanks so much.' She pulled away before he had a chance to see the effect he had on her and began walking towards the exit, squeezing past the crowds. She ignored the spiky elbows and sharp shoulders, but as she made slow progress through the mass of bodies she was suddenly shoved sideways and almost fell against the glass window.

'Hey!' she yelled.

'Sorry,' a muffled voice yelled back, but she couldn't spot the culprit. 'All this for a doughnut,' she muttered, squeezing herself up against the window to avoid any further pushes. As she did so, she noticed a bright orange poster stuck on the window, advertising cooking classes every Friday evening. It read:

No baking experience required; all products baked are included in the price. Become your own Clementine Chef! Call below for more details.

'Are you alright?'

Theo was suddenly beside her, holding out his hand, which she took. It was warm and his hand was big, it almost enveloped hers. She laughed.

'I'm fine. Some people sure do need their sugar fix though.'

'It's like queuing for tickets to see Beyoncé in here,' Andreas agreed, parting the crowd with his arms, and leading them out of the bakery.

Back on the street, Maya hailed a taxi and one pulled up straight away.

'This was lovely, thanks again,' she repeated, suddenly at a loss for what to say. Theo opened the cab door for her and helped her in.

'My pleasure,' he said, looking deep into her eyes. Suddenly she felt very hot. She wanted to say something else, but before she had a chance to think of something, he sighed and closed the door. As the taxi pulled away, Andreas gave her a knowing look which she ignored. Instead, she turned around from her seat to look back and spotted Theo still standing on the kerb, watching them leave. She replicated Theo's sigh.

'Honey, you're going to get yourself into a whole lot of trouble at this rate.'

She turned back and glowered at him. 'I have no idea what you're talking about,' she said.

'Of course you don't,' he replied sarcastically. 'But let's just say that I don't think it was *my* stunning looks, charming sense of humour and fabulous dress sense that he was interested in today.'

'How do you know?' she joked. 'You might be just his type.'

He laughed but turned in his seat to look at her, his seat belt stretching across his chest.

'Perhaps it's time to give this twelve-month ban a break for a bit. Try dating again—'

'Not happening,' she interrupted.

'He seems like a really nice guy though—'

'Then you date him.' She shot him a warning look. 'I'm happy as I am. I'm enjoying being single.'

He looked intently at her, scanning her face. 'Are you, though? Are you really, truly happy?'

The direct question threw her, and she paused before answering, somewhat unconvincingly, 'Of, of course I am.'

Andreas didn't respond, but just kept scanning her face. She felt like she was being interrogated and he could see inside her soul. A moment later, he leant back, resting his head against the seat, still looking at her. He smiled.

'Like I said, you're getting yourself into a whole heap of trouble here.'

Chapter Twenty-Nine

'You've got it made here! Free lodgings, free clothes, awesome aunt. Think I can move in too?'

Chloe was standing in front of Maya's large wardrobe wearing nothing but matching neon-pink bra and knickers, with a pile of clothes hung over her left arm and her right hand placed on her hip. She was staring intently at the contents of the wardrobe, a look of adoration on her face. She leant forward and stroked a beautiful satin dress gently.

'Hello, gorgeous,' she said, before dropping the rest of the clothes on the floor and pulling out the chosen dress. Maya, who was sitting cross-legged on her single bed, had been happily watching her own private Chloe-led fashion show for the last thirty minutes while Chloe tried on the vintage wardrobe, one piece at a time. Maya pointed at the chosen dress, a bright blue knee-length tea dress with a line of sequins around the pussy-bow collar.

'That one's too tight for me,' she said, pointing at her chest. 'If it fits, you can have it.' Chloe squealed and threw it over her head, letting the delicate fabric flow down over her slim frame. It looked amazing on her. She swivelled like a little girl playing dress up.

'I love it!' she exclaimed; her face lit up like a Christmas tree.

'Then it's yours.' Maya pretended to take a picture with an imagined camera in her hands and said, in a mock American voice, 'Fabulous, darling.'

Chloe strutted her stuff around the bedroom and they both fell into a fit of giggles onto the bed. Maya then pulled out a brown, wooden box from under her bed and opened the lid, revealing a treasure trove of costume jewellery. They both delved into it, their hands pulling out jewels like kids with a jar of sweeties, and proceeded to try on huge costume rings, long beads of pearls and flashy, gaudy earrings. There was a short tapping at the door and Aunt Sophia burst through, with Matilda the goat following closely behind. She was carrying a gold tray with three cocktail glasses perched on it.

'Margaritas, girls?'

More squealing, and Aunt Sophia joined them on the bed, handing a cocktail to each of them.

'So, have you shown her the shoes yet?' she said to Maya, nodding her head in Chloe's direction.

'Shoes?' Chloe squeaked, her voice getting ever higher.

'Not yet!' Maya took a big sip of her cocktail, the cool liquid sliding deliciously down her throat, and she sat up on her knees, addressing Chloe. 'We found a huge chest in the loft which is full of my mum's shoes from the 1970s. They are just incredible. And' – she paused for dramatic effect – 'they are all our size too.'

More squeals ensued, so excitable that Matilda the goat made a hasty exit and made a beeline for the hallway, where she rather grumpily began munching on the curtains in protest.

'Have you checked the top of the wardrobes, Maya?' Aunt Sophia said, pointing a heavily ringed finger towards the top of the built-in wardrobe that covered one entire wall of the bedroom. 'I'm pretty sure they are full of winter coats, that should be just your size.'

'I did earlier, I couldn't find anything,' Maya said, occupied by the huge shiny brooch that Chloe had just pulled out of the jewellery box. It was a mix of amber and sapphire, in the shape of a butterfly. It was gorgeous. Maya's fingers itched to touch it.

'They are definitely still there,' Aunt Sophia said, making her way to the wardrobe. She was wearing a long maxi skirt and an off-the-shoulder short T-shirt that just revealed the glint of a piercing on her belly button. As she stretched up to slide open the top wardrobe door, her T-shirt rose and Maya's eye was drawn to the faded but large scar across Aunt Sophia's lower abdomen. It seemed to stretch from hip to hip.

'Aunt Sophia, how did you get that scar across your stomach?'

At the mention of the scar, Aunt Sophia quickly abandoned her task and pulled her T-shirt low down over her skirt, her face flushing. 'It's nothing. An old scar. I had my appendix out when I was a teenager,' she said, bending down and turning her attention to the mound of scarves on the rug. She began trying to fold them into a proper pile, but the silky material made the task fruitless.

'How did I never know that?' Maya said, concerned.

'Because it was way before you were born, missy, and it was such a quick operation that I was up and about again within a few days.' Aunt Sophia gave her a quick smile and continued her task.

'I guess I was unlucky then,' Chloe said, slipping on a satin dressing gown over the top of her clothes.

'Why?' Maya asked.

'Because when I had my appendix out when I was eight, I spent two weeks in bed. It was horrid. But at least mine wasn't as big as yours,' she said, standing up and lifting her own shirt to reveal a similarly faded, but smaller vertical scar, about three inches long, to the left of her abdomen. She pointed her stomach towards Aunt Sophia for her to compare, but Aunt Sophia only gave it a cursory glance. Maya looked at Chloe's toned tummy, having seen that scar many times when they were changing, sunbathing, and through Chloe's habit of walking around half-naked a lot of the time.

'Yours looks completely different, Aunt Sophia. For one, it's horizontal, and two, it's much lower down,' Maya said, her forehead creasing in concern. Aunt Sophia shrugged.

'Well, yes, I'm a lot older than you two gorgeous girls, and operations were a bit of a botch job in my time. The surgeon had probably had a couple of whiskies for Dutch courage before beginning,' she joked, downing the rest of her glass. 'I don't really remember and it's really no big deal.' She stood up, hoisting her glass in the air. 'Now what is a big deal is that we have run out of margaritas. A travesty of the highest order! We must remedy this immediately. Who's for another round?'

Both Maya and Chloe yelled, 'Me!' and in an effort to hunt down their glasses amidst the mess that was the floor, Chloe inadvertently knocked over a cardboard box that had been resting on the desk beside her. The contents spilled out, mostly tatty paperbacks and what looked like old diaries.

'Sorry!' Chloe said, bending down to begin picking up the books, with Aunt Sophia rushing forward to help her. Maya grabbed the tray and stood up.

'You two deal with that mess, and I'll go and get the drinks.' She found the three glasses and made her way carefully through the clothes-covered floor into the hallway. In doing so, she startled the poor goat who was trying to doze, its head on the bottom step of the stairs.

'Sorry, Matilda,' she said breezily. 'Just on my way for a top-up.'

In the kitchen, she poured three new, strong margaritas into the cocktail glasses and hummed along with the tiny radio that blared some catchy boyband tune from the kitchen windowsill. Making her way back upstairs, she passed the front room in which the television had been inadvertently left on, its bright screen blaring into the dark room. If Maya had looked, she would have seen Michael's stiff smile and glazed eyes. Had she stopped, she would have noticed the slight tension on set, the way his shoulders sat a little too tense and his hands clamped together unnaturally.

But Maya didn't see any of this. She passed the door to the front room with her mind on the two girls upstairs. Matilda the goat passed her on the stairs as she made her way up.

Maya stopped and bent down to the goat's floppy ear and whispered, 'Today has been a good day.'

Matilda simply grunted in response before trotting off to find some peace and quiet.

Chapter Thirty

Day 113

Sometimes I just adore my job. Ignoring the irate passengers, the jet lag and the constant dry skin caused by cabin air, there is something to be said about getting to travel the world with my work. Tonight, I am flying long haul to New York and will be landing on Easter Saturday evening, just in time for the infamous annual Easter parade in the city. I've never been and always wanted to go! Have any of you lovely readers been? Easter bonnets, human-sized bunnies, copious amounts of guilt-free chocolate (as the walking burns off the calories) and the chance to see Manhattan at its finest. There is no better city, in my opinion, than New York. The noise, the smell (OK, maybe not the smell), the food, the atmosphere – it is like the city itself is breathing, there is motion everywhere. New York makes me smile. From the gritty sidewalks to leafy Central Park, then skywards to the crazy heights of the Empire State, each view is unique, and each visit is too. Can you tell I'm excited?!

Easter is an important time for me, for many reasons – most of them memories of a happier time, a time when life was simpler, and my concerns were few. Easter is in religious terms a time for new beginnings, and never have I needed a new start more than now. My mum always used to say, 'Travel down Easter Avenue – time to reflect, review, and renew.' Easter Avenue was a metaphorical street where, according to my mum, we should each pause and consider ourselves and our actions. Was there anything we could improve on? Or change? 'Aim to be the better person, the person you aspire to be,' she would say. We would sit around the kitchen counter, with a huge bowl in between us, and for every positive mention, we would throw a blueberry into the bowl, and for every mention of something to improve on, we would add a dollop of soured cream. She would then go on to bake the most amazing blueberry cheesecake, saying 'Life is made up of the sweet and the sour. But combine the two together and you gain the sweetest result.' She was amazing. I still make that cheesecake every year, minus the gluten, and minus my mum.

So, as you can see, Easter is a pretty big deal to me. And what makes this year even better is that my lovely aunt will be joining me on the flight to New York! She's going to bring the most fabulous of bonnets for the two of us to wear. She sews like my mum used to cook – seamlessly. I won't say what the bonnets look like now, but I will upload photos of them tomorrow (just the bonnets, no head shots).

So,. I guess what I'm saying is, Happy Easter to you all, however you choose to spend it. I hope your Easter weekend is full of love, laughter, and most importantly – CHOCOLATE!

'Cabin crew, please take your seats for take-off.'

'All you need to do is say hello,' Chloe said, clipping her belt into place next to Maya's.

'I will.'

'And ask him to join us tomorrow.'

'Chloe—' Maya warned her as the plane began taxiing to their allocated runway.

'What's the big deal?'

'There isn't one.'

'Then you won't have a problem with me asking him to join us tomorrow.' Chloe smiled victoriously at her as the plane began its descent into the skies.

'What about Dave?'

'What about him?' Chloe shrugged. 'That's old news. Nice guy and all that, but you know me, I'm not one for relationships. But you are.'

'I'm not. I am sticking to my rule—'

'Being single, blah blah blah . . .' Chloe said, interrupting her. 'Haven't you had enough of that by now?'

'In case you've had a recent severe bout of amnesia, you were the one who instigated the whole thing.'

Chloe waved away her concerns. 'But that's because you were all weepy and sad, and I thought it might help you get out of your wedding disaster funk. But look at you now! You're more confident and happier than I've ever seen you.'

Maya paused. 'I am, actually. You're right.'

'I always am,' Chloe said smugly, just as the seat belt sign turned off and she unclipped her seat belt. Standing up and straightening her pencil skirt, she turned back to Maya and said, 'Now go and say hello.'

'Hi.'

Maya noticed that he looked even better than she remembered. His hair had recently been cut and his face seemed brighter, less strained.

'Oh, hi!' Theo said, his face lighting up at her arrival. 'I was really hoping you would be on this flight.'

'Well, here I am,' she said, doing a tiny curtsey. 'You on your way to New York?' She immediately cursed herself for saying something so stupid – of course he was, why else would he be on the flight?

'Yes, I am. Meeting with the accountant, the solicitor, the manager – basically my week comprises of meeting men in suits and talking about money.' He joked, but she could see he seemed lighter. The woman in the seat next to him, in row twenty-eight, cleared her throat, nudging him gently. 'Oh, sorry! How rude of me, Maya, meet Holly. Holly is my . . . friend. She's coming to New York with me, to . . . help out with things.' He looked flustered and kept stumbling over his words.

'Hi,' Holly said. 'Nice to meet you.'

'And you,' Maya said, nodding her head in what she hoped was a friendly manner, though inside her stomach was somersaulting. Holly was really pretty, in a girl-next-door kind of way. She had shoulder-length auburn hair that sat with a slight wave to it and contrasted against her grey eyes that seemed to be flecked with the same auburn that streaked her hair. She had a kind smile and pale skin that made her appear delicate, but approachable. They made a great couple, Maya noted with a hint of disappointment. 'Well, I'd best get back to it, that drinks trolley isn't going to push itself,' she joked, pointing to the back of the plane. 'Catch you later.'

'Sure, catch you later,' Theo repeated, looking between her and Holly.

As Maya walked back to the galley, she passed Chloe, who was leant over talking to a small child in the middle seat of row twelve and whispered in her ear.

'He's not alone.'

Chloe looked up mid-sentence, eyebrows raised questioningly, but her attention was soon diverted as the little boy decided at that point to vomit all over his dungarees and the back of the seat in front of him. Maya kept on walking, her good mood from earlier disappearing quicker than the boy's spaghetti hoops from his stomach.

'Another drink?' Maya asked Aunt Sophia, who was sitting in row one, looking totally relaxed in her long flowing maxi dress, with a large, patterned headscarf wrapped around her pretty curls and an almost empty glass of champagne in her hand. A book was open on her lap, but she didn't appear to be reading it. Her eyes were closed, and she was leant back in her seat. She opened one eye at Maya.

'Why not,' she said, leaning forward and holding out her glass for a refill. Maya filled it dutifully and handed her a tube of Pringles.

'Anything else I can get you, madam?' Maya asked, mock professionally.

'You can stop calling me madam, for one,' Aunt Sophia replied, sitting back in her chair and resuming her original position, eyes closed. Maya couldn't help but smile. She realised that of all the trips to accompany her on, she was ever so grateful that Aunt Sophia had chosen this one. Tomorrow she was going to be completing her fifth challenge of the year so far and she was so delighted to be completing it in great company; with her best friend and her crazy, but lovable aunt.

Chapter Thirty-One

'I think we've outdone ourselves, ladies,' Aunt Sophia said as they made their way up the steps off the 49th Street subway station and into the bright, glorious sunshine of Fifth Avenue. Aunt Sophia was wearing one of her usual flowy dresses that skimmed the subway steps like some sort of bohemian, multi-coloured wedding gown, but for once the eye wasn't drawn to her eclectic fashion sense. On her head was a huge papier mâché bonnet shaped as a miniature version of Tower Bridge, with its trademark powder-blue steelwork and working bridge mechanism, which, if Aunt Sophia pulled a small cord at the back of the bonnet, would open and close. There was even a papier mâché pillar-box-red London bus patiently waiting to cross the bridge. It was spectacular and was so large that it had been created over the top of a motorbike helmet and was fastened securely under her chin with a black leather strap. She'd even had to pay extra to store it in a protective box in the hold of the plane.

Maya had gone more low-key, with a simple, much smaller bonnet resembling a summer garden and was adorned with beautiful faux flowers of yellows, purples, and pale pinks, all glued on with Aunt Sophia's glue gun. There were even the tiniest yellow butterflies nestled in the flower petals and a white picket fence standing upright around the perimeter of the rim. To hold the bonnet in place was a stunning purple and gold fabric that wrapped around the bonnet and tied neatly as a bow under her chin. It was elegant and understated and Maya loved it.

Chloe, being Chloe, had completely forgotten about her bonnet that she was meant to make before the trip, so had popped out this morning after breakfast at the hotel and come back with all manner of items in plastic bags and disappeared to her hotel room. When she reappeared, they all dissolved into a fit of giggles, but she insisted she was proud of her creation, and it was both practical and efficient as they could eat it when they got hungry.

So, as they walked into the busyness of Fifth Avenue, surrounded by swarms of people and yellow taxis, they were a sight to behold. One older, striking woman with thick curly hair and a bonnet that caused onlookers to stop and stare; a younger, curvy woman looking pretty in a pale pink dress with a bonnet to match; and an attractive, slim woman, dressed in tight black skinny jeans, an off-the-shoulder sparkly T-shirt and a New York Yankees yellow baseball cap which had an overabundance of American candy bars, still in their wrappers, all taped onto it, pointing out at jaunty angles.

'Great bonnet,' someone called out as they walked towards the start of the parade, arms linked together.

'Thanks!' they all trilled back, stopping to look at one another before saying simultaneously, 'He was talking about *my* bonnet!'

The atmosphere in midtown Manhattan was electric. The sun was shining, and it seemed that the entire population of New York had turned out for the parade. They had missed the 10am start time, but it didn't seem to matter one bit. People joined and left the parade at any point along the half-mile route and the speed was slow but extremely welcoming for all the participants. And Maya noticed that the Americans went all out with their costumes and Easter bonnets. She seemed to have been transported right into the middle of a cartoon, with characters and creatures walking around her like on a movie set. There were huge bonnets, with giant sunflowers being supported by careful scaffolding on people's heads, there were feathers and flowers and colourful eggs adorning every hat and head surrounding her. There were giant human Easter eggs walking around, with only feet and arms visible. There were fluffy human rabbits hopping around with baskets of chocolate eggs for all the children and there was always cheerful music blaring from somewhere.

'Isn't this fabulous?' yelled Chloe as she grabbed a Twinkie from the top of her head, ripped into the packaging and took a huge bite.

'Brilliant!' Aunt Sophia posed for her umpteenth selfie with another member of the crowd, her bonnet proving a huge success.

'Shall we stop and get a coffee somewhere?' Maya asked, as they made their way slowly down Fifth Avenue, admiring the crowds of revellers and perusing the beautiful window-displays in the shop windows.

'Sure, why not?' Chloe said, winking at a handsome man as he walked past her, his own head devoid of any bonnet.

'Let's find somewhere that sells brunch, I'm starving,' Aunt Sophia said, shaking her head at Chloe's offer of a bite of her Twinkie. 'Somewhere that offers something a bit more substantial than a candy bar.'

They continued forward until they reached the corner of 51st and 52nd Street and found themselves within a huge crowd of people. Looking upwards, they could see why. They were standing outside St Patrick's Cathedral, a stunning white stone, Gothic structure with two huge doors that were swung open to welcome in visitors. The stone steps leading up to the doors were barely visible through the throng of people gathering to pay their respects at Easter. The service had started, and Maya could hear the beautiful sound of the choir singing, even from the kerbside. Maya found her eyes drawn to the huge, intricate spires pointing up towards the bright blue sky, as if directing its viewer straight to heaven itself. To the side of the cathedral was a large white van with a camera crew filming its presenter, an attractive red-headed female who looked quite out of place in her plain two-piece blue suit and lack of bonnet. She had a bright light pointing in her direction and she was smiling away, her practised eye pointing straight into the camera lens.

'Oh, we have to get into that shot,' Chloe said, dragging Maya by the arm towards the direction of the truck.

'No, no, we don't,' Maya said emphatically. She did not want to be on camera, even if it was for a news channel broadcasting thousands of miles away from home where no one she knew would see it.

'Come on! It'll be fun. Sophia, don't you want to show-case that fantastic creation of yours?' Chloe knew that Aunt Sophia would revel in displaying her design to such a large audience and she was right. Aunt Sophia's face lit up and she marched towards the camera with a renewed enthusiasm and vigour. Maya followed begrudgingly behind them both. As they approached one of the presenters, there was a large crowd gathering, all eager to get their moment of fame and they could hear the presenter talking aloud to the camera.

'So, as you can see, I am here at St Patrick's Cathedral today to capture the amazing efforts of our fellow New Yorkers this Easter Sunday. This age-old tradition has been running for over a century now and the parade highlights the passion, the talents, and the good old-fashioned sense of unity that this city offers. From the conventional to the bonkers, the outfits and bonnets on display today truly are a marvel to see. Let's speak to some of the general public and see what they have to say about the Easter Sunday Parade.' The male presenter turned to the crowd, searching for an appropriate candidate to talk to. Aunt Sophia surreptitiously pulled on the cord to the side of her head and the bridge on her head began opening and closing. The movement caught the presenter's eye.

'Oh, will you look at that one! Please step forward, madam, and let us have a look at your creation there.' The presenter ushered Aunt Sophia forward and the crowd parted, allowing Sophia, Chloe and an unwilling Maya, who was being dragged by the arm, to walk towards the camera and bright lights.

'Hi.' Aunt Sophia beamed at the presenter.

'Nice to meet you,' the presenter said, his American accent accentuated against Aunt Sophia's strong British accent. 'Please tell us a little about your bonnet. Did you make it yourself?'

'I did, actually. Took me three days to construct and paint, but I think it was worth it.' She pulled on the cord again and a collective gasp went up around the crowd.

'Fantastic!' the presenter said. 'And do I detect a British accent there?'

'That's right. We've flown from London to come and be a part of this fantastic parade.'

'Well, with that bonnet, you sure did bring a part of London to New York. It's fantastic!'

'Thank you.'

Maya wondered how much the presenter enjoyed using the word *fantastic*. He sure was using it a lot.

'And who are you here with today?' he asked, his eyes drifting over towards Maya.

'I'm here with my niece, Maya, and her best friend, Chloe.' Aunt Sophia gestured towards them both, Chloe coming forward immediately to get her moment in the limelight and Maya standing behind her in the shadows.

'Oh, and will you look at this, er . . . this creative bonnet!' the presenter said, pointing to Chloe's baseball cap. 'How unique.' He laughed.

'It's a nod to the New York Yankees and all things American,' Chloe said proudly. 'You want one?'

'No, no, thank you,' he laughed, smiling at the camera. 'Well, isn't it just fantastic?' His eyes moved towards Maya, 'And yours? So artistic.' He gestured towards Maya. 'Come forward a bit so the camera can get a good shot!'

The cameraman moved forward a little and Maya reluctantly took a step forward, keeping her head down.

'What a stunning bonnet,' he said. 'Just like a quintessential English garden. Did you make this yourself?'

'Yes,' Maya muttered, smiling uncomfortably.

'And is it based on your garden back home?'

'I guess,' Maya answered, thinking of Aunt Sophia's huge farmland and open space.

'And are you staying in New York for long?'

'Until tomorrow,' she answered. The presenter, sensing her discomfort and clear reluctance to engage with him, turned the camera back to Chloe.

'Is this your first time in the city?'

'Oh no, we fly here a lot, we're both cabin crew for Oasis Airlines,' Chloe said, flicking her hair from side to side coquettishly. Maya paled, realising that naming their airline with her blog being so public could jeopardise her anonymity. She pulled down her bonnet even lower over her face and looked at her shoes.

'Oh, fantastic! And what's your favourite thing to do while in New York?' The presenter was still smiling back and forth between the camera and Chloe, his grin looking like a Cheshire cat who lapped up the most exquisite of cream.

'Oh, eat!'

They all laughed at this, and the presenter took that as his cue to move onto someone else. He turned away from Chloe to the family standing to the left of him.

'Well, it seems that our Easter Parade is drawing the crowds not just from our own borders, but from far and wide! And what about you, little lady? Tell me about your fabulous creation?'

And just like that, the cameraman moved away from Chloe, Maya and Aunt Sophia and the crowd shifted slightly, trying to remain in shot. Maya slid backwards through the throng of people and out of the crowd, back into the shade of the cathedral, hidden away from view just as she liked it.

Chapter Thirty-Two

Later that afternoon, the three of them were sitting on a blanket in Bryant Park, with a bottle of wine, three plastic tumblers, and sushi bought from a little deli around the corner, just as the sun was lowering behind the Empire State Building.

'I hate to say it, but I think I might have had my fill of chocolate today,' Chloe said, lying down on her back, clutching her tummy and groaning. Maya and Aunt Sophia just laughed. Chloe had not only eaten the contents of her Easter bonnet, but she had also gorged on a giant chocolate pretzel the size of her head on the way to the park. They were surrounded by other picnickers in the large grassy area, all waiting for the music to begin. The temperature was just beginning to drop, and the lights surrounding the huge stage at one corner of the park were starting to come on. Maya helped herself to another piece of sushi and rose to sit on her knees on the blanket to watch as a band walked onto the stage and began setting up.

'As days go, this one was a good one,' she said, taking a sip of her drink and inhaling the sweet smell of cut grass, flowers, and the heady fruitiness of her wine. She looked over at Aunt Sophia, who was lying flat on her back, her eyes closed, the amber glow from the setting sun lighting her hair. She looked so much like her mother in that pose.

'I've definitely had worse,' Aunt Sophia said, letting out a contented sigh. The music began, and the cool sound of jazz filled the park.

'So, Sophia. What's your deal? How can someone so hot and so effortlessly cool still be single and living remotely on a farm?' Chloe said, turning her head to one side to look over at Aunt Sophia. The abruptness of the question was not out of the ordinary for Chloe, but it still made Aunt Sophia laugh.

'Say what you think, hey, Chloe?' Aunt Sophia said, sitting up on her elbows and looking over towards the band. 'While I take the compliment, thank you very much, I often ask myself the same question. But then I remind myself that being alone is pretty awesome. Men, and women, just complicate things.'

'Yeah, I guess. But don't you get lonely?' Chloe continued.

'Being alone and being lonely are two very different things,' Aunt Sophia said, appearing to pick her words carefully, 'I experienced not being alone and that didn't work out, so I decided that I am best as I am.'

'You did?' Maya asked, her interest piqued. 'My dad told me that you have always been alone, that you preferred your own company.'

'Did he now?' Aunt Sophia said, a little gruffly. 'Well, that's not always been the case.' She lay back down and closed her eyes, indicating they were done talking. Maya's mind carried on though, trying to piece together the fragmented childhood memories in her mind.

'So, was it a guy or a girl that broke your heart then?' Chloe continued, sniffing a potential drama faster than a drug-trained sniffer-dog. Aunt Sophia didn't answer for a second, and the air between them suddenly seemed a little tense. Then she sighed, and spoke, her tone soft and sad, 'It was a guy. His name was Bertie. And he was four years older than me.' Her eyes were still closed, and Maya could imagine she was picturing him in her head.

'Bertie . . .' Chloe said. 'Was it love?'

'It certainly was,' Aunt Sophia answered, a sweet smile appearing on her face, making her seem younger. 'He was my everything. I thought I had struck gold with him, and nothing else seemed important. We existed as one,' she said, tailing off.

'And?' Maya asked, her interested now piqued.

'And that was my problem. Existing as one; no concerns, no worries, no life experience or knowledge of sex. We just lived in the moment.' She chuckled. 'We couldn't keep our hands off one another, and we were always sneaking around, finding clandestine places to meet. I craved his touch.' She pressed a hand against her chest, her eyes closed, a smile on her face. 'He would send me crazy simply by holding my hand. And when he held me . . .' She tailed off, taking a deep breath in. 'My body would pulse like a bumble bee, craving more.' Her eyes were closed, but Maya's mind wandered off to the memory of her and Theo hugging in the bakery. To how it made her feel. Her cheeks flushed warm.

'We would sneak off whenever we had the chance,' Aunt Sophia continued, 'if we weren't making love, we were talking. We loved to talk about our future. I was so happy I could have burst.' She hugged her arms around herself. 'It was perfect. He was perfect. My life was perfect,' she said, her smile disappearing. 'And then it wasn't.'

'What happened?' Chloe asked, her attention fully on Aunt Sophia. Someone tossed a red ball onto their blanket, but none of them noticed.

'Then he died,' Aunt Sophia said sadly. 'Undiagnosed heart condition, they said afterwards. No signs, no warning – just one minute he was helping his dad with some DIY, the next minute he was dead.'

Maya's chest ached for Aunt Sophia, and she wiped away a tear that she didn't know she had shed. Chloe reached out and took Aunt Sophia's hand.

'I didn't find out immediately, either. His parents didn't know about me, we'd kept our relationship a secret from everyone. Instead, I found out in the chemist of all places. I was there purchasing some antacids for a troublesome stomach ache that I'd had for weeks, when the chemist was discussing Bertie's death with a customer. I had no idea they were discussing Bertie until the customer mentioned his name in passing, as he used to mow her lawn,' Aunt Sophia said, her eyes glazing over as she walked through the memory. 'I remember grabbing this female customer roughly by the shoulder and yanking her around, demanding more, insisting it was a mistake. The chemist had to come from behind the counter and almost restrain me,' she said, a sad chuckle escaping her lips. 'It was only when he confirmed it, that I allowed it to sink in. I fainted there and then, on the chemist shop floor. With the antacids still in my hand.' She sighed deeply.

'I stayed in bed for two weeks after that day. Wouldn't and couldn't move. My parents obviously guessed that Bertie and I had been in some sort of romantic relationship, and word soon got around. Bertie's parents refused to believe it. Bertie was from a posh family, you see, and their expectations of his career, marriage, children were high. I was not anywhere close to the calibre of woman that they were hoping for for their only son. I was only seventeen.' She paused, watching a toddler playing with a balloon nearby. 'I felt terrible. I struggled on from day to day, trying to motivate myself to study, to move on, but I just couldn't. Plus, my stomach aches didn't relent.' She gave them both a wry look. 'Two months later, it was impossible for my mum to ignore. Taking me to the doctors, it was soon confirmed. I was pregnant. And almost six months gone. I was carrying Bertie's child inside me and for the first time since his death, I felt hope. But that soon disappeared once it was decided for me that adoption was the best outcome for all involved.'

Maya and Chloe looked at one another, shocked.

'Aunt Sophia,' she began, not knowing what to say, 'I'm so sorry.'

'What a terribly sad story,' Chloe said, getting up and coming to sit beside Aunt Sophia.

'Yes, well, it's all in the past. One must move on,' she said, sitting up and shaking her hair out behind her as if to shake away the memories.

'Did you ever have it out with his parents? Let them know that they had a grandchild on the way. Did they not acknowledge the baby?' Maya asked her, but Aunt Sophia nodded sadly.

'They were grieving their only child. And they refused to believe me or refused to accept me; either one ended up with the same result – they wanted nothing to do with me or the baby.'

'So, this baby was just given away? Without your consent?' Maya said, feeling enraged on Aunt Chloe's behalf. But she shook her head before answering.

'I gave the baby away for adoption as soon as she was born. I couldn't be a single mum at seventeen, with no prospects, no money. I felt tortured. But I knew that there were others who were more deserving of a baby, who would look after her, would love her as their own. I did it for her sake, not mine.'

The band finished their set, and the park went quiet, apart from the humdrum of people enjoying themselves. But for the three of them, there was no laughter or chatter, just shock.

'That must have taken such strength.' Maya said softly, thinking of the pain this must have caused. She placed her hand on top of Aunt Sophia's. She nodded a yes, tears now rolling down her pretty cheeks. 'Do you know who the adoptive parents were? Did they keep in contact?' She needed to know; her mind was full of questions. Aunt Sophia nodded.

'So where is she now?' Chloe asked, placing a hand on Aunt Sophia's other hand on the blanket. Aunt Sophia closed her eyes a moment, her tears dropping silently onto the blanket beneath her. When she opened them again, her sorrow was so deep that Maya felt her own chest constrict, her own eyes fill with tears. Aunt Sophia looked away from Maya to Chloe and answered.

'She's right in front of me.'

A new band started playing, their base notes reverberating around the park and people began to stand, to dance, oblivious to the emotional hurricane that was unfolding within inches of them. The three of them stayed seated on the blanket, their bodies frozen to the spot. All around them was revelry, but in that little spot in the park, two lives had just changed forever.

'I don't understand,' Maya said, her voice croaky and weak. Aunt Sophia continued crying, her tears flowing freely now, and she took Maya's hand and squeezed it tightly.

'Maya, don't hate me. Please don't hate me. I did it for love. I did it all for love. If you let me explain . . .' She waited for Maya to respond, but Maya simply stared at her aunt, struggling to comprehend.

'Maya, take a deep breath,' Chloe said, rubbing Maya's shoulder, her own face white with shock. She took a deep breath in herself, taking her own advice. Maya tried to but felt dizzy. She felt like she was on a moving ship, the ground beneath her unsteady. Chloe looked at Aunt Sophia, urging her to go on.

'Maya, I loved you the minute I knew I was pregnant, but I also knew I couldn't keep you. As fate would happen, my sister, your mum, had recently married and despite a year of trying, they appeared to be having trouble conceiving their own child. A discussion was had, and it was agreed that you should be given to them. Levi had a good job and Tess had always been the kindest, softest woman I know. I had no qualms that they would be perfect parents. And they were.' Aunt Sophia was trying to explain but without revealing the truth too harshly. Chloe's eyes widened, suggesting she had worked it out.

'But my parents,' Maya said. 'My parents, they loved me. They said I came from love—'

'Which you did.' Aunt Sophia added, her hand squeezing Maya's again.

'My mum, my mum was your sister . . .' Maya said, the dots finally forming a clear line. 'If she was your sister, and I came from you, then . . .' Maya's eyes looked up into eyes that were so like her own. They moved across to the unruly hair, the small waist, the memory of that scar on Aunt Sophia's lower abdomen.

Maya's whole world began to spin, with Chloe's voice fading away, as if she was moving away from her, from the park, from the city. She was on her own. The only sound was the whooshing of her heartbeat. And then the world went black.

Chapter Thirty-Three

'Maya? Maya!'

She could hear a voice, but it seemed far away, like in a dream. But slowly, it grew louder and clearer and she could feel someone shaking her shoulder gently.

'Maya, darling. Wake up.' The voice sounded familiar, but also concerned. Who was it? And why wouldn't they leave her be? Another female voice was heard, a much younger voice and she recognised that voice too. Come to think of it, there was music too, loud music. And the buzzing of a bee around her ear. It was so close to her that she could almost make out the sound of its wings opening and closing. On instinct, she waved it away gently.

'She moved her arm! She moved her arm!' the voice exclaimed, and Maya was sure she recognised the voice. She tried opening her eyes a little, and was greeted by the close-up, concerned faces of both Aunt Sophia and Chloe. She tried to sit up but they both insisted she stay put.

'Just rest. Wait until you're ready,' Aunt Sophia said, as Chloe's face moved out of focus and Maya could hear her talking to more unfamiliar voices.

'Shall we call 911? Or see if we can flag down a paramedic?' American accents were clear, and Maya instantly recalled where she was. Bryant Park. Picnic blanket. Ground. She moved her fingers slightly and could feel the soft, cool grass underneath her. Had she fainted? Why? Then it all came flooding back to her. Aunt Sophia, her parents, the adoption. Her birth mother. She opened her eyes fully at this point and pulled herself into a seated position with some effort, wanting the small crowd who had gathered to dissipate. She smiled weakly at them, before speaking, her voice hoarse.

'I'm OK. Thank you. No need for alarm. Just a little too much wine,' she said, forcing a weak smile on her face.

'Are you sure?' Chloe asked her, reappearing at her side. Maya nodded and whispered, 'Please get rid of everyone.' Chloe nodded and waved them all away, stating wine as the cause of the collapse. The crowd bought it and made their way back to their festivities.

'Maya, darling, what can I do?' Maya looked over to see Aunt Sophia's ashen face, her eyes full of concern. 'Do you want to go back to the hotel?'

Did she? So many questions were running through her mind that the thought of physical exertion of any kind exhausted her. She shook her head no. Chloe found some water and offered it to Maya, who sipped it slowly. It seemed to help, and her strength began to return. 'I'm so sorry,' Aunt Sophia said. 'So, so sorry. I never intended to tell you today, it just kind of happened.'

'Were you ever going to tell me?' Maya asked. Aunt Sophia looked conflicted, her mouth opening and closing in hesitation. 'I wanted to, believe me. But your mum and dad asked that, on agreement of the adoption, I be known as your aunt. Nothing more. Your mum really wanted a baby, and here you were, waiting to be loved. I agreed, because they promised I could remain in your life and see you as often as I wanted to. Knowing you were there to hug, to see, to kiss, made the adoption just that little bit easier. I accepted my role.' She took a deep breath in and continued, 'But when your mum died, I begged your dad to let me tell you the truth. I saw how broken you were after her death, and I thought that if you knew that your biological mother was still alive, it would help you heal. But Levi refused. He said that it was disrespectful to your mum's memory. She was your mother and should remain that way. Truth be told, I lost my temper, and we had a huge fight. He'd lost his beloved wife, me my sister, and the grief had overwhelmed us both. Words were exchanged, terrible words, and he walked out of my life seemingly forever. With you. My heart broke that day, Maya. More than you'll ever know. I retreated into myself, my farm, my animals, and from that day onwards, I lived a half-life, simply watching you from the outside, wishing I could talk to you again, or just hold your hand.' At this point, she reached out and stroked Maya's hand. Maya didn't stop her.

'So, imagine my delight when you and your dad turned up on my doorstep last new year, asking if you could stay with me. It was like a dream come true. You had come back into my life, and I hope you'll never leave it. For that, I will be forever grateful to your dad. However much he hates me. None of this was his fault, Maya. He is a good man.'

Maya looked at her face, the pain visible, the eyes fearful. She really did look so much like her. Maya didn't know what to think. Her mind was full, yet blank, and she suddenly felt immensely tired. She yearned for something, not knowing what it was, but instinctively she leant over to Aunt Sophia and allowed herself to be enveloped in a deep, tight hug. It was exactly what she needed, and she physically relaxed into Aunt Sophia's body. She breathed in her scent, listened to her heartbeat. She felt warm. She felt safe. She felt like she had come home.

Chapter Thirty-Four

The following day, Chloe discreetly disappeared for the day, and Maya and Aunt Sophia walked for hours around Manhattan, talking. They had decided that Maya would keep calling her Aunt Sophia out of respect for Maya's deceased mum, and for continuity. So much was new, that it was a relief to still revert to names they were used to. They walked for miles, their steps going unnoticed as Maya asked questions, and Aunt Sophia answered them as best she could.

They had also called her dad together. He had cried. Which made them all cry. But somehow it had brought them all closer – despite the three-and-a-half-thousand-mile divide. They had talked, openly and honestly and been frank with each other. Yet no one argued, and apologies were made. The air between them was now clearer than the air at thirty-five thousand feet. The one area Maya didn't ask about was her biological father, she could sense that that was still too raw for Aunt Sophia. But she did ask, 'Did my paternal grandparents ever reach out after I was born?'

Aunt Sophia took her time to answer, 'They did. Once. But they preferred to stay uninvolved.' It was a diplomatic answer, yet it still stung. She had been rejected without ever being seen. But perhaps that was for the best, she thought. She decided to close that chapter and not explore it any further. She didn't need to. She had the most amazing dad waiting for her back home, who loved her with every part of his soul. Knowing he had taken her in despite not being his only made her love him more. He truly was a wonderful man.

As the sun rose high into the sky, they found themselves heading into Central Park via Fifth Avenue from East 97th

Street. Immediately the chaotic hubbub of the city dulled to a muffled hum as they walked further into the park, the trees lapping up the sunshine and warmth by raising their branches skywards, their leaves a plethora of green.

'Do you ever think you'll leave the farm?' Maya asked, watching a family as they played ball with a toddler, a baby just visible in a pram beside them.

'It's not something I've ever considered, to be honest,' Aunt Sophia said, as they crossed over East Drive and made their way towards the Bridle Trail. 'I've always wanted to ensure I was near you. Just in case you ever needed me. And so that, rather selfishly, I could keep an eye on you.' Maya looked over at her, and a huge rush of love washed over her, imagining how difficult it must have been to be so close and yet not be able to truly be herself. 'Plus, I couldn't stand Michael. That git was never good for you,' she said with a scowl.

'Why didn't you tell me that, then? We could have saved a whole heap of trouble, and not to mention a whole heap of money on a cancelled wedding!'

'Would you have listened?' Aunt Sophia asked. 'Really listened? And could I risk angering you to a point where you might not want to see me anymore?' She stopped and grabbed Maya's shoulder gently. 'No, I couldn't. It was too big a risk to take. But I was always there, on the sidelines, waiting.'

Maya looked into her eyes, which were so like her own, and realised that no, she wouldn't have listened. Her blinkers were well and truly secured in place with Michael.

'What made you go out with him in the first place?' Aunt Sophia asked. 'By the time I met him for the first time, you two were well established, and the topic never came up.' They continued walking along the Bridle Trail, with the Rhododendron Mile on full display, a range of pink flowers proudly stretching forward like badges of honour for all to see. Maya looked ahead at a sea of garden pink that made her feel like she was Alice walking through her own Wonderland.

She reached out to touch the large petals gently, feeling their coolness in the warmth of the day.

'It was serendipity, really. Or so I thought,' she said, as they continued their slow walk. 'He was going for an interview, his first for a radio station as the local weatherman. I, on the other hand, was on my way home from having just arrived back on a long-haul flight from, I don't remember where now, and we were both heading down the steps to the underground. I remember noticing him, as he was frantically searching through this light-brown satchel with initials stitched into it, and I remember thinking how adorable the satchel was. He reached the bottom of the steps and frantically stopped, upturned his satchel, and watched as all the contents spilled onto the dirty station floor. By stopping so instantly, I barely had time to register it, and ended up smacking straight into the back of him, sending him flying, with him landing face down onto a floor that I can only describe as *undesirable*.' Maya made a face, twisting her mouth in disgust.

'I helped him up, apologising profusely and began picking up the contents from his satchel. I noticed a notebook, a large brown envelope, a pen, a couple of books on weather instruments, a scarf, and oddly, I thought at the time, a miniature anemometer.

'"Shit," he said loudly, and I remember it plainly, as a young boy, probably aged around seven, started repeating him, saying the word over and over, with his mum berating him. I felt so guilty. Michael looked so stressed.

'"I've lost it," he said, scavenging in the satchel to every corner over and over. He was red-faced, and his hair was flopping sweetly over his eyes.

'What have you lost?' I asked him, scanning the floor beneath people's legs, hoping to spot something lying around.

'My wallet. My black wallet. I've lost it. I can't believe this,' he said, checking his wristwatch for the time, and wincing. 'I'm going to miss my interview slot. I can't believe this,' he repeated, checking his bag again fruitlessly. I felt terrible. I had to help him. Plus, I couldn't ignore the fact that he was ridiculously cute, even more so in this flustered state. So, I said to him, 'Here, let me get you a one-day travel card. Just so you can get on your way. It's the least I can do for bulldozing you over.' My eyes noticed the dirt-stained cuff on one of the sleeves of his shirt where he had fallen, and that his plain, yellow tie now had a diagonal stripe that was the colour of dishwater grey.

'No, no. You can't do that. You don't know me. I wouldn't know how to pay you back,' he said, appearing to notice me for the first time since our encounter. He looked me up and down, and I remember feeling flushed all of a sudden. He then smiled, and instantly, I fancied him.

'Please,' I said, placing a hand on his arm. 'Let me do this for you. Call it paying it forward. We might meet again, and you can repay the favour.' I saw his expression change, and he nodded, taking another look at the time.

'Actually, that would be so great, thank you. I can't tell you how important this interview is.' He followed me to the nearest booth, and I bought him a one-day pass. He pulled out the brown envelope from his satchel as I paid and slid out two A5 single white sheets from inside. I remember thinking they looked glossy, like photopaper and wondered if he was a photographer. He then proceeded to write his name and number down on one blank sheet and nodded at me to do the same on the other. I remember feeling so nervous as we exchanged numbers and then, with a smile and an awkward handshake, he was off to catch his train, and me mine. It was only as I sat down on the train and turned the glossy white sheet over that I noticed I was correct and it was a photograph. Of himself. A headshot clearly taken professionally. And he'd pulled two out of the envelope, so I imagined that the envelope was full of them. How endearing, I thought at the time, and intriguing. Maybe an actor? Or a model? Instead of seeing him for what he truly was – an egotistical poser with a weird obsession with weathervanes – I thought he was exciting. And if I'm honest, I thought it flattering that he would even take notice of someone like me.' Maya shrugged sadly.

'I didn't actually think I would hear from him again, but, three days later, he rang me and asked if he could buy me a celebratory drink. He told me that he had managed to secure that job position and owed it all to me. How could I say no to that?!

'We met the following week in the city, and it was an instant connection. Three months later, he asked me to move in with him, and the rest, is history.'

Maya stopped to look over at Aunt Sophia.

'Well, it all sounds relatively sweet,' Aunt Sophia said, choosing her words, 'but when did he start behaving like a total prat?'

Maya laughed at her bluntness. 'I guess about a year later, I noticed a change. We had become used to staying in most nights when I wasn't flying, and I never really noticed the questions, it was very subtle. "Who are you seeing tonight? Why do you need to see them? Stay in with me, I'll be lonely without you." He was already complaining about the amount of time I spent away from him while working, so I guess I just started to become a bit of a recluse when at home. He didn't want me out of the house, and, if I'm honest, it was all a bit flattering. He wanted me to himself, he must love me so much, right? Until he started going out. On the nights I was away, he was, what he called it, "networking".' Maya air-quoted with her hands. 'He was out socialising in the city, drinking, partying, and then when I was at home and asked to go out, he would be too tired, too hungover, too skint to take me out. But I still thought to myself, I was loved. He was serious enough about me to let me move in and share the house and the bills.' She rolled her eyes at her own stupidity. 'Little did I know that I was simultaneously helping to pay off his mortgage, and free up his money so that he could socialise every week. Then he got promoted.'

She looked across at Aunt Sophia who was looking ahead, not at Maya, her face free of expression.

'Once he got promoted and into television, that's when it all changed. His confidence grew, and mine disappeared. I spent my time trying to please him, keeping the house clean and tidy, making sure his washing was done, while he spent his time working out how to get the next promotion, the next social media exposure, the next rung of the entertainment ladder.

'Looking back now, I think he only proposed so that he could travel to New York and get the exposure he so desperately wanted in America. Did you know that he was going to incorporate a weather report into his speech, and have the television station share it? Our wedding was basically a live-action advertisement for him. No wonder he was so desperate to get hitched in New York,' she said, feeling angry at him, and at herself for being so unaware.

'Oh, the irony,' she said, realising that they had walked far past the Jacqueline Kennedy Onassis Reservoir. They had inadvertently walked themselves to Belvedere Castle. 'My wedding location.'

They both stopped and stared at the Vista Rock on which the folly sat proud; its own image reflected in the clear waters of Turtle Pond. Its turret pointed skywards, and she found herself following the white trail of a passing aircraft as it made its way over New York. The idea of her marrying there seems unnatural now, almost surreal. Especially to Michael. Her love goggles had been removed and she could see him for what he always was, an opportunist with an agenda that only suited himself. She was a by-product on his pathway to success, nothing more. As she looked across at the pavilion, where she was set to marry, she no longer felt sad for an occasion missed; she felt grateful for her escape.

Chapter Thirty-Five

Ten days later and Maya was back in New York. The flight over had been good; clear skies, no needy passengers and seat 28C was filled with a friendly old man from Italy, who walked with a stick and slept for most of the seven hours.

It had been a rollercoaster of a week. First, finding out she had a mother masquerading as an aunt, and a birth father who died almost immediately after she was conceived. These sorts of things happened to other people, she thought. People from soap operas. Not normal, slightly overweight cabin crew, with next to no social life and a penchant for sugar. However, it had also been wonderful to see her dad and aunt finally come together again. Along with Gayle. It felt like she was part of a whole again. A slightly unusual whole, but she'd take it.

It had also been the first time she had worked again with Andreas and she couldn't help but recollect his words in the taxi last time they were in New York together. Was she happy? Had she convinced herself so wholeheartedly that it was better to be single than be hurt? It both annoyed and alarmed her that Andreas's words had got inside her head. She hadn't even spoken to Aunt Sophia about it as she was worried what her response might actually be. Instead, she'd spent the last nine days wandering around the farm, helping feed the animals and, if she was really honest with herself, spending far too much time talking to Matilda the goat. Maya found that Matilda was actually proving to be quite a useful ally. She kept all her secrets, ate up all her leftovers and didn't try to offer any advice. But she did, however, have an annoying habit of eating her shoes.

She knew she had a one-night stopover again, so she had decided to go it alone and plan her next challenge. This one had been easy as the idea had almost smacked her hard in the face and it involved no tall buildings, or creatures with sharp teeth. This one would be fun. This one involved sugar.

'Now for those of you who are gluten-free today, please make sure you pick the benches to the left of the kitchen, as they have all the ingredients you will need already provided.'

Maya headed over towards the left of the kitchen but was embarrassed to find that she was the only one walking over towards the workbench. As she popped on the apron, she subconsciously ran her fingers over the pale stitching on the apron, spelling out the words, The Clementine Bakery. The other five paying guests were all gathered opposite her, along the row of workbenches, chatting excitedly and tying up each other's aprons. Maya felt a little foolish for being alone. If she were still with Michael, they'd probably have been doing this together, laughing and joking about her inability to bake even a cupcake without setting fire to the kitchen. He'd always said she was the prettiest, but most awful chef. She suddenly found herself wanting to cry. She realised that she didn't want to be alone anymore. She felt an urge to run out of the bakery and not stay for the cookery class, but just as her fingers reached for her bag, a feminine voice with a deep New York accent spoke from behind.

'Hi, Maya, is it? I'm going to assist you today. My name is Shauna.'

Maya turned to see a curvaceous woman in her late fifties smiling at her. She had the most intense, startling blue eyes.

'Hi Shauna.' Her voice wobbled a little and Maya cleared her throat in an attempt to hide her near-miss of a meltdown. Shauna still smiled but Maya could feel her eyes reading her expression. She let go of Maya's hand and leant in conspiratorially.

'You're lucky. One-to-one is normally double the price for baking lessons and you've landed on your feet with me. I'm the best chef they have.'

Maya laughed and felt her shoulders relax a little.

'We're making gluten-free chocolate chip cupcakes, then,' Shauna said, pulling across a recipe sheet and placing it in front of Maya. 'If you mirror what I do, then you'll end up with the best cupcakes this side of the Hudson.' She didn't wait for Maya to respond, but simply held up the butter in her left hand and began slicing it into cubes. Maya followed suit. Then Shauna weighed out the sugar and poured it into the same bowl as the cubed butter and began combining it together with her fingers. Maya repeated the task and found the repetitive motion oddly relaxing.

'Get your hands right in there and massage that butter. It works best at room temperature,' she said, watching Maya's hands at work as she simultaneously worked her own bowl. 'So, Maya. What brings you to New York? With an accent like yours, it sounds like you've just stepped off as an extra on Downton Abbey! I assume you're not a local New Yorker?'

Maya shook her head, chuckling. 'No, I work for Oasis Airlines, and this is one of my more frequent routes. I'm on a one-night stopover, which just happened to coincide with your bakery class tonight.'

Shauna began breaking eggs into her bowl, one at a time, and Maya copied her actions.

'And how did you hear about us, then? We're not exactly based on Fifth Avenue, and last time I checked, our delivery didn't stretch as far as Europe,' she joked, handing Maya a handheld electric whisk.

'I came here a couple of weeks ago, actually. A friend – well, an acquaintance – brought me here and I saw the poster in the window as I was leaving.' She plugged in the whisk and paused, about to turn it on. 'I have set myself challenges; one a month for a whole year, to try something new and, well, I thought it was about time I learnt how to bake a cake without the fire brigade being on standby.'

Shauna laughed, a proper belly laugh that sounded wholesome and loud. The people on the workbench opposite all looked up from their mixing, with their chef rolling his eyes in Shauna's direction.

'Keep it down, Shauna,' he said, his chef whites pristine and puffs of white hair poking out from beneath his chef's hat. 'Some of us are trying to teach serious baking over here.' But Maya noted the twinkle in his eyes and the beginnings of a smile.

'And what did you think when you came a few weeks back? Did you enjoy it?'

'Loved it,' Maya said without hesitation. 'Finding a bakery as wonderful as this, and that can accommodate my dietary needs, is a rare find indeed. The food is just incredible.'

'Thank you,' Shauna said, smiling. 'I think this place is pretty fabulous too.' She indicated for Maya to start scooping spoons of flour into the mix as it whizzed around. 'I just hope the new owner thinks so too.'

'Oh, has the bakery recently been sold?' Maya asked, watching as a cloud of flour floated upwards towards her as the mix blended rapidly. Shauna leant over and turned her whisk down to a slower setting.

'Not sold, exactly. But we have a new owner who has inherited the bakery. Apparently, he's undecided about what to do with the place. He's from your part of the world actually; some architect or designer from England, supposedly. Nice guy and all that, but he hasn't a clue about the business or any interest in baking.' She turned off her whisk and signed for Maya to pour her bowl of chocolate chips into the cake batter. 'He was here a few weeks back, supposedly to try and understand a little more about the business. But I haven't a notion how a British kid, in his early thirties thinks he can run an established bakery by himself, with no experience. Thank goodness for Dave Myrrh, that's all I can say.'

Maya noticed her heart was beginning to race and her mind was piecing together Shauna's words like a game of Tetris.

'Dave Myrrh?'

'Great guy,' Shauna continued. 'He stepped in as manager when the owner got sick about a year ago and has been running the place since. Straight out of business school and thrown in the deep end, but he never complained. These kids of today sure do have some gumption.' She grabbed an ice-cream scoop from the selection of baking tools beside her and showed Maya how to scoop up the batter mix and pop it into a cupcake case. She did it with ease, while Maya's hands were trembling a little.

'Ah sweetie, it's OK. Here, let me help.' She closed her own hands over Maya's and helped her fill the cupcake cases, one by one, until half a dozen were filled. 'You try yourself now,' she said, finishing her own. They completed their tasks in companiable silence, and popped them in the oven, with Shauna setting a timer.

'Right, now you get a ten-minute, well-earned coffee break while the cupcakes work their magic,' Shauna said, pointing to a table set up through the doors into the restaurant. 'Go and join the others and I'll see you in a bit.'

She ushered Maya towards the doors and Maya found herself having to make small talk with the other participants while her mind was whizzing with unanswered questions. She surreptitiously walked away from the others and looked around the bakery. It seemed oddly quiet without the crowds of hungry customers, but it gave her a chance to take in the bakery itself. The décor was elegant and understated; with pale orange being the ultimate theme. On the walls were framed photographs of what looked like the bakery in its infancy. She stopped at one photo which had captured a moment in time, a sepia image of the *Clementine* sign being hoisted up above the shop, clearly newly built, with a group of smiling people gathered underneath. The next photograph appeared to be the New York mayor, shaking hands with an older female baker as she handed over a cupcake. A young woman holding a baby stood beside the woman, huge smiles on their faces. A third photograph showed the same woman, in her mid-fifties, with her arm around the same younger woman, who was in turn holding hands with a toddler. Next to the toddler stood a handsome man, dressed smartly in a three-piece suit. His hands were folded across his chest, and he emanated pride and strength. Each image reflected a moment in history. It was obviously a family-run business.

'Finish up your drinks please, everyone, and come on back to the kitchens,' the male chef requested from the kitchen doorway. Everyone did as they were told, and Maya headed back to Shauna.

'Can I ask you something?' Maya asked quietly, as she followed Shauna to the nearby ovens and copied her actions of removing her tray of cupcakes from the oven. She barely even registered that they had risen perfectly and were little mounds of chocolate deliciousness.

'Sure, go ahead,' Shauna said, closing the oven door and heading back to the workbench carrying her own tray.

'The name of the guy that's inherited the bakery . . . it isn't Theodore, is it?'

Shauna stopped wiping down her worktop and looked over at Maya, her brilliant blue eyes wide in shock.

'Why yes, it is! Do you know him?'

'I think so. But I don't know his surname. I met him on the flight over here a few months back and he told me how he'd inherited a business. He's the one that brought me here a few weeks back, said he knew of a great bakery that he'd recently visited.'

Shauna was shaking her head in disbelief. 'Honestly, the UK must be such a small island; you all seem to know one another!'

'It certainly seems that way . . .' Maya said, her sentence trailing off as she thought back to a few weeks ago and how Theo had managed to get them a table and told them not to worry about the bill. And how that pretty waitress seemed to be flirting with him. Maya realised now that she wasn't flirting, she just knew him and hoped to keep her job.

'Well, if you speak to him again, put in a good word for me, will you, honey? I love my job and if he decides to sell, I don't know what I'll do. I've worked here since his grandmother took me on in my teens. Baking's all I know.' Shauna looked at Maya sincerely, worry etched across her face.

'Sure, of course I will,' she reassured her. This seemed to cheer her, and her smile returned.

'So, what's he like, then? Outside of being my new boss? He sure is a looker, isn't he? Reminds me of a young Marlon Brando, but with messier hair,' she joked, nudging Maya with her elbow. Maya blushed.

'I guess. I've not really noticed.'

'You little fibber, you! Look at the flush on your face! Honey, it isn't hard to see that you like him. But then, what woman wouldn't?'

Maya was protected from having to respond by a huge crash behind them. One of the participants had dropped their glass bowl accidently and it had shattered splattering the kitchen in chocolatey, gooey icing. Shauna hurried over to help clear up the mess, leaving Maya alone and the unanswered question floating in the air along with the sweet smell of cake. Maya was relieved and spent the next ten minutes sending thankful glances to the butterfingered man nervously icing his own set of cupcakes opposite her, his apron covered in chocolate goo.

By the time Shauna had cleaned everything up and helped restore a sense of calm back to the class, she seemed to have forgotten she'd ever asked Maya anything and they'd resumed their task of decorating their cakes, piping bags in hand. Shauna was quiet, focused on piping a beautiful silhouette of a clementine on top of a cupcake. Maya found her voice, and asked, 'Theo said there had been a big dispute between his family. Was that to do with the bakery?' She knew she was being nosy, but she was trying to piece everything together from the snippets he'd given her. It must have been a pretty huge dispute for his mother and grandmother to up sticks and move across the ocean. Shauna looked a little taken aback and at first didn't answer. But then she looked around to see if anyone was nearby and began.

'Well, seeing as you already know there was a dispute, and seeing as he told you himself about the whole hoopla, I guess I can say it,' she said, lowering her piping bag and looking across at Maya. 'It was at least twenty-five years ago, I'd say' – her forehead crinkled in concentration – 'no, I need to go back to the start. The beginning of it all.

'So, my nana was best friends with the original Clementine, a Miss Clementine Carol. Miss Carol came from a wealthy family, you see, and they helped her invest in the business, at only the tender age of twenty. It was quite a thing in those days, a woman entrepreneur! But she was a natural. She was passionate, dedicated, and extremely driven. I remember she would be in the shop at 5am every day, her sleeves rolled up and her hair net on, already onto her second bake of the morning, despite hiring three renowned pastry chefs. She accepted nothing less than perfection in every single cake. She was fastidious in her work, and it showed. The food became the city's top spot, featuring in every New York paper, magazine, and gossip column. I was taken on because the bakery was busy from morning until nightfall. It took a while, but her hard work began to pay off. One of her regulars was Hank, a local accountant that visited the bakery daily. Not for the baked goods, but because he was madly in love with Clementine. They married within a year and held their reception here, with the whole neighbourhood invited. Nine months later they had a daughter, but that didn't stop her. Apparently, she was still in the kitchen preparing doughnuts on the day that her waters broke!' Shauna laughed, shaking her head. 'Barely two weeks later, she was back in the bakery, the baby strapped to her chest like the sweetest bag of sprinkles you ever did see. A total poppet.'

'Theo's mum,' Maya said, connecting the dots. Shauna nodded, and then picked up her piping bag again. As she continued with her icing artwork atop one of her cupcakes, she carried on.

'Anise was her name, but everyone called her Ani. She grew up in these kitchens, and before she was ten years old, she could whip up a meringue that would be good enough for the President himself! She had talent, just like her mother. Together, they were phenomenal.' Shauna closed her eyes, as if recalling them to mind. 'Two decades passed, the bakery went from strength to strength, and was full of laughter and joy. Until October 1994, when poor Hank died of a sudden heart attack. Gone, slumped at his desk, it was over in moments. They said he didn't suffer, but the same cannot be said for Clementine. The grief overwhelmed her. The bakery stayed closed for three weeks, which was unheard of in those days, until Ani opened it up and began to work solo. It took Clemmie a long time to step back through the bakery doors and don her apron once more. She was never quite the same though. Her spark had gone, and with it, her desire to be the best.'

Shauna sighed, as if the pain was still raw. 'Twelve months passed, and Ani found love. A wonderful man named Austin. He jumped on board with the bakery and took charge. What a relief it was for everyone! He was a hero, willing to pick up where Clemmie unfortunately was failing, and the bakery thrived again. And so did Ani. They married quickly, and before she knew it, she had her own bundle of joy strapped to her chest like a sweet bag of sugar.'

'Theo,' Maya said.

'Theo,' Shauna repeated, nodding. 'But that was when it started to go wrong.' She sighed theatrically, shaking her head as she continued her piping. 'Austin had grand ideas; you see. He wanted to expand, grow the business, open Clementine bakeries all over the country, create a brand that could then go on to sell in supermarkets, you name it, he wanted the brand to be there. To cheapen everything that Clemmie had worked so hard for. Both Ani and Clemmie were against it, they felt it was perfect as it was; a unique, family-run business with regulars that she knew the names of, loyalty discounts, a neighbourhood that they loved and who loved them. Heck, even the mayor came out one time to order a whole bunch of cupcakes for his daughter's first birthday. It caused quite a scene; I can tell you! Reporters taking pictures, a piece in the *New York Times* . . .'

Maya thought of the faded photograph from earlier. The mayor shaking hands with Clementine, the look of pure joy on all their faces. She instantly felt a jolt of loyalty to this woman who had achieved so much.

'Ani challenged him, said he was in the wrong, but he didn't agree. Then he made the ultimate act of betrayal.'

'What did he do?' Maya asked, her voice almost a whisper, her cupcakes forgotten about.

'He went to the source. The wealthy family. Convinced them of his plan, wowed them with mood boards and projection figures. Of course, the Carol family didn't get to where they were without a little investment, and they lapped up this potential for growth immediately.'

'But it was Clementine's business,' Maya interjected, feeling angry for Clementine.

'Ah,' said Shauna, 'that's where the problem lay. You see, when they gave Clementine the money to start up the business, they also took a share of the business too. Their share was 51 per cent But until that point, they had been sleeping partners, if you will, leaving her to her success and them to their old age. Everyone was happy. Until Austin came on the scene and started shaking the sands beneath everyone's feet. Clementine had siblings. Siblings who were squandering their own inheritance, and with it a lot of the Carol fortune too. And so, the parents jumped on board with Austin's plans and sold him their shares for cold, hard cash. And that's when the problems began.'

She finished her last cupcake and looked over to Maya, who had been so caught up in the story that she was still on her first one. Shauna tutted and dragged the tray over to her, so that she could continue where Maya had stopped.

'Is that why they left America? Fled to the UK?' Maya asked, watching as sprinkles were added with flourish. Shauna nodded.

'They came up with a plan.' At this, she smiled proudly. 'It was done subtly, with no hint of them doing so. You see, there was a reason the bakery was such a success, and that was down to the recipes Clemmie had tried and perfected over the years and were locked in her safe every evening without fail. Without those recipes, the bakery would be nothing more than a bog-standard coffee shop that sold sweet treats. The rift between the family was also causing a chasm between Ani and Austin. They argued non-stop, and his interest in Theo was minimal to say the least. His eyes were blinded by dollar signs. So, a few months later, with the help of me and my nana, they sneaked out of the bakery, with only a couple of suitcases and a buggy for Theo, and left on the next flight to the UK. With $25,000 in cash, and the original recipes, leaving Clementine Bakery in a total state of disarray. As you can imagine, it all blew up in the bakery when Austin read the note that Ani had left him, saying that she wanted a divorce. No one knew, other than me and my nana, where they had gone to. Austin searched and searched, even hired a private detective, but nobody imagined they would be brave enough to leave the country. Or leave her beloved business. But leave she did, and they set up a new home for the three of them in Norwich in Norfolk. And there they stayed, until Clementine's death.'

A small tear escaped her eye and dropped down onto the worktop, but she brushed it away and turned to Maya, smiling. 'I made it over there a few times to visit. They had a humble but happy life. Clementine retired to take care of Theo, and Ani worked in a local school canteen, still baking, but for littl'uns instead. She divorced Austin, requesting full parental rights for Theo, and he acquiesced immediately. He just wanted her shares in the business, nothing more.'

'And the bakery? Did it continue?' Shauna nodded.

'It did, but the pastry chefs resigned in defiant loyalty and the locals refused to visit. It was the talk of the town for months. And without the locals, the trade reduced dramatically. Plus, their products were not a patch on the original recipes, and without Clemmie or the pastry chefs, the knowledge wasn't passed on to their replacements. Yes, the bakery carried on, but it was never the same. Austin almost ran it into the ground, with us propping it up with cake dowels, so to speak, and keeping it afloat. Just.

'But when Austin died, only a few months before Clementine's own death, we were all in for a shock. Austin had left everything he owned to Theo, debts, and all. And this place!' Shauna smiled widely, finishing the icing of the last cupcake with a flourish.

'Clementine's Bakery was rightly handed back to Clementine's own grandson – and it is up to him now to ensure his grandmother's heritage. He's already made a ton of changes, but without knowing his intentions, it's hard to judge if they are for the good of the bakery or for profit. I hope it's the former.' She looked at Maya, and concern was etched on her face.

They were interrupted by the sound of scraping chairs and the gathering of personal belongings. It prompted Shauna to kick into action.

'Right, no time to finish them all, but you can take some of mine home,' she said, pulling a white cardboard box from nowhere and filling it with cupcakes. She didn't continue her tale, nor did she open up with further information. The class was finished, and Maya was ushered out with the other participants. As Maya walked towards the kitchen doors, she looked back at Shauna and smiled, with Shauna giving her a private wink.

Maya walked out into the cold night air, carrying her box of cupcakes and her heavy burden of knowledge. Poor Theo, she couldn't help thinking, her heart opening to his sad situation. And with that sympathy came something else. A fierce loyalty. Theo had got into her head already, but now it seemed he was making his way into her heart too.

Chapter Thirty-Six

Maya knew that word would get back to Theo that she had visited the bakery, so she felt drawn to message him first, which she did as soon as she got back to her hotel.

Hey Theo, I've just been for a cookery class at The Clementine Bakery and found out that you're more than just a fan of the chocolate cake there – you're the new proprietor! Congratulations. Exciting times for you!

She didn't know what else to say. She couldn't admit that she knew his whole history, and she was aware that he was fiercely private, so she kept it light and breezy. She pressed send and opened her box of freshly completed cupcakes, took one out and began munching on it. It really was one of the best things she had ever made in her entire life. She took a photo of the others still sitting perfectly in the box and sent it to Chloe with the caption – *Look what I made.*

She carried on munching, enjoying the sensation of the sugary sweetness on her lips when her phone pinged back at her. The message was from Theo.

You were at Clementine Bakery? I'm confused. Are you in NY now? Any chance we could meet for a coffee soon? I'm in the UK. Thanks, Theo.

She responded.

I am in NY until tomorrow. A coffee sounds nice, are you around this weekend? I'll be in London until Sunday evening.

Only a minute passed before his response came through.

*Absolutely, I can meet then. How about Saturday? Say, the
Natural History Museum at 10am?*

Maya paused. Would this be classed as a date? She didn't want
to break her rule, especially as she was over a third of the way
through now. But then he was with Holly now, so technically
was it OK? She felt so undecided and hurriedly resolved to
decline when another message came through.

*My friend will be joining us, I hope that's OK. He's
currently working on a PhD in historical biology and has
special access to some of the restricted areas. Might be cool.*

A friend. Theo was bringing a friend, which meant he didn't
view this as a romantic date at all and Maya could accept.

Sounds perfect. See you on Saturday at 10am.

Maya felt excited. She closed the lid of the box firmly; one
was enough for tonight. She switched on the hotel television
to see if she could find a comfort film to watch. But instead of
a cheesy sitcom or romantic movie, she found herself looking
straight into the smiling face of Amanda Avary, a large microphone in her hands. She was wearing a gown of shimmering
black that hugged every inch of her body, its tight bodice
leaving little to the imagination. Her wavy, golden hair was let
loose around her shoulders and her make-up was impeccable.
She looked amazing. She was standing on a huge stage, beside
some podium and she was lit up by a spotlight directly on her.
The sound was muted, but Maya found herself reaching for
the remote control and turned up the volume.

'Ladies and gentlemen, I am honoured to be here today to
host the prestigious Annual Television Broadcasting Awards!
In its nineteenth year now, we have seen some immense
talent pass through these doors, and I can guarantee that this
year will be groundbreaking in its ability to showcase the best
of America's broadcasters and behind the scenes teams. I am
delighted to announce that I will be co-hosting tonight's show

with none other than the extraordinary, the hugely talented . . .' She paused for dramatic effect. 'Steven St John. Please welcome him onto the stage, everyone.'

Maya watched as a huge round of applause went up around the massive auditorium and an extremely handsome man walked from stage left towards Amanda. He was wearing a tuxedo that looked custom made and his dark hair was slicked back like he had just stepped out of the shower. He was tanned, mid-thirties and wouldn't look out of place on a catwalk in Milan.

He reached Amanda and kissed her warmly on the cheek, his hand pausing just a second longer on her back before he turned to the camera and spoke to his audience. 'Thank you for that grand welcome, Amanda. I cannot tell you what a delight it is to have you travel from the United Kingdom to be with us today. I have long been a fan of your presenting work and what an honour it is to co-present these awards with you this evening.'

Amanda feigned embarrassment and continued reading from the autocue.

'Steven, you flatter me! Thank you.' She touched him gently on the arm, before turning back to the audience. 'Now let's get on with the show. First up tonight we have . . .'

Maya muted the volume at this point, but her eyes never left Amanda's. She scanned her face, her body, her gestures and compared herself to each graceful gaze, each elegant movement. In comparison, she felt like a has-been frump. No wonder Michael had left her. She reached over and opened the box of cupcakes again, grabbing the closest one to her and shoving it into her mouth. She had barely finished chewing when she was distracted by another message flashing up on her phone, this time from Chloe.

They look proper professional, Maya Moo! So proud of you x
Don't suppose any of them will make it back home, will they?

Maya gulped down the last bite of her cupcake and went straight for a third. 'Not likely,' she said aloud to the empty room, spraying crumbs all over the clean, white bedspread.

Chapter Thirty-Seven

At 9.54am on Saturday morning, Maya walked towards the Natural History Museum in glorious morning sunshine. She was feeling a lot better since her cupcake binge five days ago and she found herself cheered by her surroundings. She loved London in the spring. There was a freshness in the air, the promise of something new to come and she had a definite skip in her step as she made her way towards the museum. She had decided to dress relaxed, and had opted for jeans, a white T-shirt, and a yellow blazer of her mother's that she had found hanging in the back of her wardrobe, along with sneakers. Low-key, understated. Her curly hair was let loose around her face and her make-up was minimal; she didn't want to send the wrong message out to Theo.

As she approached the museum, she spotted him standing on the steps checking his phone. The sun was shining, and he was bathed in sunlight, as if the sun was a spotlight, only for him. He was wearing his typical attire: straight-cut jeans, trainers and a jumper, and on his head, the same battered baseball cap. She could see his dimple clearly, and there was an element of stubble there that made him look suggestively dishevelled. She immediately thought of him waking up in bed, with that stubble, adorable dimple, and not much else, and she blushed instantly. *Stop it, Maya*, she told herself. She walked past the queue of young families, tourists, and blurry-eyed students and up the steps to meet him.

'Hi,' she said, distracting him from his phone.

'Oh, hi!' He seemed genuinely pleased to see her she noted, his smile warm and inviting. He then immediately whipped his baseball cap from his head and stuffed it into the back pocket of his jeans. Maya found this ridiculously adorable. 'You're here, great. Ian is already inside sorting out access. Let's go.' She followed him inside, noting his lack of greeting; he didn't attempt to kiss her or hug her, just kept his distance but remained friendly.

They walked towards a pale man wearing a large dark rain-coat over his skinny body. He was carrying a large rucksack that was currently being searched by a security guard.

'Ian,' Theo called out and Ian turned around. He smiled at them both, but his smile seemed strained.

'Hi, nice to meet you, Maya,' he said, holding out a hand. She took it and noticed it was clammy. 'Bit of an issue here, actually. Turns out my all-access pass hasn't got the correct signature on it, so they are trying to call through to the university dean now . . .' He tailed off as another, more senior security guard began gesturing for him to follow them to a room signed *Private*. 'Oh, this is ridiculous, I've explained everything already . . .' He began to follow them but shouted back to Theo, 'You go on in. I've sorted your passes for the day. I'll come and find you both.'

The security guard motioned for them to pass him their bags, and within seconds they were in the museum's main entrance, the Hintze Hall. It was eerily empty of crowds as they'd skipped ahead of the queue and Maya took a moment to appreciate the silence. She hadn't been here for years, her last trip being with her secondary school, but the building never ceased to amaze her. She remembered being taught how the building was designed entirely of terracotta, with huge archways that led the eye upwards towards a grand glass ceiling that flooded the building with natural light. But being back there in the flesh was another thing entirely.

'I forgot how spectacular this building is,' she said, in awe, her eyes drawn towards the huge blue whale skeleton that stretched out above their heads, making them feel very small and insignificant.

'It really is,' Theo replied, walking slowly around, taking in the room and pointing at the impressive ceiling. 'It reminds me of a cathedral.'

They both stopped and stood staring upwards at the elaborate bones of the skeleton that hung above them, its skull frozen open as if catching its prey, and followed its arched spine, shaped like a wave, all the way towards its tail which pointed towards the grand staircase at the back of the hall. It was lit up in a clear bluey light, its bones emanating a blue hue. Theo noticed a wooden sign to one side and read up on the information.

'Her name is Hope,' he said quietly.

'Hope. That's nice,' Maya said, her eyes moving along the nine-hundred-inch-long mammal. 'She must have been a magnificent creature.' Maya thought about her recent encounter with the shark in America and how it had made her feel calm, at peace almost. 'I swam with sharks recently,' she said. Theo's head whipped around, surprise etched on his face.

'You did what?'

'Swam with sharks. In America. Only little ones though.'

'That's so awesome!!' he exclaimed, his voice echoing around the hall. The museum was officially open by this point and people were starting to swarm in. He got some odd glances from a few tourists trying to take photographs around them, so he walked over to Maya. 'Any other surprising things I should know about you?' he joked. 'Do you wing walk on planes? Bungee jump off skyscrapers?'

She laughed. 'Definitely not! I don't normally do anything adrenaline-focused; I'm more of a stay-at-home with a take-away kind of girl. It's just that this year has been a bit . . . different.'

'Different?'

'Different,' she repeated.

'Do you want to talk about it?' he asked, as they made their way up the grand staircase together. Maya paused. Did she?

'You sure you want to hear my whole sorry tale?' she joked. 'It's a tad depressing.'

He threw up his hands and shrugged his shoulders. 'It would be a good distraction from the mess that is my life, to be honest. Go for it.'

So, she did. She told him everything. From her relationship with Michael spanning three years, to their engagement in Cyprus, and finally, his ultimate betrayal live on air. Theo listened without interrupting, but his facial expression changed from sadness to disbelief as she continued her tale. They had walked the entirety of the blue and green zones without Maya even really noticing and found themselves in the Wildlife Garden. She decided not to mention the blog though, or her no-dating pact, only that she was challenging herself to achieve something new once a month.

'A new challenge every month? Isn't that hard to achieve?'

'For a single gal with no social life? Nope. Totally achievable,' she joked wryly. 'It's just coming up with ideas that is the trickiest part.' She looked at her watch, shocked at how quickly the time had passed while they toured the museum. 'Sorry, you should have stopped me. I tend to gabble on and on . . .' She felt embarrassed. Once she had started, she just felt the need to offload the whole sorry tale to someone who was completely impartial. She took a deep breath in and blew out noisily as they walked around the courtyard.

'Why are you apologising? What a shitty year. What a total sod!' Theo said, eyes wide with concern for her. 'You've done amazingly well, considering. I'm not sure I would be so forgiving or so . . . together.'

This time it was Maya's turn to shrug. 'I guess I had no other choice, really.'

They both fell silent, and Maya took in her surroundings. The garden was like a haven away from the busyness of the city and they were surrounded by the most beautiful colours and the air was alive with the humming of bees, butterflies, and insects. People were walking slower, taking in the peace and tranquillity of the garden. The sun was really warm now, and Theo pulled off his jumper, and so, his T-shirt lifted with it. Maya found herself staring side-on at his toned torso, at the smattering of hairs leading down towards his—

'Shall we sit?' he interrupted her thoughts, and she looked up to see he had caught her staring. There was a slight blush to his cheeks, but also a small smile playing at the corner of his lips. He pointed at a bench just ahead of them and she nodded and smiled, aware that her voice might not be as steady as she would have liked. Her brain was too busy processing (and storing) images of him as he was now, but minus the T-shirt too.

The bench was in a spot that was bathed in midday spring sunshine and as she sat down, she decided that changing the subject might be a wise idea. She asked him, 'So what about you, then? Are you going to tell me about Clementine's Bakery?'

His whole body seemed to tense up on the bench next to her and Maya noticed a vein in his neck begin to pulse. 'Oh, I don't know . . .' he began, running a hand through his thick, messy hair and sighing. 'I just don't know. I never expected any of this. Granny told me that she had washed her hands of the whole bakery after the "*big falling out*" thirty years ago.' He held up his hands to air-quote his words. 'Mum, me, and her had moved across to the UK when I was only two years old; I don't even remember New York or anyone there. Neither of them ever mentioned it. The first time I even heard about the bakery was when I uncovered a box of old photos at the bottom of my gran's wardrobe when I was playing hide and seek years ago.' He paused and Maya thought back to those sepia images hanging on the wall in the bakery. 'When I asked them both about it, they talked of having worked there when they were younger, but never that she owned it, or created it.'

An orange and blue butterfly floated down and landed on his knee, and he stopped talking to stare at it, its wings opening and closing slowly, mimicking the action of breathing. A few seconds later, it flew off to a nearby bush. Theo continued.

'Mum died when I was fifteen, and after that, it was just Granny and me. She was retired, and I was a typical teenager;

self-centred enough to not bother asking about her life before me, caught up in my own pubescent world! She seemed happy enough and we chugged along together in harmony most of the time, just the two of us. I didn't think we had any secrets between us. But then she died, and when searching through her things, I found details about this American bakery, but I just couldn't piece it all together. How had she never told me about this other life? Then, to hear the news that my own estranged father had died only weeks later and left me this unknown bakery across the other side of the world, well, it was a lot to take on. Emotionally and physically. Here I was, trying to sort through my gran's estate, which was hard enough in itself, but then being told about my father, and having to fly to New York only days after her funeral,' he paused, clearing his voice which had turned a little gravelly, 'let's just say I found those first few months difficult. A mix of grief and a general feeling of disassociation.

'Which is when I met you on Christmas day, on that flight to New York,' Maya said, piecing together all the parts of what must have been such a difficult time for him. He nodded and continued.

His will stipulated that I inherit it but left no instructions as to what to actually do with it. Should I sell it to the family? But would she have hated that? Or should I try and run it myself and uproot my whole life here? I have no business experience, nor have I ever lived anywhere other than here. Am I even capable? Do the US family hate me? If I move, will I ultimately fail and end up ruining an established, family business?' He stopped to exhale and turned towards her before saying sadly, 'You know what hurts the most? It's that she is the one person that I would have turned to in such a dilemma. It would be her safe, unbiased opinion that I want above all others. And she isn't here.'

Maya couldn't help herself. She reached out and took his hand in hers, giving it a little squeeze. 'I'm so sorry, Theo.'

He shrugged and smiled regretfully. 'These things happen. I guess it's been a bit of a shit year for both of us, eh?'

She smiled back. 'I guess.'

'What would you do if you were in my situation?' he asked her, keeping hold of her hand.

'I honestly don't know,' she said. 'I guess I would do whatever felt right.' She thought of his dad and wondered about his say in all this. 'Are the US family friendly? Is there any animosity?' She knew the answer to this but didn't want him to guess that she was privy to his personal history from Shauna.

'Those I've met so far are, yes. My grandparents died over a decade ago, but are strangers to me, I have no idea if they were good people or not' – Maya didn't say anything, despite thinking he was probably best off not knowing them – 'but I have a few cousins from my mother's side, including, as you already know, Dave. He's more like a brother to me now. And his loyalty to the business has been such a help. Not only has he proved to be a fantastic manager while things get sorted, but he's also proved to be a great friend. I'm lucky. But he refuses to help me in making a decision about the bakery.' He ran his hand through his hair and Maya wished, for a second, that she could do the same. Instead, she asked him,

'What do you want to do?' He sighed deeply and didn't answer for a moment.

'That's it, I'm just not sure. Part of me loves the idea of upping sticks to a brand-new life; experiencing a new city, new friends, no money worries; but then I'd have to leave behind everything I know and am comfortable with.'

'I thought I was comfortable with my life, and look how that turned out,' she said wryly.

'But you didn't choose to change it.'

'And nor have you,' she replied, 'but you've been given a real chance to turn something really sad into something great.'

'True.'

They fell into silence for a few minutes, both thinking.

'Do you like New York?' he asked, changing the subject.

'Yes and no,' she said, thinking about her answer. 'It's too hot for me in the summer months, but there is something magical about the city in the winter. The frosty air, the promise of snow, the festive energy and vibe. It's something special.' She was smiling. 'Ever been to Central Park?'

He shook his head. 'Not yet. I've flown over twice now, but each time I've been too busy with the bakery.'

'Well, you cannot positively make an informed decision without visiting Central Park. I insist you go.'

'OK, OK,' he said, holding up his hand in mock surrender, laughing. 'I will do. Where would you recommend I go first?'

'Well, Belvedere Castle is a must—'

'There's a castle in Central Park?' he interrupted. She nodded.

'Yep. A beautiful one. Along with a huge lake, the Bethesda Terrace, the Romeo and Juliet statue . . . all stunning.'

'Even in winter?'

'Especially in winter,' she said adamantly, nodding.

'You know, I plan to fly back to New York again soon when I have a bit of a lull with work projects. Maybe I'll check these places out.'

'Maybe you should.' His hand felt warm in hers and she was suddenly very aware of his proximity. He shifted on the bench, so he was a little closer. A spark of electricity shot through Maya, her skin prickling.

'Finally!' An exasperated voice called out from the garden path. They both turned to see Ian marching towards them, his pale face flustered and his huge backpack almost dragging along the ground. Maya instantly let go of Theo's hand and shifted along the bench.

'Ian, they've finally let you in, have they?' Theo joked, standing up to greet him.

'All so ridiculous,' he said, throwing himself down onto the bench between them with a thud. 'Apparently there are two Ian Bradshaws at the university, and they gave my all-access pass to an economics student from Wales, who is currently on a placement in Spain. It's taken hours to sort out and I've wasted half the day.'

'Really sorry to hear this, Ian,' Theo said and Maya nodded in agreement.

'Thanks. I'm heading up to the first floor of the Red Zone to meet an esteemed biologist there, want to join me?'

'Sure,' said Theo and both men stood up. Maya stayed seated. 'Actually, I think I'm going to make a move now.'

Theo looked disappointed but took it in his stride. 'Are you sure? I haven't bought you that coffee yet.'

'I'm sure, thank you. Hold that coffee for next time.' She smiled at them both and stood up. 'Lovely to meet you, Ian. I hope your day improves!'

'Thanks, you too,' Ian said, turning to walk back the way he came. Theo looked from Ian to Maya, unsure of what to do. Maya made it easy for him.

'Let me know next time you're flying, and I'll see if I'm working,' she said, smiling and walking away from them both with a little wave. She didn't look back. She knew if she did, she would find him still looking at her and she didn't like the thought one bit. Her body was pulsing with excitement and fear, and as she walked towards the exit, her left hand was still tingling from holding Theo's.

'Sort yourself out, Maya,' she said crossly out loud as she made her way back through the Hintze Hall, causing a small group of tourists to jump back and stare at her in concern.

Chapter Thirty-Eight

Before she even realised it, six months had passed of her living with Aunt Sophia. Their bond had deepened as time went on. Nothing was off-limits now, and it actually made her feel even closer to her mum, hearing how grateful she had been, and how much Maya had been loved. Even her dad had resigned himself to the fact that she wouldn't come and live with him, despite him always offering, and Maya regretted not having done it when she was younger. Aunt Sophia, along with Matilda the goat and the three cats, Cayenne, Salt and Pepper, were just a dream to live with. There was always music in the house, and the walls just breathed happiness. Equally, there was always mess everywhere and Aunt Sophia was terrible at washing and cleaning. But she was a brilliant cook and an even better sounding board.

Maya found herself going days at a time without thinking about Michael now, especially since his particular news channel had been deleted from Aunt Sophia's television. And ever since finding Theo on the plane with his new girl, Holly, she had decided to not complicate that friendship any further. It just seemed too problematic, and their lives were so different. Plus, he hadn't contacted her either, not since their non-date six weeks ago at the museum, and she didn't want to be the one chasing a man in a newly formed relationship.

Before she knew it, she found herself at the end of June, still single, still blogging, and still living with her aunt. They were currently sitting in the garden, a bottle of white wine on the table between them, their chairs pointing towards the sun that was setting over the fields, with the radio on in the background. Matilda was clopping around the courtyard of the farm, munching on thistle and Aunt Sophia's prized sunflowers sporadically, while Salt and Pepper were stretched out on the patio, enjoying the final rays of sunshine. Aunt Sophia took a deep breath in and exhaled slowly, her beautiful silver hair cascading over the back of her garden chair.

'So, Maya – what's your plan?'

'Plan?' Maya asked, taking a big gulp of her cool glass of white wine and looking quizzically at Sophia.

'Your plan, your upcoming birthday – how do you intend celebrating?'

'Celebrating? Oh, I hadn't given it much thought.'

'That's what I thought,' Aunt Sophia said, leaning forward and pouring them both another glass of wine. 'What would you like to do?'

Maya thought about it, what did she want to do? She would be twenty-nine. She was still living with a sliding-doors attitude, where she compared her current situation to what could have been. Or should have been. She felt suddenly very heavy in her soul, so took another big gulp of her wine, focusing her mind on the cooling liquid as it made its way into her stomach.

'I have absolutely no idea.'

'Again, that's what I thought. So, I have a proposal for you.'

'I don't want a party,' Maya interrupted her.

'No, I know. I'm not suggesting that at all. What I'm suggesting actually ties in with your monthly challenge of trying something new. And this is new. Well, actually it's old, but new to us.'

'I'm intrigued,' Maya said, raising an eyebrow in her direction.

'It's a ball, that takes place in an actual, real-life castle,' Aunt Sophia said, her voice and face animated. 'And it's period costume only. Like a re-enactment, but where we get to eat, drink wine till we are merry and dance with tall, dashing noblemen. What do you think?'

Images of corsets, ballgowns and horse-drawn carriages passed through her mind, and she laughed. It seemed absurd but extremely good fun.

'Is it happening on my actual birthday?' she asked.

Aunt Sophia nodded enthusiastically. 'Yep. What are the chances?'

'So, I'd be the actual belle of the ball for the night?' Maya joked.

'You would indeed, and I can be your beautiful, yet elegant escort to the ball.' Aunt Sophia made a sweeping gesture with her hand that had them both laughing.

'Sure,' Maya said, when she caught her breath again. 'On one condition.'

'And what's that?' Aunt Sophia asked, mid-sip.

'That you don't try and set me up with any gloomy Mr Darcy.'

'Agreed,' Aunt Sophia said, mock solemnly, before they both burst into another fit of giggles.

Day 184

Almost halfway through my twelve-month rule of singledom! How is it possible? I feel like I have risen above the stormy clouds at lower altitude and hit the smooth cruising altitude emotionally. The fog is lifting, and I am seeing the sun. Daily! If any of you are recently dumped, or fed up with being single, then take a leaf out of my blank dancing card. Enjoy the days, savour the sunshine, and learn to dance . . .

'Maya? It turns out there might be a slight hiccup with your birthday on Saturday . . .' Aunt Sophia began as she tightened the lacing on Maya's gold bodice.

'What kind of hiccup?' Maya asked, wanting to turn around, but Aunt Sophia had control of her waist, forcing her to face forward. She felt this was deliberate.

'Not a huge one, and definitely not one that is certain, only rumours . . .'

'Just get to the point!' Maya exclaimed.

'Right, yes.' Aunt Sophia took a deep breath in. 'Well it turns out that this ball at Arundel Castle is a bit of a hit, actually. It's getting quite a bit of attention, seeing as it is being held on midsummer's day. And well, there is going to be some media coverage there. A news channel actually . . .' She tailed off, leaving Maya to connect the dots.

Maya's heart skipped a beat, and she swung around force-fully, causing the huge skirt of her dress to swish and almost take out Matilda, perched on a chair next to her dressing table. 'Which news channel?' She looked at Aunt Sophia whose face was full of anxiety.

'Michael's news channel, NWN.'

'Yes, I know who he works for,' Maya said shortly, trying to loosen the suddenly too-restrictive corset of her dress. Heat was rising in her cheeks and her mouth felt dry.

'*They* might not be there,' Aunt Sophia said, her emphasis on the word *they* filled with meaning.

'But they also might be,' Maya said. 'I'm not going.' She sat down abruptly on the chair, just as Matilda jumped off it, her face determined. Aunt Sophia sighed.

'If you don't go, you've let them win. It's your birthday, the tickets have been paid for and the costumes have been hired—'

'I don't care.'

'You can't hide away forever on the off-chance you might bump into them—'

'I can,' Maya said, her bottom lip childishly jutting out and wobbling precariously. 'Take this costume back.'

Aunt Sophia sighed and leant over to give her a hug, which was awkward as they were both strapped into period dresses. She stood back up and placed her hands on her hips.

'So, what's the alternative? You stay at home on your birthday? Sulk and cry? Unwilling to move on?' She sounded exasperated. 'Do you know what you should actually do? You should go. Go and show them both that you have moved on, that you are better off without him and that they are nothing but a passing memory now. That's the ultimate win.'

Maya listened to her, but she couldn't speak. Aunt Sophia could see her struggling to keep her tears at bay, so continued, this time her tone much softer.

'How about we still go and have a great time, hey?'

Maya shrugged. 'But say Amanda Avary is there presenting and she spots me, I'll be seen as the pathetic, single ex, who has to rely on her aunt for dates.' She realised how that came across, 'No offence meant.'

'None taken,' Aunt Sophia said, smiling. 'But why don't you prove her wrong?'

'How? I am pathetic and single.'

'And feeling very sorry for herself,' Aunt Sophia scolded, wagging a finger in Maya's direction. 'Look, you're not pathetic, you're amazing and Amanda Avary doesn't even compare to you . . .' She grabbed Maya's phone from the bed and scrolling through until she landed on what she was searching for. 'And as for the single status, that can easily be remedied with one phone call.' She turned the screen around so that Maya could read the name on the screen.

'No,' Maya said.

'Why not?'

'Because he's with someone now. Remember? I met her on the flight.'

'All the more reason. Firstly, make it abundantly clear that you're not looking to get romantically involved, but that you are simply asking for a favour; and secondly, knowing he's already in a relationship with another girl, you are effectively still sticking to your rule of singledom.' She crossed her arms across her chest, looking very smug and pleased with herself. 'It's a win–win situation, agreed?'

Maya stared at the name on the screen for a few seconds, running through the notion of attending the ball with him on her arm and showing Amanda that Michael was a thing of the past. It might work. It certainly would make her feel better.

'Oh, sod it,' she said, pressing dial on the phone screen and holding the phone up to her ear. The recipient answered on the third ring.

'Hello?'

'Hi Theo. It's Maya.'

Chapter Thirty-Nine

'I still can't believe he agreed to this,' Maya said nervously, tugging on the multitude of frilly lace on the cuffs of her dress. Aunt Sophia was adding the finishing touches to Maya's make-up, adding a third layer of mascara to her already made-up eyes.

Maya had visited a hairdresser earlier that afternoon, and her hair had been meticulously styled so that she had a single, thick plait running from one ear to the other, across the crown of her head and the rest of her hair was left in her natural curly state to fall just below her shoulders. In between the layers of the hair braid, the hairdresser had woven in thin ribbons of gold and cream which matched her dress perfectly.

'Well, from how you've described him, he sounds like a lovely guy.'

'He is.'

'Then that's why. Plus, he still owes you for making that complaint last Christmas.'

'He's already apologised for that.'

'But it's not exactly a chore now, is it? He gets to accompany a beautiful woman to a fabulous event, where there is free-flowing wine and great food. I wouldn't exactly worry too much about it.' Aunt Sophia finished her make-up and took a step back to admire her handiwork. 'There now, all done. Exquisite.' She smiled and handed Maya a mirror so she could take a look herself. Maya had to admit that she did actually look quite pretty. Her eyes were emphasised by a smudged, dark liner and thick lashes, while her olive skin glowed from the summer sun they'd been having recently. Her lips were lightly brushed with a pale pink gloss and there were tendrils of curls falling around her face.

'It's just missing something . . .' Aunt Sophia said, tapping her index finger to her own, plump lips.

'Oh?' Maya asked, checking for smudges or blemishes.

'Yes, this.' Maya lowered the mirror to see Aunt Sophia standing before her holding in her hands a small, thin, square box, wrapped in gold paper and with a red ribbon tied around it. 'Happy birthday, sweet Maya,' she said, softly.

Maya's eyes grew wide as she took the box in her hands and fondled the soft ribbon gently and slowly.

'Well, open it then!' Aunt Sophia laughed. Maya pulled off the ribbon and tore into the paper until she was staring at a blue velvet box with a gold clasp. She opened the lid and found herself staring at the most beautiful necklace made of gold, with a delicate chain from which three rings sat against the plush cushioning in the box. Each ring was the same size, no bigger than a button, but each was different, one rose gold, one silver and one yellow gold. She lifted the necklace gently out of the box and held it up to get a closer look. On each of the rings were an initial; one with M, one with S, and one with T.

'One for each of us; you, me and your mum, Tess,' Aunt Sophia said quietly. 'You were her proudest achievement,' she added, her eyes tearing up.

Maya felt her own eyes prickling with tears, but this time she smiled; the necklace was beautiful, but it was so much more than that; it signified a bond with her aunt that had developed quickly and fiercely over the last six months. A bond that meant she also felt closer to her own mum again. And it wouldn't have happened if Michael hadn't dumped her. For the first time since it happened, she almost felt grateful to him for what he did, as it had opened opportunities with Aunt Sophia that she might never have experienced.

'I adore it,' she said, indicating for Aunt Maya to help fasten it around her neck. 'Truly, I do. Thank you.' The necklace fell softly onto her skin, sitting comfortably on her breastbone and they both admired it before Maya stepped forward and gave Aunt Sophia the biggest, warmest hug. After a moment, Aunt Sophia took a step back and said, gruffly,

'Enough of all that mushy stuff. I have one more present to give you before we leave.' She disappeared out of the Maya's bedroom as quickly as her own swishy gown would allow, leaving Maya waiting. She appeared moments later, this time carrying a much larger box, wrapped in the same gold paper, her arms apparently struggling a little under the weight. She plonked it down on the desk in Maya's room and said, 'Ta dah!'

Maya stood up and ripped off the paper in excitement to find herself staring at a shiny, black, beautiful typewriter. The keys were weathered and worn, the letters almost indecipherable, but Maya thought it was one of the most beautiful things she'd ever seen.

'Now your dad went in and paid half, so you must remember to thank him too,' she said gracefully, 'but I had these made for you myself.' She lifted the typewriter a few inches and Maya noticed a thin pile of papers underneath. 'Pull them out,' she said. Maya did so and noticed the papers were blank apart from the heading, which had her name printed on in beautiful calligraphy. 'For your next chapter. Both literary, and emotionally.' She plonked the typewriter back down with a flourish and checked the clock on the wall. 'We'd best be off if we don't want to keep your young man waiting,' she said.

'Aunt Sophia, you've been so kind, so generous—'

'Hush, hush now. I'm not one for emotional outbursts,' she said, gathering her skirt and heading for the hallway. 'Let's get going and dance ourselves back into the nineteenth century.'

Chapter Forty

As Maya and Aunt Sophia approached the long sweeping pathway towards the castle, Maya looked up at the impressive, eleventh-century, grey stone fortress. Situated high atop a hill overlooking the glorious West Sussex countryside, it sat proud, its intimidating turrets, huge keep and towering castle wall making Maya feel a little nervous. It was huge. But her nerves were more to do with the fact that Theo had agreed to meet her at the entrance, and she was only moments away from seeing him again.

Alongside them were other couples, all dressed in extravagant nineteenth-century ballgowns and costumes, all walking up the gravel path towards the castle. Maya suddenly became hugely aware of her own outfit. While it was a beautiful combination of gold silk and silver lace trim, with intricate pearl beading, the corset underneath appeared to be designed for a woman less well endowed in the chest area. Maya's poor bosom was simultaneously squished and forced upwards, so that her cleavage was spilling out over the top of the dress, almost indecently. She'd always been blessed/cursed with a large chest and she had long since learnt how to hide it under jumpers, high-necked T-shirts, and well-placed scarfs. This was a huge step outside of her comfort zone. But Aunt Sophia had insisted that she looked amazing, declaring that that was how the corsets were supposed to sit, so she had gone along with it, clearly having no other option. And she was aware that her birthday necklace simply drew the eye towards her chest.

The ballgown itself was beautiful though, she couldn't deny that. The silk fabric was pattered with tiny, silver hand-sewn birds that were dotted around her skirt as though mid-flight, and the sleeves themselves were puffed on the shoulders with sheer lace that flowed down to her wrists. The dress was tight around the chest and waist, but then flowed out widely down to the ground. She liked how it swished when she walked and liked it even more when she realised she could wear her trusty off-white sneakers under the skirt, concealed from the world. With her hair styled professionally and her make-up flawless, she did feel pretty. A rare feeling for her. Gone was the dowdy, often bare-faced Maya and in its place for tonight was a graceful, elegant beauty.

Aunt Sophia had opted for a wildly garish ballgown, in ruby-red silk and purple trim. With her waist-length grey curls cascading down her back, and a red fascinator in her hair, she looked stunning. Together, they were a captivating couple, and Maya linked her arm through Aunt Sophia's as they approached the entrance, feeling her shoulders relax at the lack of any media presence, or NWN vans. Perhaps they wouldn't be coming after all.

At first, she didn't spot him. A crowd had gathered, a bottleneck of a queue where people were showing tickets and having bags checked before continuing through to the castle and she found herself craning her neck to find him. What if he bailed on her? What if he couldn't come? Aunt Sophia squeezed her arm supportively.

'He'll be here, I'm sure of it.'

Maya simply nodded, a strained smile on her face, but then she heard her name being called from behind her. She let go of Aunt Sophia's arm and turned to find herself staring at Theo. But not Theo as she remembered, a Theo that looked like he'd walked straight off the set of some period drama. He was wearing tight, beige trousers that were tucked into knee-high, dark brown riding boots and a light blue tailcoat with ornate gold buttons on each side of the lapel. Underneath the tailcoat was a waistcoat of blue and beige, and under the crook of his left arm he was holding a top hat that matched the colour of his trousers. His hair, as always, was ruffled and messy; and Maya could see he hadn't shaved, giving him the air of a rugged gentleman that had just travelled the length of England on a horse to meet her. The overall look was extremely sexy. He should look ridiculous, Maya thought, but standing against the backdrop of the castle and with a crowd of similar Victorian-dressed humans surrounding him, he stood out for all the right reasons, and she could feel her pulse quicken.

I fancy him.

The thought appeared in her mind uninvited and unwanted. But as he stepped forward towards her, the thought grew like a balloon being filled with the air of insight. His eyes were wide and his smile broad.

'Maya, you look fantastic. Thank you for inviting me.' He went to kiss her on the cheek, but her petticoats were so wide that he had to lean in quite far and it all became a bit uncomfortable. He barely reached her cheek before he pulled back.

'Don't thank me, you're already doing me a huge favour by coming along to this ridiculous event.'

He shook his head in protest, 'Are you kidding me? I studied Victorian history as part of my final year, I love this era!' He genuinely did seem excited. It was endearing and only added to his sexiness. 'I mean, I'm sure there will be some wildly inaccurate interpretations of late-Victorian traditions tonight, but that's not to say I am not willing to partake in them . . .' They both laughed and Aunt Sophia cleared her throat.

'Theo, this is my Aunt Sophia.' Maya gestured to her. Theo smiled and offered her a tiny, nineteenth-century bow.

'Delighted to meet you,' he said, gallantly holding out an arm. 'May I escort you lovely ladies into the ball?'

'We'd be thrilled,' Aunt Sophia said, folding her arm through his and winking at Maya. Maya took his other arm, and they headed in the direction of the castle entrance, through a stone archway at the stone castle gates. A Regency soldier was standing in front of a wooden sentry box checking off names on a clipboard.

'Welcome to the Arundel Midsummer Ball. Please make your way towards the formal courtyard.'

'Thank you,' Maya said, before moving forward and walking the sandy stone path towards the impressive, towering castle. One of the square turrets had a brightly coloured flag waving gently in the evening breeze. As they made their way up the slope, they could hear music coming from inside the castle walls. The obvious lack of media presence lifted Maya's spirits, and she smiled at Aunt Sophia, starting to think that this evening was actually going to be a whole heap of fun. She laughed as Theo reeled off historical facts about castles, and she couldn't help but find his childish enthusiasm attractive and she listened as he talked emphatically about turrets.

As they entered the courtyard, all three were taken away at the magnitude of the event. It had been transformed into an open-air ballroom, with lanterns hanging above their heads attached to a huge metal uncovered gazebo that stretched the length of the courtyard. Flaming lanterns lined the periphery of the dance floor, so that the orange hue flickered off the moving guests and everywhere, in every archway and corner of the space, there were huge vases filled with a plethora of summer flowers of every colour. The scent was amazing. There was a string quartet playing fancy music and already a large crowd were dancing, making Maya realise that she could in no way be tempted to dance without looking a fool. Instead, her gaze landed on a bar that had been set up to the left of the dance floor, with what looked like large barrels of wine being poured directly from a tap inserted into each barrel.

'Shall we grab a drink?' she suggested, not really waiting for a response. After three large red wines had been poured, they clinked their glasses together with Aunt Sophia declaring, 'Happy birthday, dearest Maya.'

Theo looked shocked, his glass frozen in his hand, 'It's your birthday today? You never mentioned it on the phone.'

Maya shrugged. 'I don't like a fuss.'

'Well, now I feel bad that I've come without a gift.'

'Don't be silly. And besides, where would I put a gift?' She gestured to her tight bodice and teeny velvet pouch that hung from her wrist which was only just large enough for her phone and a lipstick. She noticed Theo's cheeks flush as he made his way over her tight corset.

'Then I insist that I buy the next round.'

'I'm not going to argue with that.'

'Nor me!' agreed Aunt Sophia, downing her glass in one go. 'Ready when you are.' Theo looked surprised, but laughed and downed his glass too, before turning back to the bar.

'Right, let's get this birthday started.'

Chapter Forty-One

An hour later, and Maya was both tipsy and happy. She had revelled in the admiring glances from other guests and it boosted her confidence that every time she searched out Theo, he was watching her. It was incredibly erotic. Her cheeks were flushed from the alcohol, but her body was glowing for him.

'Do you want to dance?' Theo asked her, reaching out a hand for her to take. She nodded, but self-consciously moved across the dance floor, her only thoughts were for his hand in hers. Coming to a stop, he turned towards her and placed his other hand around her waist. Despite the thick material of the bodice, it felt like his fingers were touching her naked skin, and as they began to move, she fell into a natural rhythm with him, their bodies moving in unison. The rest of the room disappeared, and it was just him in front of her, him pulling her closer against him. It wasn't the bodice this time causing her to feel breathless.

After what seemed like only moments, the dance was over, and Theo let her go. For a moment, she could see a flash of disappointment in his eyes, and she knew she felt the same. She wanted him to take her back and hold her close. His eyes found hers, and her lips parted. He stepped forward, his eyes fixed on hers, but then his gaze broke, as Aunt Sophia rustled up beside them.

'Come on, Maya. Shall we at take a turn around the gardens?' Aunt Sophia was looking flushed and stumbled a little in her heels.

'If you like,' Maya said, quickly scanning the courtyard around them. Everyone was drinking and enjoying the party atmosphere. The sun was beginning to set, and the castle stone was lit in a beautiful pinkish hue.

The three of them made their way, following wooden signs hammered into the soft ground that stated *The Midsummer Gardens*. It led them out of the castle and into the most beautiful gardens Maya had ever seen, Signs took them this way and that, and they meandered their way through a rose garden that was filled with roses of every colour and a scent so strong that Maya wanted to bottle it as a perfume to be used forever. They stumbled across a kitchen garden that was bursting with fruit and vegetables from every angle. And as they made their way around the formal gardens, structured like a leafy maze, they found themselves following a group of wooden signs with painted arrows, all oddly titled *The Stumpery*. Maya felt like she had stumbled back into the nineteenth century.

'What on earth is a stumpery?' Aunt Sophia asked, still holding a huge full glass of wine.

'I have no idea. A pub?'

But as they turned the corner, they soon found out what it was. A huge arrangement of tree stumps turned upside down and arranged in such a way that they twisted and turned this way and that, as if tangled together by nature. Out of the stumps burst the most beautiful of flowers, all in bloom. The effects were quite stunning and the atmosphere in the garden was one of awe and tranquillity. Which was very soon disrupted by the sound of footsteps from behind them and a shrill, controlling female voice barking instructions loudly.

'Hurry if we're to catch this evening light. This glow will be perfect for accentuating my tan . . . come on, people.'

Maya turned her head to find herself staring straight at the approaching form of Amanda Avary and a small camera crew scurrying behind in her shadows. Her body stiffened and her heart raced, she wanted to run yet she felt rooted to the spot. Amanda hadn't even noticed them standing there, she was too busy stretching her long neck around to try and find the perfect spot to film. Maya analysed Amanda's seemingly perfect figure which was highlighted by a pale cream bodycon dress that showed off her beautiful legs. The dress was knee length and had a high collar, so ticked all the boxes for being demure enough for the channel's daytime viewers, but sexy enough that they could envisage easily what was hiding underneath. Maya suddenly felt ridiculous in her fancy dress outfit with its huge skirt and too-tight bodice. She wanted to leave, right that second.

'Please, let's go,' she whispered to Aunt Sophia, who had also clocked Amanda. Her cheeks were flushed in anger to the point they almost matched the silk of her dress and Maya could see her muttering under her breath, but she nodded briskly and took Maya's hand in hers. Theo, completely unaware of the developing atmosphere, seemed excited at the prospect of being on television. He was straightening his waistcoat and running a hand through his hair. When he turned to Maya though, his expression changed and was replaced with concern.

'Maya, are you alright?'

'We need to leave. Now.' She spoke quietly, but her tone was clear.

'Sure,' he said, hastily walking in the opposite direction from the camera crew and Amanda.

Maya turned to follow suit, but in her panic, she forgot that she was wearing a heavy, ballooning skirt and in her haste, she accidentally stepped on its hem and lost her balance. She desperately tried to reach out for Theo, but he was a couple of steps behind her and didn't react fast enough. Realising she was going down, she let out an anguished, 'Oh, shit' and fell straight into a particularly large lavender bush to her left. As her hip made contact with the ground, she heard a sickening rip of silk and a moment later, a matching rip of pain spasmed through her right side. 'Fuck,' she groaned. She had landed on one butt cheek and had face-planted the lavender so that she could feel sprigs of it sticking into her arms, face and hair, the sweet smell overwhelming so close. She was instantly transported straight back to her grandmother's vanity drawer where she always kept little bags of dried lavender.

'Maya!' Aunt Sophia yelled, and Maya could hear footsteps crunching on the gravel path, getting closer. Moments later, she felt strong arms gather her around the waist and lift her up out of the bush.

'Shit, are you OK?' Theo asked, his face full of concern. He got her back on her feet, but he didn't let go of her waist. She tried to act all nonchalant, brushing any captured sprigs of lavender from her dress and hair, but really wanting to just crawl under a rock. Her face felt flushed, and she felt stupidly embarrassed, but that embarrassment suddenly turned to ice-cold fear when she heard a voice approach them.

'Oh, my goodness, are you alright? We all saw you fall.'

Amanda Avary and her crew were fast approaching her. Maya wondered how she didn't fall over herself with those stupidly high stilettos sinking into the stony path, but she tried to stand up tall and quickly turned her face away from them.

'I'm fine,' she said, tossing off any concern with a backward wave of her hand. She kept her head turned away from Amanda, inspecting the back of her dress. In horror, she noticed a huge tear in the join between skirt and bodice, her fleshy midriff making a bid for freedom. She covered it quickly with her left hand and began to back away from the gathering crowd.

'Maya, seriously, are you OK? Maybe you should sit down?' Theo turned to Aunt Sophia. 'Don't you think Maya should sit down?' His concern was lovely, but she really wished he would stop saying her name aloud.

'Maya?' Amanda's voice cut in sharply. 'As in Maya Madeski?' She let out a surprised laugh. 'Well, of all the places to see you . . .'

Maya froze, her face still turned away, but she could see Aunt Sophia looking past her towards Amanda, a furious scowl on her face. So, with her free hand, she pushed back the curls from her face and turned to face her.

'Amanda.' It was neither a greeting nor a welcome, but it was all she could manage. She watched as Amanda's large, sparkling eyes rose up and down her outfit, taking in the whole messy picture. She had a look of mock concern on her face.

'Darling, are you OK? That was a bit of a tumble.'

'I'm fine,' Maya mumbled, managing a straight, closed mouth smile.

'Well, that's a relief,' Amanda said, looking completely unconcerned. 'And don't you look just lovely, minus the foliage of course.' A laugh tinkled out of her pink lips and her eyes moved across to Theo. 'Are you here alone?'

Maya marvelled at how such an innocent question could be loaded with so much undertone. She tried to stand up a little taller, but the pressure on her left hip was causing it to throb angrily.

'No, no. I'm here with my aunt and my er, my friend, Theo.' She gestured to Theo who smiled handsomely and took a step forward to shake her hand. Amanda accepted it, but her eyes didn't leave Maya's.

'Delighted to meet you, Amanda Avary. I watch you most days . . .' he began. Maya realised he was fawning over her presence and clearly hadn't felt any of the animosity between them. 'I can't believe you're filming here tonight. Fantastic!'

Amanda's focus changed and she looked at Theo properly for the first time. Her smile switched up a notch, realising she was in the presence of a fan. 'We are indeed. The whole crew are here actually to film a live show. There's me, obviously.' She let go of his hand and placed it on her chest, patting it. 'And the wonderful Samuel Stinson, who is currently getting ready in the van.' She then turned back to look directly at Maya. 'And then we have the weather being covered live tonight from the castle by the fantastic Michael the Weatherman. It's going to be a ball, pardon the pun!' The camera crew all laughed, and Maya felt suddenly very sick. Michael was here. Actually here. And she was standing in a ridiculous, ripped outfit, covered in twigs and with scratches up her arm and on her cheek.

'That's amazing. I've always wanted to be on television. Where are you filming?' Theo asked innocently, completely unaware that Maya was struggling, and Aunt Sophia was reaching boiling point.

'Oh, up at the castle in the courtyard. We just popped down here to capture the opening sequences,' Amanda said, 'speaking of which, we must crack on before we lose this wonderful light.' She turned to her crew who started setting up. 'If you like, we could always interview you live on air later?' she directed the question at Theo, clearly enjoying the way it made Maya squirm.

'Sure! We'd love that, wouldn't we, Maya?' He looked over at her and clocked her expression, then turned to Aunt Sophia and registered her thunderous glare at Amanda. The poor man looked totally confused. 'Oh, um, well, we'd better get Maya back up to the castle to see if there is any first aid.'

'Oh yes, you must! Poor Maya. Always getting herself in a bit of a pickle, aren't you?'

Maya didn't answer. She couldn't. Amanda waited for a moment before turning around to her crew. 'Right, let's not waste any more time, let's get to work.'

She walked away in the direction of the rose garden. Aunt Sophia walked over to Maya and wrapped a supportive arm around her shoulders. Theo shook his head.

'Maya, you're hurt. Let's get you back up to the castle.' He came forward and put out his arm for her to loop hers through. She did, feeling suddenly exhausted. They began their slow walk back to the castle, making sure they weren't in Amanda's eyeline. Once back in the courtyard, he found a stone bench hidden away under an archway and sat her down gently.

'I'm going to see if I can get some help, and then perhaps someone can tell me what is actually going on?'

His face was so full of concern that she felt guilty for keeping him in the dark. She nodded. He left and Aunt Sophia walked over and joined her on the bench.

'I've scanned the area, he's not here.'

'Thank you.'

'She is toxic.'

217

Maya nodded.

'And a total bitch.'

Maya continued nodding.

'What do you want to do? Do you want to leave?'

Maya was wondering the same question. Did she want to leave? She did, but part of her knew that leaving would give Amanda the satisfaction that she had won. But if she did stay, there was the problem of the ripped dress and bedraggled hair.

'I just don't know. I mean, look at me.'

Aunt Sophia scanned her face and her body. 'Well, that's easily sorted.' And she disappeared back into the crowd leaving Maya alone on the stone seat, wondering if she'd ever had a worse birthday than this one. She was pretty sure she hadn't.

Chapter Forty-Two

'So, Michael Simmons is your ex-boyfriend? The fool that dumped you live on air?'

'Yep.'

'And Amanda Avary is the woman he left you for?'

'Correct again.'

'And you knew they might be here tonight filming, and you only asked me along so that you didn't have to appear single in front of them?'

'Yes,' Maya said quietly, blushing. 'I'm so sorry.'

Theo sat back on the stone bench, leaning against the castle wall, staring ahead, taking it all in. He had returned with a first aid kit and wiped clean any scratches or cuts, but they were minor. The biggest pain seemed to be in her hip, but she hadn't bothered to check that, preferring to stay in the shadows.

'I'd understand if you want to leave,' she said, looking sideways at him, feeling so embarrassed. He didn't answer. Instead, he just sighed deeply and looked down at his hands in his lap before turning to Maya, his eyes full of compassion.

'You have really had a shit time of it. What sort of man would I be if I also abandoned you, like he did? Absolutely no way. If *you* want to stay, then I am staying with you.'

He seemed resolute and smiled. Maya didn't know how to respond, she felt so utterly grateful to him. She was interrupted from responding by Aunt Sophia bustling back over, her huge skirts swishing along the stone courtyard, with a young woman in her wake.

'Don't panic, I've got you sorted.' She gestured to the woman to step forward. 'This is Lexi. She is the make-up artist for NWN and has a wonderful, magical make-up box with everything we need to fix you.'

'Hi,' Lexi said, lifting her huge, silver make-up box and rattling it gently. 'I'll be your fairy godmother for the night.' She had a strong Scottish accent and a sweet smile.

'You work for NWN?' Maya asked, looking around Lexi to see if Amanda was hiding in her shadow.

'I do,' Lexi said, loudly, but leant forward to whisper conspiratorially into Maya's ear, 'but I cannot stand Amanda Avary. She's a total cow.' She winked a perfectly made-up eye at Maya. 'Let's get you sorted.'

Maya stood up to follow her and Theo stood up too. 'Shall I get the drinks in, ladies?'

'Sounds splendid, darling Theo,' trilled Aunt Sophia, leading Maya away from him and in the direction of the parked NWN vans on the outskirts of the castle.

Twenty minutes later, Maya walked back into the courtyard in search of Theo, feeling completely revived. Lexi had done a miraculous job with the help of her magic bag, and Maya's dress had been stitched back together with the use of a hardy needle, some gold thread and one of the gold ribbons taken from her hair. Her scratches had been cleaned and dotted with some tattoo cover-up and her make-up had been re-touched so that it looked even better than before. Lexi had added some curl oil to Maya's curls and used her curling tongs to give them definition so as she walked, they cascaded down her back like those of a girl from a renaissance painting. She felt amazing. She spotted Theo standing at the bar and walked towards him, just as he turned around and spotted her. His eyes widened.

'Wow,' he said. 'You look phenomenal.'

'Thank you,' Maya said, blushing. Having his eyes scan her that way was making her skin prickle and the hairs on the back of her neck stand on end. She broke his gaze and took the full glass that he had waiting for her on the bar. She took a sip. 'I did have a bit of help though.' She turned to look for Aunt Sophia and Lexi, but they'd both disappeared into the crowd.

The courtyard was brimming with people now, with the makeshift dance floor full of nineteenth-century dancers all twirling and waltzing in their brightly coloured costumes. While scanning the crowd, her eyes landed on someone she'd been dreading seeing for the last six months. The same someone who was staring right back at her with familiar hazel-grey eyes agog. The same crew cut that he'd had since his teenage years and refused to deviate from. The same broad shoulders and narrow hips in his standard dark trousers and plain shirt. It was Michael. Her Michael. And he was walking straight across the dance floor towards her, his eyes not leaving hers.

Chapter Forty-Three

'Maya. Of all the places to bump into you!'

Michael's face was full of surprise, and he leant in for a kiss on the cheek. The familiarity of his lips touching her and the musky scent of his aftershave sent her pulse into overdrive. She let her eyes close for a second and she felt transported back into a time where every afternoon, before he left for work, he would kiss her cheek and say, *whatever the weather, always take an umbrella!* She felt that recurring lump appear in her throat and when she opened her eyes again, he had pulled away.

'You look fantastic,' he said, and she could see he genuinely meant it. He was scanning her from top to bottom and it felt very intimate.

'Thank you, Michael. So do you.' She hadn't meant to say it. She didn't want to ply him with platitudes, he was still the arsehole who dumped her, but she couldn't help it. He did look amazing. He was wearing his usual attire for work, and he stood out from the period costumes around them, but in a good way, like a modern-day actor stuck on the set of a period movie scene. He was tanned, muscular and with just the tiniest of traces of make-up on his cheeks. Someone cleared their throat behind him, and she suddenly remembered Theo.

'Oh, I'm so sorry, Michael please meet Theo, Theo this is Michael. He's an . . . old friend.'

Michael baulked at the term *old friend* and his smile wavered for just a second, but his professional background kicked in and he took a step forward to shake Theo's hand. 'Theo, nice to meet you.' He dropped his hand quickly and turned back to Maya. 'So, how have you been? I've felt so dreadful about how we left things . . .'

How *we* left things? Maya thought to herself. *We?* It didn't feel very united at the time, with him sneaking behind her back and dumping her on air. She could feel her anger bubbling up, her rage flushing her cheeks. She wanted to retort, but she felt Theo's arm suddenly appear around her waist and him kissing her on the cheek.

'She's been amazing, actually. We've been amazing. Almost six months now of being together, isn't it, sweetheart? We couldn't be happier. You did us a favour in all honesty, mate. If you hadn't dumped her, I wouldn't have found my one true love.' And as Maya turned to him in confusion, Theo pulled her forward and kissed her directly on the lips. It was like a firework exploded in her veins, her blood felt electrified, as if every cell had come alive and begun fizzing. His lips were warm, and he tasted like a blend of wine and sweet cherries. The kiss was determined, and she could feel the hint of his tongue and she melted into it, wanting more. Just as she leant into him, their bodies pressing together and her skin tingling, he pulled apart. But his eyes never left hers. 'I'm one lucky guy.'

She didn't respond, she couldn't. Her lips were still prickling.

'Well, that's just . . . great to hear,' Michael began, his forehead creased in thought, but his smile still plastered across his face. 'I'm really pleased you're happy, Maya. I am.' Maya looked at him finally and noticed suddenly how fake his tan was, how his eyebrows were shaped too perfectly. He reminded her of a tropical Ken doll. 'And you look just fantastic,' he said, this time more softly, his eyes tenderly scanning hers. Suddenly his phone rang, causing him to jump a little, as if interrupting his thoughts. He pulled it out of his trouser pocket and clicked to answer it, not before sighing at the name displayed on the screen.

'Yes? No, I know. Yes, yes. I'm coming right now,' he spoke in a strained voice, his tone clipped. 'I'm coming!' He ended the call and looked down at the now-black screen, his mind elsewhere. 'I have to go, we're about to go live down in the rose garden,' he said, looking at Maya again. 'It was so great to see you.' He lifted his free hand and gently took hers. She could feel Theo stiffening beside her, his grip around her waist tightening, but he didn't say anything. Michael squeezed her hand lightly and looked as if he was about to say something more when he let go abruptly and walked away from them both.

As Maya watched him leave, she felt herself exhale. She hadn't realised it, but she'd been holding her breath for what seemed like forever, and only now that he had gone, could she breathe properly.

'Are you alright?' Theo asked, his hand still holding tight around her waist, his body still touching hers.

'I think so,' she said, before continuing, 'you kissed me.'

'I know,' he said, looking shifty, 'but I just couldn't bear the thought of that arsehole pitying you. I wanted to make him think you'd moved on. I took the role of fake boyfriend a little too seriously. I'm sorry, it was out of line.'

But she shook her head. 'No, it was genius, thank you. It's why I invited you, after all, you were simply playing your part. It's just that . . .' She trailed off, raising a hand to her lips and gently touching her fingers against them.

'Yes?' he said, the intensity in his eyes building as he followed her fingers.

'The kiss . . .' she began, almost whispering, and he pulled her a little closer towards him, her chest touching his.

'Yes?' he repeated, and she could feel the warmth of his breath on her face.

'Maya! There you are!' Aunt Sophia bustled up to the bar with two people either side of her, her arms threaded through each of theirs, oblivious to any tension and clearly a little drunk. Maya pulled apart from Theo instantly, as if she'd touched a flame, and turned her attention to Aunt Sophia who was leaning quite heavily on a thickset man. 'This lovely couple have offered to teach us to dance the waltz! Meet Esther and

Donovan, they're professional dancers hired for the evening to teach people to dance. Theo, you go with Esther and Maya, you take Donovan.' She gestured for them to step forward, which Maya did, with Donovan smiling and holding out a hand. 'Go, go, have fun, birthday girl! I'll just grab another drink and watch.'

As Maya was led away from the bar and onto the dance floor, she couldn't help but look back over her shoulder at Theo, who was also being led away. He was smiling at his new dance partner and nodding politely to her questions, but as Donovan began teaching her the beginning steps of the dance, she couldn't help but find her eyes being drawn over in his direction, and when she did, she was both delighted and distressed to find him staring right back at her.

'Oh, Maya,' she mumbled to herself as Donovan spun her around in a figure of eight. 'What are you doing?'

Chapter Forty-Four

Day 188
Reader, I saw him.
My ex. My once betrothed. Is there anything worse than seeing
an ex when you're not looking your best? Quite frankly, no.
I have managed to go six months without seeing him, yet why
is it that on the first night since he so publicly dumped me, I
bump into him barely an hour after crawling out of a bush.
And I mean literally, not metaphorically. I couldn't make it
up. There he was, looking all dashing, handsome and familiar,
and there I was, scuffed knees, a ripped dress that I had no
chance of getting my deposit back on, and a purpling bruise on
my left buttock the size of New Zealand. You probably think
that I made up for all that by showing him what he was missing
with my witty conversation and clever retorts. Guess again. I
managed a measly two sentences at most, and none of them will
have me winning any literary awards any time soon. And I
can't even say that I wasn't prepared because I was. I knew
there I was a chance I might bump into him at this event yet
I still wasn't prepared for actually seeing him in the flesh. To
hear his voice and smell his familiar scent.

But I have to admit, that despite ALL of that, I haven't
woken up this morning full of regret and tears. It could have
gone so much worse. I could have begged him to come back to
me. Or caused such a scene that he left, thankful that he'd
made such a wise decision. Or simply been seen and ignored
– the ultimate insult.

So, despite my clear incompetence to manage a normal conver-
sation or walk like a functioning adult without falling over, I

feel that our meeting was the first step to me trying to gain some closure from him. I may have muddled through, but I did it.

Reader, I saw him. And that's OK.

The following morning, Maya woke with three realisations. One, that it was the first day of July. Two, her left buttock was throbbing to such an extent that she wondered if Matilda the goat had been pummelling her during the night, and three, she definitely felt attracted to Theo. None were encouraging realisations, and each came with their own set of problems. She was due to fly to Boston the following day, and the notion of being on her feet for hours on end with a dodgy hip might prove problematic, and continuing to see Theo would only encourage her romantic feelings to grow, which would put her rule of singledom at risk. Her blog had gained traction over the last few months, and she had followers in the tens of thousands. She couldn't back down now. She was halfway, only another six months to go. And there was always the problem of Holly. As far as she was aware, Theo was with Holly still, and she would never be the other woman. Never.

So, after dragging herself into the kitchen to make herself a large coffee, she pulled out her phone to text Theo. After their near-kiss experience, the rest of the evening had run smoothly and with no further attempts at closeness. Theo had been the perfect gentleman, dancing with Aunt Sophia and her equally and at arm's length. And at the end of the night, he had walked them both back to the taxi rank and kissed them on the cheek, but his lips hovered just a second longer on her cheek. But he had acted brilliantly in front of Michael, and for that she would be forever grateful. Her mind was swirling with contradictions and in the end, the message took three attempts to get right. It read,

Hi Theo, thanks so much for last night. I'm so grateful to you on so many levels. For agreeing to come, for picking me out of a bush, for acting the part in front of my ex – not

*your average night out, hey? You are a lovely friend. Say hi
to Holly for me. Speak soon, Maya.*

She pressed send. She waited until the two ticks appeared,
showing it had been both received and read. Then she burst
into tears.

Chloe turned up at Aunt Sophia's house a few hours later
and Maya was feeling a lot better. She had run herself a hot
bath and, with the pamper set given to her by Gayle, she had
indulged in a face mask, body scrub and full-on soak. Her hip
was sporting a country-sized bruise already and the water helped
soothe her aching limbs. After her bath, she had padded down
into the kitchen to find a full fry-up waiting for her, cooked
by Aunt Sophia, who was out tending the chickens. There
was a note pinned to the plate, along with two painkillers on
a side plate, telling her to *Eat! Back after lunch.* She did as she
was told, and so when she answered the door to Chloe, she
was feeling relaxed and relatively pain-free.

'Happy birthday!' Chloe screamed, as she bulldozed her
way through the front door with a huge cluster of brightly
coloured balloons floating behind her. Her arms were laden
with a cake box, a brightly wrapped present and her oversized
handbag. Maya couldn't help but laugh as Chloe tripped her
way down the hallway towards the kitchen.

'What is all this?' she said, following behind, trying not to
get knocked by all the balloons.

'Well, I missed your birthday, didn't I? So I'm going to
make sure that I make up for it today.' She dumped everything
on the kitchen table and came forward to give Maya a hug.
'Happy birthday, gorgeous girl.' She pulled back and looked
at Maya's outfit which consisted of denim shorts and a baggy
T-shirt. 'But this just won't do,' she said, wagging her finger
up and down Maya's body. 'I'm taking you out, you need
to change.'

'Why?' Maya exclaimed.

'Just because.' Chloe shrugged, her eyes dancing with excitement. 'C'mon, Maya. I want to make a fuss of you. You deserve it.' She pulled the present across the table and handed it over. 'Open, open, open!' She was like an excited kid, jiggling on her toes, her sequinned sandals tapping on the stone tiles.

'OK, OK!' Maya laughed, finding her excitement infectious and she ripped into the present. She gasped as she saw what it was. Lifting it out of the box, she examined the ornate, gold frame and ran her finger over the glass. Behind it sat an off-white, slightly pearlescent piece of paper with delicate writing scrawled across it. It was Maya's first ever blog post, titled *Flying Solo*. Seeing her words actually typed out and holding a physical copy in her hands felt utterly surreal and she just kept staring at it.

'Don't you like it?' Chloe said, looking nervous.

Maya shook her head. 'I love it! It's brilliant. Thank you.' She went in for a huge hug, but Chloe pushed her back.

'Have another look in the box, that's not all.'

Maya did so, popping the frame upright on the kitchen table and delving back into the box, excitedly. Under a layer of tissue paper, there was a folded, bright orange, high-visibility jacket. She picked it up, confused. 'Please don't tell me this is some new fashion trend?'

'Nope,' Chloe said, opening her own handbag and whipping out a matching jacket and holding it out in front of her. 'These are for this afternoon. I am helping you complete your next challenge!' She threw the jacket over the top of her cotton jumpsuit and pushed the cake box across the table and lifted the lid to reveal a delicious-looking chocolate cake. 'But first, we eat. You'll need to keep your strength up.'

Chapter Forty-Five

After gorging on a huge slice of chocolate fudge cake and being told to change outfits into 'more suitable attire' involving trainers and trousers, Maya found herself being driven by Chloe towards a local woodland nature reserve.

'Are we nearly there yet?' Maya asked for the umpteenth time.

'Maya – enough with the questions, you're like a petulant child. We'll be there in a few minutes,' Chloe scolded, her eyes on the road. But she looked excited. A few moments later and they pulled into the large car park in the forest, the thick jungle of trees almost blocking out the summer sunshine and keeping the air cool. When Maya stepped out of the car, she tried to guess what Chloe's plan was for the day; tree climbing? Den building? Hill hiking? She just couldn't see anything that indicated what they would be doing.

Chloe opened the car boot and pulled out some sturdy trainers and put them on and then said, 'C'mon, it starts in five minutes.'

'What does?' Maya said.

'You'll see.' Chloe winked and slammed the car boot shut before heading off in the direction of the thick forest, away from the forest café, gift shop and visitor centre. Maya followed a few steps behind her, feeling grateful she had changed out of her flip-flops and into her sturdier trainers, but with each step, she could feel her hip ache. The car park soon disappeared from view and the sound of other people became muted in the thick undergrowth, with the smell of the forest feeling fresh and clean. Chloe was following a small trail and there were wooden arrows pointing them in the direction she was heading. After five minutes of walking, Maya spotted a clearing ahead of them with a large wooden cabin positioned in the centre, facing towards them. Two rangers, dressed in green overalls, one male, one female, were handing out clipboards and forms to four other people beside them.

'Welcome, welcome,' the male ranger said, smiling through his huge, bushy beard, his bald head gleaming in the bright sunshine. 'You must be Maya and Chloe, the last of our party. Let me grab you your forms and then we can get started.' He took two clipboards from the female ranger and handed them over to Chloe. 'If you could just sign the health and safety questionnaire and the waiver of liability form, then we can get started.' He was extremely excitable for a man who appeared to be in his late sixties, Maya thought.

'Waiver of liability?' she hissed to Chloe. 'What are we doing?'

'Just sign. It's all fine,' she said, scrawling her signature on the forms without reading them and handing them back to the man. Maya looked down at the forms in her hands and read the first line on the form, '*Waiver of Liability for the Use of Segways on Private Land*'.

'We're riding Segways today?' Maya looked over at Chloe who was almost bouncing on the tips of her toes with excitement.

'We are! Happy birthday!'

Maya laughed, feeling relieved. Riding Segways actually seemed less frightening compared to what she thought Chloe might have planned for them both. She quickly signed the forms and handed them back over to the ranger, who took them and dropped them all inside the cabin.

'Right, if you can all follow me around the back of the cabin, where the Segways are all lined up and we'll show you all how to use them.' The six of them followed both rangers where they found themselves standing in front of a Segway each. Maya was surprised at how big they were. It seemed quite daunting as she looked up at it. But ten minutes later, she was riding it slowly in tandem with Chloe, following the lead of Arnold and Maria, their rangers for their ride, and loving it. With a maximum speed of twelve miles an hour, they were following the forest path together and she couldn't help but enjoy the freedom of feeling the warm wind rushing through her hair and the only sound being the collective whirring of the eight machines as they made their way through the forest. It was an odd sensation though, leaning forward to go faster and pulling back to slow the machine down.

'Isn't this great?' Chloe called out, her blonde hair fanning out behind her, her cheeks flushed with excitement.

'It's brilliant,' Maya yelled back. They were at the back of the group, with only Arnold behind them, keeping an eye on them all. They were all staying very linear, keeping in a straight line, but Chloe began to swerve a little from side to side, her confidence building.

'We can try a few turns, if you like,' Arnold called out and Maria began to slow, causing everyone else to follow suit. They then proceeded to show the group how to safely turn around in circles and learn to swerve safely. Chloe threw herself into it, but Maya didn't want to, preferring to stay safe. Her hip was still throbbing quietly and mentally she wasn't prepared to take any huge risks. So, while everyone else was swirling around like mechanical ballerinas, she decided to pause for a bit, choosing instead to pull her phone out of her pocket. Still standing on her Segway, she scanned her messages. There were two. The first was from Theo.

Hi Maya, it was my pleasure. It was an interesting night, and I am happy to help you ANY time. I'm flying again on August 10th; will you be on my flight? Seat 28C.

The second message caused her to gasp. It was from Michael.

Hi M, I still can't believe I saw you last night, I haven't been able to stop thinking about you since. You looked so beautiful. Can we meet? X

＊

Two men. Two very different messages. Maya stared at the screen with disbelief. Theo didn't get the hint at all, leaving her wondering how she should respond. And Michael's message seemed to be unstitching her only recently healed heart again. Instinctively her first response was to tell him to get lost, that he was a no-good loser whose loyalty was as non-existent as a snowstorm in July, but her irrational emotions were roller-coasting through her internal systems like a steam train. Should she meet him? What harm would it do just to meet for a drink?

'Maya? What's wrong?' Maya jumped as Chloe pulled up alongside her in her own Segway. 'Why have you stopped?' She saw her looking at her phone. 'Are you kidding me? We're out in the middle of a forest, together, and you are on your phone? C'mon.' She looked thoroughly displeased and Maya quickly popped it back in her pocket.

'Sorry, sorry. It's just that . . .' she began, wondering whether to tell Chloe.

'That what?' Chloe looked impatient now, they only had hire of the Segway for an hour and she did not like standing still.

'That . . . nothing. Let's go.'

As they completed their hour, Maya kept smiling and acting like she was having a great time, but in her head, there were two men fighting for attention. At a time when she should be swearing off men altogether, here she was with her mind full of them.

As their hour came to an end, and Maya and Chloe headed back towards the café for a well-deserved cold drink, Maya made a decision. And when Chloe went up to the counter to pay for their drinks, she took out her phone and pressed delete on both messages.

'There,' she said to nobody in particular. 'Decision made.'

Chapter Forty-Six

August came around and before she knew it, she was scheduled to work the Heathrow to JFK flight on August 10th. So
was Chloe, who always made the flight more bearable, but as
Maya did her final pre-boarding checks before the passengers
got on the plane, she felt full of nerves. She kept glancing out
of the cabin windows as she passed each aisle. She paused at
row twenty-eight and ran her hand over seat C.

'Maya, they're coming on board now. Positions, please,'
Nigel Edwards, her onboard manager said, gesturing for her to
come to the front of the plane, which she did, after straightening
the hem of her skirt and making sure her collar was done up.

As they welcomed passengers onto the plane, Maya scanned
the faces to see if she could spot Theo. Despite having deleted
his message, she hadn't been able to stop thinking about him
over the last few weeks. Turns out Theo's face was never that
far from her mind, whether she was in Spain, Thailand, or
Africa. Just as the last passenger boarded, she breathed a sigh of
relief. It looked like he wasn't coming. She turned to head into
the galley when she heard heavy footsteps running through the
passenger boarding bridge towards the plane. Looking around,
she came face to face with a hot and sweaty Theo.

'Shit, I thought I was going to miss the flight entirely.' He
was panting heavily and there were a few nervous glances at
him from some of the other passengers. He handed over his
ticket, not making eye contact with her. She noticed but didn't
let her resolve slide.

'Well, you've just made it. Go and take your seat, we're just
about to taxi out.' At this point he did look at her, scanning

her face questioningly and she felt her cheeks flame, until his expression turned aloof.

'Sure. No problem.' He headed to his seat without so much as a glance back at her and Maya knew she had offended him. But work took over, and for the next few hours she was grateful for the distraction.

After the initial chaos of the flight, once the meals had been cleared away, the lights went down to offer the passengers a chance to sleep. Normally Maya revelled in the respite of these few quiet hours, but she couldn't seem to relax. She was covering the front section of economy but that didn't include Theo's row and most people wanted to either sleep or immerse themselves in a movie.

'Just go and say hi,' Chloe said to her from the galley as they restocked the fridges. 'What harm will that do? I've said hello, it looks weird that you haven't.'

'I know it does,' Maya said. 'It's just how do I explain the fact that I completely ignored his message?'

'Just say you've been busy. That you've been out of the country on flights. That you caught bubonic plague, I don't know. Who cares? Just go. I'll cover you.' She pushed Maya slightly, encouraging her to go.

She made her way towards row twenty-eight and noticed Theo with his eyes closed, head tilted back, earphones in. He looked adorable. She touched his shoulder gently and his eyes sprang open.

'Hi,' she said quietly, careful not to disturb any of the other passengers.

'Hi,' he said, pulling out his earbuds. His smile seemed polite. 'How are you, Maya?'

'I'm good, thanks. You?'

'All good,' he said, nodding. 'Is there something I can help you with?'

'No, no. I just wanted to come and say hi.'

'OK, hi,' he said, smiling briefly.

'Are we OK?' she asked him, aware that the passenger in the middle seat next to Theo was throwing them both irritated glances. Theo looked at her hard.

'Of course, it's good to see you again. It's always nice to see a friendly face when travelling.'

'It's just you seem a bit off with me, that's all.'

'Me off with you?' Theo said, his tone frustrated. 'Maya, you're the one who asked me for a favour, used me to get back at your ex, and then completely ghosted me once you got your use out of me. Excuse me if I don't jump for joy when I see you again.' His voice rose and Maya flushed.

'Theo, it's not that simple. I didn't mean to use you, it's just that . . .' She tailed off, wanting to explain her blog, her reason for why she had to stop herself before she broke her pact altogether. And the fact that there were at least two others tied up in this mess – Michael and Holly.

'It's just that what?' he said, looking hurt.

'It's complicated,' she whispered, aware that they now had a small audience enjoying a bit of mid-flight drama.

'How?' he said, looking at her squarely.

'Well, for one, I'm not in a position to date right now, and two, there's Holly to consider . . .' She tailed off, waiting to see his expression change, for him to admit to already being in a relationship. 'I just didn't want to be that person, you know?'

'I clearly don't,' he said heatedly, his forehead creased in frustration. 'What person?'

'A person that comes between two people. I didn't want to complicate things for you.'

'Maya, there's nothing to complicate,' he said, his voice strained. 'Holly is a friend. Her mum and my mum met when we were only toddlers, and we grew up together.' He paused. 'She also happens to have a girlfriend called Bethany. She was coming out to New York with me as a favour, to try and help me decide what I should do with the bakery business. You messaging me back wouldn't have been a problem, I assure

236

you' – he turned his face away before adding – 'but it would have been polite.'

'Oh,' was all she could think of as his words sank in. They stung, and she could feel her professional resolve beginning to crumble. 'I'm so sorry. I didn't mean to ghost you, I just didn't want to be the "other woman". I know how painful that feels,' she said, feeling tears threaten. She blinked them away and smiled at a passenger in the row behind him who was beginning to look concerned. It was not a great look for a member of the cabin crew to look upset or unprofessional. She switched on a smile and turned back to Theo, whose expression had softened. 'So, you're not attached?'

He took a moment to respond, scanning her face, but then his usual, lazy smile returned. 'Nope. I am as single as a lighthouse on a deserted island,' he joked. 'Sorry, bad cartographer joke.'

Maya smiled and the tension broke between them.

'I really am sorry,' she repeated. 'I should have messaged you back.'

'Yep, you should have,' he said, and his directness only made her feel worse, 'but I'll let you make it up to me with a drink. Tomorrow night?'

She paused, thinking about the twelve-month rule, but instinctively answered, 'Sure, I'd love that.' Out of the corner of her eye, she spotted Chloe making panicked hand gestures to her, with Nigel Edwards heading in her direction. 'Just message me, OK?'

'As long as you reply,' Theo joked and Maya left his row smiling.

At the end of the shift and when the plane touched down at JFK Airport, she realised she was still smiling. She stood at the open door with Nigel and, after most of the passengers had already exited the plane, Theo approached her.

'Thank you for flying Oasis Airlines, we hope you've had a pleasant flight,' said Nigel stiffly.

'Oh, I really have,' Theo said. 'The staff have all been incredibly helpful. I have no complaints.' Maya stifled a giggle and Nigel shot her a warning look.

237

'That's always great to hear, thank you. We appreciate all feedback, good and bad, and endeavour to improve.'

'Well, the feedback is all positive, I assure you.' He smiled at Nigel and gave Maya a quick wink as he passed her and left the plane.

'Well done, Maya,' Nigel said as they completed their post-flight briefing. 'You've really turned it around over the last few months. After a dodgy start to the new year with that passenger complaint, it's good to see you've improved with your customer service skills, and your writing skills. The company are proud of you. As am I.'

'Thank you, Nigel,' Maya said with a straight face, but she could see Chloe silently laughing behind his back. If only he knew.

Chapter Forty-Seven

Maya had arranged to meet Theo at the rooftop bar of her hotel, the Lexington Lodge, at 8pm. She felt this was a safe bet, to keep it on her home ground and she had also wrangled Chloe into coming along too, which had been a hard task as the rest of the crew had headed out together for a proper drinking session. But Maya felt that with Chloe present, then it wasn't really a date, as such, and she wouldn't be breaking her pact. But it still didn't stop her spending over an hour getting ready. She had chosen a pair of beautiful tan-coloured, palazzo trousers with a cream sheer blouse that was floaty, but also sexy. She had asked Chloe to help with her make-up, and for once, her hair had played ball and curled just as she liked it. She had matched the outfit with a pair of flat gold sandals that were both comfortable and stylish. Chloe had gone all out and was wearing a brightly coloured wrap dress that clung to her narrow hips and large bust. She hated flat shoes as much as she hated complex carbohydrates, so she was wearing giant wedge sandals, in a shade of hot pink.

As they walked through the glass doors out into the rooftop terrace, Maya scanned the bar for Theo. She found him straight away, perched on a barstool against the backdrop of the city. The Queensboro Bridge was lit up in the summer evening, and she could see the silhouette of Queens in the background. It was still humid, despite it being late, and she was glad she had chosen loose-fitting clothes.

Theo had a beer in front of him and looked so attractive, in a simple tight-fitting white T-shirt and black jeans. But his trademark scruffy hair was still messy, like he'd just rolled out of bed. That image made her flush. He spotted them both and stood up smiling and they walked towards him.

'Hello, ladies,' he said, kissing them both on the cheek and pulling out two stools for them to join him. 'What can I get you to drink?'

'A Lexington Lush, please,' Chloe said, scanning the rooftop terrace for any men worthy of her attention.

'Make that two, please,' Maya said, addressing her order to the barman who'd appeared as if from nowhere.

'So, how's the bakery business going? Have you made a decision yet?' she asked him. He sighed loudly.

'Not quite yet. There is so much involved, and probate is proving especially difficult as there are those that are contesting wishes to let me inherit it all. I'm having meetings with lawyers this week to see what the next steps are. But in the meantime, I am going to try to enjoy my time in New York as I'm here for three weeks. I need to explore it and get a feel for what it would be like to actually live here.' He took a deep breath in. 'It's such a huge decision.'

'You know what I would do?' Chloe interjected, smiling broadly at the waiter who had just placed her cocktail glass on the bar and taking a large sip.

'I genuinely don't,' Theo said. 'What would you do?'

'I would jump at the chance of starting a new life. You've been offered a chance of a successful business and a life in a city that is buzzing and alive. It's a no-brainer to me. You're not married, you have no kids that you've mentioned, I can't see what the issue is.' She shrugged in her usual, nonchalant way and took another sip. 'Fabulous cocktail, by the way.'

'You're very direct, aren't you?' Theo said, smiling.

'As direct as a flight from New York to Los Angeles. Life is too short to spend your days deliberating. Make a decision and stick to it. Don't you agree, Maya?' Chloe looked at Maya, who was staying quiet up until this point. She could tell that Chloe was bored already.

240

'I think that it's complicated. And Theo needs to do what feels right for him. No one else can make his decision for him.'

Chloe rolled her eyes and ordered another round of cocktails.

'So, what do you have planned to do over the next few weeks, to get to know the city?' Maya asked.

'Oh, loads actually. I'm going to see the Yankees play at Yankee Stadium, a visit to the Museum of Natural History, the Guggenheim Museum, explore Greenwich, Chinatown, Little Italy . . . basically eat and walk, a lot.'

'Sounds fun,' Maya said.

'Should be. Also, I want to experience New York at different times of the year. I've seen it in spring already, but it will be good to see it in the heat of summer, and autumn. I hear New York in autumn is amazing.'

'They call it the fall here, not autumn,' Chloe said, 'and yes, it is awesome.'

'Thanks for the heads-up,' he said, politely. 'Shall we grab a table?' He pointed to a recently vacated table and Maya nodded, but Chloe checked her phone.

'Actually, I'm going to head off. Andreas and the gang have managed to get access to that new bar downtown called Atlas. He says it's incredible.' She stood up and drained the dregs of her second drink. 'So why don't you two stay on here, and I'll meet up with you later, yeah?'

She didn't give Maya a chance to respond before she kissed Theo on the cheek and disappeared in the direction of the exit, leaving a haze of Chanel and vodka fumes behind her. Maya couldn't believe the audacity of her, that she would leave knowing Maya wanted her to stay. But she couldn't say anything in front of Theo, so she just grabbed her drink and headed in the direction of the small table situated under a large gazebo with trailing lights. Sitting down, she felt suddenly awkward.

'Chloe's definitely strong-willed, isn't she?' Theo asked, sitting himself down with a second beer.

'That's one word to describe her,' she said wryly. 'I prefer stubborn and opinionated.' They both laughed at this. 'But

241

she's fiercely loyal and incredibly kind, too,' Maya continued. 'I couldn't be without her.'

Theo nodded kindly but said, 'Well, no disrespect to her, but I'm glad she's gone.' He was looking at his beer glass, his fingers catching the trails of condensation that ran down the glass like mini rivers, his eyes suggestive. 'I wanted it to be just us two.'

'Oh.' That was all Maya managed, feeling herself grow even hotter. His eyes rose to meet hers.

'I really like you, Maya. More than just like you, actually. I know you said you weren't ready for a relationship, but is there any chance you'd just give me a chance? One date, that's all I'm asking.' His gaze was sincere, but sexy, and she couldn't help but stare at his soft lips as he ran his tongue over them out of nervousness.

'Theo, I really want to . . .' she began, and his face lit up, 'but I just can't. It's complicated.'

'Complicated how?' he asked.

'Complicated in that I swore I wouldn't date again for a year. I said to myself that I'd give being single a chance. So, if I date you, and believe me, I want to, then I would be breaking that pact.'

Theo didn't speak for a moment, taking her words in. 'A whole year? When did you make this pact?' he asked.

'Christmas Day, last year,' she said sadly.

'So, you would turn down the chance of happiness just because you made yourself a deal when you had only just had your heart broken?' he looked confused, like he couldn't make sense of it, which, Maya realised, was understandable. It did all sound a bit crazy. But she nodded anyway. 'But who would know, other than yourself? Just break the pact,' he declared, giving her a sexy, suggestive wink.

'It's not as simple as that,' she replied, laughing at him, but feeling her body respond.

'Why?'

'It just isn't.' She was frustrated. She wanted him. But she wanted to be loyal to her blog. But at this moment in time, watching his fingers circle the cool, sweating glass, she found it hard to even think about anything else. But she had to. She had committed to both the blog and the agreement with Oasis Airlines. She had to keep writing, and in doing so, she had to remain single. She felt disloyal for even being here with him right now, having thoughts about him that would definitely not agree with her single status. Her blog was still anonymous, and she wanted it to remain that way. Theo leant back in his chair, scanning her face, trying to figure her out.

'You are one complex woman, Maya,' he said, taking a large gulp of his beer. She sighed.

'I know. But I do really like you,' she said quietly.

'Well, that's a start, I guess,' he said wryly. 'Another drink?'

'Sure, why not?' she said, and passed over her now empty glass, their hands touching. It took all her resolve to stay rooted to her seat. She could see by his dilated pupils that he had felt it too. But the moment broke as she let go and busied herself with a tendril of hair that had come loose. He smiled and turned towards the bar, and despite her best intentions, she couldn't help but observe just how great his bum looked in those jeans and how hard it was going to be to keep to this pact.

An hour later and another cocktail down, Maya was feeling much more relaxed. More than she'd felt in a long time, she realised. As the sun had gone down, so had the tension in her shoulders. Theo was easy-going and the conversation flowed.

'So, are you still doing your monthly challenges?' he asked her. 'Any crazy antics other than Regency balls and baking lessons at New York bakeries?'

Maya laughed. 'I am, but lower key this time. Just a bit of forestry fun on a Segway.'

He raised his eyebrows admirably. 'So, what's next? What's this month's challenge?'

'I actually don't have one yet. Any suggestions?'

'None that come to mind . . .' he began, his face screwed up in mock thought. 'But if I think of anything, I'll let you know.'

'I look forward to it,' she said, flirtatiously, without thought. She was finding it harder to resist him as the evening went on. At that moment her phone rang, which broke the building tension between them. It was Chloe.

'Hi Maya, are you coming downtown to join us? This place is awesome.' She was shouting above the loud, bass music pumping in the background. Maya sighed; she really didn't fancy it. She looked across at Theo who was trying not to listen in. He looked so sexy. Maybe it was best she cut the evening short with him before she did something she would regret.

'Sure. I'm on my way.' She heard Chloe squeal and shout back to the others that Maya was coming, and she hung up the phone.

'I have to go.'

'Sure,' he said easily, smiling and downing the rest of his drink. 'Let me walk you to a taxi.'

'Thanks,' Maya said, finishing her own drink in a few large gulps. As they entered the lift together, they rode down in silence, the hot, sticky atmosphere only heightening the sexual tension. She really had to resist pressing the button for her hotel room floor and cancelling any further plans. But she didn't and before she knew it, they had stepped out of the hotel and onto the sidewalk, where there was an abundance of waiting taxis. Theo walked to the nearest one and pulled open the door for her.

'Thanks for tonight,' he said, looking intently at her. 'I've had a great time.'

'Me too,' she whispered, not daring to speak as her legs were starting to tremble a little. She paused, wanting to hold his gaze just for a moment, to soak up his smell, his face, his whole body, and as she did so, he leant in suddenly and kissed her. The kiss was warm, gentle, slightly open-mouthed but not probing – just perfect. He pulled back after only a moment, and she felt her cheeks were hot to the touch. She noticed he looked rattled too. He was still holding the taxi door open for her and they were a few steps apart, but Maya felt like an invisible thread was drawing her to him. Every cell in her body wanted to kiss him again, to step forward and grab his T-shirt and pull him towards her, and her body was aching for his touch. Her skin prickled, and her blood coursed through her veins, the rhythmic pulsing audible only to her.

They both jumped as the taxi driver yelled back at them, his palm pressing angrily on his steering wheel horn. 'Are we goin' anywhere this evening, folks? I don't get paid for sitting stationary, y'know.'

'I'd better go,' Maya said reluctantly, taking a step forward to climb into the taxi.

'Absolutely,' Theo said, his voice husky and full of desire. She climbed in and he closed the door, still staring at her.

'Atlas Bar, East Thirty-Seventh Street, please.'

'Sure thing.' The taxi driver pulled away from the kerb and away from Theo. Maya didn't look back. She didn't trust herself. She knew if she did, she would find herself jumping out of the cab and into Theo's arms. With her lips still tingling, she whizzed across town knowing that things were about to get a lot more complicated.

Chapter Forty-Eight

The next day, Maya was with the rest of the crew eating breakfast in the hotel restaurant. Most of them were hungover, some were still drunk, and she appeared to be the only one both alert and fully sober. She had barely slept, yet she didn't feel tired, and she wanted to get out and clear her still-buzzing head. She knew she should write, she hadn't written a blog post in over a week, but she couldn't formulate the words. Not without admitting that she was coming dangerously close to abandoning the blog altogether, if it wasn't for her contract with Oasis Airlines. The crew weren't all due to fly home until tomorrow morning, so she knew she had a whole day to herself while the rest nursed their hangovers and slept most of day, so she finished her coffee and made her excuses to leave. Chloe hadn't even surfaced from her room yet.

Stepping out into the morning sunshine, she was surprised to hear her phone chime with a message so early on. It was the middle of the night still in the UK. She pulled out her phone from one of the pockets of her sundress and her pulse quickened when she saw it was from Theo.

> *Challenge accepted. Meet me at the entrance to Central Park, corner of East 59th Street. Grand Army Plaza at 11am.*
> *Allow yourself five hours. Bring a sunhat and a large bottle of water. Wear sun lotion. All will be revealed . . .*

'What the . . .?' Maya said aloud to the busy street. Images of last night had been consistently rolling through her mind like a camera roll but hearing from him again so soon made the images go from slightly blurry to crystal clear. She realised she wanted to see him again. Sooner rather than later, too. She replied,

I'll see you there.

As she approached the Grand Army Plaza entrance to Central Park, she spotted Theo straight away. He was standing beneath the golden Sherman Monument, trying not to get knocked by the hordes of tourists swarming around him, all clearly desperate to find some shade from the oppressive summer heat. He was wearing smart linen pale blue shorts, a white T-shirt, dark aviator sunglasses and on his head was the baseball cap that he seemed to adore.

'Hi there,' he said, a genuine smile on his face. He kissed her gently on the cheek. 'Are you ready for your next challenge?'

'It depends what it is,' she said. 'I'm a little nervous.'

'There is absolutely nothing to be nervous about. You're going to enjoy this,' he said, reaching out his hand to lead her further into the park. She took it and a little shiver ran up her arm. It felt nice, holding hands with him. They headed towards what Theo told her was the Thomas Moore Statue. Walking under the large canopy of branches offered some cooling relief and Maya looked around at the pockets of people gathered on blankets, all hiding from the midday heat. Theo was looking ahead at the monument, clearly searching for someone. His face lit up and he said, 'That must be him, he looks just like his profile picture.'

And he pulled Maya gently in the direction of a tall man, with wispy white hair and limbs that looked far too long for his body. He was wearing all white, with a crisp linen shirt, matching trousers and around his neck was a vibrant yellow cravat. As they got closer, Maya could see he was standing on a large rock and there were a group of people, of varying ages, all looking up at him excitedly.

'Edmund Eddison?' Theo called out, and the man in question looked down at them both. Maya noticed his huge, bushy eyebrows that almost covered his eyes completely. He nodded briskly. 'I'm Theo, and this is Maya. We're enrolled on today's course.'

Edmund said nothing in return, but let his steely gaze run up and down them both slowly, taking in their outfits. Maya felt scrutinised, but they were clearly deemed acceptable as his face broke into a friendly smile and he said loudly, 'Welcome, both of you, to the Eddison Art School of Excellence.' He fanned out one of his extra-long arms and gestured to the whole group, standing like a starfish. 'Now we are all here, we can begin today's watercolour class. If you could all follow me for the short walk to our proposed location at Gapstow Bridge.'

The group of amateur artists all excitedly gathered their bags and belongings and followed him north. Maya and Theo remained at the back, trailing behind some ancient, eccentric man wearing a three-piece suit and bowler hat, despite the heat, and a large woman whose long, greying hair was in a beautiful updo, but was held in place by actual paintbrushes. Maya noticed her dress was patterned with paintbrushes too. She looked to her left and spotted the pleasing sight of The Pond in the distance, the twinkling, azure blue water looking glorious in the sunshine.

'We're attending a painting class?' she said to Theo, who was walking beside her, still holding her hand.

'Not just any painting class,' he exclaimed excitedly. 'Edmund Eddison's painting class! Do you know how hard it is to get a class with the painter himself? We were so lucky to get these spots, with next to no notice.'

'Theo, I can't paint,' she said bluntly, deciding honesty was the best policy here. 'Like, at all. I can barely colour in a dot-to-dot picture.'

'Well, this will be the perfect opportunity to learn then.' He seemed unperturbed by her obvious reluctance, not slowing his pace.

'I have no equipment, no pencils or paintbrushes,' she continued.

'All provided,' he said, giving her a side wink and squeezing her hand. 'Don't worry, this'll be fun.'

Maya wasn't convinced. But she didn't say anything else, she didn't want to come across as ungrateful. He'd obviously gone to a lot of trouble organising it since they talked last night. The group turned a corner on the path, and she found herself staring at a beautiful stone bridge that looked like something from a movie, its shallow arch hovering just above the water, connecting one side of Central Park to another. In front of her, Edmund had stopped beside a group of wooden easels, with crisp, white paper already in place and a collection of paints adorning each easel. Beneath each easel was a folding chair, lying on the lush grass.

'Here we are. Choose an easel of your liking and get comfortable.' He gestured again with arms and legs astride, like a starfish, a pose that he clearly liked standing in, she noted.

'You will each have five hours to sketch the view before you, with a one-hour break for lunch. I suggest a pencil outline to begin with, and then I recommend the full use of your watercolours provided. I want to see shadowing, grading, and blending of your paints. Do not be shy in unifying them, what you think might not work could come together in a beautiful hue that accentuates your painting. I will be on hand to help with any queries and suggestions.' He looked at his watch. 'And begin.' At this command, he took a grand bow and Maya couldn't help but stifle a laugh. He belonged on a stage, this one. But his eccentricity was infectious, and she decided to give this her best shot.

'I don't know where to start,' she whispered to Theo as they chose easels next to one another.

'Work from the bridge out,' he whispered back, picking up a pencil and drawing a line across his page. Maya followed suit, picking up her pencil and placing the point onto the centre of her white paper. She took a deep breath in and closed her eyes. Opening them again, she looked ahead at the view and drew her first line. It felt good.

Chapter Forty-Nine

Six hours later, Maya felt sweaty, slightly sunburnt, and her arm was aching from consistently raising it to make brushstrokes. But she also felt incredibly proud. What she had produced on paper actually bore a passing resemblance to the view in front of her. Not a mirror image in any way, or something that anyone would describe as 'worthy of talent' but she still felt proud. She looked across at Theo's painting and couldn't believe how good he was. His painting resembled a Constable for its detail, with his use of colours matching the blend of greens and blues to perfection. Even Edmund had been complimentary, stopping at Theo's easel repeatedly throughout the day to give him hints and tips.

'Please, everyone. Put down your paintbrushes and take a step back from your easel. We will now collectively assess each other's work.' Maya felt like a contestant on *The Great British Bake Off*, standing in a line with the other contestants, waiting to have her work judged, except there were no sugary treats on offer. Just polite criticism. And Edmund wasn't Mary Berry sweet either, he was harsh, scathing at times, but she agreed with everything he said. She even walked away from his feedback with tips for how to improve and found herself wanting to pick up her paintbrushes and start again.

As the rest of the class rolled up their pieces of parchment and popped them inside the cardboard tubes, Theo asked her, 'So, did you enjoy your challenge, then?'

'Actually, I did! I haven't drawn anything since school, but I forgot how relaxing it can be. Thanks for organising it.'

'My total pleasure,' he said, smiling, his tanned arms flexing as he rolled up his own parchment paper, 'I took art classes when I was at university and stumbled on Edmund's work. He massively influenced me back then, and I've been painting on and off since. I found out earlier this month that he was offering classes in Central Park, and so when you mentioned you needed a challenge, I looked him up. Turns out he'd had two cancellations only this week for today's class. It was like it was meant to be.' He looked so animated that she instinctively wanted to kiss him.

'Definitely meant to be,' she said. But she found she wasn't just referring to today's challenge. 'Do you want to grab a drink? I'm feeling really dehydrated.'

'Sure. Let me just thank Edmund for a great class.' He headed off to speak to Edmund and Maya quickly took a photo of her own painting and uploaded it to her blog. She tapped out a blog post and pressed upload.

Day 230
Challenge No. 8 accepted and completed. (See below photo)
Painting lesson 101 – with the esteemed Edmund Eddison, no less. In Central Park too. I can't take the credit for this one, it came organised by a friend of mine and was a bit of a surprise. I thought my art skills resembled those of a pre-schooler, it seems there might be more to my hidden talents than I initially thought. I can paint! Who would have thunk it? I will add it to my ever-growing resumé of talents of rock climbing, glass blowing and bush diving (this last one is less of a talent, more of a clumsy, can't-walk-in-a-straight-line kind of gift).

Seriously though, I feel proud of this one. It's no Constable, don't get me wrong, but it's not so horrific that I have to pass it off as deliberate abstract art. I did good. And I definitely don't say that often enough. I did good. And if I hadn't tried it, I would never have known. And I was definitely inspired by my surroundings. Central Park is just beautiful. What you see in the movies actually does match up to the real thing. The lakes, the pathways, Belvedere Castle, it's all food for the soul. I feel like Central Park has breathed a bit of life back into me,

without me knowing how much I needed it. Because of this,
I'm thinking that with my remaining challenges I should aim
to see the world. I travel all the time, but rarely do I travel
alone. I didn't think myself capable of it. But why? If I have
survived the last two-thirds of a year, then I can survive travel-
ling solo. Perhaps that could be the next blog theme! Travel!
A hike up a volcano, a sleepover at an ice hotel, the sky's the
limit! (Except skydiving, that one has already been vetoed . . .)

'Shall we get that drink then?' Theo had appeared back by
her side, and she nodded, rolling her parchment paper into a
scroll, and popping it into her own tube.

'Where do you suggest?'

'I have no idea! Shall we just walk and see?'

'Sure, sounds good.'

They made their way back the way they had come, through
Central Park and towards the Grand Army Plaza Entrance, then
out onto the corner of Fifth Avenue and East 60th Street. As
they approached the busyness of Manhattan, the change from
birdsong and general park pleasantness to horns blaring and
people shouting was perceptible, and Maya noticed a shift in
her own walking. Any calmness from her day was seeping
out of her like melting paint and she just wanted to be somewhere cool and quiet. Theo saw a sports bar and pointed at it.
Maya was just grateful to step off the busy sidewalk and into
a hopefully air-conditioned building. Which was lucky really,
as Theo's choice of bar turned out to be a bit of a dive.

It was occupied by only five other people, and they looked
as grim as the wallpaper and sticky floor. There were small
TVs angled above the long bar sporadically, with some sports
or news channel and the atmosphere was dire. Even the two
bartenders were silent, one reading a newspaper and the other
with earbuds evident.

'Do you want to look elsewhere?' Theo whispered as they
stood by the entrance, the bright sunlight blocked out by the dark,
heavy door. But Maya felt so thirsty that she shook her head.

'This looks fine,' she said, knowing full well it didn't. 'It'll do for one drink, anyway.' Theo didn't seem convinced but followed her silently to the bar. They both hopped up onto barstools and Theo tried to catch the attention of one of the bartenders by clearing his throat. Neither even looked over in their direction, so he tried again, louder. The one closest to them, the one reading his paper, actually rolled his eyes, threw his paper down onto the sticky bar top and walked over to them. He was in his mid-fifties, bald and his left hand was covered in tattoos.

'Yeah?'

'Can I get a glass of white wine and a bottle of your finest beer, please?' Theo asked, attempting banter. The bartender neither smiled nor answered back, but simply grunted and moved away from them to, Maya assumed, make their drinks. He was surprisingly quick though and only a moment later, he plonked their drinks down onto stained bar mats.

'Thank you,' she said, taking a sip of her wine. It was warm. She looked over at Theo, who was wincing after taking a sip of his beer. She stifled a giggle. She tried to distract him. 'So, would you move out here permanently if you decide to take on the bakery or will you distance manage from back in England?'

'It would be impossible to manage from afar. I'd have to move out here. The current temporary manager, you've met before, is my cousin Dave Myrrh. He works easily fifty-hour weeks and is in the bakery more than he is at home. There's no way I could not be there if I really want to make a success of it.'

'What about Dave though? Will you effectively take away his job?'

At this, Theo removed his baseball cap and brushed his fingers through his messy hair, making it stand on end. 'Ideally, I'd like him to stay on and remain as active manager, while I get my head around things. But then he's told me he only stepped in as a favour and has plans to travel. He says he'll stay, but he might only be saying that as he is the nicest chap ever.' He sighed, took another large gulp, and winced again.

'This really is disgusting.' Maya laughed and pushed her wine glass away from her, noticing the rim of her glass was dirty. Her stomach squirmed a little. She looked up at the television screen above them and noticed it was on some news channel called *NYN, New York News*. The screen was on mute, but her eyes were drawn to the rolling news ticker along the bottom of the screen, highlighting the day's entertainment news. She gasped as she saw a familiar name flash across the screen in vivid blue and white. It read,

★UK's Amanda Avary steps into New York role★

'What's wrong? Is the wine that bad?' Theo hissed, following her gaze to the television screen. The three presenters were muted but animatedly chatting and there was a large headshot of Amanda Avary in the background with the words *NYN Welcomes New Presenter*. 'Oh, I see,' he said quietly, his face filled with compassion. They both continued watching in silence, Maya feeling more nauseous as the seconds ticked by. Amanda Avary was moving to New York, which meant Michael would no doubt be moving with her. Would she ever be rid of them, or was life going to keep throwing up rude reminders every time she tried to move on?

'Do you mind if we leave?' she said, downing the rest of her glass without thought and immediately regretting it as the contents wanted to return up her oesophagus and spurt out all over the bar.

'Sure,' he said, wisely choosing to just push his glass away without finishing it. 'Let's go.'

As they stepped back out into the bright sunlight and onto the busy sidewalk, Maya felt suddenly sad. What had been a wonderful day with Theo now felt tainted. She wanted to go back to her hotel room and lie down.

'I think I'm just going to make a move if that's OK?'

'Of course,' he said, placing a hand on her shoulder. 'Do you want me to walk you back to the hotel?'

'No, no,' she said. 'I'm fine.' She smiled at him, but as she did so, a large bus pulled alongside him and she found herself staring at a poster on the side of the bus with the image of Amanda's huge, perfectly aligned and no doubt cosmetically enhanced face. Maya leant forward and kissed him gently on the cheek before turning around and walking away from him. She wondered if she would ever be able to move on from Michael and his cheating ways. All thoughts of romance towards Theo were forgotten as she trod the hot, dusty sidewalk in the direction of the hotel. She pulled out her phone from her skirt pocket and dialled Chloe, who answered on the second ring, sounding sleepy.

'Michael is moving here, to New York,' she said. And then she burst into tears.

Chapter Fifty

It turns out she wasn't wrong. By the time she'd flown back to England and broken her rule of switching on the NSW News Channel, there was a noticeable shake up of presenters. Gone were Amanda Avary and Michael and in their places were two presenters that she didn't recognise. Was that why Michael had texted last month? Was he going to tell her he was leaving the country? Should she have met him for that drink after all?

She hadn't seen Theo again before leaving New York, and knew he was staying out there for a few more weeks, but her flying schedule wouldn't be sending her back there until the end of the month. Her mind kept tormenting her with *that* kiss, the feel of his hand in hers and wanting more. Her mind kept juxtaposing the two men; her past with Michael and her potential future with Theo. What did she actually want? Her head hurt with it all. So, she decided to do what felt right, she decided to ignore it all and focus on what was important, her writing, her challenges, and her friends. She switched off the television, took herself into the kitchen and plonked herself down in front of her laptop. Time to write.

Day 252
As we head into the month of September, I find it hard to believe that I am almost three-quarters of my way through my challenges. They've been enjoyable, surprising, frightening, stressful at times, but above all, really enlightening. Who would have thought it? I've decided to highlight here what I feel they have taught me so far:

- *I still hate heights. No bungee jumping or plane walking for me.*
- *Sharks are beautiful, with eyes that are reflections of their soul. But still terrify me.*
- *Baking gluten-free can actually taste great, it just takes practice. Being a coeliac does not need to hinder me or make me feel inferior.*
- *I love a good ol' fashion parade and think a lot of this country's problems could be solved if everyone just kicked up their heels once in a while and held a big, musical, all singing all dancing parade.*
- *Painting is therapeutic but paint is a nightmare to get out from both your cuticles and hair.*
- *Being only 5'3", wearing floor-length gowns will never be a good choice.*
- *Hedges or bushes are not my friends.*
- *Wearing a bracelet that you actually made by hand in an actual cave is hugely empowering. And personal. Totally recommend it.*
- *My stomach muscles are far too inferior for the regular use of a Segway. I ached for a week afterwards.*
- *Opinions can change.*
- *People are surprising.*

I am going to spend the afternoon searching the internet to see what my next challenge will be. All I know is, is that it needs to be a break from the norm.

I found out this week that my ex has moved away. Like far, far away. Thousands of miles in fact. So, I don't need to worry about bumping into him at the supermarket or catching glimpses of him in the street. It's a good thing, he's now out of my life for good, right?

Then why do I feel so sad? Shouldn't I be feeling like this is the perfect opportunity to move on? And just suppose I had happened to find a really great guy, why do I feel the need to push him away? Urgh, if you've come to this blog in hope of *inspiration or great advice today, then I'm afraid you're not going to find it. I'm a gal in need of guidance! Advice welcome!*

She uploaded the blog and took some time to read through the comments and messages. Her likes were in the thousands now, and the comments easily in their hundreds. Before she knew it, an hour had passed with her scanning through them all. She then moved onto her messages. Most of them were spam, or to be ignored, but she noticed two that proved really interesting. One was from a local radio station, stating they had seen her blog and would love to interview her on air to discuss her blog and her Rule of Singledom. They offered to keep her anonymous and were offering a small fee for the interview. The second was even more exciting. It was from a mainstream tabloid magazine, called *The Write Way*. It read,

> *Dear Flying Solo,*
> *We have been following you for a while now and found both your blog and your adventures fascinating. Everyone gets dumped, but not everyone decides to use it as an opportunity like you have! We love your writing style, your wit, and your ability to personally reach out to your audience. Based on this, we wondered if you would be interested in being part of a feature for our magazine? We understand you want anonymity, which we would respect, but we could tie it in with Oasis Airlines and work alongside their marketing team. We hope that you would consider working with us. Please see below for our competitive rates of pay.*
> *We look forward to hopefully hearing from you soon.*

Maya sat back in her wooden chair, exhaling loudly, causing Matilda's ears to poke up from her curled position nestled beside the Aga. A magazine article and radio interview? Just from her silly old blog? She couldn't quite believe it.

Aunt Sophia walked in from outside, through the back door, her arms full of freshly laid eggs. 'Morning, Maya Moo. Omelette for breakfast?' she said, holding up the large tray, feathers sticking out of her cardigan and hair at all angles.

'Sure. But first, what do you think of this?' She pointed at her laptop and Aunt Sophia dumped the tray onto the worktop and walked toward, leaning over Maya's shoulder to scan the messages. As she took in the information, she whistled through the small gap in her front teeth.

'Wowee, girl. That is exciting! Do you want to do it?'

'I don't know. Do you think I should?'

Aunt Sophia pulled out a chair and sat down, resting her head in her hands.

'Well, the way I look at it, what have you got to lose? They both said they would keep it anonymous, so you won't get found out, and it may even offer up more writing opportunities. What is it your mum always used to say?' she asked, one eyebrow raised.

Maya smiled, 'She always said, "*opportunities are like snowflakes, each one unique. But you have to catch them while you can.*"'

'Well, it looks like you just found some fresh snow,' Aunt Sophia replied, smiling back.

Chapter Fifty-One

The radio interview proved to be both fascinating and terrifying in equal measure. She had been ushered in like some sort of celebrity, along with a representative from Oasis Airlines, and placed in a soundproof room with a huge microphone and an equally huge cup of coffee. The radio presenter, a woman in her late forties called Emma, had been welcoming and approachable, respecting Maya's decision to keep her anonymity, and referring to her only as *our talented guest*.

Surprisingly, Maya found it easy to talk once she relaxed and began to trust the presenter. She talked about her passion for writing, her desire to remain positive, and made light of the challenges so far, having the presenter in stitches at times. She loved it. The whole thing lasted just an hour and she was back home with promises that it would air later that week.

The magazine article seemed even easier. They only wanted a few quotes from her and permission to quote some extracts of her blog and the rest was left to the editor in charge. But Maya did get to see a proof of it before it went to print, and she was delighted. Not only did they keep her anonymous, but they also made her sound confident, brave, and empowered, which were not words she would use to describe herself on a daily basis.

Both the interview and the article came out in the last week of September, which was extremely exciting and as she walked through the airport on her way to departures on the last day of the month, she stopped at WHSmith to buy herself a copy of that week's *The Write Way*. Leafing excitedly through the pages, she found the article on page twenty-eight. It was a whole page spread, titled *Flying Solo* and while there wasn't a photo of her, or any indication as to her identity, she squealed a little and wanted to shout out to the weary passengers passing her that *she* was in a nationwide magazine. Seeing her words in print was surreal, but amazing. Her interview had also gone down a storm, with the comments and followers on her blog page almost doubling overnight. It all felt a bit overwhelming.

Which was why she was almost relieved that she was heading out of the country with work and that her September challenge was remote, quiet and, much like the end result of the task itself, giving her a much-needed chance to breathe.

An hour later and Maya was boarding her flight to Genoa airport, for a one-night stopover in Italy. Chloe was already in San Francisco on a two-night stopover, but Maya had been so pleased when she'd received the rota to see that she was flying with Andreas today. He was always a huge amount of fun. And when she'd suggested he help her with her next challenge, he'd jumped at the chance. They were on a night flight, which meant they had a whole day and night in Italy, before returning home the following morning, and Maya had arranged it all. Andreas was already onboard and almost skipped down the aisle towards her.

'My feet are tingling at the thought!' Andreas exclaimed excitedly, as Maya placed her holdall into one of the overhead compartments. 'And I even had a pedicure this morning, to make sure my toes are in tip-top condition for it.'

'You do realise that your feet are going to be in a right old mess after it though, don't you?' Maya asked, as she headed towards the galley to lock the containers in place. He followed her and began switching on the coffee machines.

'It's not about how you finish things, it's about your attitude when starting. And my attitude is that if you look brilliant, you'll do the job brilliantly.' He spoke with such conviction that Maya turned to look at him. With his perfectly coiffed black hair, manicured eyebrows and clearly exfoliated face, she knew that styling was key to his daily routine. She instinctively raised a hand to her own uncared-for, bushy eyebrows and her short, bitten-down nails. Even her last haircut had now grown out and returned to its usual, frizzy curls once again. Thankfully the airline uniform ensured she changed out of her leggings every so often, otherwise she would live in oversized T-shirts and fluffy socks.

'I'm sure you'll be the best dressed there,' she said, squeezing his arm and heading towards the cockpit to check on the pilots, 'but for now, we've got work to do.'

The flight had been brief, with no hiccups or issues and after a one-hour bus trip to Portofino, and a five-hour nap in her hotel room, she stood waiting at a bus stop along with Andreas for their minibus to collect them. Andreas was yawning loudly, and Maya heard his stomach growl.

'Are you sure we don't even have time for breakfast? I love the Italian hotel buffets!' he moaned, rubbing his soft tummy. Despite his love of the beauty parlour, his love of food tended to overrule anything else. He had a little potbelly that he tried to hide under waistcoats and jackets, and he couldn't pull off skinny jeans, but Maya loved him all the more for it. There was something so endearing about him, and Maya felt he gave the greatest hugs. This morning he was wearing dark blue linen shorts and an olive-green polo shirt that was stretched over his stomach.

'No time, I'm afraid, the email was very specific. We needed to meet here at 9.15am so that we have time to get there for 10am. It's going to be a busy day. But here you go . . .' She dug into her backpack and pulled out a large chocolate bar that she picked up in duty free earlier. 'Open this. That should keep you going for a while. You're going to need all the energy you can get.'

Andreas didn't need telling twice. He ripped into the foil packaging and snapped off a whole row.

'Thanks, doll.'

The minibus rolled up and they climbed aboard, sitting themselves together among an almost full bus. Most of the occupants were young adults, their bronzed skin and worn clothes indicating they were most probably on gap years. Maya felt like the oldest one there in her red polka-dot tea dress and bright white trainers which, on reflection Maya realised, might have been a huge mistake.

As they made their way through the Italian countryside, Maya couldn't help but take in the beauty around her. Despite the already building heat in the minibus, she felt excited. Italy was one of her favourite countries to visit, but she hadn't ventured further than the cities before this. This challenge was going to be tiring but seeing the row upon row of olive trees and orchards whizzing past, she was really glad she had chosen it. Andreas dozed for the journey, and she used it as an opportunity to check her blog page. She had updated her blog with links to both the article and the radio show before she flew and was thrilled to see such positive feedback already. Her words were reaching people.

The minibus took a sharp right onto a dust track, and they passed row upon row of vines, neatly lining the fields like green lines on yellowing exercise paper that seemed to go on forever. After what seemed like an age, two huge barns came into view, their stone walls dusty yellow, and there were a group of people waiting just outside the entrance to one of the barns. As the minibus slowed, it pulled up alongside a sign with the name La Vendemmia Vigneto scrawled on it. Nudging Andreas, they climbed out of the minibus into the dry heat of the morning to be met by a tall, stocky, middle-aged man wearing denim dungarees.

'*Ciao* and *benvenuto* to you all,' he said with a strong Italian accent. 'Welcome to La Vendemmia Vigneto, *The Harvest Vineyard*. My name is Mattia, and we are excited to have you all join us here today for this monumental event. Our entire calendar year builds up to this one event and we hope you find the event as rewarding and fascinating as we do. Please follow me inside the barn and we'll show you what we do here.'

The twenty or so crowd followed Mattia and his co-workers into the welcome cool and darkness of the first barn where, once her eyes had adjusted, Maya took in the sight of four deep, circular, large paddling pool-sized wooden tubs that were waist height, the wood stained a deep red.

'Today, you will be participating in our two barns, across eight tubs, in the art of pigéage, or as you might know it better, in grape-stomping. This method of grape-pressing is thousands of years old and is actually a softer, more controlled way of ensuring the grapes are squeezed, rather than crushed.' He went on to explain the reasons for the methods involved, but Maya was barely listening, she was looking over at Andreas who was like a kid in a sweet shop, stroking his fingers across the many, many bottles that lined the walls behind them. She stared up close and some of the dusty labels read as far back as the early 1920s. There were barrels and bottles everywhere and the smell was strong with fruity, woody aromas and the air felt thick with fermenting grapes. It was almost enough to make her feel light-headed.

'There are some that believe that this process of using our feet is unhygienic, but I can tell you that that is a myth. All bacteria or potential dirt are removed in the fermenting technique so please don't worry.' He gestured to the three other colleagues surrounding him. 'Now, my colleagues here will separate you into groups and we will break for lunch, which will consist of typical Italian salad, all grown on our farm, and, of course, our own beautifully produced wine. Enjoy!'

He moved aside and the group were separated into sets of four and taken to a tub, where they were asked to remove their shoes and socks and roll up any clothes that may touch the grapes or get stained. Maya's group consisted of her, Andreas, and two backpacking boys that looked extremely hungover and with such dirty feet that Maya wondered how powerful the fermenting process was to eliminate that sort of filth. Thankfully, she was asked to get in first, with Andreas. Mattia was their guide and with the use of a small stepladder, he helped her climb into the huge tub. She felt odd standing there, in an empty tub and she wriggled her toes in anticipation. Andreas climbed in next and they both giggled, him standing opposite her, waiting. One by one, Mattia began pouring in large barrels of huge, green grapes that looked fit to burst. As Maya took her first step onto the grapes, there was a large squelching sound that made everyone standing around the tub laugh. It sounded rude, slightly disgusting and it echoed around the cavernous barn. Cold fruity flesh seeped between her toes and as she continued slowly pressing down, she found it extremely satisfying. The coolness was refreshing against the muggy heat in the barn and as more grapes were poured in, the cool liquid began to gather at the bottom.

Andreas was in his element, with his heavier frame more efficient in pressing the grapes and squeezing the juice out of them, their skins tearing easily under his weight. They both started off slowly, taking tentative steps as they found their balance as best they could with the lack of a solid base, but as they continued walking around in a circular motion, they got more confident. Grape juice was beginning to spread up her legs and she pulled the hem of her dress up, just in case. It felt both cooling and disgusting. Andreas was clearly loving it by the way he was squealing with each step, his face full of childish delight. But it was also exhausting. Before long, Maya found herself sweating and puffed out; it was like wading through jam. Her legs grew tired and before long it was suggested they swap with the two backpackers, who jumped in without the need for the stepladder.

'How much fun is this?' Maya said to Andreas as they were handed towels to wipe down their sticky, sopping legs.

'So much fun! You are just full of surprises, Maya. I wouldn't have you pegged for getting down and dirty. I mean, could you imagine Chloe doing this?' They both laughed at the image. Chloe would have hated having her perfect pedicured feet and freshly waxed and spray-tanned legs subjected to such sugary mess.

'I wouldn't have done it this time last year, but I would have been missing out. This is great fun.' And it was. She remembered to take a photo of the barn quickly to upload to her blog.

They all stopped for lunch before continuing with their stomping. Sitting in the Italian sunshine, eating a plate of fresh salad, mixed with plump olives and the sweetest sun-dried tomatoes with an array of cheeses so large, Maya was sure she could hear the table groaning under the weight, was just sublime and washing it down with some cooling, crisp white wine was perfection. Andreas was sat beside her, slathering the crustiest bread with salted butter and slicing large chunks of cheese.

'Maya, you can ask me to join you on any of your adventures if they include food and wine. I'm game,' he said, ploughing the bread straight into his open mouth. 'I need to find myself an Italian farmer. I'd be happy forever.' She laughed at this. 'And what about you? Any developments with that hunky mapmaker of yours? The one with the fabulous hair?'

'Theo,' she said. 'Yes and no. He kissed me,' at which point she held up her hands to calm him. 'But it isn't going anywhere.'

'And why is that?' He lowered his voice into a horrified mock whisper. 'Is he a terrible kisser?'

'The opposite, actually.' She blushed at the memory. 'It was amazing. It's just that I'm not ready.'

Andreas put down his huge slice of bread and sighed. 'Darling girl. Michael has right royally screwed you over, hasn't he? Don't let him ruin future opportunities of finding love for you because he acted like a complete ass. I get it, your confidence has been knocked, but you can't continue being heartbroken forever. He is definitely not worth that.' He picked up his bread again, speech clearly over, and took another bite.

'I know, you're right,' she said quietly. She just needed to convince her broken, confused heart to believe him.

Chapter Fifty-Two

The afternoon grew hotter, and the work became harder as they continued with their grape-stomping. They had both almost finished their latest turn in the tub with a fresh batch of grapes, with Maya's feet becoming tired. Even Andreas had slowed his pace, focusing his efforts of treading down deep for the maximum effect and they had worked out that balancing was easier if they joined hands, facing one another. They were almost done, when Maya heard a huge crash in front of her, towards the back of the barn and she looked up in surprise. Andreas swirled round at the commotion too, but his feet must have slipped on the slimy, wet base and he fell backwards, in comical slow motion towards the squelchy mush. However, because they were still holding hands, he took her down with him. Falling head first into a mushy mess of green slush was awful. It went up her nose and, in her mouth, and she was hit in the side of the head by Andreas flailing his arms around to try and stand up. There was no sound, it was like her head was stuck in a balloon. Suddenly, she felt two strong arms wrap around her waist and pull her upright and she grabbed onto those arms, her eyes gloopy and blurred.

'Are you OK?' Mattia was looking at her worriedly, and her first instinct was to burst into laughter. She felt disgusting, with grape segments dripping off her face and chin, but as she glanced across at Andreas, who was equally slime-covered and resembled some sort of giant, slippery monster, she couldn't help but find the whole situation hilarious. Her tea dress was stuck to her, and her curls were dripping green sludge, but it was Andreas who looked worse. His face was screwed up in disgust and he was spitting out pips and grape flesh, his whole face green. Maya noticed his front tooth was covered in grape skin, making him appear like he was missing said tooth. His normally perfectly styled hair was flopped forward into his eyes, and he was looking aghast at his clothes.

'I'm absolutely fine,' she laughed. 'Are you OK, Andreas?' He looked up at her as if noticing her for the first time and his eyes widened. A second later he, too, burst into laughter and before they knew it, they were leaning on each other, laughing so hard that they could barely stand.

'Darling, we're totally sloshed,' he said, as he dripped grape juice from his body, nodding at Mattia's outstretched hand offering help. He waded over to the stepladder and began the difficult task of climbing out, his body weighed down by his wet clothes. Maya followed suit; her dress stuck to her legs as she climbed out. The rest of the barn had stopped to watch the commotion and a young Italian man stepped forward with a wad of towels for them. He smiled shyly at them both, his eyes hovering just a fraction longer over Andreas.

'Tommaso, show them to the washrooms. *Rapidamente!*' Mattia bellowed, and the Italian man nodded curtly, gesturing for them to follow him. Andreas clocked Tommaso and his eyes widened. They both followed him out of the barn towards the farmhouse, which had a separate outbuilding converted into a washroom.

'I'll leave you to clean up and see if I can find any spare . . . what do you call them . . . Overalls?' Tommaso stuttered over the unfamiliar words, his Italian accent thick and deep, and he reminded Maya of some sort of Italian movie star from the 1950s, in his faded, ripped jeans and tight T-shirt. He was very handsome. But she also noticed his eyes weren't drawn to her at all, but more to Andreas, who was staring right back.

'Thanks so much,' she said, smiling and pushing Andreas into the cool outhouse.

'He is totally crushing on you!' she exclaimed, stripping out of her dress with difficulty. Andreas blushed, which was very uncharacteristic of him.

'No, he isn't. Don't be daft.' He pulled off his T-shirt and began unbuttoning his shorts.

'He absolutely is. And he is gorgeous.' She continued, 'What was it you said you wanted? A handsome Italian farmer?'

Andreas swiped her with his soggy T-shirt, and she laughed, wringing out her hair into the sink.

'*Mi scusi*? Hello?' Tommaso's deep, soothing voice could be heard from just outside the door and Maya went to answer, poking her head around the door so that her modesty was still intact. Not that he would have been interested. 'I have some clothes for you to wear.' He handed over two folded pairs of light brown overalls and stood there.

'Thanks so much. We'll be out in a moment.' Maya smiled. 'Won't we, *Andreas*.' She emphasised Andreas's name clearly and Tommaso nodded. As he turned to walk away, she swore she saw him mouth the word, *Andreas*, silently. She knew she was right. She walked back in and handed over a pair of overalls to Andreas and, after scrubbing themselves down with some towels, they got dressed, with most of the splodges of grapes removed, leaving them with a tinge of slime and a faint green hue.

'He likes you. You need to ask for his number.'

'That's ridiculous,' Andreas answered. 'I am clearly older and fatter. He would never go for the likes of me.' He buttoned up his overalls, which were not the most flattering outfit she'd ever seen him in.

'Now who's being ridiculous. You're gorgeous, as is he. And there was a definite spark there.'

Andreas paused before answering. 'But look at the state of me. I'm sticky, dressed hideously, and stink of mouldy grapes. Who would want this?' He gestured up and down his body.

'Well, there's only one way to find out, isn't there?' She lifted an eyebrow determinedly and did the last button up before grabbing her soiled clothes and marching back out into the sunshine. 'C'mon. Let's go and get you a date.'

★

Turns out love really does appear in the strangest of places. Buoyed by repeated glances and timid smiles from Tommaso over the next hour, Andreas did go over and speak to him at the end of their day, his body reeking of drying grape juice and his hair now gelled upwards by naturally occurring sugars. They shared a glass of wine, along with everyone else, to celebrate their hard day's work, but Maya could clearly see that the rest of the crowd had disappeared in their eyes. They had tunnel vision for each other.

They left La Vendemmia Vigneto with smiling faces, tired limbs, and a crateful of wine each, but Andreas left with something even more exciting: Tommaso's phone number.

Seeing how happy he was made Maya think. Did she really want to give up the chance of feeling those attraction butterflies in the pit of her stomach, those furtive glances that hint of something more? Was she allowing Michael to dictate her future?

As they rode the journey back to the hotel in the minibus, each lost in their own thoughts, Maya wondered if it really was time to let him go. But which him?

Chapter Fifty-Three

October seemed to fly by for Maya, which was ironic as her flying schedule felt like it was the busiest it had been in months. It wasn't, but she had been scheduled to fly lots of short-haul flights to cover illness, so she was making lots of little flights here and there, which was actually more exhausting.

She hadn't given much thought to her October challenge at all. But in the second week, she was sitting in Aunt Sophia's kitchen, lazily watching as she made a huge lamb tagine and scrolling through social media, when a message from Theo popped up.

Fancy a drink in town tomorrow night? I could get the train in and meet you in Waterloo Station at 6pm?

'Say yes.' Maya jumped as she realised Aunt Sophia had wandered over from the Aga and was reading over her shoulder.

'Aunt Sophia! Stop snooping!'

'Say yes, and I will.' She shrugged, grabbing a half-drunk bottle of red wine from the kitchen table, and pouring herself a glass. Maya rolled her eyes.

Sure, sounds lovely. See you there.

Standing under the huge, multi-faced Waterloo Station clock, Maya realised she felt really nervous. On the train into town, she'd convinced herself that this was just two friends meeting up, but deep down she was hoping he would kiss her again. His train arrived on time and she scanned the crowds for his face. Seconds later, she saw him, and it hit her how handsome he was. That lazy smile, his floppy hair, the deep, kind eyes that drew you in. She fancied him.

He greeted her with a kiss. Just a gentle, quick kiss on the lips and it surprised her, but before she even had time to respond, he had pulled back and was smiling.

'Hi,' he said softly. 'So, I thought we would try out somewhere really quite special,' he said, taking her hand and leading her towards the row of taxis all lined up outside the station. 'I think you're going to like it.'

Twenty minutes later, they were riding up in one of the lifts of the so-called Walkie-Talkie building on Fenchurch Street, situated in the banking district of the city. The lift was rising at quite a speed and Maya could feel her stomach flipping slightly as she watched the digital display above the lift doors count up quickly. She was confused as to why he would bring her to what looked like an office building. But the lift was full of people, so she assumed Theo was taking her somewhere that offered more than just a fax machine and a photocopier. After only a few moments, the lift slowed and stopped on floor thirty-five. As the doors opened, Maya gasped. In front of her was a ginormous rooftop conservatory that was like a glass rainforest, with palm trees, fronds and green foliage of varying types that filled the entire top floor of the building. They had arrived at Sky Garden.

There were varying levels, with cafés and bars dotted on each level and the natural light poured in from the glass panels that rose from floor to high ceilings. Each pane of glass grew larger as Maya's eyes rose to the ceiling and the sky was a beautiful autumnal blue that was growing deeper towards the horizon.

'This place is phenomenal,' she exclaimed, as they slowly walked around the level they were on, taking in the urban landscape of the city.

'Isn't it? Take a look at that skyline,' he said, pointing out the tiny buildings below which made Maya feel like she was on top of the world. She followed the Thames River as it snaked its way through the city, and she could see for miles. Despite the chaos of rush hour, she couldn't hear anything and there was a tranquillity that came with viewing a bustling city from afar.

'Let's get a drink,' he said, inviting her to follow him down to the next level where there was a bar and a large, outside terrace where people were gathering with drinks and enjoying the late afternoon heat. He ordered two glasses of wine and they decided to sit inside, Maya feeling a little wobbly at the idea of sitting outside, so high up. The first glass went down easily, and she bought the second round. Theo was such an easy listener, and she found her eyes kept getting drawn to his lips, that were just so kissable, she had to resist leaning across the table and grabbing him. It reminded her of those canvases sitting in the art gallery back in New York. Fuelled by wine, she asked him, 'So, what made you stop modelling for M. M. Milner then?'

He spluttered into his drink, his eyes wide in shock. 'How . . . what . . .?'

'Dave and Chloe,' she answered, watching his face put the pieces together.

'But . . . but how? I was assured that they were no longer on display or for sale.' he said, looking severely flustered by this point.

Now it was time for Maya to flush. 'Um, they took me to the gallery, and I got the opportunity to meet M. M. Milner in person, and she showed them to me herself.' She paused, taking in his awkwardness. 'But they are really good. The artist is very talented. And you looked . . .' she paused again, unable to think of a word without making it obvious that she was almost drooling over them '. . . the part. You're a natural.'

He looked down at his wine glass, swirling the contents around slowly with his hand. 'It was a long time ago,' he said quietly. 'It was only a few years after my mum had died, and I needed the money for university,' he began, but she interrupted him.

'Look, hey, I'm sorry. I shouldn't have asked. Let's just forget the whole thing,' she said, taking a resolute gulp of her drink to indicate she was done talking.

'No, it's OK. It's just a long time ago, that's all. But the artist was amazing, she totally took me under her wing. Like

273

an aunt, I guess. She could sense my loss. She had just lost her sister that autumn, so together, we were able to talk, and drink, and . . . yeah, she was amazing.' Maya nodded, showing she was listening. 'It really helped. And I am proud of the images. Mortified, but proud,' he said, a little grin appearing across his face, his dimple reappearing. 'She did manage to make me look quite good in the end.'

'She made you look incredible,' Maya said, without thinking, and looked across shamefully to see he was staring at her, one eyebrow perfectly arched.

'Oh yeah? You think so?' he said, his voice dropping, and he leant forward onto the small table between them, his forearms stretching his shirt in a good way.

'I do. In fact, I wouldn't say no to buying one of those canvases, for art purposes only, of course.'

'Of course,' he said, leaning in even more. She could feel his knee rub against hers and in the warmth of the orange sun, she looked deep into his eyes, realising that she wanted to kiss him so badly.

As the sun set over the city, she felt like this was one of the most perfect dates she had been on. If it was indeed a date. In the whole three years of dating Michael, he had never taken her anywhere like this, even though his work exposure often offered him opportunities to try new places. He did go himself, but he used the excuse that it was a networking opportunity and her being there would only bore her. What a stupid excuse, she realised now. And she had gone along with it, gullible and supposedly in love, so she had stayed home in her pyjamas with a microwaveable meal, while he had wined and dined in some of the best places the city had to offer.

As the Sky Pod Bar grew busier, Theo suggested they go for a walk along the river, so they made their way towards the lifts. Maya could feel the effects of the wine hitting her mostly empty stomach, and she grabbed his hand for support as they walked into the lift. He looked at her and a frizzle of sexual tension shot between them. The lift arriving startled her and as they walked in, they found themselves alone as the doors closed. As the lift began its fast descent, Theo wrapped his arms around her waist and pulled her close, kissing her softly to begin with, but as the lift continued its dropping, so did her resolve. She leant into him, their bodies pressed together, the heat rising. He smelt amazing, his aftershave intoxicating and as his tongue found hers, she found her hands automatically making their way up around his neck, her fingers sliding into his thick hair. Every part of her body wanted more; her skin alive for what felt like the first time in months. The kisses grew more intense, his hands strong against her back, pulling her into him. But suddenly the lift shuddered to a stop and the doors pinged open to a crowd of queuing people. A couple of people cheered, and one person wolf-whistled, causing the queue to laugh. Maya and Theo pulled apart sheepishly, Maya's cheeks flushed, and Theo looked embarrassed. They exited the lift and made their way out of the building quickly, Maya's eyes firmly focused on the ground. Once outside, she looked at him self-consciously.

'Well, that was embarrassing,' she said, breaking the tension. But Theo was still looking intensely at her, his eyes clearly wanting more.

'I think it was about time, actually.' He moved closer towards her and pulled her in for another kiss. This time she didn't hesitate. She had to agree, kissing Theo felt good. It felt well overdue and more importantly, it felt right.

Chapter Fifty-Four

Day 292

'Happiness is a gift and the trick is not to expect it, but to delight in it when it comes.'

Charles Dickens

When I started this blog, over ten months ago, I really believed that I would complete it. Twelve months of being single? Easy. My heart was broken, and I had no intention of dating again, and certainly no desire to. I swore off men, closed my heart, and limited my viewpoint to a 'men equal heartache' mantra.

Yet, without wanting to, I stumbled upon a man who, despite my many attempts to dissuade him, has found his way into my life. He is romantic, sexy, kind, and the complete opposite to my ex. Plus, he comes with free cupcakes. Is he perfect? Definitely not. He is obstinate and stubborn, and has an odd, over-affection for his baseball cap. Yet he seems to accept me for who I am, warts and all, and while there is a strong possibility he will be moving to the other side of the world before too long, he is certainly making me smile again. And it feels like it's been a long time since I really smiled.

For those of you that have been with me since the start, I hope you're not disappointed that my rite of singledom has veered off course. I will still be completing my challenges each month and I will continue to blog regularly.

Am I scared I'll get hurt again? Yes.

Am I terrified I'm doing the wrong thing? Absolutely.

But life is strange, and unpredictable, and having this blog means that I currently have the confidence to give it a try.

Now I'm off to find a challenge to complete before the month is out!

Watch this space . . .

'Dad, any idea on what my latest challenge could be? I'm stumped and I have two days in which to achieve it.'

Maya was sitting on her dad's ancient sofa with a curled-up Smithy on her lap and a mug of hot chocolate balanced on a cushion. Her dad was sitting in his armchair, his newspaper resting on his lap, his reading glasses perched on his head. They had just finished a huge Sunday roast, cooked by Gayle, and were now all flaked out in the living room. Gayle was out in the kitchen, adding the finishing touches to the trifle that nobody had the room for.

'How about you challenge yourself to wash the dishes?' he joked. 'Save me a job.'

Maya rolled her eyes. 'I'm thinking something a little grander than just scraping dried bits of Yorkshire pudding off a tray, Dad.'

'Then I've no idea. Learn how to change a tyre? Rewire a fuse? Fix a lawnmower?'

At this point, Gayle walked into the sitting room carrying a tray with a large glass bowl full of creamy trifle and three bowls balanced on it. Her apron was covered in blobs of gravy and there was a smear of cream on her cheek.

'Stop listing jobs on your to-do list, Mr Madeski, Maya needs to find her own challenge, not finish overdue jobs of yours.' She playfully tapped him on his shoulder and said, 'Now who wants trifle?'

After a huge portion of trifle, they all collapsed even further into their seats. Gayle began reading the newspaper that had fallen off Maya's dad's lap and onto the floor as he fell into a food-induced nap. She was rifling through the pages while Maya tried to find a good movie to watch on the television when Gayle exclaimed, 'Hey! This could be something to do!' She tore out a page from the paper and handed it to Maya who scanned the black-and-white print.

'An advert for haemorrhoid cream?' Maya questioned; one eyebrow raised.

'No, silly. Look at the advert next to it.'

Maya did and read the following:

St Nicholas Church, Oddstone, is auditioning for new members for their church choir.
No previous skill required, however an ability to read music is an advantage.
Wednesday, 30th October 7.30pm.
Auditions in the Church Hall.
Please bring own song choice.

'Absolutely no way,' Maya said, tossing the paper to one side. 'Have you heard me sing?'

'Actually, I have. You always sing when you're in the shower. You're not bad.'

'But I'm not good either. I'll make a complete fool of myself,' she exclaimed.

Gayle shrugged. 'All I know is, you have two days left of October in which to complete a challenge. I don't see many more ideas coming your way, do you?'

Maya considered her words. What with her spending most of her free time now with Theo, when their schedules allowed, the last week or so had just flown by.

'Do you want me to come with you?' Gayle asked.

'Would you audition too?'

'Sure,' she said, shrugging again. 'I'm too old to feel embarrassed these days. Why not?'

At this point, Maya's dad let out a huge snore that almost rattled the ornaments from the mantlepiece.

'And maybe your dad could audition as a baritone.'

At this, they both burst into laughter, making her dad wake up and look at them suspiciously.

Chapter Fifty-Five

Day 309
Challenge decided!
And this might be my most nerve-wracking yet. I think I'd rather swim naked with sharks while covered in Chum, than do this. I am sincerely regretting my choice for this month's challenge.

For tonight, I am off to (stupidly) audition for a village choir, in a little village close to me. I say stupidly, as I can't sing. Well, I can sing, but neither in tune nor key. My mum used to say that I could recite poetry like a cherub, but I sang like a braying donkey. And she was being kind. When I was a kid, every Christmas nativity saw me cast as either a silent sheep, or a voiceless shepherd. One year, I was even cast as the stable door, I kid you not. Carol services were a logistical nightmare, with teachers trying to surreptitiously place me as far away from microphones as possible, unbeknown to me. I have improved slightly but let's just say that I wouldn't be your first choice for the karaoke.

So, tonight will be . . . interesting. I am taking comfort from the fact that it isn't a big deal. Other than a few locals no doubt, it'll be a small village affair where the choir mistress will let me down gently and I'll be home within the hour, watching re-runs of The Voice *from the safety of my own home.*

I would say wish me luck, but I think it would be safer to wish the choir mistress a pain-free audition.

What was I thinking?!

*

At 7.25pm, Maya and Gayle were standing outside St Nicholas's Church in their village of Oddstone and Maya was feeling decidedly foolish. She was about to embarrass herself in front of a group of strangers. She could feel the sweat already beginning to form under her armpits and the back of her neck, despite the almost freezing temperature outside.

'This is stupid,' she said for the umpteenth time since they had left the house together.

'It may be, but sometimes it's good to be foolish. We all spend far too much of our time being serious. C'mon, let's go in.'

Gayle stomped past her and up the steps to the doors of the church hall. She pushed open the door, and Maya could hear the echoes of a piano playing, alongside a male voice singing. She looked back at Maya, holding the door open and gestured for her to follow her. As she paused, an old man, dressed in a smart three-piece suit and with a matching trilby hat perched at an angle on his head, walked past her towards the steps. He doffed his hat to Gayle as he passed, thanking her in a very posh voice.

'Come on!' Gayle hissed, her breath causing puffs of smoke in the darkness. 'It's freezing standing here.'

Maya reluctantly forced her feet into moving and walked up the few steps towards the church hall. As she passed Gayle and walked into the bright, fluorescently lit hall, she felt nauseous at what she was about to do. There was an old lady with bright purple hair sitting behind a makeshift desk to the left of the doors.

'Your name, dear?'

'Maya Madeski.'

'And what piece of music will you be singing for Joseph Jackson today?'

'Away in a Manger.'

'Lovely. Please take a seat and wait to be called. Thank you.' She pointed to a row of chairs which surprisingly were all full. There were a lot of people queuing for a small village choir.

Maya counted at least a dozen. It must be a popular church, she supposed. She waited for Gayle who confirmed her name and that she would also be singing the same carol. Gayle was also directed to the growing queue.

'This sure is busy for a small village choir,' Gayle said aloud, voicing Maya's thoughts.

'I know,' Maya whispered, butterflies forming in her tummy at the thought that she was actually going to sing in front of other people. She hadn't done that since school when they had to sing in assembly, or when she drunkenly sang karaoke in Malaga with Chloe a few years back, but that was so hazy a memory that she had to rely on Chloe's holiday photos to prove that she actually did sing. She cleared her throat nervously.

The connecting door to the main church swung open and two girls in their mid-twenties walked out, looking crestfallen, but shocked. Once the door closed behind them, the skinny, blond-haired one turned to her red-haired friend and said, 'Did we actually just do that? In front of *him*?'

'We did!' the redhead said, and they both squealed, grabbing each other's hands, and jumping on the spot. The old lady with bright purple hair manning the door rolled her heavily lidded eyes and called out to them. 'Please move along so the next group can audition. I'm sorry you weren't successful this time around.' She stood up with some difficulty and grabbed her clipboard from the table. Walking over to the connecting door, she opened it a fraction and waited for a signal before nodding.

'Can the next six people in line go through into the church please.'

Half a dozen people in the queue all stood up and made their way into the church, with Maya, Gayle and the remaining four all shuffling along the row of chairs as if they were playing an adult version of musical chairs. Fifteen minutes passed and five more people arrived through the doors, with the bright purple-haired lady having to get quite forceful with one guy who kept insisting that he wanted to bring his huge camera in with him.

'Why would he want to bring that in?' Maya whispered to Gayle.

'No idea. Perhaps he's from the local paper? Maybe a choir audition is entertainment in Oddstone.' She shrugged. Ten minutes later, the connecting doors swung open and the six people re-emerged. Four were looking downcast while two older men, clearly in their advancing years, were smiling and congratulating themselves, their deep baritone voices clearly evident.

'Who would have thought it?' one of them said as they passed Maya and Gayle.

'Well, I never. I heard he moved into the village a few months back, but I never dreamed he'd take an active part in the community. Audrey is going to have a meltdown when I tell her when I get home . . .'

They passed Maya so she couldn't eavesdrop any further, but her interest was now piqued. One of the four unsuccessful participants was crying and was being consoled by her friend. Purple-haired lady rolled her eyes again, her tolerance for theatrics clearly low. She stood up again, this time with a puff, and made her way over to the connecting door. Opening it a little, this time she paused as if she was listening to someone talking, and then she turned to the waiting crowd.

'Please can the next six in the queue step forward into the church.' The old woman tried to smile, but it appeared more as a grimace and Maya stood up with some trepidation, wondering what she was getting herself into. She followed the others towards the doors and into the church, with Gayle trailing behind her.

The church itself was beautiful; a stone building set out in a traditional cross format, with the main aisle running up the centre, facing the pulpit. There were rows of solid wooden pews facing forward and the church was lit by beautiful tall candles standing in large, wrought-iron stands. Stained-glass windows lined the walls, their intricate depictions of Christian events were just breathtaking, even without the sunlight beaming through them. It felt peaceful and quiet. On the left-hand side was a chapel where there was a large, upright piano and a man sat behind it, only the top of his head visible.

'C'mon over,' he said, not looking up from behind the piano, waving an impatient hand to beckon them over. The six of them shuffled forward, their footsteps tapping on the grey stone floor. 'Sit down in the front pew.'

They did as they were told and only once they were all seated, did he stand up. An audible gasp went up from them all. It was *the* Joseph Jackson: 1970s pop star extraordinaire turned philanthropist, synonymous for marrying one of his fans that he chose out of a crowd of thousands to sing a duet to in his early years of fame. That love affair had lasted over fifty years and he gained a name for himself as being the nicest pop star in the world. Supposedly he was a great person to work with and he had continued producing music that had stayed in the charts for five decades. He and his wife had even started their own international singing school for those less fortunate. He believed in the motto *Capability not Capital* and had helped tens of thousands of young stars find their way to follow their dreams. He had also been extremely handsome in his younger days, with luscious, wavy locks that sat on his shoulders and seemed to have a mind of its own on stage. He had eyes the colour of molten amber with contrasting long, dark lashes. His signature outfit was wide denim flares with big-collared black shirts, worn with kerchiefs of every colour. He had been on every magazine cover, every entertainment show, even been knighted by royalty for his services to charity. And right now, he was standing directly in front of her, smiling.

'Thank you for coming today, I'm sure I'm not who you expected to see this evening.' A few murmurs and chuckles of agreement rose from the six seated in front of him. 'I hope I'm not too much of a disappointment!' he joked. 'The St Nicholas's choir mistress has asked if I can step in and help this week, as she has just had an operation, so I accepted the challenge with joy. This is a wonderful church and as I am new to the village, I am excited about getting to meet the inhabitants of Oddstone.' His smile was genuine and broad. 'So, if you'd like to stand up, one by one, and come over to the piano, let's hear what you've got to offer.'

He walked over to the piano and sat back down, with the first auditionee stepping nervously forward. It was a man in his fifties, wearing a bright orange jumper that stretched almost down to his knees. He handed over a song sheet to Joseph Jackson and moments later, the familiar tune of 'Amazing Grace' rung out through the church. The man began singing the words and his soulful, deep voice echoed in perfect tune. It was beautiful. Maya felt more nauseous with each verse, knowing she was next in line to sing.

The man finished his song and Joseph looked up from the piano, smiling. 'Very nice, indeed. You, sir, have a beautiful voice and the choir is in need of extra tenors. You're in.'

The man punched the air in glee. 'Fantastic! Thanks so much.'

'My pleasure. You will be an asset to the choir. We'll be in touch.' And he gestured for him to take a seat. His amber eyes then turned towards Maya, beckoning her forward. 'Please come forward.'

Maya honestly felt like bolting. She stood up and her whole body wanted to run out of the church and into the darkness and obscurity, but her legs seemed to work of their own accord and headed towards the piano.

'Your name?'

'Maya Madeski,' she said, her voice quiet.

'Your occupation?' He narrowed his eyes, assessing her.

'Cabin crew. For Oasis Airlines,' she said, wondering why it was relevant to her audition. His eyes widened a little, but his face remained passive.

'And your song choice?' he asked, holding out a hand for her sheet music, of which she had none. She tried to speak, but only a terrified grunt escaped her lips.

'Uh, I don't have any music,' she managed, her voice hoarse, 'but I'd chosen to sing "Away in a Manger".'

He looked at her sternly. 'You've come unprepared, I see. Interesting. Can you sing?'

'Um, not really,' Maya said, blushing crimson. 'This was kind of a dare, of sorts. But I'd like to give it a go if that's OK?'

He smiled. 'That's just fine with me. I think together we can wing it.' He began tinkling the opening bars on the piano and nodded his head rhythmically in her direction. 'Ready when you are.'

It was at this point that stage fright kicked in in all its glory. Maya's throat tightened and her eyes bulged. She couldn't move, let alone make a sound. She was holding her breath, her ribs contracting painfully. She managed a panicked shake of her head to show him she couldn't do it. He stopped playing, placed a hand gently on her arm, and smiled knowingly. 'It's OK. Take a deep breath in for five, and exhale for ten. You can do this,' he whispered, only audible to her. 'Ignore the others.'

She tried to do so, but her throat felt tight. He could see her struggling. 'Do the same as me,' he said, getting her to make eye contact with him and locking her in. As he ran his fingers up his diaphragm, he took a breath in and held it, counting down seconds silently with his fingers. He did it again and this time she felt she could copy him. *In through the nose, out through the mouth*, he repeated quietly. He did this five times and she found herself still, her body calmer. He lowered his hands and began playing again. It took all of her control and might, but she began quietly singing the opening lines of the song. She was so quiet she was barely audible.

'Louder,' he said. 'Project to behind my head, towards the back of the church.'

She tried, but the louder she became, the less tuneful she was. She could hear her attempts to remain in key were fading fast and with each new verse, it was harder and harder to hit the notes her brain was trying so hard to achieve, yet her voice box stubbornly ignored. The nerves were making it worse, her voice trembling and scratchy. At one point, she noticed

Joseph Jackson actually flinch. But ever the professional, his smile stayed steadfast and encouraging.

After what seemed like hours, she finally finished the carol and the last note reverberated around the stone walls, like an awful, offkey echo. Joseph Jackson finished playing and the church fell silent. She didn't look back at Gayle. She was sure she'd been laughing silently. Her eyes landed on Joseph, her cheeks flushing crimson with embarrassment. He stood up and came around the piano to where she was standing.

'Well, that was very . . . brave, well done. It was a good effort and a lovely song choice,' he said, encouragingly. 'However, I think your voice might need a bit of an improvement, and I'm disappointed to say you're not right for the choir at this point in time.' He turned to the awaiting auditionees and raised his voice so that they could hear. 'Nevertheless, I applaud anyone who is courageous enough to step outside their comfort zone and try. So, well done.' And he did something that Maya really didn't think she deserved, he began to applaud her, smiling. The others behind her joined in and she turned to them, blushing even further, mouthing the word thank you in their direction. Turning back to Joseph, she was surprised when he leant forward and whispered something in her ear, so that only she could hear over the clapping. He whispered,

'I read your blog earlier, *Miss Flying Solo*. I love it. Bravo on challenge number ten. You did it!'

Maya's eyes grew wide in shock. 'How did you know?' she whispered.

'I'm a frequent flyer with Oasis Airlines, darling girl,' he said, giving her a wink, 'and there aren't too many villages that are auditioning on this very night. Chances are I wondered, nay, hoped that you might pop up at my audition.'

He took a step back to look to the next auditionee, which was Gayle. He nodded for her to come forward. Maya was totally stunned, still standing there, wondering what sort of surreal, out-of-body moment she was experiencing where a

286

hugely famous pop star was reading her blog and following her journey. She was dumbfounded.

As Gayle brushed past her to step into position, as Maya made her way robotically back to her seat. Joseph Jackson had just listened to her sing, and he'd read her blog, and he knew who she was. Could life get any more bizarre?

It turns out it could.

Chapter Fifty-Six

Day 316
*What a month, and we're only a week in already! There I was
thinking that meeting a famous pop star was the highlight of my
year so far, when things have just got more and more extraordinary with each day of November. Firstly, the iconic superstar
and total gent went on to mention my lowly little blog on one
of his podcasts the day after my audition, causing my blog count
to skyrocket. This was then picked up by a national radio station,
who asked me to come on LIVE and talk about my blog! Little
ol' me! They kept my anonymity as requested and since then,
I've seen my blog page inundated with comments from local and
national press, wanting to find out my identity and come interview for them. It's been a whirlwind; I can tell you!*

*Secondly, one of my closest friends who came on my last chal-
lenge with me (remember the grape pressing in Italy?), well, he
has seemingly found the love of his life. Despite them living in
differing countries, speaking different languages and both working
long hours, they seem to have fallen head over heels for each other.
I couldn't be happier. Love really is the strongest emotion, eh?*

*While I can't say that my heart is as open as my darling
friend's, I can say that I feel I am starting to heal. I am considering opening myself up to finding romance again. Not love,
not yet. But romance? Yes. I forgot how wonderfully heady the
first few weeks of a romance are. The excitement, the electricity,
the anticipation . . .*

Am I nervous ? Yes, I am.

Will I keep you posted? Yes, I will . . .

On every single detail? Absolutely not . . .

Once the flight had reached cruising altitude at thirty-five thousand feet, Maya walked the aisle towards the galley to begin her duties of preparing the hot drinks. But as she loaded her trolley with the hot-water jugs, she heard her name from behind.

'Maya?' Maya turned to see Ivy, a fellow cabin crew regular who looked after first class, standing next to the blue curtain.

'Hi Ivy. All OK in first class?' Maya asked, filling her trolley with sugar sachets.

'Yes, yes, all fine, thanks. It's just I have a passenger asking for you specifically to come and see him.' She shifted uncomfortably. Maya stopped what she was doing and looked at her quizzically.

'Who would be asking for me?'

Ivy paused before saying, 'It's Michael Simmons. He's on this flight.'

Maya's eyes widened. Michael was on this flight? Asking for her? With Theo sitting in economy too? Ivy continued. 'He's quite insistent. I wouldn't normally even tolerate the idea of you seeing him, but he spoke to Nigel Edwards who insisted that you must remain professional, whatever the circumstances.' She changed her voice to try and mimic Nigel. 'If someone in first class wants something, then we must try our hardest to accommodate them.'

'What about my section?' Maya asked, grasping at any straws that meant she had to stay put.

'Nigel is coming down to step in so you can come back with me.' She looked so apologetic that Maya felt sorry for her. At that point, Nigel stepped through the curtain.

'Off you go then, Maya. I'll cover you. We must be accommodating to any VIPs that fly with us,' he said pompously. 'Whatever links or personal history we might have with our passengers, we must remain professional at all times.' He gave her a glare that meant business, and Maya felt torn. She wanted to see Michael. However much he had hurt her, she wanted to know why he was asking for her. So, she handed over the tray of sugars to Nigel and followed Ivy through the galley into first class, her heart thumping in her chest.

Michael was seated in row one, seat C, and as she approached, she could see his long legs stretching out into the aisle, with seemingly no thought for anyone wanting to walk past. She rolled her eyes at his carelessness.

'Hi, Michael,' she said quietly, careful not to disturb the other passengers. Michael glanced up with a look of pure elation that she had come.

'Maya, hi! Thanks for coming to see me.'

'I didn't really have much of a choice. You spoke to my manager,' she said drily, which he chose to ignore, his eyes running up and down her body, which made her uncomfortable.

'You look amazing.'

'And you look just the same,' she said, noting he really hadn't changed. The only addition was that he now appeared to be wearing foundation, which Maya thought made him look a little ridiculous. 'Michael, what do you want? I have work to do.'

He seemed totally unfazed by her lack of enthusiasm in seeing him. 'I rang the airline to see when you were flying, I wanted to make sure you would be on my flight.'

'Well, that's a huge breach in protocol and against company policy—'

'I just wanted to ask if you'd be willing to finally get that drink with me tonight, in New York. I have tickets to this new bar opening and would love to take you there.' He cut her off, brushing away her concerns with a flash of his hand. 'Would you join me? I miss you, Maya Moo.' He used her pet name, which was infuriatingly familiar. It took her straight back to times gone by. He continued. 'Look, I know things have been . . . difficult since we broke up, but I feel I owe you an explanation.' He stared at her, his eyes wide and pleading. 'Please, Maya?' He looked adorable. She could feel herself relenting.

'I don't think that would be a good idea . . .' she began, the sunlight streaming through his window and causing her to turn away. As she did so, he reached out and took her hand, squeezing it affectionately.

'Just one drink, that's all I'm asking. Let me make it right.'

She sighed, her hand feeling so familiar in his. 'Fine. One drink. That's all.'

He looked delighted; his face lit up. 'Fantastic. I'll text you the details of the bar. See you then. Thanks, Maya.'

She turned to leave then, walking back down the aisle, when she heard him call for her again, affection thick in his voice, like honey. 'Maya?'

'Yes?' she said, her heart jolting a little and turning back.

'Could you sort me a whiskey and Coke on your way past the bar please?' He gave her a wink. 'Thanks.'

By the time Maya had settled into her hotel room at the Lexington Lodge, she felt exhausted. She had panicked that both Michael and Theo would somehow meet when exiting the plane when it landed, and she hadn't had a chance to see Theo since her debrief. He had taken a taxi straight to the Clementine Bakery and they had plans to meet up for lunch tomorrow.

Lying down on the hotel bed, she checked her phone, the blue light illuminating her face. She had three messages from Andreas and two from Chloe. She opened the message from Andreas. There were three photos attached of him in Italy, one with his arm around Tommaso, both looking loved up and two of them eating in various restaurants. The message from Chloe was an image of a beautiful pair of gold, sparkly heels with a half-price sticker attached and then the words SQUEAL! written at the bottom of the message. Maya chuckled. She then checked the company website, and selected the blog section, and was amazed, as always, to see the hundreds of comments under each blog post, taking her break reading through each one. It was a real morale booster. And very much needed.

Originally, her plan had been to get an early night in the hotel and be rested for her date Theo tomorrow in Central Park, as Theo was meeting with the Clementine Bakery lawyers for a dinner meeting later that night, but now she found herself showering and getting dressed for her drink with Michael. While she hadn't intended on making any sort of effort for him, she couldn't help but choose her auburn wool jumper dress that clung to her curves and finished just above the knee. It was a polo neck, so she justified wearing it as it didn't show any skin, as such, especially when she paired it with thick, black tights and ankle boots. She curled her hair properly though and spent far longer on perfecting her make-up than she intended to do.

She made her way across Manhattan to the new bar, appropriately called Rendezvous. She exited the cab and found Michael waiting for her by the entrance, dressed in tight jeans and a navy blazer buttoned up over a crisp, white T-shirt. He came forward when he saw her and kissed her directly on the lips. She pulled back in surprise.

'Michael, what are you doing?' She pressed her hand to her mouth as if to stop him trying again.

'Sorry, old habits,' he said, looking mock horrified. 'I just couldn't help myself. You look amazing tonight.'

His ability to be so over-friendly had thrown her and she immediately felt on the back foot. He placed a hand on her lower back and led her past the bouncer, declaring his name which was on some list, and they were allowed into the building. The bar itself was up a large flight of stairs and was spread across the entire floor of the brownstone building. Exposed beams and floorboards were clearly a theme, and there were high-backed velvet booths designed in such a way that every single booth was positioned so that each party had their own privacy. The lighting came from dimly lit uplighters in the floor, and waiters floated around each booth silently. There was low-level jazz music playing in the background and the whole bar screamed exclusive and expensive. And, Maya thought, totally pretentious. But she let him lead her towards a booth which was positioned facing the huge, floor-to-ceiling glass window that overlooked the city. It was clearly the best booth in the bar. A bottle of champagne was already on the table, along with two glasses.

'Champagne?' she questioned, one eyebrow raised. 'Is that meant to be a joke?'

'No? I just wanted to spoil you, that's all.'

Maya found all this very disconcerting, so decided to try and take charge of the situation. 'So, where's your new fiancée this evening? Are you both settling well into New York life?'

It worked; Michael looked suitably uncomfortable. 'Look, Maya. I haven't come here to talk about my life with Amanda. I've come here to apologise to you. What I did last year was wrong on so many levels, and for that I am so sorry.' He looked contrite enough that her resolve melted just a little.

'Why didn't you just tell me? Why not finish with me first?' Her questions came out husky, brittle almost.

He shook his head mournfully. 'I just don't know. I should have done. I know I should have done, but at the time, I just got caught up in the excitement with Amanda. She was' – he corrected himself – '*is*, so intoxicating.'

'So, instead of facing a difficult situation and being brave, you decided just to run away,' she said scornfully.

'I did,' he replied, honestly. 'I was selfish. You are too good for me, Maya, and I took you for granted. You were always there, never arguing, always trusting. You balled my socks, made my dinner, ironed my clothes. You were my still anemometer in a category five hurricane. You calmed me, kept me grounded.'

Maya rolled her eyes at his weather reference. Trust Michael to refer everything back to bloody meteorological conditions.

'Basically, I was your housekeeper then. Nothing you've just said talked of love, or romance. I gave you three years of my life, and you repaid it by dumping me in the most disrespectful way possible. Do you have any idea how humiliating it was for me?' Her voice cracked at the last question, and he instinctively placed his hand over hers on the table. He began circling the soft part on the back of her hand with his thumb, like he used to do when she was anxious. She didn't push him away.

'I can imagine,' he said. 'I did try to call you. On what should have been our wedding day. But you never answered. I wanted to say then how sorry I was.' Maya remembered that missed call on her phone when she was lying in her hotel bed all those months ago. 'But by then, things had escalated. Amanda had convinced me that we needed to unite and move to the US, and I just got caught up in the whirlwind of it all. She really doesn't take no for an answer. In anything,' he said and Maya noted a hint of resentment in his tone. He was still circling her skin slowly but he seemed distracted, his gaze wandering off into the New York skyline.

'But why didn't you try again?' she whispered. He sighed unhappily before continuing.

'Because Amanda told me that you left a message asking me categorically to not contact you again. You asked for a clean break, she said. She also went on to say that when you came to my house that night to collect your things, you commented how you wished I had broken it off sooner. That you'd already moved on with a guy from work, and you were relieved that it didn't have to be you to end the relationship. She said you had been secretly dreading our upcoming wedding and was so relieved it was all over.' He looked pained at the recalling of this memory. 'And she said when you left, the relief on your face was obvious. Apparently, you even laughed at how stupid we had been in thinking we had a future together.' He looked sad. 'You actually laughed.'

Maya felt shocked at this revelation. Amanda was a good news presenter, but who knew she was such a great actress too? To spin a whole web of lies to her fiancé was a new low.

'And then when I saw you at the Regency ball in June with a new guy,' Michael continued, 'I presumed he was the man you'd moved on with. It was so painful to see you there, looking stunning, with him. It just proved what Amanda had said all along . . .' He tailed off.

'Michael, I never said any of those things. She lied.' Maya moved her hand away from his and it on her lap. 'When I came over to your house that night, I barely spoke two words to her, before she blurted out that you were moving on. I was heartbroken.'

Michael looked at her, wide-eyed. 'You hadn't moved on with a guy from work?' he asked and Maya shook her head no. 'What about commenting on how stupid our relationship had been?'

'All lies,' Maya said.

Michael took a long gulp of his drink and leant back into the booth with some force, looking shocked. 'The conniving cow,' he said.

Maya nodded in agreement. 'But it still doesn't excuse your behaviour. It takes two to tango, and you knew what you were getting yourself into. You still cheated on me,' she said.

'I know,' he said, turning his gaze towards her, with what looked like tears in his eyes. 'And I regret it every day. If I could turn back time, then—'

He was interrupted by his phone ringing in his blazer pocket. He shook himself and pulled the phone out. In the dim lighting, Amanda's name flashed up brightly on his phone. He didn't answer it, instead he cancelled the call. Maya felt torn. What had he been about to say? The call seemed to throw him off balance and he poured himself another glass of champagne, ignoring her own nearly empty glass.

'What were you going to say?'

He looked at her, confused, his mind elsewhere. 'Sorry, she calls ALL. THE. TIME,' he emphasised those final three words with an animosity that did not match the voice of a man in love. Clearly, all was not rosy at home. Maya suddenly felt weary. This was all so draining. Michael was draining.

'Well, I'd best be off, I think,' she said, sliding her bottom along the booth to leave. 'Thank you for at least trying to explain. I do appreciate it.'

'No, don't leave!' he said, grabbing at her hand again. 'Stay for another drink. Please.'

'No, but thanks.' She stood up and he jumped up too.

'Let me take you back to your hotel, at least.'

'Again, no. But thanks. I'll grab a cab downstairs.'

As they both made their way out of the bar, with Michael quickly paying with a black Amex card, she noticed, Maya had to dodge a huge crowd that were now queuing to get access. Yellow taxis lined the sidewalk and she walked over to the closest one at the front of the queue. She went to open the door, but Michael stopped her.

'Maya, please. I want you to know, I did love you. Always. I was just a fool.' His face was full of concern, and it felt like he wanted her to believe him. She nodded but didn't speak for fear of getting tearful. Without warning, he leant in and kissed her softly on the lips, his mouth open slightly, wanting more. Her eyes were wide with shock and a flash of light startled her into action. She pushed him away with both hands on his chest.

'No, Michael,' she said, angrily. 'You can't do this. You're with Amanda now.' She forcefully pulled open the taxi door and looked at him one last time. 'You made your choice. Go home to her.' She climbed into the taxi and slammed the door shut, her eyes facing forward. 'Lexington Lodge, please. Near Queensboro Bridge.'

She didn't look back as the taxi pulled away. She couldn't. She could still taste him on her lips, the familiarity, the passion. As they snaked their way through the busy streets of Manhattan, her eyes were blind to the impressive towering buildings and bright lights of Broadway. Instead, they were downcast, full to the brim with tears.

Chapter Fifty-Seven

The next morning, she awoke with a raging headache. When she had arrived back to her room after her encounter with Michael, she had dived into the minibar, and it was clear that mixing any sort of mini bottles together had been a bad idea. She greatly needed hydrating, and quickly. Theo was due to meet her downstairs in an hour. Guilt flooded her system like a wave as she recalled Michael's kiss last night. Not that she invited it, or wanted it, but kissing Michael had made her realise that she no longer wanted him. She mourned the loss of their relationship, but she didn't miss Michael as a person. Last night only solidified what she had gradually realised: he was selfish, egotistic, and self-absorbed. She actually felt a little sorry for him. He clearly didn't seem that happy with Amanda.

But as she showered and got dressed, she felt calmer than she had in months. Meeting Michael had given her some closure. She felt surer of herself, more confident. If the last eleven months had taught her anything, it was that she needed to trust her judgement a little more and learn to take chances and not settle. She had settled with Michael because, deep down, she was scared that she wouldn't find anyone as 'good' as him. She now knew that she was good enough and, when finding someone new, she had to be confident enough to judge whether *they* were good enough for her. Her perspective had shifted. And so had her mindset. She would tell Theo about last night, she decided, but only to show him that she was totally over Michael now. She finally felt ready to commit to their new relationship, with no previous hang-ups.

An hour later, she walked out into the lobby of the hotel to see Theo standing there, looking so handsome in his black jeans, grey sweatshirt, and dark charcoal double-breasted coat and all thoughts of Michael, and last night, just disappeared from her mind. He was holding his battered, grey baseball cap in one hand, a large sports bag in his other hand and he was facing outside, looking unbelievably sexy.

'Hi, you,' Maya said as she sidled up behind him and wrapped her arms around his chest. Her arms barely came together, and she felt a tingle at what lay beneath those layers. He turned around and kissed her straight on the lips, a full kiss. It was so different to last night with Michael; this felt connected, emotional – right. When they pulled apart, he took a look at her, which was so sexy as she felt his eyes scan her outfit. She was wearing jeans and a bright burnt-orange jumper but had covered it over with a large, cream duffel coat. She had paired it with knee-high boots and a large, orange pashmina.

'Hi. You look beautiful,' he said, and she could see he meant it. 'But you might need a change of outfit later on,' he said, winking at her.

'A change of outfit?' she asked, looking down at her sensible choice for the time of year.

'Yep. We are off to do something very festive, very unique, and very American,' he said, feigning an American accent. 'I have something planned that might just work as your November challenge too.'

They walked out of the lobby into the busy street. The sky was an ominous grey with a tinge of orange, hinting that snow might be on the way.

'I am suitably intrigued,' she laughed. 'But why the change in outfit?'

'Because you're going to get very sweaty while doing it.'

'Ooh, now I'm properly intrigued,' she said, winking at him. 'Are we doing it together?'

'We are,' he said, before chuckling, 'with a whole team of cheerleaders in tow, too.'

'Theo, please tell me!' she exclaimed as they both climbed into a taxi. 'Where are we going?'

'Radio City Music Hall, please. Thanks.'

'Radio City Music Hall?' Maya asked, her interest piqued. 'Are we seeing a show?'

'Not quite. But it is something that involves dancing,' he said. 'You'll see.' He wrapped an arm around her shoulder, and she snuggled into him, feeling excited. She trusted him. She pulled out her phone from her coat pocket and opened her blog website. Sat in the back of the taxi, while they trickled through the streets slowly towards Broadway, she typed out a new blog post.

Day 318

I am literally sitting in a yellow cab pootling my way across New York towards my penultimate challenge as I write this! And I am ridiculously excited. It's been organised by my new friend, let's call him Mr X, and supposedly it's dance related.

Now, I might not be able to sing, or bake, or wear Regency costume successfully, but one thing I know I can do, is dance. I love dancing. Stick on a tune, and I'm there, on the dance floor, my hips gyrating like a 1980s Jane Fonda extra from one of her aerobics videos. It is my favourite thing. I don't do exercise as a rule, but if I did have to, then dancing would be my first choice. I love Latin dance, salsa, ballroom, you name it. I am a huge Strictly *fan and* Dancing with the Stars *is always my go-to watch when I'm here in the US. Dancing makes me happy. I think I'll find it hard to mess this one up, but time will tell . . .*

As always, I'll keep you all posted.

She uploaded the post and checked her messages. She sat suddenly upright, shook herself a little and reread the message. Letting out a tiny, involuntary scream, she exclaimed, 'Oh, my goodness!'

'What's wrong?' Theo asked, resting a hand on her shoulder. Maya turned back to look at him, tears in her eyes and a huge grin on her face.

'Nothing. Only the best news ever!' She turned her phone around to show him a photo. It was of Gayle and her dad standing in front of the London Eye with her dad holding Gayle's hand up towards the camera. Sitting on Gayle's ring finger was a thin band of twisted gold, with a small diamond at its centre. The photo was captioned with the words, SAVE THE DATE – DECEMBER 18TH. WE'RE GETTING MARRIED!

'Who are they?' Theo asked, smiling at the photo while Maya was excitedly jiggling in her seat.

'It's my dad and his girlfriend. I mean, his fiancée! They are just perfect for each other.' She sighed happily. 'When my mum died, he was a total wreck for a long time. He was lonely and so sad. But then Gayle came along, and he came alive again. You know when you see two people together and realise that they were just meant to be? That they are a picture-perfect match?'

'I'm starting to,' he said, rubbing a hand gently along her back. She realised what she had said and turned to look at him. His expression was totally serious, and it made her blush.

'You are?' she whispered, leaning into him a little more.

'I am,' he said, pulling her into him and kissing her. Her phone and her dad's big announcement were forgotten in an instant and the rest of the taxi journey was silent.

Chapter Fifty-Eight

They pulled apart as the taxi came to an abrupt halt in midtown Manhattan and the cab driver yelled at them that they'd arrived. Maya looked out of the now-steamed-up window to see they were directly outside Radio City Music Hall, with the banner of brilliant blue lights that curved horizontally across the front of the building, and the iconic words 'Radio City Music Hall' illuminated in bright yellow.

'What are we doing here?' Maya asked, staring up at the towering building as they made their way inside. It was only late morning, and it was clear that there wasn't a show about to begin. The sidewalk was empty too.

'You'll see,' Theo said, leading her into the grand foyer of the hall. Maya gasped as she looked around her. The foyer was immense; art deco in style and painted in red and gold. The huge red walls were broken up by ginormous floor-to-ceiling mirrors that worked to only make the foyer feel even more impressive and the staircases were decorated in what looked like gold leaf. The overall effect was one of opulence and luxury.

'Welcome to Radio City Music Hall!'

Maya had been so engrossed in looking upwards, that she hadn't noticed a beautiful, skinny woman standing beside the huge, gold ticket kiosks wearing a red leotard, covered in diamanté sequins, short skirt and skin-coloured tights with gold tap shoes. The leotard had thick straps that emphasised her narrow shoulders and muscular arms and was decorated in gold, sparkly poinsettia fabric flowers that laced their way from her right hip to her left shoulder. Her make-up was pristine, with a bright red lipstick that emphasised her pale skin and heavy eyeliner paired with extravagant, false lashes. Her blonde hair was tightly secured in a perfect chignon, with delicate gold and red poinsettia hair clips fastened in flawless lines to the left of her head.

'Hi,' Theo said, coming forward and shaking her hand, 'nice to meet you.'

'And you!' she said, with a thick, New York accent. 'You must be Theo and Maya. I'm Noelle, and I'll be giving you both your 101 Rockettes dance class this morning!' Every sentence sounded like an excited exclamation. 'Are you ready?'

'A Rockettes dance class?' Maya repeated, looking at Theo. 'We're having a dance class by a real-life Rockette?'

Noelle nodded enthusiastically, her feet jiggling as if she was on fast forward.

'We sure are! Your boyfriend booked it as a surprise for you! A one-hour dance lesson with me, to learn some of the steps from our spectacular Christmas show.' She did a tiny little spin for them. 'Happy Thanksgiving!' She gestured for them to follow her up the large staircase. 'We have changing rooms next to the dance studio for you both to change.' She bounded up the stairs as if she were filled with helium, whereas by the time they had reached the mezzanine, Maya was already out of breath. But Noelle's excitement was rubbing off on her and she felt excited about getting started. Theo unzipped his sports bag and pulled out a brown paper bag and handed it to her. Looking inside, Maya could see a shoe box, a pair of black Lycra leggings and a bright blue sports T-shirt. Opening the box, she noticed the trainers were her actual size, as was the sportswear. She looked at him, surprised.

'I texted your aunt,' he said sheepishly. 'She gave me your correct size.' Maya was both impressed and touched. Theo really was so thoughtful.

'Let's do this!' she said, matching Noelle's excitable tone. An hour's dance lesson seemed relatively easy, she thought. How hard could it be?

★

302

Forty-five minutes later, Maya and Theo were both dripping in sweat, their muscles aching. It turns out a Rockette's dance lesson is really, really hard. Noelle had them learning a whole dance routine from their latest Christmas show and it was gruelling, but immensely satisfying. Maya had a renewed respect for the dancers who, during this time of year, danced up to four shows a day. They had twirled, tap-danced, strut-kicked, and they'd just attempted an eye-high kick, but poor Theo looked like he'd sustained a groin strain in doing so and had disappeared off to the loo, which Maya was sure was an excuse for a break.

'Let's take five while we wait for Theo, yeah?' Noelle said, her pristine make-up still in place. She didn't even look hot, let alone sweaty.

'Sure,' Maya said nonchalantly, but ruined her indifference by collapsing onto the floor near her water bottle and leaning back against the mirrored wall.

'You're so lucky to have found a guy as sweet as Theo. He's a total doll. And that British accent, yum!'

They both laughed and Maya nodded in agreement. 'He is lovely.'

'How long have you been together?'

Maya wasn't sure how to answer this. Technically, she'd known him for almost a year now, but they hadn't exactly been friends from the first time they laid eyes on one another. 'It's still quite new, actually.' She decided to keep it brief.

'Well, don't give him up easy. Good men are hard to find. Trust me, I know.' Noelle looked sad suddenly, her tone serious, and she unconsciously rubbed her ring finger. Maya noticed a tan line where she guessed there once sat a wedding band but was now naked of jewellery.

'I'll try,' she said, just as the door opened and Theo came walking back in. Noelle jumped back into Rockette mode and plastered a smile back onto her face.

'Right, we have fifteen minutes left, guys! Let's give it our all and see if we can smash this routine!' She jumped up, switched the music back on, and ushered them both into position. Shouting above the music, she counted them in, 'And five, six, seven, eight.'

Once their hour was up, they made their way back into the grand foyer, with Noelle chatting away excitedly about her plans for Thanksgiving the following weekend. Neither Theo nor Maya had decided to bother changing back into their original clothes, especially as they were both sweaty and still hot. As Maya walked down the huge staircase, she gazed in wonder at the building's décor and had to pinch herself mentally. Had she really just danced inside the actual iconic Radio City Music Hall? As they reached the ground floor, she turned and took a quick photo for her blog. This was a moment that she wanted to remember. Both Theo and Noelle had continued walking, both engrossed in chatting about the various pros and cons of the Thanksgiving parade. Maya caught up with them just as Noelle stopped at one of the kiosks where she was handed a red envelope from a young guy who stared dreamily at her.

'So, here are your tickets for one of our shows. They are valid for a year, include a voucher for popcorn and a drink of your choice, and you can book them any time, so next time you're in New York, look me up. Obviously, the shows with me starring in them are the best!' They all laughed at this, with the guy behind the kiosk glass joining in.

'Too right, Noelle!'

'Oh, wow. That's fantastic!' Maya said, excited at the prospect of seeing Noelle in her element.

'All part of the package, doll,' Noelle said, coming forward and giving her a hug. 'I hope you've had a great session and if you're ever in town again, look me up!' She leant in and hugged Theo too.

'Of course, we will,' Maya said, feeling like she'd just made a friend. Noelle seemed genuinely lovely.

They pushed through the doors and stepped out into what appeared to be a snowstorm. The sidewalk was already covered with a thick layer of slushy snow and the cars driving past were going at a careful, slow speed, with mounds of black slush already forming at the sides of the road. There was a strong wind too, blowing the snow almost horizontally into their bodies as they stood on the sidewalk.

'What the . . .' Theo said, as snow pummelled his face silently. He pulled out his baseball cap and popped it onto his head. Maya was already shivering and tightened her coat around her.

'Was this part of your plan?' she yelled above the wind, noticing large snowflakes caught in his long eyelashes as he tried to blink.

'Definitely not,' he exclaimed, pointing at the nearby entrance for the Rockefeller Center Station. 'Let's get out of the cold.'

They made their way cautiously and slowly towards the subway stairs, trying not to slip on the now treacherous sidewalk. It was packed with people all trying to avoid the storm and instinctively Maya pulled out her phone to check for any work emails. Their flight home wasn't until tomorrow, but she needed to stay ahead of any updates. However, her phone had no reception in the subway.

'Fancy heading to get lunch? I know of a brilliant New York bakery where the food is free if you're dating the owner . . .' Theo joked as they were jostled and pushed their way deeper into the subway.

'Delicious. Sounds good to me.' She kissed him on the cheek, and they made their way towards the approaching train. Climbing in, she felt hot and sticky once again, the carriage was packed with travellers trying to avoid the snow. She checked her phone again, still no reception. Theo had managed to find them two seats and as he stared ahead, his hand reached over and folded over hers. It was a small movement and her cheeks flushed with warmth.

'Are you really going to move out here then?' she asked, knowing that avoiding the big questions was great and kept them in their happy little bubble, but life was moving fast, and she needed to know where she stood. She felt his hand tense a little.

'I think so, yes.' He looked over at her then, a sadness in his eyes. 'I hope I'm doing the right thing.' Maya nodded encouragingly but found that irritating lump in her throat was back again. He would be living on a whole different continent to her. He pulled out his wallet from his jacket pocket and opened it, sliding two photos out from an inside pocket, and held them up. One was of a woman with a young baby in her hands, her face almost identical to Theo's, but with the feminine touches of longer eyelashes and higher cheekbones. It was a well-thumbed photo. The other was a more recent one of Theo as he looked now with his grandmother. There was a clear resemblance between them, the eyes so similar, yet the older woman had a fierce, determined look that suggested she was hot-headed and strong-willed.

'These two women gave me everything. They made me who I am today.' He sniffed and popped the photos back into his wallet. 'I can't give up on their legacy, on everything they worked hard to achieve.'

'I get that,' Maya said quietly, as the train rattled through the tunnel.

'Do you think you'll come and visit me?' he asked, looking suddenly nervous.

'Would you like me to?' she asked, her heart flipping like a fifty-cent coin.

'I really would. I want this' – he pointed back and forth between them – 'to not end. I really like you, Maya. More than like, actually.'

'I really like you, too,' she whispered, her heart speeding as fast as the train. He looked instantly relieved.

'That's so good to hear.' He kissed her gently on the lips. 'So, I've found an apartment just two blocks from the bakery. Huge bay windows with views of the Hudson just visible if you stand on tiptoe. The landlord is a regular at the bakery and even knew my grandmother, so gave me a great rate.' He looked at her intently. 'Would you like to come and see it?'

She nodded. 'That sounds really great.' He kissed her again, this time more deeply. The noise of the train and the travellers just disappeared, and Maya could think only of Theo and how much she wanted this to work. Her hand made its way onto his chest, and she felt his heat. She wanted more.

Suddenly the train screamed itself to a halt and they broke apart to see they were at their stop.

'This is us,' he said, his breathing ragged. Maya stood up silently and exited the train, enjoying the feeling of his hands holding her waist from behind. It was even busier on the platform, but for the first time she didn't care as she felt Theo's hot breath on the back of her neck, her hairs standing on end. They shuffled forward slowly, his hands never leaving her and before long she felt a rush of cold air hit her face as they climbed the stairs towards the street. She turned once to look at him and could see the desire in his eyes. She quickened her pace.

They finally reached the surface, and it was clear by the howling wind and heavy snow falling that the storm hadn't weakened. If anything, it seemed to have got even stronger.

'The bakery is only a block from here,' he said, pulling down his cap and shoving his hands in his pockets to keep the frostbite at bay. 'This way.'

Maya followed suit, tugging the zip of her coat up as high as it could go and shoving her hands in her deep coat pockets too. As they started walking, she could feel her phone vibrating repeatedly with notifications in her coat pocket, but she ignored them as the icy cold was almost painful on her face and exposed ankles. It was only a minute or so to the bakery, but when they reached the familiar orange frontage, they almost fell inside the door in an effort to feel some warmth. The employees behind the counter recognised him immediately and called out greetings of hello. He smiled back and collapsed into a table in the almost-empty bakery. Maya joined him.

'I am totally frozen,' he said, rubbing his hands together and blowing on them to warm them. A waitress appeared immediately at their table.

'Hi Theo, what can I get you?'

'Hi, Brielle. I would love two of your best hot chocolates please. All the trimmings.' He gave her one of his friendliest smiles and she winked at him before disappearing towards the counter. At that point, Dave pushed through the kitchen doors and noticed Theo.

'Theo! You're here. Brilliant. Can I have a quick word with regards to our Christmas menu? We need to finalise on the candy cane sprinkles.' He beckoned Theo over and disappeared back through the swinging doors.

Theo sighed. 'Do you mind? I'll be two seconds.'

'Sure, you go,' Maya said, waving him off, just as the most delicious hot chocolate was placed in front of her, the whipped cream peak so high she wondered if she'd need a shovel to eat it. It looked delicious. She took a sip through the red and white striped straw. It was as tasty as she imagined it would be and as the hot liquid hit her stomach, she relaxed back into her chair. Her phone vibrated again in her coat pocket with yet another notification and she decided to check in with work. She assumed the storm was causing havoc with the airports, so pulled out her phone. She gasped. She had seventeen missed calls, eleven voice messages, and twenty-three notifications. Unlocking her phone, she scrolled through the messages.

Chloe – *What were you thinking???? RING ME BACK NOW.*

Andreas – *Darling girl, were you drunk?? Why go back? What happened with Theo?*

Dad – *Maya, please call me. I'm concerned. The phone hasn't stopped ringing.*

Aunt Sophia – *You fool. Have I taught you nothing this last year? Poor Theo. Call me.*

Michael – *Maya, we need to talk. Urgently. Amanda knows. Everyone knows.*

What on earth had happened? Maya felt her chest tighten, unsure of what was going on. She had messages from numbers she didn't recognise, and before she even attempted to listen to the first voice message, another message from Chloe popped up. Maya read it wide-eyed.

You're trending everywhere. WHERE ARE YOU?

She had attached a link to a national UK newspaper and Maya clicked on the link. As the article loaded, she lifted a hand to her mouth in horror, her gasp audible. The girls behind the counter looked over at her with interest and a couple of diners two tables away stopped their discussion to see what had happened. But Maya didn't notice, staring horrified at a close-up photo that was plastered over the tabloid front page. A high-quality photo in colour and with every detail clear for the world to see. A photo of Maya and Michael standing on a New York sidewalk, frozen in time, caught in an embrace, kissing. The tagline read,

BREAKING NEWS
US TV Star Amanda Avary's fiancé, Michael Simmons, Cheats with Unknown Woman.

Maya could feel the panic rising in her chest and pins and needles started prickling her hands and feet. She wanted to run, but where to? She looked outside, expecting to see reporters hunting her down, desperate for more, but there was no one, just an empty sidewalk with a slow-moving taxi trickling past. With trembling fingers, she typed Michael's name into the internet and, instantly, the same image appeared on newspapers, entertainment sites and gossip columns, internationally too. The image of her unwanted kiss was trending everywhere. She felt sick, the hot chocolate burning now in her throat. She went to stand up, but as she did so, Theo appeared back through the kitchen doors, laughing at something Dave had just said. He looked so happy. She wanted to cry. He sat down and took a big gulp of his own hot chocolate before looking at her. His cheerful face instantly turned to concern.

'Maya, what's wrong?' He reached out to her, but she flinched. She couldn't cope with his kindness and tears fell from her eyes down her cheeks.

'Theo, I'm so sorry.' The girls behind the counter were really invested now, this scene before them the most exciting thing that had happened that day. Theo's face grew more grave.

'What for?'

But Maya couldn't trust herself to speak again, the tears flowing silently down her face. Instead, she passed the phone over to him, the screen still lit up with her image. He looked at the phone, not understanding at first, but then realisation hit. He looked up at her and then down at the phone again, this time scrolling through the taglines.

'When did you . . .?'

He tailed off and she whispered, 'Last night.'

'Last night?' he repeated, still staring at the image, his face screwed up in pain. 'But you had an early night at the hotel?'

She shook her head no. 'Michael was on the flight. He asked to meet. Just for a drink. One drink.'

'Looks like he got more than just a drink,' Theo said slowly.

'I didn't kiss him, he kissed me. I pushed him off straight away. The photo doesn't show that—'

'I see,' he said tightly, dropping her phone onto the table as if it was on fire. 'You sure look comfortable there though.' He pushed up suddenly from the table, his chair tipping backwards with the force, and stood up. They now had the attention of everyone in the bakery. Even Dave had come off his call and was looking over in concern. 'I trusted you, Maya. I was willing to give you everything. I wanted this to be . . .' He gestured to the bakery but stopped. 'I wanted you to be . . .' But he couldn't finish, his voice cracking.

He pressed his lips tightly, his face strained. He looked at her then, with such hurt, such pain, that she felt like she couldn't bear another second of his gaze. But then he turned away and walked out of the bakery and into the darkness of the street, disappearing from view.

Maya lowered her head onto the table slowly and began to sob.

Chapter Fifty-Nine

Theo didn't return to the bakery, despite Dave's repeated calls to try and contact him. His phone appeared to have been switched off. It didn't take long for the staff at Clementine's to realise something bad had happened and when one of the girls recognised Maya when scrolling through her social media, the tone changed in the bakery from concern to a cool chillness that meant Maya felt obligated to leave.

Standing in the street, with snow falling around her, she was at a loss at what to do. So, she did what she always did when she felt sad or scared, she called her dad. He picked up on the first ring.

'Maya? At last! Where are you?' He sounded fraught, and she instantly felt guilty. She found an alcove in a closed-down shop doorway and hid in there to avoid the storm.

'I'm OK. I'm still in New York.'

'And are you alright? Are you safe?'

His concern was too much, and she burst into tears. 'Oh Dad, I didn't do it. Michael kissed me; I didn't kiss him. We are definitely not back together. You believe me, don't you?'

'Of course I do, darling. You're with Theo now.'

'I am. Well, I was.' Her tears flowed even faster. 'He just walked out on me.' She had snot streaming down her face as well as tears and she tried unsuccessfully to wipe her face clean. She was trembling. She desperately wanted to be home in her dad's house, with his big strong arms around her. She thought of Theo again and the tears came thicker and faster. 'Dad, I love him.' It was the first time she had said it aloud, and as she did so, she realised she meant it.

'Oh poppet. You really have got yourself into a bit of a pickle, haven't you?' he said, sounding sad. Maya nodded silently. There was a bit of a kerfuffle with the sound on her phone and she wondered if she had lost reception when Gayle's voice suddenly appeared.

'Maya? It's me. Now, as much as I love your dad, he's not the best for giving advice in difficult situations. But I am.' Maya could hear him trying to protest but getting shushed by Gayle. 'Here's what you're going to do.' Her voice was firm, strong, and it made Maya stop sobbing for a second. 'You're going to go back to your hotel and stay put until your flight home tomorrow. Once home, we'll meet you at the airport and you're to come and stay with us until this all blows over. Just in case anyone traces you back to your aunt's house, you're best off not being there right now. We'll keep you safe and this'll all blow over in a matter of days.'

'But what about Theo?'

'Give him some space. You have to come home tomorrow anyway as you're working. Isn't he due to fly home on the same flight?'

'Yeah, he is,' she hiccuped.

'Well then, that'll give you the opportunity to talk to him then. Explain everything. For now, get back to your hotel.'

'OK,' Maya said, feeling exhausted. She signed off with the promise of messaging them in an hour and hailed a passing taxi. As they trundled through the almost empty streets of Manhattan, she touched the envelope in her bag that held the tickets to see the Rockettes. That felt like a lifetime ago, not just a few hours. Taking the tickets out of the envelope, she ran a finger over the gold embossed lettering and delicate paper and began to sob again.

As the taxi pulled up outside the Lexington Lodge, she climbed out with heavy limbs and the beginnings of a migraine. She barely even noticed the snow as she walked into the lobby of the hotel, ignoring the greeting from the reception staff, and headed directly for the lifts. But sitting in an armchair in the lobby, his back to the reception area, was Michael, dressed all in black and wearing black sunglasses indoors. He looked stupid and shifty. Maya tried to ignore him, but he jumped up and slid into the lift alongside her.

'What are you doing here, Michael?' she hissed, pressing the button for her floor with such force that she thought the button would break. It annoyed her that he knew Oasis Airlines always used the Lexington Lodge as a base for their cabin crew and had done for years. He knew so much about her.

'We need to talk, and you weren't answering any of my calls or messages.'

'What do we need to talk about? You kissed me. You got caught out,' she said, furiously. 'And you've ruined my life. Again.'

'It was an accident. I didn't know any reporters would be there, did I?' He pulled off the sunglasses and his eyes were strained, but she couldn't tell if he was being genuine. He had always been a good liar, she realised.

'It doesn't matter. The tabloids will make a story of it whatever the truth is.' She felt trapped in the lift and hated being so close to him. 'Just go back to Amanda.'

'I can't. She threw me out,' he said, gruffly.

'Don't for one second think I'm going to feel sorry for you,' she warned, giving him an exasperated look.

'I don't. I just wondered if maybe you could just speak to Amanda, let her know that it wasn't deliberate. That it was an accident on your part, perhaps . . .'

Maya's eyes widened as she took in what he was asking. Shaking her head at him, she was saved from answering by the lift doors pinging open at her floor. She walked out, away from him towards her hotel room.

'Maya, please,' he said, following her. 'I don't know what else to do. I'm trying to make a go of it out here with my career. This scandal will set me back—'

'I don't care,' she said, still walking ahead of him.

'And I don't expect you to either. But I'm pleading with you. This is my work. You know how passionate I am about my career.'

At this, she swung around to look at him, her eyes flashing in anger. 'What about my life? My passion?'

'What passion?'

'My writing. This will potentially destroy my anonymity.'

Michael shook his head, confused. 'I don't understand. You're a writer now?'

She went to speak, but a door to her left opened abruptly and an American family looked shocked to find them standing there, yelling at each other. She quickly unlocked her own hotel door opposite and pulled Michael into the room with her, shutting the door quickly.

'Look. You have your life, I have mine. When you dumped me, I felt lost, heartbroken; so I started a blog, and what I intended to be a private diary of sorts went on to become something that's blown up bigger than I could ever have anticipated.' She looked at him proudly. 'I have followers in the tens of thousands now and have been interviewed a few times, too.'

Michael looked at her in shock, taking it all in.

'You have been writing? To thousands of people?'

She nodded.

'What's it called?' he said, looking anxious. 'Please don't tell me you've been dragging my name through the mud daily to the whole of the UK?' He suddenly looked panicked.

'No, don't worry. You have never been mentioned by name,' she said bitterly. 'But it has been a surprising success. It's called *Flying Solo*.'

Michael sat down on her bed, taking it all in, shaking his head in shock. 'I can't believe this. Who would have thought?' he was mostly talking to himself, but he looked up at her, pride in his eyes. 'Well done, Maya. I'm proud of you.'

His words were so surprising that she didn't answer immediately. She just nodded back at him. Neither of them spoke for a few moments, until her phone rang again. She rushed to check the caller and her shoulders dropped when she saw it wasn't Theo, but her dad. It had been well over an hour now and she hadn't messaged them.

'I need to get this,' she said, moving into the bathroom and speaking to her dad quietly, reassuring them both she was fine. She made no mention of having Michael in her hotel room though. She ended the call and returned to the bedroom. Michael was on his phone, his gaze intense. On her return, he stood up suddenly and cleared his throat.

'I think I should go, actually.'

'OK,' she said, surprised at his change of heart.

'I just worry that if the press work out we are here together, then it'll only stir up more of a media shitstorm. I should get back to Amanda.' He walked to the door and looked back at her. 'I am sorry though, Maya. Truly, I am.'

'Fine,' she said, feeling confused, but he had opened the door and disappeared before she had a chance to say anything further. She watched him from the doorway to her room as he made his way down the long corridor towards the lift, and she hoped against hope that that would be the last time that she ever had to talk to or see Michael Simmons again.

Chapter Sixty

Theo never turned up for the flight home. His seat lay empty, and his phone remained switched off, leaving Maya on the flight home without any answers to where he might be or what he was doing. It was a horrid shift, with her colleagues keeping a distance from her but whispering behind the curtain or in the galley whenever they could. It was a long seven hours and she had never been so grateful to see her dad and Gayle waiting for her at the airport on her arrival. They both wrapped her up in their arms and bustled her into their car, taking her home.

Later that evening, they sat down together to eat, with Chloe and Aunt Sophia also gathered at the table. It was the first time Maya's dad and Aunt Sophia had socialised together in decades and the conversation felt a little forced. But they were making an effort, at least.

'Another slice of pie, Sophia?' Maya's dad asked, offering her the pie dish, but she refused.

'No, thank you.' Her eyes focused on Maya. 'So, are we agreed then that you do not respond in any way? To the press, the media, or Michael? He doesn't deserve your help.' Murmurings of agreement echoed around the table and Maya nodded, her plate still almost untouched. 'And, Chloe, you're going to try and contact Dave again, to see if we can get to Theo through him, yes?'

'Absolutely,' Chloe said, nodding to Gayle for second helpings and holding out her plate.

'If we handle this correctly, the news will have nothing else to go on, and it should all blow over relatively quickly. We just need to keep Maya hidden.' They all nodded at this, but Maya did not feel confident. She knew what mainstream gossip media was like and she also knew what Amanda was like.

'What about Amanda? She could totally make me out as a villain in all this,' she asked the table and none of them answered. Instead, they shot furtive glances at each other, with Gayle speaking up first.

'Well, she hasn't said anything yet. And the latest news is she's carrying on as normal, disputing the claims. She doesn't want her pride hurt, so I'm sure she'll want this over as soon as we do.' Cue more nodding heads.

'We'll be here the whole time, Maya. All of us, protecting you,' her dad said, looking over at Aunt Sophia who nodded in agreement.

'That's right, all of us.'

'But now it's time for you to get some rest,' he continued. He looked at Chloe. 'Are you happy to stay?'

'I sure am, Mr M. I haven't had a sleepover at yours since that last time when I got a little tipsy on your home-brewed beer and threw up all over your beloved yucca plant, remember?' They all laughed, with Maya's dad flushing.

'Well, yes. Quite. But I think it best if we get Maya to bed now so she can rest. It's been a tough few days.' Chloe nodded and jumped up, pulling Maya gently up from her chair and linking arms with her.

'Come on, you. Let's get upstairs to bed.'

Maya didn't argue. She felt exhausted. They went upstairs and got undressed into the pyjamas that Aunt Sophia had thoughtfully brought over in a bag from the farm. Climbing into her old childhood bed felt as comforting as a hug. Chloe climbed in beside her, as if they were children, and slid her arms under the covers. She found Maya's hand and clasped it in her own.

'Chloe? Do you think Theo will ever talk to me again?' she whispered as Chloe switched off the bedside table lamp.

'I'm sure he will. Once we've explained everything, he'll understand.' Maya didn't respond but let her heavy eyelids close for a second as she enjoyed the comfort of having Chloe and her family around her. 'And when this blows over,' Chloe continued, 'I think we should get away for a bit. Have a holiday together. Your dad's invited me for Christmas, along with Sophia, can you believe it? All of us under the same roof – amazing. But after Christmas, I think we should book a holiday. Get away for some winter sun somewhere. What do you think? Sand, sea, and copious amounts of sangria. Sound good?'

But Maya didn't respond. She was already fast asleep, totally exhausted, her hand still clasping Chloe's.

Chapter Sixty-One

'Maya? Are you awake?'

Maya opened one sleepy eye to find Chloe's face right up against her. Maya groaned as everything came flooding back and she attempted to roll over, away from Chloe and back to sleep where she didn't have to think or remember. But Chloe stopped her by placing a hand gently but firmly on her shoulder. 'Maya? I need you to take a look at this.'

Maya noted the alarm in Chloe's voice and opened her eyes. The room was still dark, with the curtains drawn, and she could hear rain pelting the bedroom window.

'What time is it?' she rasped, her voice sounding croaky and hoarse.

'Almost eight a.m. But I really think you should take a look at this, Maya. The story broke last night on New York time.' She brought her phone up to Maya's face and the brightness of the screen made her flinch. But the sound of Amanda Avary's clear voice reverberating into the dark room was enough to startle her into an upright position, accidentally knocking the phone out of Chloe's hand and onto the floor. Chloe scrabbled around to pick it up again.

'Chloe, what is this?' Maya felt uneasy, her heart racing. Chloe didn't answer, but just picked up the phone and restarted the video. Amanda was sitting in a comfy, plush chair being interviewed by an equally thin, and glamorous TV presenter.

'So, tell us how it felt when you initially saw the infamous photo of your fiancé kissing another woman.'

Amanda sighed dramatically, flicking her perfectly coiffed hair to one side. 'I was heartbroken. As a recently betrothed woman, and innocent to it all, I felt broken and betrayed. Especially as I recognised the other woman instantly.'

The presenter looked surprised. 'You did? Who is she?' She leant forward, pressing her tanned elbows onto her cream pencil skirt.

'She is his ex-girlfriend. A girl called Maya Madeski. He broke up with her well over a year ago, but she clearly hadn't moved on.'

The presenter's eyes were wide in fake shock. 'Do you think he still has feelings for her though? That kiss didn't look one-sided.' Amanda smiled sweetly at her, shaking her head from side to side.

'No, definitely not. He told me afterwards that she had only met up with him so that she could promote her writing. She used him as a marketing ploy.'

'Her writing? What do you mean?'

'When they originally broke up, all seemed amicable, so he tells me. Then, months later when he proposes to me, it became apparent that she clearly wasn't as over him as she had originally made out. She became jealous and vented through the only way she knew how - this desperate, sad little blog of hers.' She sighed theatrically, turning to the audience and evoking their sympathy. 'And I'll admit, it's actually quite good, in an amateurish way. Her lack of clear style or proper prose seemed to appeal to the mass market and her blog gained traction in the UK. However, she must have realised that she was limited to the UK market only, which is why Michael and I believe she used him as a platform to gain more worldwide coverage. The kiss was purely purposeful to gain attention.' The sad smile didn't falter.

'Please don't name it, please don't name it,' Maya mouthed. The presenter looked down at her notes.

'This blog, called *Flying Solo*, currently has over fifty thousand followers and the writer has so far remained anonymous. All we knew up until now, was that it was associated with Oasis Airlines and it referred to one of their cabin crew employees. However, it seems that Maya Madeski is looking to find international success, using both her employer and her ex-boyfriend as a means of achieving her goal. Amanda, what would you like to say to Miss Madeski if she is watching this evening?'

Amanda looked directly at the camera and spoke kindly, appealing to her audience. 'Maya, I'm not cross, I do understand. Michael was caught off guard, but he does understand the reasons you acted like you did. We all want to make a success of ourselves, but your writing speaks for itself. You don't need Michael to propel you forward.' She took a deep breath. 'We both forgive you.'

'You're amazing,' the presenter said, reaching out to Amanda and squeezing her hand in a moment of solidarity. At this point, Maya felt like she was about to throw up. She covered her head with her arms. Chloe quietly turned the phone off.

'I'm so sorry, Maya. She is such a cow.'

'It's all lies,' Maya said, her voice muffled. 'He kissed me. I pushed him off me.'

'I know,' Chloe said quietly. Maya started to sob.

'Why are they doing this to me?'

'Because they're selfish gits with only one goal in mind. They are well suited. Shit always sticks to more shit. Rather than admit Michael acted like a cheating bastard, they have decided to put a positive PR spin on it.' She sighed. 'How did he even know about your blog? Did you tell him?'

Maya nodded, her lips tight. He was total scum. He'd seen an opportunity to show himself in a good light, and further both his and Amanda's coverage by going to the press.

'What do I do now? This is going to go viral. Everyone will know who I am. Everyone will know my innermost thoughts and feelings.' She could feel the onset of panic rising in her throat. All her emotions of the last year were written in that blog knowing it was anonymous. Her lows, her tears, her healing. All there on her blog. Her sobs came faster, and she could feel herself beginning to hyperventilate.

'Maya. Calm down, sweetheart. We'll get through this.' But Chloe looked unsure. This was bigger than any of them had anticipated. Last night, they were only aiming to keep Maya hidden, but now her name was splashed about over the internet, with anyone and everyone believing she was some cheating, immoral writer who had hurt the wonderful Amanda Avary. Not to mention the fact that her blog was on the company website as well. Nigel must be going crazy. She'd probably be fired. There was a knock at the door and Aunt Sophia opened it slowly, letting the light from the hallway blaze into the darkness of the bedroom.

'Girls? Are you awake?'

'We are,' Chloe answered, while Maya continued to sob. Aunt Sophia walked in, and Maya could feel the bed dip as she sat down at the end of it.

'So, she's seen the news, then?'

'I've shown her,' Chloe answered.

'What does she want us to do?'

'What can we do? Amanda is very believable. The public trust her.' This just made Maya cry even harder. Aunt Sophia didn't respond. Maya could just about hear the phone ringing downstairs.

'How about a nice cup of tea?' Aunt Sophia asked, rubbing Maya's leg over the My Little Pony duvet cover.

'Good idea. I'll come down and help you.'

Maya could hear them leave the bedroom together, her arms still covering her face. She kept replaying the images from the interview over and over in her mind. Amanda's smile was imprinted in her mind, taunting her. She finally calmed down and stopped crying, just a few hiccups now and again. She could hear the phone continuously ringing and the voices of her dad, Aunt Sophia, Gayle, and Chloe all talking in hushed tones filtering up the stairs towards her. What was she going to do? What could she do? She didn't have the exposure Amanda had, and no one would listen to her anyway. She didn't have a platform.

Or did she? Amanda had highlighted her blog as a reason for her supposed cheating, but why couldn't she use that same blog to speak the truth? To give her side of the story? She sat bolt upright and pulled out her laptop from her bag next to the bed. Booting it up, she watched with stinging, red-rimmed eyes as the screen came to life. Ignoring all emails, including an ominous one from Oasis Airlines, she logged straight into her blog page and was shocked at how many followers she now had. It had doubled overnight. But she didn't care. She didn't even look at the most recent messages or comments, she instead opened a new blog post, and without pausing to think, she just started to write.

Day 320
I'm sure you've all seen the interview with Amanda Avary by now. And if you haven't, just search for it. I want you to see it. What she said last night was completely untrue. So let me give you the real version of events, not one that has been cleverly orchestrated to suit their (Amanda and Michael Simmons's) situation.

Yes, Michael Simmons is my ex. He dumped me live on air, almost a year ago to the day, when he proposed to Amanda Avary (search for that video too, it's available on the NWN website). But he wasn't just my boyfriend, he was my fiancé. We'd been engaged for months and were only weeks away from our wedding in New York. He broke my heart. And on the week of our cancelled wedding, he ran off with Amanda.

Just let that sink in for a minute. An already engaged man proposing to another woman. That day my whole world fell apart and I was not only heartbroken, I was totally and utterly embarrassed. Yes, I did write the blog as a cathartic way to deal with my grief, that much is true, but I never did it as a reason to get Michael back. I didn't want him back. He is a low-life cheater who was only out to look after number one. I just wanted to move on, and my blog became a way to process my emotions and find the strength to realise that I was just fine on my own.

The challenges were a monthly reminder that I could be whatever I wanted to be and, up until two days ago, I felt buoyed by the fact that my twelve-month plan was almost complete. And ironically, I kept him anonymous, out of respect to him.

Michael's version of events is totally untrue. He did ask me to meet him, yes, but he explained that it was an opportunity for him to apologise, to explain his reasons for leaving me. And to be honest, I needed it. I needed the closure. But in having that drink with him, it became apparent that he was the selfish, pretentious idiot that he always was. And that realisation was all the closure I needed. I left early and it was only as I tried to find a cab, that he kissed me. I pushed him away and hoped that I would never have to see him again.

But the press had different plans.

Did I organise the photographer? Of course I didn't.

Did I do it for the money? Absolutely not.

When the photograph appeared in the press the following day, Michael also appeared at my hotel, asking me to lie for him, to help him. I couldn't do it. He was no longer my problem and his relationship with Amanda was not my concern. My biggest error at this point was not that I tried to use him for my own gain, but that I trusted him enough to tell him about my writing. By mentioning my blog, I opened my personal life up to him and in doing so, I gave him an opportunity.

My blog has been, and always will be, an honest account of my life. Nothing more, nothing less. I am just trying to fumble along as best I can, documenting my life and hoping I strike a chord with many others who have been dealt the same raw deal of heartbreak. I am not after a magazine deal; nor am I hoping to become famous. It's just me. Still writing. Still blogging. Flying Solo.

Thank you for reading.

She quickly scrolled through her most recent photos and found a selfie of her in at Radio City Music Hall, smiling broadly with the grand foyer in the background. Her hair was messy, and her make-up wasn't perfect, but she exuded happiness. She uploaded it to the blog and published it without pausing to think if it was a good idea. She was already at rock bottom, what difference did it make whether she posted or not? She wanted people to judge her based on her own words, not Amanda's.

Feeling instantly better, she slammed the lid of her laptop shut and rolled herself out of bed. She felt grimy and emotional. What she needed right now was a fresh shower and a good dose of freshly brewed coffee. Dealing with the world could wait until later.

Chapter Sixty-Two

The next few weeks passed painfully, with an uncomfortable meeting with Human Resources at Oasis Airlines, who, despite their webpage receiving hits triple to what they normally received, felt that they needed to explain her position within the company and ensure that she wasn't out to promote promiscuity and scandal. She made it acutely clear that she was the innocent party, and in doing so, she was allowed to continue with the blog until the twelve-month completion date, providing they continued with the story of 'good girl scorned'. She argued that that was actually the case, but the truth seemed less important than their reputation. And they couldn't deny that a bit of drama and scandal had helped with their advertising.

Because of this, the airline lined up three long-haul flights for her, as an advertising tool to show that they believed and sided with her. She was inundated with passengers asking questions, enquiring after her wellbeing, and the majority had good intentions, which was a relief as both Andreas and Nigel, surprisingly enough, were there within seconds if anyone decided that they had their own opinion on the matter. She felt paraded, used, loved, protected, and conflicted.

When at home, she had reporters turning up at her dad's house requesting quotes, numerous requests from news agencies for exclusive interviews, so many strangers. Yet zero contact from Theo. Maya kept calling him but he never answered and Chloe's repeated calls with Dave achieved nothing except a renewed affection sparking between them again. She refused all interviews and avoided the news. She didn't even log into her blog to check the comments or see the responses. She just couldn't face it. Chloe stayed by her side as much as her flying schedule allowed and moved into Aunt Sophia's spare room, along with Maya, just to support her. And Maya absolutely appreciated it. Aunt Sophia, Chloe, her dad, and Gayle became her shield from the outside world, and if they did hear news about Michael or Amanda, they certainly didn't pass the news on. It was a strange, lonely, and unsettling few weeks. Maya kept writing messages to Theo, but every time she did, she found it hard to press send.

> *Theo. Please forgive me. But not for what you think I did. I never wanted Michael back in my life . . .*

> *Theo, I wasn't honest with you. And no relationship can thrive without honesty . . .*

> *Theo, I never gave us a proper chance, and now I want to. Please contact me. Please . . .*

The messages were all in draft in her phone. She felt that each message wasn't enough to convince him. Each time she went to reach out, her confidence left her, and his silence only worsened the situation.

Before she knew it, it was the morning of December 18th, and she awoke to what would be her twelfth and final challenge. This one was the most important of all and the most emotional. For the first time in weeks, she pulled out her laptop from the bottom drawer of her bedside table and switched it on. With shaking hands, she logged into her blog. Her message box was inundated, but she ignored them all and simply opened a new blog post and began typing.

Day 357
Sorry for the lack of posts. It's been a challenging time. I write today with two intentions, both emotional.

Firstly, when I started this blog almost a year ago, I did it with low expectations and with the sole aim of remaining single. I had experienced the searing pain of heartache and there was no chance I would open my heart to being damaged again. Yet, I met a man who, little by little, showed me that love is unpredictable. I tried to push him away, to tell myself that I wasn't interested, and spent many a day convincing myself that I didn't want, or need, love.

But love is a strong emotion. The strongest of them all. By opening myself to him, I found all the sadness and fear beginning to dissipate and instead, I found my smile. I told myself not to fall for him, not to lose control. But it happened. I fell. My heart burst open again and without realising, I fell in love with him. But the biggest realisation for me was that I thought I'd experienced love before. When previously engaged, I believed I was happy. I kept ignoring the niggling voice that told me I wasn't. I felt comfortable and secure, and I mistook that for love. But experiencing what I have in these last few months has shown me that love is so much more. It's passion, it's trust, it's feeling like you've come home every time you meet. It is knowing that life is brighter with that person in it. It's the feeling of awfulness if that person ever feels or experiences pain.

Which is why I am writing this.

I hurt him. Not purposely and certainly not intentionally. As you know from my previous blog, I had, and still have, no intention of reigniting anything with Michael. Those fabricated lies have only deepened my belief that Michael and Amanda are very well suited, and I no longer harbour any feelings for either of them. But I did hurt my new love by not telling him what had happened. He found out like most people, via the press, and that must have been so confusing and brutal. If I can make one plea via this blog, it's that this post reaches him.

I'm sorry.

Secondly, I want to end this blog as I originally intended. With my final challenge.

Twelve months and twelve challenges later, I feel like I am ending on a high with my most significant challenge to date. Today, I am best woman to my darling dad and his delightful fiancée. They are getting married at the church in the village where he has lived for over forty years. I am both honoured and extremely nervous about doing them both justice on what will be their most important day. My speech is written, and my outfit is hanging on my wardrobe door. I'm off to have my hair done in a bit. As challenges go, it requires little effort from me other than not losing the rings and smiling. But the big deal is the speech. Can I really write about love when my own life has been a total disaster in that field? Can a girl who's had her heart broken twice before she turns thirty really have any right to talk about the art of love? Time will tell. Wish me luck and please send positive vibes for approximately 4pm today. This blog may have started with a failed wedding, but I hope it ends with a perfect one.

An hour later, Maya was having her hair styled into some sort of updo at the only hairdresser's in Oddstone. Gayle was in a chair to her left and Chloe was to her right. She was desperately trying to feel some of the happiness radiating from Gayle's excitement, but she just couldn't. She was so happy for Gayle and her dad, but her heart felt even more broken than it had nearly a year ago. She missed Theo terribly and thought of him constantly.

But, for today, she had to put all thoughts of Theo out of her mind and focus her attentions on her dad. He had asked Maya to be his best woman a few weeks ago, and Chloe was jokingly asked to be the flower girl. Even Andreas had been invited to join them for the day and had agreed to be the usher. The whole village had come together to celebrate this winter wedding of two of its inhabitants. The weather was cold and clear, with the temperatures not expected to reach higher than just above freezing and Maya was grateful for Gayle's decision to put both Chloe and her in warm velvet long-sleeve dresses. Both dresses were a deep plush red, with sweetheart necklines and floating knee-length skirts that swished when they walked. They had matching velvet high strappy heels and removable beaded collars that wrapped around the neckline comfortably.

But for now, Maya was just wearing baggy jogging bottoms and a jumper that was so old, one could assume it was fashionably distressed. It also had a dried egg stain crusted onto the cuff, from her recent breakfast bap. But her hair looked impressive, so that was a start. She looked at herself in the large mirror facing her and a tired, red-eyed, sad woman stared back at her.

'Are you pleased with the style?' Gayle asked her, leaning over from her chair, and touching her arm. Maya nodded enthusiastically, her smile not quite reaching her eyes.

'Oh, absolutely.' Her hair had been twisted into a tight swirl at the back of her head, with individual curls strategically left to frame her face. Dark sequinned rose clips had been fastened to one side and when she turned her head, the sequins caught the lights of the hairdresser's and sparkled festively. She forced a smile onto her face and looked across at Gayle. 'And you just look stunning,' she said, honestly. Gayle had already had her make-up done earlier that morning, and her normally frizzy, greying hair had been styled into tousled waves that sat gently on her shoulders. On one side her hair was fastened with a similar clip to Maya's, but larger and the rose was solid gold. Her face shone with happiness.

'What's so strange is that I don't even feel nervous. I thought I would, you know,' she said, shrugging.

'It just goes to show that it is meant to be,' Maya said, kindly. 'You and Dad are made for each other.'

Gayle looked at her and took a deep sigh. 'Your words mean more to me than you could ever know.' Her eyes were intent. 'Your dad still loves your mum, you know.'

Maya felt a huge lump appear in her throat and her eyes filled with tears. 'I know,' she said, nodding her head. 'He is just blessed to have found two perfect women. Mum would be happy that he's happy.' She stopped speaking, not trusting herself to say anything more. Despite knowing Aunt Sophia was her birth mother, she still considered her mum to be the most prominent maternal figure in her life. Nothing could take away those memories and feelings of being loved. She missed her terribly.

Gayle looked equally emotional, and they just sat there, holding hands, silent for a moment. The door to the hairdresser's flew open, letting in a gust of icy air and Andreas bounded in, his dark blue suit and crisp white shirt making him look so handsome.

'Come on, ladies. Your chariot awaits. Let's get your glad rags on, it's almost time to get you to the church!'

Just before 4pm, Maya climbed out of the hired Rolls-Royce and accompanied her dad up the steps of St Nicholas's where the vicar was waiting for them in the vestry. He greeted them warmly and encouraged them into the warmth of the church. Maya gasped as she entered and saw the twelve real Christmas trees standing proud in the side aisles, decorated in twinkling lights. At the end of each pew in the centre aisle were the most beautiful Christmas garlands consisting of holly, ivy, and large gold bows. The church was already almost full of wedding guests and Maya smiled nervously at their expectant faces. Looking over at her dad, she could see his face full of joy, not a trace of nerves in sight. She pressed her hand into his and squeezed it.

'I'm so happy for you, Dad,' she said, kissing him on the cheek.

'Thank you, Maya Moo,' he said, looking the happiest she'd seen him in years. As they made their way towards the altar and settled into position, the church organ changed its tone from typical wedding orchestral music to a more contemporary piece that seemed so familiar to Maya. She looked over to the organ which was situated behind the choir stalls to her left and found herself staring at Joseph Jackson, the ageing pop star who only a few weeks earlier had admitted to following her blog. As if on cue, Joseph Jackson, wearing a pale jade velvet suit and glasses, turned his head to look over at them and saw her staring. He winked and she stifled a giggle.

'Dad, what is Joseph Jackson doing at your wedding?' she whispered. Her dad shrugged, clearly having no clue who he was.

'It's the weirdest thing, actually. Apparently, he called the vicar this morning and asked if he could switch with the organist and play. He said he had read your latest blog post and wanted to show his support for us all. I couldn't say no!'

Maya was shocked. Joseph Jackson wanted to be here because of her! What a sweet guy. Before she had a chance to say anything more, the congregation shushed, and she could feel them shuffle in their seats to turn around. She followed suit and saw Gayle standing at the back of the church, with Chloe standing behind her. She looked phenomenal. The music changed again and as Joseph Jackson began to play, Gayle began her slow stride down the aisle, her eyes bright with love. Maya felt tears fall onto her cheeks and didn't try to stop them, but this time they were tears of happiness. The love in the church was palpable and she couldn't have been happier that two people that she loved so dearly in all the world were finally getting their happy ever after.

Chapter Sixty-Three

The reception was held at the only hotel in Oddstone. A small, boutique hotel with only five bedrooms and a cosy restaurant with an adjoining library that had floor-to-ceiling shelves. The wedding party was small but intimate, and there were four round tables in total and in the middle of each table was a centrepiece made up of twelve giant mince pies on a three-tiered cake-stand decorated with holly. After the wedding breakfast, Maya stood up to say her best woman speech. This was the part of the day that she had been most anxious about and nobody, not even Chloe, had been given a chance to hear what she was about to say. She coughed nervously into her napkin, pulled out her folded piece of paper from her tiny, sequinned bag and tapped her spoon onto her wine glass. The room grew silent, and all eyes turned towards her.

'Ladies and gentlemen, it is such an honour to stand here today and speak about my wonderful dad and my equally wonderful new stepmother.' She paused as a small murmur of applause reverberated around the room. 'I think we can unanimously agree that my dad certainly scrubbed up well for the occasion, whereas Gayle looks simply beautiful.' She looked at Gayle, who blushed and looked down at her hands in her lap. 'When my mum died seventeen years ago, our world shattered and neither of us thought we could recover from it.' Her voice caught in her throat, but she continued. 'Birthdays went unnoticed, and Christmases became something that others enjoyed, but we endured. Life continued, and we fumbled on as best we could, but we felt separated from the rest of the world.

334

'But then three years after she had left us, a new person came into our lives under the guise of working for Dad. And she was like a spark of joy. She reminded us that birthdays were memorable and to be celebrated, and that Christmases were the magical days that I remembered them to be. Her infectious laugh made us smile once again and her warming dinners soothed our broken hearts. She never pushed or overwhelmed us, but instead she became a constant quiet presence, patiently waiting until we were ready to accept her. And accept her, we did.' Maya paused and turned the page of her notes.

'Gayle's positivity is infectious and when around her, you can't help but smile. She makes everything good, and I couldn't be more grateful that she taught my dad how to love again. Every Christmas, without fail, she unboxes my mum's Christmas angel tree topper and places it, pride of place, on the top of our tree. Every Christmas, without fail, she pours an extra glass of wine at the table and toasts my mum before we eat. And every Christmas, without fail, she reminds us that Christmas is a time for kindness and compassion for others. It has always been her favourite time of year, and, because of her efforts, it is now also ours.

'So, it couldn't be more fitting that they chose to get married at Christmastime. Christmas is the time of year for being thankful for having those we love around us and for celebrating another year gone by. And I couldn't be more thankful to be standing here today watching the two people I love most in the world marry each other.' She paused, a wobble of emotion escaping her lips. But she composed herself and lifted her glass of champagne into the air. 'Please can you all join me in raising your glasses for the toast?' The room all lifted their glasses as she continued. 'To the bride and groom.'

'To the bride and groom!' chorused the bridal party, and the room went silent as everyone took a sip. Maya turned to her dad and Gayle and blew them a kiss.

'Happy Christmas to you both.'

Happy Christmas, they mouthed back to her, their eyes swimming in tears. Maya sat back down in her seat, her hands trembling a little and Chloe squeezed her hand under the table.

'A beautiful speech, Maya,' she said softly. 'Your mum would be so proud of you. Your mum is so proud of you.' Chloe nodded in the direction of Aunt Sophia, who was dabbing her own eyes with a napkin.

Maya nodded, but at that moment in time, she felt incredibly lonely. As soon as she could, she slipped quietly out of the restaurant and into the beautifully landscaped hotel gardens. The winter sun had already set, and the ground was becoming icy under her feet. In the darkness, she found a wooden bench and sat down and pulled out her phone. With her fingers feeling icy cold, she typed out a single text and pressed send, her breath coming out in white puffs in the freezing temperatures. It read. *I miss you. I don't want to be solo anymore.*

Footsteps startled her in the darkness, and she turned to see Andreas and Chloe walking towards her.

'There you are!' Andreas exclaimed, holding a glass of champagne in each hand, and clearly trying hard not to slip on the icy ground. He handed her one of the glasses, which she took with a shiver. Chloe had her duffel coat hung over her arm and she placed it around Maya's shoulders.

'It's freezing out here, you dafty. Why are you on your own?'

Maya took the coat gratefully and as she did so, the first few flakes of snow began to fall around them.

'Snow!' Andreas exclaimed, his eyes lighting up like an excitable child. Chloe sat down beside Maya.

'We wanted to give you something. Call it an early Christmas present from us both.' She had an envelope in her hand and placed it on the seat between them.

'But it's not Christmas yet,' she said, lifting the gold envelope up and turning it over in her hands. Her name was scrawled on the front.

'Correct, genius. But we felt like today of all days, you might need cheering up,' Chloe said. 'It's from both of us.'

Maya opened the envelope and pulled out a piece of paper. Skimming the wording, she could see it was a fully paid enrolment for a novel-writing course at their local college.

'What is this?' she whispered. Chloe and Andreas looked at one another, before he stepped forward.

'You have a talent, Maya. Your writing is inspiring, and you clearly have a gift with words. We want you to keep it going. We think you'd write a great novel.'

'But if you do, it must include a totally glamorous and beautiful best friend,' Chloe declared.

'And a clearly handsome, svelte gay man,' he joked, nudging her on the shoulder. They all laughed. Maya shook her head in shock.

'This is amazing. You guys are the best,' she said, staring at them both.

'Oh, we know,' Chloe said mock seriously. 'Which is why we expect to be the first names in your acknowledgements.' Andreas nodded in agreement.

'Agreed,' Maya said, laughing. She jumped up and pulled them both into the tightest hug. This time, the tears that filled her eyes were ones of gratitude and what felt like the tiniest sparks of excitement again.

Chapter Sixty-Four

Day 363

My Next Chapter

It's Christmas Eve and the year is almost complete. The mince pies are out, and the mulled wine is being poured. I celebrated Christmas with my family today, a day early, as tomorrow I am scheduled to fly to New York.

I don't mind, really. It's probably best that I spend the day thirty-five thousand feet high, with little to no phone reception and be kept busy with air-sick, excitable passengers hoping for glimpses of the old man in the red suit flying past.

But I do have one question running around my head like a festive merry-go-round. Should I stop this blog or keep it going? Is one year enough, or do you want to hear more? And should I set myself another year of challenges? I start a writing course in January, so will need a creative outlet! Do let me know in the comments below!

But back to Christmas. We land in New York approximately mid-afternoon US time tomorrow, so I intend to spend the rest of the day with my two best friends (fellow cabin crew) and gorging on festive treats until the jet lag kicks in. There is nowhere more festive than New York at Christmas. We hope to go ice-skating at Rockefeller Center and in Central Park. We'll even climb the Empire State Building. There is no better view of the world than observing it from the clouds. Believe me, I know . . .

Happy Christmas to you all (especially you, JJ. You know who you are. I owe you a BIG thank you. You are a total star (pun intended)).

Chapter Sixty-Five

Good morning, ladies and gentlemen and welcome on board Oasis Airlines, Flight 340, direct from London, Heathrow to JFK airport, New York. Flight time today will be approximately seven hours, forty minutes and the weather in New York is currently a balmy two degrees above zero. My name is Captain Cane, as in the candy, and on behalf of the Oasis crew, may we take this opportunity to wish you all a very merry Christmas! Leaving these snowy skies behind us, we should have a smooth flight once we hit the Atlantic and our predicted arrival time in New York is approximately two in the afternoon. Our crew will be here today for all your festive needs. Please take a moment to read the safety leaflet in the pocket of the seat in front of you . . .

Maya finished her pre-flight safety demonstration to her section of the plane and walked down the aisle checking all seat belts were correctly fastened as the plane began its taxi towards the runway. She paused just for a second at row twenty-eight, noticing seat C was already taken by a lanky teenager with headphones as big as bagels on over his ears. He was already asleep. Maya swallowed hard and continued forward.

Cabin crew, prepare to take your seats for take-off.

Maya walked to the back of the plane and plonked herself into the fold-down seat next to Andreas. Fastening her seat belt securely, she leant her head back and sighed.

'Oh, darling. You didn't actually believe he would be on here, did you?' Andreas asked her, his perfectly pristine eyebrows raised.

'No, not really. But there was always that smidgen of hope, you know?' She looked sideways at him, and he nodded. 'But I'm so glad I'm spending Christmas with you,' she said.

'Me too, doll.'

They took off without incident and before long she was busy pre-heating the dinner plates and loading up the trolley.

'Maya?' She turned to see Ivy standing between the curtain to first class and the galley. 'A passenger is asking for you in first class again.'

'Sorry?' Maya said, her hands full of steaming trays, wafts of reheated turkey filling the small space.

'A passenger in first class,' she repeated. 'Can you come up before we start serving lunch?'

Maya shook her head, unwilling to move. 'Please tell me it's not Michael Simmons.'

Ivy laughed. 'No. This time, it's not him! Hurry though, I'm already ten minutes behind schedule.' She disappeared behind the curtain, leaving Maya alone. She dumped the trays down onto the narrow worktop and looked for either Chloe or Andreas to ask for their help, but they seem to have disappeared. She loaded up the trolley as best she could and quickly made her way into first class. She passed Ivy in the aisle, who told her to head for seat 1E. She couldn't see who it was that was asking for her, but as she reached row one, she noticed a man in a bright red Christmas jumper bending down over the seat to an old, brown weathered bag underneath.

'Can I help you, sir?' she asked.

He sat back up and she gasped, her hand rising to her mouth. It was Theo.

'Hello, Maya,' he said, smiling nervously.

'Theo. What are you doing here?'

'I have a rare sleepwalking condition,' he said, mock serious. 'I appear to have sleepwalked into the airport, bought a ticket and now I find myself halfway to New York.'

'No, really Theo,' she said, matching his smile. 'Why are you here?'

'I came back to England to sign off the sale of my grandmother's house, but I'm now on my way home again.'

'Home? You've moved permanently to New York then?'

He nodded. 'I have. Time to start a new life.'

He was looking at her in a way that unnerved her. She couldn't read him. But he was still smiling.

'Theo, I'm so sorry. Truly I am. I did try to contact you—'

'I know,' he said, putting up a hand to cut her off. 'And I handled it terribly. I know you weren't at fault. I just – it all came as such a shock. But I should never have acted like I did.'

'No. I was wrong not to tell you what was going on. I was just so happy with you that I didn't want anything to ruin it.'

'You weren't. I should have listened . . .' He tailed off and they both looked at each other, wanting to say so much but not sure how to say it.

'I'm sorry,' he said.

'Me too,' she replied, and it took all her willpower to stand there in her professional capacity and not kiss him. She exhaled, feeling like she had been holding her breath for weeks.

'Can I ask one question though?' she said, and he nodded. 'How on earth can you afford to fly first class to New York?'

He chuckled. 'I can't! A *friend* of yours helped me with my seat,' he said, nodding his head in the direction of the twitching first-class curtain.

'Chloe knows you're on this flight?' she asked, astounded. Chloe had never managed to keep a secret for longer than five minutes throughout their whole friendship. She automatically looked back towards the middle of the plane to see both Chloe and Andreas's heads peeking out behind the curtain. She shot them both an exasperated look and Chloe shrugged, smiling brightly.

'She's been really nice, actually. Scary, but nice,' he said chuckling. 'I was so hopeful you'd be on this flight, Maya. I did message Chloe before I booked the tickets just to check. She even upgraded my seat, as 28C was already taken,' he said, reaching back down into his holdall. 'Anyway, so here I am. And I wanted to give you something.' He pulled out a small, book-sized present from his bag and handed it to her. It was wrapped in brown paper packaging and there was a hessian ribbon wrapped around it. 'Happy Christmas, Maya.'

She took the present from him, still dazed. A call bell rang a few rows back, but Ivy walked past her, stating, 'I've got this, don't worry.' Maya opened the package slowly, unravelling the ribbon and unfolding the paper. Underneath was a simple brown box. She opened the lid to reveal layers of cream tissue paper. Lifting off the top layer of tissue, she spotted a single gold key on a key chain shaped like an orange. She lifted the key chain up and held the key up to her face. Her eyes widened like Christmas baubles.

'Keep looking,' he said, indicating there was more in the box. She looped her index finger through the key chain and pulled off another layer of tissue paper. Underneath was a silver-framed photograph of a beautifully decorated bakery, its brightly coloured door surrounded by a flowery garland, with two orange bushes standing firm either side of the door. It was Clementine's Bakery. She looked at Theo questioningly. 'There's a note under the photo frame,' he said, nodding towards the box. She lifted the photo frame from the box and a pale cream envelope lay underneath with a large gold question mark embossed on the front. She placed the box on Theo's lap and opened the card with trembling hands to see three simple words written on it in his neat handwriting. It read,

Our Next Chapter?

Maya didn't speak, she couldn't. Her whole body was trembling. Tears were falling silently down her cheeks, and without thought, she leant down and kissed Theo, her tears salty against his soft, sweet lips. He returned the kiss with enthusiasm and the whole of first class erupted in applause, but neither of them heard nor even noticed. They continued kissing, their heads high in the clouds.

'I love you, Maya,' he said, through their kisses.

'I love you, too,' she whispered back, her heart soaring.

After a whirlwind year of trying to remain single, she had inadvertently fallen head over heels in love. Maya Madeski was no longer *Flying Solo*.

Acknowledgements

I dedicate this novel to all the strong women in my life —
but most importantly, my mum. My staunchest supporter
and brilliant hug-giver. The best cake maker and awesome
gift-buyer (even though you always leave the price tag
on!) Your strength is phenomenal, and your love is fierce.
Thank you.

To the rest of my family, my dad, my stepdad, my Nanna,
my siblings, and extended family. Growing up with your
support made me believe that, with hard work and courage,
I could follow my dream to becoming a writer. And to my
brothers who showed me what sibling loyalty is (but can I
have the heads of my collection of My Little Ponies back now,
please?) How we managed to not burn the house down when
we were younger still baffles me and there's no one I would
rather share my Appletiser with. Whenever I throw my dinner
out of the window, I think of you.

To Liz, Debbie and Nikki, I treasure your friendship and
love you dearly. Liz, you are fiercely loyal, always calm, and
I love you not just because you make a brilliant chocolate
mousse, but because I know you are always there when I
need you (and often with wine.) Nikki, you taught me what
it was to fly without stepping on board a plane, thank you
for putting up with my endless cabin crew questions. Your
patience is what makes you such a brilliant flight attendant
and friend. Debs, I honestly don't know where I'd be without
you. You've been there for every big life event, but also for
the small stuff too. My dino-loving, film buddy; my book-
shop partner and beverage spiller (always on the carpet Debs,

always!) There's no one I'd rather receive a WhatsApp video message from. Thank you, girls.

It is important to add a nod to my Book Club ladies too; the heady concoction of laughter, wine and cake every month has kept me on my creative toes and brought me such joy. Our joint love of all things book-related has been my literary tonic over the years. For that, I am forever grateful.

To my wonderful editor, Rhea Kurian. Your faith in my book has been truly humbling, and I love that you saw something in my characters what others didn't. Your enthusiasm for Maya and Theo has been joyous and I'm honoured that you took me on board. And to the Orion Team, thank you. Writing the book is only part of a long process, and your dedication has brought it to where we are today. I feel honoured to work with you all.

Finally, I finish with a dedication of love to my gorgeous children. Your hugs are epic, your jokes hilarious, and your laughter is my most favourite sound. I couldn't be prouder. Holidays, duvet days, all the days... Team Knowles all the way! But please pick up a book now and again, yeah?

And to my husband. Your support is endless, your patience continuous. Thanks for all the cups of tea. This book is written both for you and to you. Thank you.

"I was just taking her hand to help her out of a car and I knew it. It was like magic."
(Sleepless in Seattle)

Orion Credits

Joanna Knowles and Orion Fiction would like to thank everyone at Orion who worked on the publication of *Love is in the Air* in the UK.

Editorial
Rhea Kurien
Sahil Javed

Copy editor
Laura Gerard

Proof reader
Jane Howard

Audio
Paul Stark
Jake Alderson

Contracts
Dan Herron
Ellie Bowker

Design
Tomás Almeida
Joanna Ridley

Editorial Management
Charlie Panayiotou

Jane Hughes
Bartley Shaw

Finance
Jasdip Nandra
Nick Gibson
Sue Baker

Production
Ruth Sharvell

Sales
Jen Wilson
Esther Waters
Victoria Laws
Toluwalope Ayo-Ajala
Rachael Hum
Ellie Kyrke-Smith
Sinead White
Georgina Cutler

Operations
Jo Jacobs
Dan Stevens

Credits

Sleepless in Seattle. Directed by Nora Ephron. Written by Nora Ephron, David S. Ward, and Jeff Arch. Produced by Gary Foster. TriStar Pictures. 1993.